HEARTS
of
RESISTANCE

ALSO BY SORAYA M. LANE

Voyage of the Heart

Wives of War

HEARTS *of* RESISTANCE

SORAYA M. LANE

LAKE UNION
PUBLISHING

Text copyright © 2018 Soraya M. Lane
All rights reserved.

Published by Lake Union Publishing, Seattle

www.apub.com

Amazon, the Amazon logo, and Lake Union Publishing are trademarks of Amazon.com, Inc., or its affiliates.

ISBN-13: 9781477805107
ISBN-10: 1477805109

Cover design by Emma Rogers

Cover photography by Richard Jenkins

Printed in the United States of America

For all my wonderful readers – thank you.

Throughout France the Resistance had been of inestimable value in the campaign. Without their great assistance, the liberation of France would have consumed a much longer time and meant greater losses to ourselves.

– General Eisenhower, US leader of the Allied invasion into France

PROLOGUE

FRANCE

1944

'Run!' Rose hissed as the deafening bang of the explosion fired behind them.

Sophia gasped as Hazel roughly snatched her hand, pulling her along. She stifled a scream as her ankle collapsed, twisting on something that snared from the ground, but she didn't slow down. They had to move fast.

They were surrounded by the enemy. If they didn't find their way to safety soon, they were as good as dead.

'It'll take time for them to regroup,' Sophia managed, panting as she whispered. 'We'll be gone before they even start searching for us.'

The silence from the other two women told her they weren't so optimistic, but Sophia refused to be anything other than certain of their survival. She'd faced worse odds before – they all had – and there was a reason they were all still alive when so many others weren't. They'd have dogs sent to find them soon though, men scouring every blade of grass for them, so they didn't have long.

'Hazel—'

'No!' screamed Rose, leaping in front of Sophia and pushing her back.

The Nazi had appeared from nowhere, pistol raised, the barrel pointed skyward now as Rose fought against him, pushing him away. As Sophia staggered to her feet, the gun went off, the blast making her ears ring, making everything silent around her as she watched Hazel move behind the soldier. The silver of Hazel's blade shone brightly.

They'd talked about death, about whether they were capable of killing a man with their bare hands the way they'd been trained to do. Sophia swallowed the bile rising in her throat as she watched Hazel's hand tremble.

It was kill or be killed.

PART ONE

CHAPTER ONE

SOPHIA

BERLIN, GERMANY

LATE 1942

Sophia watched Alex from across the room of her apartment. He was stretched out over her chair, one foot resting over the arm of it, the other on the zebra-skin rug. She'd always hated that particular furnishing – a gift from her father that she knew better than to dispose of – but the way Alex was rubbing his toes across it, she was starting to think he might wear a hole into it if she didn't get him out of her apartment soon.

She stifled a laugh when he scrunched up a piece of paper and threw it at her, watching a smile touch his lips as he returned her stare. She had no idea how the poor man could still be so jovial after being cooped up in her apartment for so long, seeing only her, day in and day out. He didn't seem to mind terribly, or else he was the world's greatest actor.

It seemed a long time ago that she'd crept in through his window in the dead of night, begging him to flee Berlin. She'd known what was coming and had desperately tried to warn all of her Jewish friends and their families, but Alex's father had been stubborn and refused to leave the city he loved. She swallowed, blinking away the familiar sting of tears whenever she thought about that night. If only she'd fought harder, maybe they would have listened. She wouldn't have Alex with her now, but at least his family might still be safe and alive.

He threw another balled-up piece of paper at her, and she set down the glass she'd been holding and crossed the room to join him. He did it again, only this time she was fast enough to catch it and throw it back at him.

'Stop it,' she said, glaring at him and trying to appear angry.

'I'm too bored to stop,' Alex said. 'Besides, you're beautiful when you're angry with me.'

Sophia sighed and stood, hands on her hips. 'I know how hard this is for you,' she said, shaking her head. 'But . . .'

'Don't,' he said gently, rising from the sofa and holding out his hands to her. 'We don't talk about the past, remember?'

She took them willingly, never needing any encouragement when it came to touching Alex. She'd been in love with him since she was a young girl visiting his father's shop with her mother and she'd grown into a young woman who loved him more fiercely with each passing day. Sophia let him pull her close and press a warm kiss to her lips, his hands sliding down her body and up again before stopping to rest on her shoulders.

'I am so lucky to have you,' he murmured, then kissed her again. 'Every single day that I'm here, alive and safe, is a good day. Don't you ever go feeling sorry for me, Sophia.'

Sophia stroked his cheek, looking into brown eyes flecked with green. 'How do you stay so positive all the time? When so many terrible things have happened to the people you love?'

It was something she thought about constantly, wondering all the time how he managed to keep smiling, to stay so strong when he'd lost so much. When his family had finally realised it was time to leave the city, it had been too late. The Rubensteins had tried to flee, but their shop had already been destroyed and when the Nazis had come looking for Alex's father, he'd been beaten and dragged away, trying to protect his wife and daughters. Alex had arrived back home to see them being taken, had seen his mother mouth the word *Go* to him as they'd been hauled away. And so he'd run, hiding in the shadows until he'd managed to make his way to Sophia's apartment – and he'd never left.

'Because I have to,' he said, taking a step back but leaving one hand on her shoulder. 'Because there are people in this world worth believing in.'

His hand fell away and Sophia kissed his cheek, gently pressing her lips to his skin and hoping he knew how much she loved him.

'One day it will be over,' he said, turning to look out the window. She watched as he leaned on the low bookcase, careful not to get too close to the glass in case he was seen. 'One day, people like you will be remembered, revered even, for what you've done.'

'The others like me, we're just doing what any decent human being would do,' Sophia replied. To her, she was doing nothing special by rescuing Jews and securing them safe passage. But she was doing more than many, who were too afraid to stand up for what was right.

'Do we have any more visitors coming?' he asked, turning back to face her.

She shrugged. 'That's for me to know and you to wonder.'

'Don't tease me unless you can handle the consequences,' he replied with a wink.

Alex ran for her and she pounced in the other direction, running away from him. She burst out laughing when he caught her around the waist, giggling when his teeth skimmed her neck as he pretended to bite her.

Knock, knock, knock.

Sophia froze as the rapping echoed through her apartment. At the same time, Alex scrambled, instinctively making for the middle of the room. A scream ached in her throat, desperate to be released as she silently swallowed it instead. She lived in fear of a knock at her door, knowing that at any moment the precious world she'd so carefully crafted could come crashing down around them.

'Just, ah . . . ,' she stammered, trying to pull herself together, knowing that she needed to keep herself calm. 'Just a moment,' she called out loudly.

Sophia watched as Alex disappeared into the large rectangular ottoman in the centre of the room, positioned between her sofa and the armchair. She darted after him to help, carefully putting the end back together and folding a blanket to place on it, the hem hanging down to cover the entrance to the secret compartment. They were fast – they had to be – and within seconds she was back on her feet and hurrying across the room.

She took a deep breath as another knock sounded out, before pulling the door open, smile fixed perfectly, though her body trembled.

'I'm sorry, I was . . .' The words died in her throat as relief washed through her. It was only her neighbour, a young boy from the same apartment block whom she'd seen numerous times with his mother.

'Can you help me?' he asked, big eyes fixed on hers as he spoke. 'Mama said to ask if you had any food to spare? She's sick and it's been too cold for her to go out.'

Sophia remembered that his mother had been expecting. The other woman had always smiled and said hello when they'd passed each other, and Sophia knew how desperate she must be to ask for help. Residents had been fortunate to still have a reasonable supply of food in Berlin despite the war, although rations still made life less comfortable than many were used to.

She nodded, bending so she was eye level with him. 'Has your mother had her baby yet?'

He shook his head, hands wrapped together tightly at his chest.

'Let me get you something and I'll be straight back out,' she said. 'Wait here.'

Sophia gave a sigh of relief and shut the door on the boy, leaving him alone for a moment. She let her back rest against the timber, eyes shut as her hands slowly stopped shaking. She'd been certain this time that it would be them. That the Gestapo would be standing there with their evil eyes and their grinning mouths, ready to storm her place and find her secrets. She'd helped so many people now, had been the overnight stop for so many Jews who needed somewhere safe to hide, but it was Alex who was her biggest secret of all. She'd had him hidden in her apartment now for so long, right under everyone's noses. Even her father, the loyal Nazi that he was, had been sitting in a chair while her boyfriend was folded into his hidden compartment only footsteps away. She could still remember the smile on her father's face as he'd sat across from her, placing his cup on the ottoman that had been Alex's safe place for so long, while she fretted that one sneeze or cough would give their secret away. She'd wondered at the time if her father would murder her himself if he ever found out, but she'd consoled herself with the thought that even he couldn't harm someone he loved.

She pushed off from the door and crossed the room, bending low beside the ottoman. 'Alex, it's nothing. I'm just going to get the boy some food.' She paused, waited for him to tap twice to indicate that he'd heard her low whisper. She placed a hand against the soft fabric, trying to give him some of her strength. 'I'll be as quick as I can.'

Their rule was that he had to stay hidden. Whenever she wasn't there or if there was any danger, he had to stay out of sight, for her safety as much as his. Being crammed into a piece of furniture wasn't ideal, but it was the only way.

Sophia collected some things together in a cloth napkin – bread and cheese, some cold meat, and a piece of chocolate. It wasn't as much as she'd have liked – because she was supporting Alex secretly, they often didn't have any surplus food.

She returned to the door and passed the boy the bundle. 'Take this straight back to your mother,' she said, patting his head, then shut the door and locked it behind her. Then she dashed to the ottoman and helped Alex out.

Alex looped his arm around her, and she leaned into him as he dropped a kiss into her hair. His lips lingered, his breath hot against the top of her head. They didn't need to say anything; they both knew how high the stakes were.

'I have to go and see my mother in a few days' time,' Sophia said, still holding on to him. 'Will you be okay here alone? Do you think it's too much of a risk?'

She'd been putting off saying anything to Alex, but if she didn't visit soon, her father might become suspicious. She was in Berlin to study and she knew that not visiting her family outside of term time could easily blow her cover. They lived on a beautiful estate in the country, and it wasn't unreasonable for her father to expect her to spend longer periods at home. Growing up, she'd had an idyllic childhood, surrounded by luxury and with her parents doting on her, but now the grand estate felt more like a prison, her father no longer the sweet, kind man she remembered.

'I'll be fine,' Alex assured her.

He turned her around in his arms, kissed her again, his lips sending ripples of warmth through her body.

'You know I'm going to marry you when this war is over, don't you?' he muttered. 'One day we'll be telling our children all about my time in your apartment, how I endured it all to survive and marry their mother.'

Sophia could see it as clearly as a picture: a brood of children gathered around them, listening to their handsome father sharing tales of the war and what they'd done to survive. But she knew how easily that pretty scene could be shattered.

'One day at a time,' she whispered against his lips. 'Every day we have together is worth it.'

She was tired but knew how bored he must be, and so she sat with him as he talked about his plan to create another compartment somewhere in the kitchen, somewhere safe for her to conceal not just him, but whomever else she brought home. She listened to him speak of his mother, his eyes lighting up as he imagined her finding safe passage, being hidden by someone as caring as his girlfriend, escaping from the clutches of the Nazis. Sophia, in her heart of hearts, wanted to believe in his words, but she knew the truth of what was happening out there.

The Jewish camps were awful, filthy and full of starving, sick people. They were places so bad that she couldn't even imagine a dog surviving there. But she never said a word, because if Alex didn't have faith, then he'd never be able to survive.

'Sophia?'

She blinked and realised he was asking her a question. 'Sorry?'

'Are you going out tonight?'

She nodded. 'If I get the signal.'

Alex knew not to ask for details, and she never told him. He didn't know about her false papers, or if he did he never said, and he didn't know where she went or whom she met with. It was safer that way. For everyone involved. Her work was what kept her going and made her believe that the Germany she loved would one day return.

'I'll prepare dinner for us, then it's time for me to go,' she said. In other words, it was almost time for him to hide in his box again – only this time it would be for hours.

Sophia rubbed at her chest, using the heel of her palm. She'd had a tightness there for months, a pressure that she couldn't disperse no matter how hard she tried. It was there at night, weighing her down when she tried to fall asleep; it was there when she carried on as normal during the day and tried to pretend she was a model German citizen; and it was most definitely there when she slipped out into the cover of darkness when she should be safely asleep inside her apartment.

She dropped her hand and took a deep, shuddering breath. It was only recently that she'd insisted on hiding Alex away whenever she left the apartment, but she wondered if he merely went along with it until she'd gone, and then got out. She wouldn't blame him if he did, but she'd had a strange feeling lately, a certainty that her apartment was going to be searched. Nothing had been said, but the last time her father had been to visit he'd questioned her about her beliefs, as if to make certain that his daughter wasn't harbouring a softness for Jews. His hatred was so deep, so real, that it made her stomach curdle just thinking about it.

If only my dear father could see me now. She clenched her fists, tapping her pocket again to check for the hundredth time that she had her identity card on her. At night she was Heidi Becker, and she prayed every time she went out that no one she came across would recognise her. If they did, she'd be found out for sure.

Tonight she'd received the call she'd been expecting. Her phone had rung once, then stopped. She'd listened for it, waited, and then, sure enough, it sounded out again for just one more shrill ring. That was her signal and she'd known that once again she'd be sneaking out and playing her part in another rescue operation. Alex hadn't asked where she was going. He'd simply kissed her goodnight, a long, sweet press of his lips to her forehead, and she'd disappeared without knowing if she'd make it home to him again.

The thought sent a shudder of fear through her, but she didn't let it stop her. She walked quickly, her footfalls light as she rushed along the pavement. She was to walk in the shadows to a church and hide by a gravestone until she was met by a man she knew only as Horse. He was a big man, large enough to win a fight but with a heart full of kindness.

He had a reputation for saving more Jews than anyone else in Berlin. When she'd been recruited by like-minded students, Horse was the first person she'd been officially introduced to. She'd had to prove herself to him, and she'd never forgotten how intimidating that first meeting had been as he'd questioned her hard and fast about her beliefs. The jobs had started out small, but as they'd lost members and she'd slowly earned his trust, she'd quickly become more involved in his secret operations.

Sophia heard a noise and froze. The sound of her own breath roared in her ears, her heart racing as she slipped into a doorway. She pressed her back to it and stood immobile in the shadows as voices travelled to her on the breeze. Being out at night was more than dangerous – it was a death sentence; only people with something to hide were out sneaking around. The voices slowly disappeared, but she was too scared to move in case they were looking for her, in case they were waiting for her to step out. After what felt like the slowest minutes of her life, Sophia straightened her shoulders and forced herself to walk, deciding to move confidently instead of shuffling in the shadows. Surely she'd look less guilty if she wasn't lurking?

There was no noise now, the street deserted as she hurried across the cobbles to the cemetery. The last time, she'd caught an afternoon train out of Berlin and had to make her way into the woods. It had been less terrifying since she wasn't technically doing anything wrong by using the train, heading in the same direction as her family's estate. She used her own identity papers during the day, so all she had needed to do was smile, be polite and mention her father if she needed to. But once she was in the woods and following her orders, as night had fallen, her nerves had started to get the better of her. But she'd kept her chin up, met the small group of Jews – two families – and taken over as their guide to get them to where they needed to go. They all had their role to play, and hers was just one piece in the puzzle to get them to safety.

She smiled to herself as she thought about smuggling them, certain they would have made it safely to Sweden. They'd been hidden in boxes of furniture that were being transported by train. They might have had an uncomfortable wait in the bushes and an even more uncomfortable trip tucked into wooden crates, but hopefully they'd made it and they were alive. It was all that mattered to her, that they'd been given a chance to live, and when she'd retraced her steps to make certain no one had followed them, she'd felt incredible knowing the small role she'd played in attempting to get them out of Germany.

Sophia glanced around before darting across the road, crossing into a park and breaking into a run as she made her way through the dark. She was scared of the inky blackness around her; always had been, always would be. The thought of someone grabbing her, of not being able to see who or what was around, terrified her, but she gritted her teeth and kept moving, so close to where she needed to be. Besides, this was the easy part. The hard part was going to be making her way home with another person in tow.

Sophia gasped as she finally reached the cemetery, climbing the fence as quickly as she could and ducking down low. She made her way between the gravestones, hand reaching out to touch each one as she passed. And then she stopped, breathing heavily as she slid down and waited.

I'm missing my mother terribly. I wanted to be close to her. I've just found out my husband and I are expecting, and I don't know how I'm going to do it without her help.

She said the lines over and over in her mind, ready to sob out her cover story if she was caught, if anyone found her and questioned her. Sophia felt the weight of the gold band on her finger, the ring she wore to go along with her story, her nocturnal identity as much a part of her as her real life.

And then she waited. The signal was a whistle, a soft bird call that she was ready to mimic to identify that she was indeed the courier.

She sat in the cold, lying in wait in the dark, praying that she wasn't about to feel a rodent scuffle over her shoes, a spider fall from a tree or a member of the Gestapo haul her up to her feet and demand to know what she was doing. And that was without worrying about the new identity papers she had sewn into her skirt to give to the person she was about to meet.

Sophia started. That was it. The whistle was soft, but there was no mistaking it in the otherwise silent night-time air. It sounded too obvious, but maybe that was because she was the one listening for it. When it sounded a second time, she did her best to softly repeat it, and after waiting for a moment, taking one last sharp breath, she stood. A torch shone in her eyes for a moment and then everything went dark again, the sudden change clouding her vision with bursts of white.

'You made it,' a rough, deep voice said.

Sophia's heart was hammering in her chest. 'Yes. Shine the light down for me, please.'

She could make out only silhouettes in front of her, and she needed to move quickly to get the papers. If they were caught, these documents might be the only thing standing between them and death. She picked at the stitching of her skirt, opening up the secret pocket she'd made. She took out the papers and passed them over.

'Here you go,' she said with a shaky voice.

'Thank you.' The second voice was male but soft, that of a younger man, maybe only a teenager from the sound of it.

She'd glanced at the identity papers so she'd have enough information in case they were stopped, but she always preferred to know as little as possible. If she was found out, taken and tortured, she didn't want to know anything that she might be forced to share.

'We have a new arrangement,' Horse said. 'This boy is the first one I've bought from the Nazis. It seems some of the guards will do anything if you offer them enough American cigarettes.'

Sophia swallowed. 'And you trust this man? This *Nazi*?' She turned, strained her eyes into the dark. Wasn't bribing a guard putting her, *all of them*, in even more danger? 'It could have been a trap. Are you certain you weren't followed?'

Panic was rising within her, the hot taste of bile in her throat making her want to be sick. The urge to flee surged through her body, but she forced her feet to stay rooted to the spot.

'I've had him in hiding for days,' Horse said. 'No one followed us here.'

'So will we have more to help? How often will you be negotiating?'

He made a low grunting sound. 'Wait for the phone to ring. The less you know . . .'

She nodded. *The better.*

'Come on, let's go,' she whispered, holding out her hand to the young man.

He grasped it, and she could feel how thin he was, his freezing, bony skin against her palm.

'Safe passage,' Horse murmured as he disappeared into the night.

'Follow me, move when I move, and don't say anything unless you have to,' she whispered. 'If anyone asks, we've been to see my mother's grave, and you're . . .' Sophia paused, seeking out his features, wishing she could see his face properly. 'You're my cousin, and you're terribly sick.' It was the only thing she could come up with. Why else would a German boy be this painfully thin? 'You've been sick for months, and I'm scared of losing you now that Mother has gone.'

She kept hold of his hand as they rushed back the same way she'd come. The frigid air was chilling her right to the bone, but she was thankful not to be as thin as her new friend. Tonight she would feed him, tuck him safely away for the night and hope and pray that by some miracle he would be safely smuggled out of the city to Sweden before anyone found out what she was doing.

There were some Jews living in Berlin – the roundups had temporarily ceased – but it was still so dangerous for him to be here. She moved faster, desperate to reach home. She would do anything she could to stand against Hitler, but there was nothing that she liked about being in charge of another person's life and safety. Gambling with her own life was one thing; anyone else's was another matter completely.

'Thank you.'

The words were so low they were barely audible, but they brought tears to Sophia's eyes. 'You're welcome,' she murmured back.

This young man might have lost his entire family. He might have been certain he'd die before the week or month or year was out. At least now he had hope, even if it was just a glimmer.

'You'll have to hide in here.' Sophia had downed a glass of gin, and her hands were shaking less now than when she and the boy had first burst into the apartment. It always took a few drinks to settle her nerves after a rescue.

'If we're searched,' Alex said, giving her a worried look. 'She means you'll have to hide there *if* we're searched.'

The young man nodded. 'How long will I be here?'

'A night, maybe two,' Sophia replied, finding her voice. 'Any longer and the chance of you being discovered is . . .' She didn't finish her sentence. The truth was that he'd probably be safer staying here long-term, but if she did that then she couldn't help another.

'You'll be moved soon. Sophia will wait for her signal and then you'll be transported quickly,' Alex explained.

She nodded, thankful that Alex had spoken for her even though he knew little about the logistics. The rescues were starting to affect her more and more, the terror of being caught starting to weigh heavier each time. Even though she didn't tell Alex much, he'd figured out a lot of what she did.

'Would you like something to eat, or do you want to go straight to bed?' Sophia asked, clenching her fists to stop the trembling.

'Food, please,' he said. 'I can hardly keep my eyes open, but I'd do anything for something to eat.'

She warmed soup for him and sliced a piece of bread and some cheese. She and Alex didn't have a lot, but the extra she'd bought on the black market had given them enough to share this week.

'Tell me about your family,' she asked. 'How are they faring?'

He took the food she passed him and started eating, snatching mouthful after mouthful.

'Whoa,' Alex said, taking the bowl from him. 'Slow down or you'll bring it all back up.'

The boy nodded, eyes still fixed on the food that had been whisked away, as if he thought he'd never get it back.

'Have a little something to drink,' Sophia said, filling a glass with water and passing it over. She went to sit across the table, folding her arms as she watched him.

He sipped from the glass, slowly, and she smiled.

'I haven't seen my family,' he said, voice low. 'My father disappeared first. He was seen being beaten in his store, and we never saw him again.'

Sophia glanced at Alex, saw the grim set of his mouth.

'And your mother?' she asked.

He shook his head. 'We were separated. She was taken with my sister. The only family I've seen since is my uncle.'

'I was parted from my family, too,' Alex said, his voice low. Sophia had heard the story so many times, knew it like it had happened to her personally, but it still cut deep every time. 'My parents didn't want to leave, especially my grandmother, but when she passed away we made the decision to try and get my mother and sisters out of Berlin.'

She saw Alex's hands shaking and stood to find him a glass. She poured him a small amount of gin, and he took it gratefully and downed the lot.

'Do you know what happened to them?'

'I know that my father is being worked to death in a camp somewhere. He was part of the roundup. I wasn't home when they came for us, and I hid until it was safe enough to come to Sophia. I've been here ever since.'

Alex didn't share that he'd been told his sister had been raped, or the fact that he had nightmares every day about hearing her scream and being helpless to do anything before she'd been dragged away. Or the fact that his mother had had the butt of a rifle slammed into her face as she'd been taken. Sophia knew his guilt, had cradled his head and held him through so many nights, but he was alive, and she was doing everything she could to help him.

'There's little we can do once they're taken,' Sophia explained, reaching for Alex's glass and pouring more for him. She took a sip herself, savouring the burn as the liquor scalded her throat. 'It's the ones still hiding here in Berlin who we can help. Sometimes.'

She watched as Alex pushed the plate back towards their guest. This time he ate more slowly, chewing each mouthful more carefully.

'Thank you for risking yourself tonight to hide me.'

Sophia nodded. 'We all need to do our bit.'

Alex downed the rest of his drink, and Sophia stood to tidy up, needing to busy herself and do something to stop from worrying and overthinking everything.

'You might be here two hours, it might be two days. But this place is as safe as it gets,' she heard Alex say.

'I'd better get some sleep, then. It'll be the first decent rest I've had in a while.'

Sophia showed him to her bed, ignoring his protests. She wasn't going to get a wink of sleep until he was gone, and it was best that he was rested before he left, whenever that would be. She turned and walked out of the room, wanting to give him at least a little privacy for now. She had no idea what he'd been through, what horrors he'd faced in his life, and she wanted to leave him be.

'Come here.'

Sophia went gratefully into Alex's arms.

'Every day gets worse,' she said.

'You did a good thing tonight,' he whispered into her ear. 'A wonderful thing. You've been so brave.'

She tried to ignore her fears as she stood in his embrace.

'I have something to show you,' he said, touching her hand. The smile on his face made it easier to push her worries aside.

'What is it?' she asked.

'I've been working on a new place to hide,' he told her. 'I think you'll like it.'

Sophia laughed despite her worries. 'You've been working on something in secret?'

He shrugged, but she could tell he was pleased with himself as he opened two cabinet doors and bent down, pointing in. 'I've made this false wall here, one I can hide behind. It used to be the back of the cabinetry, but I've moved it forward, and now I can fit in behind it and lie down instead of being folded in half in that damn ottoman.'

Alex moved back as she crouched down to inspect it.

'You're a genius!' she said, standing up and leaning against him as she kept staring at his handiwork. 'Now we can safely hide you *and* anyone who's staying with us.'

Unless you looked carefully, you wouldn't know how deep the cupboard once was. It was a perfect facade, making a long space for him to stretch out in.

His kiss brushed her cheek. 'I know.'

Sophia felt selfish standing in his arms, knowing that she should have forced him to leave the city months ago, as soon as she'd started playing her part in smuggling Jews out. But he'd wanted to stay in Berlin, wanted to wait until it was safe, to find out more about where his family was, and she hadn't the heart to tell him they were probably all long dead, and that he should be getting out while he still could.

'We need to rest,' she said, thinking more of herself than Alex now. At any stage within the next forty-eight hours, the phone would ring. Their safest way of getting Jews out was via freight trains, and when a suitable one was passing through, that's when she'd receive her orders. Someone higher up would have a schedule, and that's why her pickup had been tonight. The boy would be moved between safe houses, and eventually he'd spend a night hidden in the woods before being placed on a train with other rescued men and women, or maybe even children. Sometimes they were able to secure documentation to register a Jewish person as someone else, but mostly the only way to keep them alive was to smuggle them out and pray for the best.

CHAPTER TWO

HAZEL

LONDON, ENGLAND

1943

Hazel sat and smiled at her future mother-in-law, then continued sipping her tea for something to do. Her cheeks were red, she could feel how hot they were, and she wasn't sure if it was because the room was so stuffy or because of the subject matter at hand. Or maybe it was because of the awkwardness of this gathering – her parents, prospective in-laws and the fiancé she barely knew any more all squeezed into the front room of her family home. Perhaps it was all three.

'Look, I think it's one thing to have to help while the men are away, but surely these women won't expect to continue doing such work after the war?'

Hazel opened her mouth to say something and received a sharp look from her mother. She knew better than to say anything contradictory, had always been the good daughter doing what she was told. Her face burnt more and she balled one of her fists, her nails digging hard into her palm as her mother-in-law's words echoed through her mind.

'Mother, once the war is over, they'll be back to being housewives,' John said. 'We can't have women taking jobs from men. Imagine it!'

Hazel forced a smile when her fiancé laughed and squeezed her hand, probably wondering why she wasn't laughing along with him. Her father was smiling, his mother was giggling, and her mother was still giving her a sharp look as if daring her to say the wrong thing. She should have behaved – it would have been easier – but ever since she herself had started working, something had begun simmering within her, something that she was finding impossible to stamp out. She almost laughed, remembering the time at the start of the war when she'd offered her services to the cause at her local recruiting office.

She smiled at the men standing around, waiting their turn in line, and then spied a very dapper-looking older gentleman in full soldier's dress uniform. Hazel quickly made her way over to him.

'Excuse me, sir,' she said, smiling at the rather stern expression on his face when he turned to her. She watched him stroke his fingers across his neatly clipped moustache as he considered her.

'If you want to have your boyfriend excused from fighting, then I suggest you go and find someone else to cry to,' he said sternly.

Hazel felt a hot blush creeping across her cheeks as she shook her head. 'No, sir. I, ah, well, my fiancé is off to fight for our great country, but that's not why I'm here.'

He stared at her, looking impatient.

'Is there anything I can do? I mean, is there a place for women in the army doing anything?' she asked, feeling stupid. Her words were coming out all wrong, her face on fire as embarrassment spread across every inch of her skin.

'Let me get this straight,' he said with a chuckle. 'You want me to issue you a uniform and send you off to war, love?'

Hazel glared at him. How dare he treat her like this! She wanted to do something to help, not be laughed at.

'I don't appreciate your mockery, sir,' she said bluntly. 'I was simply enquiring whether I might be of assistance in some way.'

'Well, then, how about you run along and offer to help in the canteen?' he suggested, still chuckling. 'Unless you want to tell me specifically what it is that you think you can do for us? Were you thinking of joining the armed forces or the navy?'

Hazel was furious, but she didn't let him see how much he'd hurt her. She could cry later, but she wasn't going to let so much as a tear escape now, especially not with him and the other recruiting officer nearby laughing at her.

'Very well. I'll find somewhere else to be of use,' she said. 'Mark my words, though – if this war goes on for years, you'll be begging women like me to come and do our bit.'

Now, women didn't have a choice – unmarried ones anyway – but back then she'd been the source of much amusement.

'Women are running farms singlehandedly, and joining the air force,' Hazel said, clearing her throat and meeting John's gaze, unable to hold her tongue any longer. 'Is it so impossible to believe that women are actually as capable as men?'

Hazel saw the horrified look on her mother's face, and then the horror mirrored on her fiancé's face, and wished she'd just kept her mouth shut. But the way they spoke about young women, as if the work they did were somehow inferior to a man's, drove her crazy. All the young men were away fighting and yet somehow women had stepped perfectly into their roles, and they were doing a damn fine job of it, even if they were being paid less! It wasn't that she didn't want their men home, but she didn't like to be told that women weren't capable.

'Sweetheart, I know you're proud of your little job with the air force, but no one will want women hanging around trying to play at working when the men come home,' John said, in a voice that he no doubt thought was soothing, but that she simply found annoying. Had he changed since she'd fallen in love with him, or had she simply grown up?

If her blood could have boiled, she was certain steam would have been coming out of her ears and nostrils by now.

'Of course, we're very proud of you for helping, too,' his mother said, nodding in agreement with her son. 'It wasn't our intention to belittle you.'

No, she thought. *It was your intention to belittle every woman who's working to keep our country running!*

Hazel took a deep breath and forced a smile. *Remember your place,* her mother would have cautioned her. 'I shouldn't have taken offence,' she lied.

'Hazel's been working long hours,' her mother said, suddenly nodding so rapidly she looked as though her head was in danger of falling off. 'Another reason women aren't built for men's work!'

John chuckled and she suddenly, vividly remembered what it had been like before the war, when their romance had blossomed. Back then it had been all about stolen kisses and long summer nights with friends, going for a walk after dinner and feeling as if her heart would burst. Before the war, he'd been fun and carefree. Or perhaps they'd just been young, with hardly a care in the world.

'You should leave your window open tonight,' John had said one evening, his whisper grazing her skin. 'Perhaps I could sneak in after dark.'

Hazel had grasped his hand, equal parts horrified and excited. 'John!' she'd scolded. 'If Mother caught us she'd never let you near me again!'

'Come here, then,' he'd murmured, tugging her behind an oak tree, hidden from sight for a few moments until their friends caught them up.

'John . . . ,' she'd started to protest, but his fingertips were so soft against her cheek, his lips even softer.

'You're so beautiful,' he'd whispered, before kissing her, brushing his lips against hers and stroking her lower back.

'Hey!' One of her friends found them and Hazel jumped back, but not before catching John's eye, smiling at him as he winked at her and backed away.

She'd thought nothing would ever change things between them, not even the war.

Hazel blinked when she heard her name mentioned, no longer listening properly. She was well aware that her opinion didn't seem to matter, except to her father, who at least feigned interest and didn't treat her like a hopeless woman. When everyone had laughed earlier, her father had given her a wink that made her proud she'd at least tried to have a voice. The John she'd carried on with and naively imagined a perfect little future with probably would have rolled his eyes and winked, too. Which was why she was so confused about the feelings she was having about him, about whether she'd made a dreadful mistake in agreeing to marry him.

'Would you all mind terribly if Hazel and I took a moment to walk around the garden?' John asked.

Hazel blushed and stood as their parents tittered away, then took John's hand and followed him out when he nudged her. He infuriated her sometimes, and often when she wrote him letters she felt as though she was corresponding with a stranger, but holding his hand felt nice, soothed her worries somewhat. They'd been courting for almost nine months before she'd waved him off to war, and this was only the second time she'd seen him since then.

He squeezed her hand and smiled down at her, unleashing butterflies in her stomach. When they were outside, out of sight and earshot, he took her other hand and pulled her gently towards him.

'I've been wanting to do this for hours,' he said, bending to kiss her.

John's lips were warm against hers, moving slowly, gently, in a sweet kiss that sent goose pimples down her spine and reminded her of those memories she'd held on to for so long. His words had infuriated her, but his touch did the exact opposite.

He pulled away, wrapping his arms around her instead and kissing the top of her head. 'How much longer do we have?' she whispered. It was the first time they'd been truly alone together, the first time she'd been able to touch him freely, and it had taken only a moment to remind her why she'd fallen for him so quickly in the first place.

'I leave the day after tomorrow,' he said, sighing and stroking her hair. 'For God only knows how much longer.'

They were silent then, and Hazel couldn't help but think how much he'd changed. The man she'd said goodbye to had been desperate to serve, excited about what lay ahead, but she could tell he had no desire to return, not this time.

'Do you ever think about the day you left?' she asked, her voice a low whisper.

He nodded. 'Often.'

She sighed and leaned into him, breathing in his scent, feeling his strong, warm chest against her cheek. 'I was so upset that you were going before you'd been called up. Back then I was more concerned about missing our wedding date than the war.'

He chuckled. 'And I was so desperate to fight. If only I'd known what I was going into, I'd have stayed home and married you.' John kissed her forehead. 'I'd have been better off waiting until I was called up.'

She looked up into his dark brown eyes and was warmed by the steadiness of his gaze. She'd often wondered how different things might be if they'd simply brought their wedding forward. Perhaps she might have even had John's child by now. But at the time, it had seemed logical to wait – she'd been young and they'd been engaged only a short time after all.

She still loved John, but her expectations had changed. She'd been brought up to expect a comfortable life as a wife and mother, and now she was relishing the independence and responsibility that came with her work. It wasn't that she didn't want to be married, but she no longer felt that being a housewife was all she aspired to be.

'What are you thinking about?' he asked, holding her at arm's length.

She smiled up at him. 'I wondered that day if I'd ever see you again. It's almost a surprise to have you standing here.'

'And I thought our wedding would only be delayed by a few months and life as we knew it would resume,' he said drily. 'How wrong was I?'

Hazel leaned in again, arms encircling his neck as she drew him in for another kiss. Here with him like this, her worries seemed to fade away, the things that had annoyed her earlier disappearing. Perhaps he just said such things to impress her parents or his? Surely he didn't believe all women were only capable of keeping a home and caring for babies.

'I'll miss you,' John whispered.

'I'll miss you, too,' she replied, jumping back when a door banged. Her father appeared and gave them a stern look.

Hazel folded her arms around herself and smiled at her father when he walked closer.

'It's almost time for you to leave for work,' he said. 'Time to say your goodbyes.'

Hazel nodded and waited for her father to go back inside, before taking John's hand and studying his fingers, imagining a wedding ring there, imagining them married, trying to go back in time and recall how excited she'd been when he'd proposed. She'd seen a perfect little house and four perfect little children back then, but now she wondered whether life would ever seem so simple.

'I'll see you tomorrow before you go?' she asked.

He leaned in and stole one last kiss. 'Tomorrow.'

Hazel walked to work, thankful to be out in the fresh air. She would miss John, but she was starting to wonder if they'd ever be married.

Perhaps other couples were the same, separated for so long and left wondering what things would be like once the war was over, or at least that's what she liked to tell herself. But she was starting to struggle with what was expected of her, feeling as if she was playing the perfect daughter, perfect fiancée routine, when she felt a yearning to do something more. What that was, she didn't know, but now that she was alone she couldn't stop the earlier conversation from playing through her mind.

What she hadn't told anybody, including John, was how her work with the Women's Auxiliary Air Force had changed. She'd quickly moved on from packing parachutes to working as a plotter, tracking the positions of enemy aircraft and taking over communication duties, and recently she'd started to hear whispers about women working under-cover. About women working in roles as important as any man's. Her superior, Officer McLeod, had asked her more than once about her language skills, and she had wondered whether the rumours were true, whether she might be selected. Her higher-ups had been surprised at her knack for working radios, and only a month earlier when one of their best plotters had disappeared without any explanation, Hazel had been certain the girl had been recruited for something bigger.

She'd only just stepped into work when she heard her name called. 'Hazel, I need a word.'

She immediately went over to Officer McLeod. Her heart started to race, excitement building. Why did he want to see her again?

He moved to a quiet spot and she stood expectantly in front of him.

'It's been brought to my attention that you would make an excellent translator.'

'Yes, sir, I believe I would.'

'Can you confirm that you are absolutely fluent in the French language?'

'Yes, sir. I am.'

'*French* French, not school French?'

She nodded. 'Is this to do with undercover work, sir?'

Hazel felt her cheeks start to burn when he gave her a stern look. She knew she was probably turning beetroot red, unsure what she was supposed to say.

'Excuse me?'

'I suppose I didn't really want to say, but I thought "translator" was code for something bigger, something more, well, important and *undercover for our country*.' She said the last part quietly, wondering if she'd made a big mistake even mentioning it.

'I see. Well, let me tell you that such things, if they existed, would be by invitation only.'

She nodded again, not sure at all what he was telling her.

'I understand,' she said with some uncertainty. What was his sudden interest in whether or not she could speak French fluently?

'Report to the Northumberland Hotel tonight at 1700 hours.'

'Yes, sir.'

'You'll be meeting with a man known as Smith. Wait in the lobby and he'll find you.'

'Thank you, sir.' Hazel watched him walk away, a little stunned by what had just happened. She had no idea how the process worked, but something told her that her job description might be about to change. This might be her chance to do something big.

She went to her desk, this time with a spring in her step. She only hoped that her French was still as good as it had once been, and that John would forgive her if she took a job he felt should be reserved for men.

Hazel sat very still. She was trying to act relaxed and pretend as if sitting in the lobby of the Northumberland Hotel was the most normal thing in the world, but the truth was that she was a bundle of nerves. No amount of pretending was going to stop her from digging her nails into her palms and clenching her toes tightly in her shoes to avoid jiggling her legs.

She'd been punctual arriving, careful to ensure she had enough time to be waiting promptly at 5 p.m. But she was still waiting some time later, and no one had come looking for her.

'Good evening.'

She hadn't noticed the man approaching her from behind the chair, and she gave him a quick glance.

'Good evening,' she replied, not wanting to engage. As he sat down next to her, she noticed he was well dressed, his trousers nicely tailored and his tie knotted perfectly.

'You're waiting for someone?' he asked. 'I've heard there are some meetings here tonight.' He stretched out, looking comfortable.

Hazel turned and gave him a tight smile. 'I wouldn't know. I'm waiting for a family friend.'

'Oh. Sorry to bother you, then. *Profitez de votre soirée.*'

Hazel laughed. 'I'm sorry, but I don't speak that language. Is it French?' She was acting calm; she knew she was doing a good job of fooling him, but inside she was on the verge of blowing up. She dug her nails tighter into her palm. *Enjoy your evening.* She'd known exactly what he'd said.

'Very good instincts,' he said with a chuckle, before holding out his hand. 'I'm Smith. Come with me.'

Hazel made a noise that sounded like a whimper, a big breath sighing from her lungs. She'd been suffocating there, trying so hard to put this man off the trail, worried she would give away something that was so secret, and it had been a ruse!

'You did well,' he said as he walked quickly. 'I'm impressed, and I don't impress easily. You thought fast on the spot.'

'Ah, thank you, sir,' she said as she hurried alongside him. He opened a door and indicated for her to walk through, bending closer as she passed.

'The clenched fists were what gave you away. Other than that?' He shrugged. 'Pretty good.'

Hazel took a step into the room and stopped. She looked around, then at the man she knew only as Smith. There were two chairs in the room, as if the rest of the furniture had been swallowed by the stark white walls. She moved cautiously when he pointed to one of the chairs, her nervous excitement making way for a pit of dread in her stomach. Hazel glanced back at the door as Smith locked it and came closer, sitting in the opposite chair.

'What comes to mind when I say the word *Nazi*?' he asked, staring straight at her.

She felt a line of sweat bead across her forehead.

'Hatred,' she said simply. 'Evil men who must be stopped no matter what the cost.'

'Do you resent your fiancé being sent to war?'

'Well, I did resent the fact he signed up so quickly.'

'So you don't want him to serve our great country?'

She gasped. 'That's not what I said! But we had planned to be married and . . .'

'Your marriage is more important than fighting this battle?'

Hazel shook her head, ignoring the tears that had sprung to her eyes. He was trying to get under her skin, and she wasn't going to let him. This was her one chance to prove that she was strong, that she could do something more to help bring the Nazis down. She wasn't some pathetic woman more worried about a pretty wedding gown than fighting for what was right!

'I am willing to sacrifice my own life for the people of our country,' she said firmly. 'Do I miss my fiancé? Of course. I would prefer him to be at home, but once and only once this war is won.'

He nodded. 'You lied to me in the lobby. Is this something you do often?'

'No, sir.'

'Where did you learn to speak the language fluently?' he asked in French.

She smiled. 'When I lived abroad in Paris,' she replied in the same language.

'Who did you live with there?' he asked, in English this time.

She took his lead, answering in her native tongue. 'I lived with a family. The daughter, Rose, was a close friend of mine when they lived in London, and when her family returned to Paris my parents arranged for me to go with them to broaden my language skills.'

'Who is this Rose?' he asked, switching languages again.

Hazel replied immediately in French. 'She is from a nice family, and I had the most wonderful time there. She married a businessman who unfortunately passed away recently.'

'Do you know anything about her husband?'

'Nothing that I imagine would interest you.'

Smith chuckled. 'You'd be surprised. Were you aware that he was affiliated with the Resistance? That he was a passionate supporter of this underground movement?'

Hazel considered his question. 'No, I was not aware. But it doesn't surprise me. He was a very wealthy man, but he was also very cultured and had a strong sense of humanity. I attended their wedding and I very much approved of Rose's choice of husband.'

'Do you feel that you know Paris well?'

She nodded. 'Yes.'

'How well do you know other parts of France?'

She gulped, not used to answering such intense, rapid-fire questions. 'Well, I know Paris very well, as well as I know London in fact. And yes,' Hazel said, trying to stay calm and answer the questions without racing, 'I did explore other parts of France. Rose and her husband had a beautiful home on the coast, near Brest, and I was fortunate enough to have an extended holiday there with them after they were married.'

'What would you do if a Nazi was running towards you?' he asked in English.

'Do I have a gun in this hypothetical situation?' she asked back.

He smiled. 'Yes.'

'Then it's a simple answer. I'd shoot him,' Hazel said bluntly. 'Make no mistake, I hate the Nazis with all my heart, and as unskilled as I might be in the field, I'd do my best to shoot him dead.' She was pleased not to hear a quiver in her voice, because the truth was that she'd hate to be put in a situation that required her to take another person's life, Nazi or not.

Smith stood and walked around the room, no longer looking at her. He kept firing questions at her, tirelessly over and over, as if he had a hundred things ready to ask her. He was relentless. When he stopped pacing and stared at her, she took a deep breath and waited.

'And what would you do if I asked you to leave here with me and disappear tonight? Would you come with me?' His gaze was cold.

'No,' she said. 'Because I don't know who you are. All I know is that you're asking me all sorts of questions, that I have no idea who you work for or what you do, and I still don't know what role I'm auditioning for, or if one even exists.'

He folded his arms across his chest. 'Maybe my sources were right about you.'

She had no idea what *sources* he could be talking about. She sat still, staring at him, pretending to be more confident than she was.

'Thank you for your time. I'll be in touch if I need to be.'

He crossed the room and opened the door, beckoning for her to walk out. Hazel stood and tried to walk as slowly as she could, head held high. She had no idea if the interview had been a dismal failure or if she was still in with a chance, so she stopped and looked him directly in the eye.

'Goodbye, Hazel.'

He smiled and shut the door behind her, leaving her alone outside the room. She breathed a sigh of relief, realising how long she must have been holding her breath. There was a clock in the lobby, and when she passed it she saw she'd been in the room for at least forty minutes.

She could only hope that this elusive Smith, whoever he was, had liked what she'd said. Because she had a feeling this was the kind of job you got only one chance of securing, and either she'd blown it or managed to impress the person deciding her fate.

CHAPTER THREE

ROSE

BREST, FRANCE

1943

Rose stood at the window and stared out. She'd always imagined coming back here with Peter when the war was over. Naively, she'd expected everything to return to normal – for her husband to return unscathed, for them to retire to their home near the coast at Brest so he could rest. And she'd also expected the fighting to be well and truly finished by now.

How wrong she'd been. She shook her head. His role as a soldier might have been over, but Peter had continued to fight, and his bravery and dedication to their country had ended up costing him his life.

Rose touched a hand to her stomach, the action alone making tears burn her eyes. *Peter.* She let them fall silently, wiping her cheek. When they'd met, at a party with friends, she'd not immediately noticed him. But when he'd insisted they all hear her opinion on the politics of the day, when every other man in the room had rolled his eyes at her, she'd known he was the man she'd one day marry. They'd spent the entire evening from that moment on talking about anything and everything, sipping wine and laughing, heads bent together. The very next day she'd found out that he was the millionaire businessman who'd been hosting the extravagant party they'd attended, and by midday she'd received the biggest bouquet of roses she'd ever seen in her life.

She smiled thinking of all the dates and gifts, all the ways he'd tried to win her heart. What he hadn't seemed to understand was that she'd fallen for him because of the way he let her have a voice, the way he listened to her and liked the fact she held her own opinions about the world. That was what had made her love him.

And now here she was, pregnant with the child they'd desperately hoped for, but with Peter never to return home. She touched her wedding band with her thumb. It somehow gave her comfort knowing he'd placed that ring there and she'd never, ever taken it off.

Rose turned and almost expected to be standing in her kitchen in Paris. She could see the sparkling bench, the kettle boiling and Maria, her long-time maid, smiling and asking her if she wanted a cup of tea. Only here there was no Maria to keep her company. The kitchen was dark, the fire not set, the house cold. It had been a beautiful retreat for her and Peter, their beloved home on the coast, but without him, and without any help to set about dusting and cleaning and tending to the fire, it seemed forlorn.

But she needed to pull herself together. Her brother, Sebastian, was coming to stay with his wife the next day, and she didn't want them feeling sorry for her. Rose touched her stomach once again, the only thing these days that seemed to comfort her. She gave herself one last moment to remember Peter, not wanting to forget his touch, his smell, his larger-than-life personality.

'Darling, it's time.'

Rose had been dreading those little words all morning, had been trying to pretend as if Peter was just leaving for work, that he wasn't leaving her again. It terrified her even more now than it had when he'd left in uniform while he'd served for the French Army.

'I don't know what I'll do without you.'

He tucked his fingers under her chin and tilted her head up. 'You'll be fine. I won't be so long. Besides, you need to hold the fort here for me – you'll be too busy to worry.'

She smiled even though she felt like weeping. This was something he had to do, which meant it was useless making a big fuss. She kept herself together, as she always did, knowing there would be plenty of empty hours to cry and fret to herself once he was gone. She'd not slept a wink all night, and it was making her irrational.

'I love you. More than you'll ever know,' she said, staring into the brightest blue eyes she'd ever seen. Those eyes were filled with tears and they made hers prickle right back, but she refused to let one fall. She wanted his lasting memory to be of her smile, not her sobs of emotion. He could be gone for weeks, maybe longer if something unexpected happened.

'You're certain you don't want me to come down to the station?' she asked. 'I can be there with you until the very last moment.'

He shook his head. 'It's only a business trip. You need to think of it as nothing more than me leaving for work. Besides, I want to remember you just like this,' he said, kissing her and running a hand down her back. 'In a silk robe, just roused from bed and with your hair all tousled. That's what got me home last time despite all odds – knowing this was waiting for me.'

She laughed. 'It was a lovely last morning,' she teased, running her hands down his lapels. He looked so handsome in his suit. 'I'll think of it every time I go to our bed.'

They'd made love, then sipped coffee and eaten breakfast together, before he'd bathed and dressed. If he hadn't been about to leave, it would have been the perfect start to any day.

'Stay safe,' she murmured against his lips, knowing it wasn't a promise he could keep but wanting to say it anyway.

'You know I will.'

Peter waved to her and opened the door. She stood, motionless, and watched him as he left, as he blew her a kiss and shut the door behind him. Rose sank to her knees once he'd gone, sobs making her body heave, her shoulders shaking as she stifled the screams struggling to burst out. She clamped one hand to her mouth, her palm silencing her pain, the other pressed to the floor as she tried not to fall forward.

'I love you,' she whispered, even though he was long gone now. 'I love you so much.'

They were words she'd spoken to him so many times, he knew them as deeply as she did herself. But still, she would have given anything to tell him one last time. To hold him just a few minutes longer. Because something felt wrong this time. He'd been so careful, so clever to go undetected until now, but she wasn't sure how long his luck would last.

Rose slipped to the ground, sinking against the cool, hard tiles. This couldn't be happening. He was supposed to stay safe. He was supposed to stay home. They were supposed to have their whole lives ahead of them. Why had she left Paris and thought it best to come here, alone?

She dropped her hands to her stomach and sobbed. He'd never even know that they had a child.

'Rose?'

Rose heard Sebastian's call and stared at herself in the mirror. She had her trademark red lipstick on, and her cheeks were ever so slightly rouged to disguise how hollow they were. She touched her hand to her hair as she studied her reflection, hoping she'd done enough to fool her guests into thinking that she was coping. When he called again she hurried down the hall to the front door. The moment she saw her handsome raven-haired brother standing there, she rushed into his arms, hugging him tight. She stood a moment, indulging in his warm embrace, before pulling back and turning to his wife, Charlotte.

'It's so good to see you,' she said, hugging her sister-in-law with as much love as she'd shown her brother. 'I've only been here two days and I'm like an old lady rattling around alone.'

Sebastian laughed. 'You're hardly an old lady.' He brought their cases in and Rose led the way through into the drawing room. The fire was blazing, and she was pleased that the house looked so different to when she'd first arrived.

'You've settled in?' Charlotte asked.

'I have. It's taken me all this time to tidy up, but it feels more like home again now.' Rose kept her smile fixed, not wanting her guests to feel sorry for her. They weren't long married and she wanted them to enjoy their stay instead of worrying about her. She didn't mention the fact that on her first night here she'd curled into a ball after crying her eyes out and slept on the cold kitchen floor.

'Show Charlotte the guest room,' she said to Sebastian. 'And please, make yourself at home. Anything you need, help yourself.'

They disappeared, chatting as they went down the hall, and Rose took a deep breath, trying to keep her emotions in check instead of falling back into her grief. It had been only weeks since she'd received the dreadful news, but she'd spent her entire life being headstrong and independent, and she wasn't about to start cracking beneath her pain now.

A knock echoed, followed by laughter, and Rose smiled as she listened to her brother and his wife. She remembered what it had been like when she and Peter were first married. They couldn't keep their hands off each other, and it had been like that right up until the last time she'd seen him.

'Darling, you're a wonderful nurse. You haven't lost your temper in days.'

Rose smothered a laugh. 'Careful, my love, or I'll find some crockery to throw at you.'

They both chuckled then, Peter's eyes meeting hers as they stared at one another from across the bedroom. She sat in front of her mirror, applying make-up, while he sat propped in bed watching her. They'd made love all morning, her husband finally over the dreadful flu that had kept him in bed for days, and she felt so close to him after the hours spent tangled, naked, beneath their sheets.

'My parents called you as sweet and delicious as a peach,' he joked. 'If only they knew what went on behind closed doors.'

He was right. She did have a temper with him sometimes and the sweet disposition she usually displayed could easily be turned into anger if Peter did something to annoy her. He'd become particularly careful with the attention he gave to beautiful women after she'd slapped him at a café.

'Speaking of disagreements,' she said, trying to keep her voice light so she didn't raise his suspicions, 'I've been hearing a lot about women assisting with the Resistance.'

Peter sighed. 'For heaven's sake, Rose. Can't you just let a man convalesce in peace?'

She set down her lipstick and smiled at him. 'Darling, you're hardly convalescing now and, besides, it seems ridiculous for me to sit here doing nothing. Can't I do something to help the war effort?'

He smiled. 'Yes, darling, you can knit socks and send them to the poor men at the front.'

She could feel her temperature rising, her cheeks starting to burn. 'Don't speak to me as if I'm only capable of knitting,' she said, fuming, but trying to keep her voice low. 'I will not be told what I can and can't do, Peter. I was simply trying to be diplomatic about it instead of going behind your back.'

'You're my wife,' he said, voice as calm as could be, as if they were having a simple discussion about the weather. 'And it seems to me you're going to do this whether I like it or not. But this is me, for once, Rose, putting my foot down.'

'You don't have the right to, to . . .' She grabbed her hairbrush and threw it at him. 'I'm your wife, not your slave!'

'Oh, Rose.'

'Don't you "oh, Rose" me!'

'But you're so gorgeous when you're cross with me,' he said. 'That sweet little nurse routine didn't last for long, did it?'

Rose took a deep breath, trying to hate him and failing when he winked and beckoned her closer.

'Sweetheart, please,' he said, circling his arms around her once she had come and settled down beside him.

She looked up at him. 'Is it so wrong to want to help?'

'No. But you're behaving as if I don't have the right to be worried about you,' he said gently. 'I love you, Rose. Is it so wrong that I want to do everything I can to keep you safe? That I want to know you're here, protected, instead of doing something reckless?'

She sighed, her frustration mounting. 'I can't sleep at night, knowing what's going on out there right beneath our noses. We need to do more. I need to do more.'

He nodded. 'I know.'

'You knew who I was when you married me,' she said softly. 'If you wanted to marry a society princess with no conscience, then you picked the wrong woman for your wife. I need to feel like I'm doing something that will actually make a difference.'

Peter laughed. 'Sweetheart, I know exactly what type of woman I married.' He dropped a kiss to her lips and ran a hand through her long hair. 'I love that you want to help, that you're so passionate and aware, but . . .'

She looked up into his eyes, knowing that he was telling the truth. One thing she couldn't fault her husband for was the way he loved her. He looked at her and truly saw her – he always had – and he'd never expected her to change herself for anyone. She'd been brought up by parents who had appreciated her opinions, but they'd always been worried about how a husband would cope with how outspoken she was. The fact they'd sent her to a top finishing school was evidence enough of how much they wanted her to marry well. Peter had more than passed their expectations, but she knew how worried they'd always been about her opinion on everything from politics to a woman's right to do as she pleased.

'Darling . . . ,' he started, then let out a loud breath.

'What were you going to say?' she asked, pushing him back a tiny bit, palms flat to his chest. 'You have a look on your face, like you're keeping something from me.'

'We're doing something already. To help, I mean.' He sighed again. 'I don't want you to think I'm sitting by and not thinking and feeling the same things you are. We want the same things, you and I, and I want you to know we're not at odds here.'

She went still, eyes on his. 'What do you mean?' Had he been keeping something from her?

'I thought it was best that you didn't know, so you could never be questioned about it.'

'What have you done, Peter? What haven't you told me?'

'I've been helping the Resistance,' he said in a low voice, as if he was worried someone could be listening. 'Financially, I mean. And very handsomely, I might add. They need weapons, and I had the contacts and the money to assist.' He hesitated and shook his head, as if he couldn't believe he was telling her. 'Some of my business trips, well, they've been to arrange funds for them and to assist with organising arms. I didn't tell you because the less you knew, the better if you were ever questioned.'

Rose stared at him. 'You what?'

'I thought you'd be happy. I—'

'Peter! How could you?' She slapped at him, furious, then grabbed a pillow and beat him with it around the arms.

'Rose!' He laughed and fought her off as she laughed back and kept hitting him. 'Rose, stop!'

She threw the pillow aside and leapt into his arms, wrapping her legs and arms around him. She planted a big, long kiss on his lips. She didn't care that he knew people who could supply arms and make those kinds of deals in secret. All she cared about was that they were doing something.

'You should have told me,' she muttered. 'You shouldn't keep things like this from me.'

He kissed her back. 'Well, now you know.'

Rose blinked away tears as she held on tightly to her husband, her cheek to his chest as she listened to the steady beat of his heart.

'I'm so scared of losing you,' she whispered.

'You're not going to lose me,' he said, and kissed the top of her head. 'I'm very careful.'

She knew that being careful had a loose meaning. They were all in danger, every single one of them, and Peter even more so now.

'If something was to happen then – to you, I mean – do you expect me to carry on what you're doing? Should I keep sending them money?'

He shook his head and pushed her back, holding her at arm's length now and staring straight into her eyes. 'No, Rose. You mustn't. I'm not having you put yourself in danger. What I've already done for them is enough.'

She nodded. 'You needn't be so worried about me, Peter. I can be careful.'

'Promise me,' he demanded. 'Promise me that I won't have to worry about you doing anything reckless whenever I'm away on business.'

'I promise,' she said, the words catching in her throat and making her cough. She hated lying, and the last thing she wanted was for her husband to lose faith in her.

'What is it?' he asked.

'I was just, well, wondering if driving an ambulance would constitute recklessness or not.'

'An ambulance? Christ, Rose, are you out of your mind? Why can't you be content helping like you already are? Like we already are?'

'For the same reason I couldn't bite my tongue the night you met me,' she said, standing and smiling down at him. 'I won't do anything silly, but I thought the least you could do was pay for an ambulance so I can provide extra assistance if it's needed. Or we could do something else . . .'

Peter had given her a look that told her she might have pushed too far, but she didn't care. He'd forgive her; he always had and she was certain he always would.

'Rose?'

Rose turned, wiping away a tear. She found herself standing in the middle of the room, so lost in her own thoughts she hadn't realised Sebastian had come up behind her. When she turned she saw Charlotte standing there, too, a worried look on her face.

'Sorry, don't mind me,' she said quickly, brushing at her cheeks and forcing a smile. 'My thoughts, memories, they just sneak up on me sometimes.'

Charlotte closed the space between them and put her arm around her, hugging her. 'Come on, let's get that water boiling and make something hot to drink.'

Rose nodded and hugged her sister-in-law back. Right now her grief was raw, but she was determined to stay strong. She had a baby on the way, a child that needed all of her strength and love. She wasn't ready to tell her brother about it just yet, wanting to keep the secret for herself a little while longer.

'I didn't want to bring this up right away,' Charlotte said as she settled into a chair in the kitchen and Rose set about making coffee, 'but, Rose, we're only here for a night now.'

Rose glanced up as her brother came into the room. 'You came all this way for a night?' she asked. Paris was over six hours away and they'd mentioned coming for a week.

She watched the pair exchange glances and then it was her brother who spoke. 'Rose, I'm not sure how much you're aware of, but there's an underground network of sorts operating in this area,' he said.

Rose spooned coffee into the pot. 'I'm not so naive that I don't know about the Resistance.' But it did surprise her to know they were so active near her home.

Charlotte laughed. 'I told your brother exactly that on our way here.'

She swapped glances with her sister-in-law. There was a reason she liked Charlotte so much.

'Were you aware that your husband—'

'Was funding them?' Rose finished, smiling. 'Yes, Seb, I was.'

Sebastian looked speechless for a moment. 'Well, did you know it was me who asked him for the funding in the first place?'

This time he had her. 'No. I didn't. He wouldn't have wanted to risk mentioning you, perhaps? But I'm aware of all his . . . *business* dealings.'

'You've unwittingly ended up in a dangerous area, Rose. I just wanted to warn you that there are covert operations happening around here. We're passing through, legitimately able to say we're here to visit my grieving sister, but we might well be disappearing after this for some time.'

Rose's hand shook as she reached for the kettle. She couldn't stand the idea of losing her brother so soon after her husband.

'I see.' She took them their coffee and sat down across from Charlotte. Sebastian joined them.

'Peter was very clear that he didn't want you involved in any part of this,' Sebastian said.

'He would hate to think you were in danger,' Charlotte added.

When Rose's hand instinctively fell to her stomach and she looked up at Charlotte, she realised how easily she'd just given up her secret. Rose shook her head and Charlotte nodded. It seemed the other woman understood that it wasn't something she wanted to share.

'You'll be gone in the morning?' she asked.

'Very early in the morning, before dawn,' Charlotte replied.

'We'd best make the most of it then,' Rose said, forcing a smile. She looked between them, remembering the first time she'd met Charlotte. Even then, she could tell her brother was in love, and the fact the two of them were working undercover together told her that her first instincts about the other woman had been right. If only their parents were still alive; they'd have loved their daughter-in-law. They were used to their own daughter being confident and abreast of world affairs, and their mother would have appreciated that in her son's choice of wife.

'You'll be fine here on your own?' Sebastian asked.

'Of course. And if there is anything, anything at all, you or your fellow . . .' – she struggled to find the right words – '*freedom fighters* want or need, you're to ask me. I'd like to do whatever I can. It's not an empty offer, either. You're to call on me for anything, be it money or any other assistance. I want to help.'

Rose reached out and touched his hand. She might be pregnant, but if there was anything she could do to help, her resolve to be of use hadn't wavered. In fact, after losing Peter, she wondered if she was starting to feel more determined than ever to do something useful, so that his death and thousands more hadn't been for nothing.

Sebastian nodded and held up his cup. 'Perhaps after this we should move on to something stronger, then.'

Rose laughed, standing and heading for their little cellar. She was certain Peter would have something suitable tucked away. 'I remember another time we said the exact same thing.'

'The day we all figured out what that bastard Hitler was doing,' Charlotte called out. 'I don't care what happens to me, but if I can help stop him, I'll do anything.'

Rose leaned against the wall in the cellar, her eyes shut, remembering as if it was yesterday the day she'd gone to meet Sebastian and his journalist friends once Peter had left for work. It must have been six years ago, but the memory was crystal clear.

She entered, scanning the café until she saw a table of four in the corner, heads bent together as they talked. He didn't see her as she walked towards him, but she was surprised to see that one of the other three was a woman.

'Sebastian,' she said, after waiting for him to look up.

'Rose!' He stood and gave her a big hug before pulling back to kiss her cheeks twice and then twice again. 'You look wonderful.'

She sighed as she stared at her brother. 'Well, you don't,' she replied, wishing he'd look after himself better and live on more than coffee, cigarettes and whisky. 'Your clothes are hanging off you.'

The rest of the table was watching them now and, as her brother pulled another chair over, the woman she'd noticed stood.

'You must be Rose,' she said, kissing her cheeks as she introduced herself. 'I'm Charlotte.'

'Lovely to meet you. You're a journalist, too?' It surprised her to see a woman working alongside her brother and his male colleagues, and she felt a pang of envy. How fabulous it must be to have an exciting job.

'I am. We've just returned from a trip to Poland. We were in Vienna before that.'

'Was it terrible? Is it truly as bad as they say?'

Rose gulped at the pained look on Charlotte's face. She moved her chair closer to her brother, glancing at him, realising now that perhaps it wasn't the alcohol and unhealthy lifestyle that was making him look so gaunt. She could tell he didn't want to talk to her about it, because when she glanced back again she caught him shaking his head to his female colleague.

'Sebastian, she has a right to know,' Charlotte insisted, reaching for a cigarette and offering one to her. Rose took it, holding it carefully between her fingers. She hadn't smoked in years, but the urge to draw on the cigarette hit her hard. 'If you won't tell her then I will.'

The other two men, journalists she had met before, smoked their cigarettes and sipped their coffee as Rose turned to her brother.

'Is this woman your girlfriend?' Rose asked as politely as she was capable.

He shook his head, grinning at Charlotte behind her. 'No.'

Rose reached out and gave him a slap across the head. 'Stupid man. She ought to be.'

That made everyone except her brother laugh, and Rose settled into her chair, intent on finding out everything she could from this interesting woman now seated across from her.

'Sebastian, more coffee please,' she said, throwing her brother a sweet smile. 'For both of us.'

Charlotte's smile told her that she'd made a friend.

'Now tell me, what did you see when you were away? What will you be reporting from your trip?' Rose asked.

'Hundreds of thousands of Jews are arriving in Poland. They don't have passports, or if they do they're marked with a J. The Germans are just getting rid of them, running them like farm animals across the border to be done with them.'

Rose's hand shook as she bent to light her cigarette. She took a slow, steady puff before lowering her hand again.

'So it's all true. Everything we're hearing is true?'

'I'm afraid so. But the reality is far worse than what anyone is hearing.'

'Worse?'

'Many of the sick and elderly, they're living in old stables near the border. It's atrocious, and worse still is what's happening in Germany. They're beating Jews on the street, torching their businesses, destroying everything they have. What they don't destroy, they take for themselves.'

Rose was certain her husband had been trying to shelter her from everything that was going on in the world. He was a businessman and was surrounded by influential people who would know precisely what was happening. She hated being left in the dark, liked to know the latest news.

'There are even more fleeing the atrocities in Austria and Czechoslovakia, but many fear that they won't be able to get out.' Charlotte blew out an audible breath. 'And there are rumours of camps, terrible places that the remaining Jews will be sent to. It's only going to get worse.' She lowered her voice. 'So much worse.'

'Surely someone is doing something about that awful man. Not all Germans can be so cruel, can they?'

'I don't know.' Charlotte shrugged. 'I'm awake all night remembering what I've seen, trying to get the images from my mind of old men being beaten trying to protect their families, synagogues burning and streets of people saluting their leader as if he's just taken over their minds somehow.'

'But what use is all of that knowledge if we can't get our photographs out?' Sebastian said, finally breaking his silence. 'We can't write what we need to, and we can't show the world what we've seen. They confiscated everything when we left.'

'I think we should be drinking something stronger,' Rose announced, her hands shaking from what she'd been told.

'Now you know why I start drinking so early in the day,' Sebastian muttered drily as he waved the waitress over.

Rose felt a surge of love for her roguish brother. For all the idiotic things he'd done in his life, risking himself to see what was truly happening in Germany wasn't one of them.

She reached for his hand and held it tight. 'I'm so proud of you, Sebastian.' She looked around at the rest of the table. 'Of all of you. You're doing something brave, something that needs to be done.'

They all nodded, but she could see they weren't so sure they were doing the right thing. Perhaps if she'd been haunted by the images they'd seen, she'd understand better.

'Brandy, five glasses,' Charlotte said when the waitress finally made her way over to them.

Rose would normally have declined, but for once she didn't want to flee the café that was a favourite amongst her brother and his kind. Her husband was at work for the day, and the last thing she wanted after what she'd just heard was to go home to an empty house.

That night, she'd lain awake, with Peter asleep beside her, wishing there was something they could do, believing so strongly that the rest of the world wouldn't let such atrocities keep happening. And quietly fuming that her husband had pretended that he wasn't so worried about war breaking out, when he must have known the facts. And now, years into a war that felt endless, she couldn't help but wonder what could have been done differently if people had taken the German leader more seriously.

Rose grabbed a bottle of wine from one of the cellar's shelves and took a deep breath, walking back to the kitchen with a heavy heart. The last few days, weeks even, she'd been living in a bubble of the past, remembering conversations and moments with Peter or with her brother, but she needed to pull herself together and face what was happening head-on. If there was something she could do to help the Resistance, she would, and before he left she needed Sebastian to understand just how very important the underground movement was to her.

CHAPTER FOUR

Sophia

Berlin, Germany

Late 1942

Two days after she'd rescued the young Jewish man, Sophia checked her skirt in the mirror and did a silly little twirl for Alex. He was sitting on her bed watching her, and the upturn of his lips made her grin straight back at him. She'd smuggled their visitor out during the night, to be passed to another person working within their secret network, so it was just the two of them in her apartment now.

'I wish you were taking me out,' she said, sighing and running her hands down the fabric to smooth it. 'Lunch, a walk in the sunshine, anything but this.'

'Is that all you wish for?' he said with a laugh. 'I'm wishing you were taking that skirt *off* instead of putting it on.'

Sophia swatted at him when he reached for her, loving his playfulness. Joking with him like this took her mind off everything else that was going on, especially the worry of not knowing whether their young visitor would ever make it out of the country alive.

'Sophia, come here,' Alex said, standing and holding out his hands.

Sophia took the few steps back towards him and let him hold her. He touched one palm to her cheek, the other pressed to her hand.

'I can't wait to marry you.'

She smiled, her heart beating so fast it sounded like a drum thumping away inside of her.

'Me too,' she said without hesitation. 'But not here. I don't know, but maybe we should start over somewhere else when we get the chance?'

'So long as we're together,' he said, and kissed her lips. 'And you're my wife.'

Sophia wished she could stay tucked up in the apartment with him all day, but she needed to go. Her mother missed her terribly, and Sophia missed her just as much. She was looking forward to seeing her even if it was only for a short time. One day she'd tell her mother everything she'd done, and she knew without a doubt how proud she'd be.

She gave Alex one final, lingering kiss and then went to gather her things. Today she was playing the part of a perfect Nazi daughter. Her mother would see right through it and be smiling secretly to herself, but to the rest of the world she was her father's delightful Jew-hating daughter.

She stopped in front of Hitler's portrait, the only thing she hated about her otherwise beautifully furnished apartment.

'You are an evil, vile little man,' she whispered, childishly poking out her tongue at him and making Alex laugh. She hadn't realised he was still watching her, his eyes trained on her from where he stood by the bed.

'A vile *pig*,' Alex added. 'Although, that could be a mean thing to say. I mean, there are probably lovely pigs out there in the world.'

'Stay safe,' she whispered, and blew him a kiss. 'And stay hidden. Promise?'

He pretended to catch her kiss, pressing it to his cheek and being as silly as ever.

'Promise,' he replied.

Sophia slipped out and locked the door. She stood for a moment, gathering her thoughts, catching her breath. Sometimes she wondered if Alex collapsed to the ground after she left and cried; sobbed for what he'd lost and the pain of being stuck in one place for so many months. It was like a jail cell for him in there. She knew there was only so much any person could take, and one day she worried he'd reach that point and go stark raving mad.

She set off to catch the train, exhausted from the night before and knowing she had big circles under her eyes from lack of sleep. There was only so much she could do with make-up, but these days she was far less interested in being the glamourous heiress she'd once been, and more interested in making a difference. Maybe it would all be for nothing, everything she'd done, but at least she could say she'd tried.

Sophia walked down the road later that day, liking the freedom of taking her time and making her own way to the house from the train station. Their estate wasn't far – it had taken her only half an hour of walking in the sunshine, and she'd enjoyed soaking up the sun as she strolled. With everything that was happening, sometimes it was the simple act of being alone in the fresh air that let her clear her mind. She smiled, thinking about her mother; it had been hard being parted, and for some reason her mother had become reluctant to leave the countryside, so it had been a long time since she'd come to Sophia's apartment in Berlin.

She started up the driveway, her forehead slightly clammy from her stroll in the sun. It was moments like this that she felt alive, could imagine living in a world that was free of the evil she was so tired of seeing with her own eyes. She remembered the first time she'd come home to visit, when she'd first begun studying at university in the city.

'Sophia,' her mother said, a warm hand touching her daughter's shoulder before stroking her long blonde hair. 'It's so good to have you home.'

Sophia turned and smiled at her mother. She still remembered how elegant she'd looked with her hair falling over her shoulder. Her father had always called her his beautiful French wife, so proud of her, and Sophia had always hoped she shared some of her mother's elegance.

'Is Father well?' Sophia asked. She'd been staying in Berlin with her aunt at the time and wondered how in her absence her mother had become so thin, her cheeks so hollow.

'Of course,' her mother replied. 'Your father is happy supporting our wonderful Führer.'

Sophia heard the sarcasm in her tone. 'You can't talk like that,' she whispered, keeping one hand on her mother's arm. 'You need to be more careful.'

Her father had never raised a hand to her, had always been so kind to both her and her mother, but now everything had changed. He had sworn to put his country before his family, and that meant abiding by everything their leader believed in, no matter what his wife's private thoughts might be.

'I am careful. It's only with you that I let my guard down.' Her mother took her hand. 'Can I let my guard down with you, Sophia?'

'What's wrong, Mama?' Sophia asked as her mother took her hand, stroking her thumb across her skin.

'We must never forget what's in our hearts,' her mother said in a low voice. 'Do whatever you have to do to survive, I will never judge you for saving yourself, but don't ever lose faith in who you really are.'

Sophia gulped. She knew what she was being told because she'd always known that her mother didn't agree with her father's unwavering allegiance to the Nazi Party. It wasn't that her mother had ever said it outright before, but Sophia had seen her look away, seen her shudder as if her skin was crawling, watched as she had mumbled when before she would have spoken her opinions loudly for all to hear.

'Does Father know?' she asked. 'How you feel? What you think?'

'No.' Her mother shook her head. 'Of course not.'

'So all those times, all those parties we've had here and all the times you've smiled and been the hostess and . . .' Sophia could see her mother, dressed in beautiful gowns and dripping in jewels, laughing and smiling, kissing Goebbels on the cheek, blowing kisses to Adolf Hitler's portrait when she was in front of a crowd. All for show. She'd always wondered, and now she knew for sure.

'Mama?'

Her mother was blinking away tears and she gripped Sophia's hand more tightly. 'I'm telling you this because I gave all our servants the morning off and your father isn't here. We must never, ever talk of this again, Sophia, but I needed you to know how I feel. Do you understand?'

Sophia's hand shook as she took it from her mother's, so she quickly wrapped both arms around her, holding her tight. Her mother was everything to her. Her friends had been raised by their nannies, comforted by someone other than their own mother, but not Sophia. She was her mother's only daughter, and she had seen how kind-hearted she was, how caring, on a first-hand basis all her life. Of course she didn't believe in stripping their Jewish friends of their citizenship, their businesses and their homes! So many of their friends, families she'd known since she was a girl, had disappeared now, fleeing for France or wherever else they could escape to.

'What's happening to them? What have the Nazis turned us all into?' Sophia whispered. 'How can they be so cruel to other humans?'

'It's happened ever since man was created,' her mother replied. 'And it will continue to happen until people are brave enough to stand up for what they believe in, no matter what the consequences.'

'I saw a sign, in a coffee shop in the city. It said "Jews Forbidden",' Sophia whispered, choking on the words. 'I was standing there staring at it, and someone muttered as they passed about it being high time that they kept them out. Then another street over, the Jewish shops were vandalised, the shopkeepers' goods set alight in the street like a fun bonfire.'

'What did you do?'

Sophia folded her hands into her lap and dug her fingernails into her palms. 'I said nothing,' she admitted. 'I wanted to scream at them and hit someone, but I swallowed it down and said nothing. I watched' – she sucked back a breath, blinking away tears – 'and did absolutely nothing.'

'Good,' her mother praised.

'Good? I was a coward!' she muttered, meeting her mother's gaze. 'I wanted to stop it, I wanted to do something, but . . .'

'But you can't. Not yet.' She watched her mother's shoulders rise then fall. 'You are no good to anyone dead or in prison, and that's what would happen to both of us if anyone knew we didn't support the Nazi Party and Hitler.'

'I would have shot them, Mama,' she said, tears that she refused to let fall burning in her eyes. 'If I'd had a gun, I would have shot them simply for laughing like that. For thinking it's normal for men in uniform to treat other people this way!'

'They are hypnotised by that little man,' her mother said quietly. 'I've seen it time and again, the way their eyes glaze over and their brains become foggy as they salute him and absorb his words. He is good at talking, I'll give him that.'

They sat in silence, the only noise the chirp of birdsong outside the window.

'Is it wrong that I still love Father so much? Even though he is a part of this?'

Her mother shook her head, her smile sad. 'No, my love, it's not. He's your father, and if he didn't support Hitler then who knows what would have happened to us by now? That man has poisoned him as he has almost every other man, woman and child out there.'

Sophia did love her father. He had always been kind and loving to her, shown her so much warmth and respect, but to know that he was involved with what was going on, that he could be directly issuing orders that ruined the lives of so many Jewish people?

'You must never say anything to him, never challenge him or give any-one reason to think that you don't support Hitler implicitly.'

Sophia swallowed. 'I know.'

'I'm proud of you, Sophia. So proud.'

They embraced again and her mother stood, tears that she didn't bother to dab away shining in her eyes.

'What do we do now?' Sophia asked.

'We pretend everything is fine, and know in our hearts that we hate Hitler and what he does with every bone in our bodies.' She sighed. 'What of Alexander? Have you heard from him or his family lately?'

Sophia slowly filled her lungs, not sure whether this was the right moment to tell her mother that only a week earlier she'd snuck out to see him. She'd never told her mother they were more than friends, but Sophia was certain that she'd guessed. Part of her had always wondered if her mother didn't want to know, simply so she couldn't be accused of hiding it from her husband if she was ever questioned.

'He's still in Berlin,' she said. 'I'm hoping his family might leave soon.'

'They should. I wish we could somehow click our fingers and transport them all to somewhere safe. Only the Nazis hate the Jews so vehemently, Sophia. Only the Germans.'

'I know.'

'If you love him, then don't stop. Promise me you won't stop loving him because of who he is?'

'I promise,' she whispered in reply.

'But don't ever tell your father about him, will you? I don't even want him to know you were ever friends with him. He would never forgive you.' Her mother's voice was husky, deeper than usual. 'He could have awful things done to Alex's family, Sophia. Things I don't ever want to imagine happening to someone we know.'

'I understand.'

The gravel crunched beneath Sophia's shoes and she looked up to the big house ahead of her, memories fading. She always struggled with the clash of thoughts inside her mind and today was no different; growing up, her home had been full of laughter and love, but it all seemed so fraudulent now. How her father could have been so kind to her, so gentle and full of praise, astounded her when it was so at odds with the man he'd become. Not to her, but to others. She hoped that once this was over he'd reflect and realise the wrongs he'd done.

She saw someone running up ahead, darting out of the house and screaming something. Sophia squinted and tried to hear. Was that Greta? The woman had worked in their home for years, had been very loyal to her mother and kept the house running despite the shortages and loss of staff. Sophia started to walk faster, then broke into a run.

'Greta!' she called out. 'Greta! What's wrong?'

'No!' Greta screamed, running full steam towards her now. 'Go! You can't be here.'

Sophia slowed before she crashed straight into the other woman. She was crying, her eyes red and swollen, so puffy that Sophia could tell she'd been upset for some time. She wrapped her arms around her to hold her, but Greta pushed back, her face full of terror.

'Sophia, you must go. Your father, if he sees you, if . . .'

'What is it, Greta? What's got you so upset?'

Why would her father not want to see her?

She looked at the house, heard men shouting and wondered what it was that Greta was so scared of. Sophia started to walk, had a feeling in the pit of her stomach that she shouldn't run away, that she needed to see what was going on in her home.

'No!' Greta yelled, snatching at her hand and holding her tight around the wrist.

'Tell me what's going on or I'll find out for myself,' Sophia snapped, struggling to pull her arm away.

'Sophia, it's your mother. She's . . .'

Sophia felt like all the blood had drained from her face, her entire body frozen as she stood and stared at Greta. Something terrible had happened, she knew it.

'My mother?' she managed to splutter.

'She's been hiding Jews,' Greta said. 'All this time, she was hiding them right under your father's nose, in the cellar. He thinks we all must have known but we didn't!'

Sophia yanked her hand away and ran, her arms pumping at her sides as she dropped her bag and sped as fast as she could to the house. The front door was still wide open from when Greta had burst out, and she kept moving, straight through the entrance, skidding on the floor as hands reached out at her – soldiers surprised to see her come bolting towards them.

'Let me go!' she screamed, slapping at their hands and breaking free, not about to let them hold her in her own home.

She could see outside, could see men standing on the lawn, surrounded by beautifully manicured hedges. Sophia pushed the door open and fell out on to the patio, staring at them, wondering what they were all looking at. Walking now, she moved across the grass, her shoes sinking into the soft ground.

'Get her out of here!' a deep male voice commanded.

She saw her father then, watched his mouth moving, saw soldiers rushing towards her, and she looked up. First she saw shoes, then legs.

She tried to scream but it died in her mouth, and all that came out was a gurgling noise. They were strung up by their necks, nooses connecting them to the tree. An entire family. There was a woman, a man, two little children and . . .

'No!' she screamed as the soldiers caught her and her legs buckled. 'No! Father, *no!*'

Her mother was there too, standing on tiptoe on a wooden crate. Why was her mother there? Why was her beautiful, kind mother connected to the tree? What was he doing to her?

'No!' she screamed again. 'Get her down! Take her down from there!'

'Do it,' she heard her father snarl. 'And let this be a lesson to anyone hiding Jews. There will be no exceptions made!'

Sophia drooped, forcing her eyes to stay open as she saw the crates kicked out from beneath the prisoners, watched her mother struggle, her fingers frantically clawing at the rope around her neck. The two children stopped moving first, then their parents, but it was her mother who struggled the longest.

'*Let me go!*' Sophia sobbed, trying to stand, doing her best to push them away.

'Let my daughter go,' her father said, storming over to her, not seeming to care that he'd just murdered her own mother in front of her.

'Did you know?' he demanded, grabbing hold of her arm and yanking her to her feet, fingers curled tight against her skin.

'Know what?' she mumbled, tears still streaming down her cheeks. 'What have you done? *Why?*'

'Your mother was a Jew lover. All this time she's been keeping them here, under my nose, in my own home!' His face was red, eyes bulging, veins standing to attention across his forehead. 'Your traitor mother made a fool of me!'

She stood taller, using her one free hand to wipe the tears from her face and look her father in the eyes.

'I will never forgive you. How could you *kill* her? How could you?'

Sophia broke free and tried to run to her, wanting to touch her, get her down and hold her lifeless body. But she was pulled away, the soldiers quick to capture her.

'If I find out you or anyone else has been doing the same . . . ,' her father started.

'What? You'll kill your own daughter, too?' she screamed at him.

He didn't need to answer her. He'd been married to her mother for three decades, and he hadn't hesitated in hanging her beside the poor family she must have fought so hard to conceal. How could she not have known her own mother was doing the very same thing as she? Risking her life to save others? No wonder she'd refused to visit the city!

Sophia collapsed on to the steps. She stayed perfectly still and waited for the men to forget about her. She blocked out their mutterings and laughter, filled with enough fury already without listening to their hateful words. Her tears had disappeared, though she knew they were only frozen for later. With her fists curled tight and her chin thrust up, she sat there, refusing to look at her mother. She couldn't bear to see her face like that, her head at such an unnatural tilt.

Sophia took a deep breath and finally stood, her entire body shaking, and slowly walked towards her mother without making a sound. She bent her head, whispered a prayer and stood on tiptoe to reach for her hand.

'I love you, Mother. I'm so proud of you,' she whispered. 'We'll see each other again. I promise.'

Sophia quickly slipped her mother's rings from her fingers, thankful they were slightly loose. She put them straight on to her own fingers before anyone saw what she was doing, head down like any normal grieving daughter.

'God bless you all,' she murmured to the family. 'May you all rest in peace.'

She thought of her mother, so bravely hiding them in her own home. How long had they been here? How many times had her mother been bursting to tell her but not been able to? All the time Sophia had imagined confessing to her that Alex was hiding in her apartment, her mother had held her own secret. Sophia's own fear of her mother knowing, of putting her in a position of having something to hide, had always stopped her, and now she was certain it had been the same for her mother, too.

'Get her away from them!' her father yelled out. 'How many times do you need to be told?'

Sophia heard the order and voluntarily moved away, shaking her head and putting out her hand before anyone had to take her. 'Leave me alone! I will go to my room.'

She hurried past, letting her tears fall now as she turned her back on her mother and fled. She entered the house in a hurry, eyes blurred, and dashed up the stairs. Voices called out to her, but she ignored them and hurried to her mother's room. She allowed herself a moment to pause at the mirror, reaching for her mother's perfume and spraying a quick mist on to her wrist. She'd smelt it all her life, would for ever be able to conjure that scent and think of her mother holding her close.

She shut her eyes, letting the aroma waft around her. She could still remember her mother singing, getting herself ready for the day and staring down at their grounds from her window. Sophia had often walked up beside her and pressed her forehead to the glass, looking down at birds bathing in a fountain at the entrance to their garden. She remembered thinking that from her mother's window, everything seemed so normal still. In their home, the only thing that had changed was the portrait of Adolf Hitler hanging in the hallway, the Führer's face staring solemnly at them when they passed.

Tears streamed down her cheeks as the memory of her mother faded, replaced with the sinister image of what she'd just witnessed. Sophia saw a handkerchief and stood, reaching for it and spraying her mother's perfume all over it and then tucking it into her blouse for safe-keeping. Then she rummaged in her mother's jewellery case, taking her other rings and diamonds, pushing them into her pocket and hurriedly looking around. There was a scarf on the bed and she snatched it, then took her mother's best warm coat from the closet. It wasn't much, but it might be the only chance she would get to take what she needed. She couldn't find any money, but the items she had would be enough if she needed something to sell at least.

She dug her nails into her palms as she fled the room, the weight of her mother's rings her only comfort. Then she quietly walked down the stairs again, careful to behave sedately in case anyone saw her. Only once she'd disappeared out the front door and saw that no one was around did she start to walk faster. She hurried away, grabbing her bag from where she'd dropped it, until she was out on the road. She was carrying her mother's coat, too hot and flustered to wear it now, and although she wanted to run she didn't want to draw any attention to herself. She needed to get home and figure out what on earth she could do about Alex. If he was found because of her, she'd never forgive herself.

CHAPTER FIVE

HAZEL

LONDON, ENGLAND

1943

Hazel noticed the smile on Officer McLeod's face the moment she saw him. He looked amused, or . . . She stared back at him. She wasn't sure what – maybe it was a look of smugness – but whatever it was, she was about to find out because he was beckoning her over.

'Is there a problem, sir?' she asked.

It had been a week since her interview with Smith, and just under a week since she'd waved her fiancé off for the third time, and she hadn't heard a thing since. But she'd thought about the meeting plenty, including who might have recommended her for the job other than the man standing in front of her.

'Seems I was right about you,' he said. 'You have another interview. In two hours' time.'

She tried to stop her jaw from dropping. 'Today?'

'Yes. They don't muck around.'

Hazel nodded. She hadn't even thought about the possibility of a second interview or what would happen next. She'd imagined she would have heard already if they wanted something more from her. 'So does this mean . . . ,' she started.

'It means,' her boss said, lowering his voice, 'that they checked you out through MI5 and you were passed by the powers that be. It also means you were one of the few women to impress them in that first interview. I don't put anyone forward lightly, but I've been watching you.'

'Why?' she asked, regretting the question the moment it had passed her lips.

'I had a good feeling about you the moment I saw you plotting for the first time on your own, and the fact you speak fluent French is a huge advantage.'

Hazel felt her cheeks flush from his praise. 'Well, thank you, sir. I'm honoured to be, well, to even be considered for this type of position.' The truth was she still didn't know what she was actually being considered for, but it was something secretive and important, and that meant it was something she needed to be doing. That is, if those in the know thought she was a suitable candidate.

'You're dismissed for the day to attend the meeting. If you don't return, good luck and Godspeed with whatever it is you are assigned to.'

He dismissed her with a nod and a smile, and she walked away in a daze. She felt she was on the verge of something huge. Women in particular seemed to be in demand for this Resistance movement – perhaps because the higher-ups felt women could go more under the radar, so to speak, than men – and the very thought of being involved in something so covert, in the field, was enough to send her heart racing and her stomach swirling.

'Thank you for seeing me again at such short notice,' Smith said.

Hazel felt more nervous this time than she had the first. Maybe it was because she somewhat knew what to expect. Or maybe it was because she knew her life might be about to change for ever.

'Are you able to tell me why I'm here now?' she asked, proud that her voice sounded so strong.

His mouth tilted upwards slightly from its previously straight line. 'What do you know of the SOE?' He cleared his throat. 'The Special Operations Executive.'

She stared back at him. What was she *supposed* to know about it? 'Well, I know it's a secret operation, that it's part of this whole Resistance movement.'

'In short, what you need to know is that the SOE is about getting close to the enemy,' Smith said, sitting in the chair and looking more at ease than he had the other day. This time around felt less like an interrogation and she was relieved. 'It also involves working in France.'

Hazel smiled. 'I see. Which is why you wanted to know about the depth of my language skills and understanding of more than just Paris.'

'Before we go any further, I need you to know that if you want to be part of this, if we take you on and send you to France, there is a great risk you won't make it back to London alive.'

She gulped, her heart starting to race though she tried to stay calm. 'What are the odds?' she forced herself to ask.

'It's a fifty-fifty chance,' he said. 'I'm not going to sugarcoat the probability of any of our field agents' making it back safely.'

'I see,' she replied, not sure what else she possibly could say.

'These are clandestine operations, and you would be in the thick of it, for the sake of a better description. Your language skills are what make you most attractive to us, and the fact that you have already spent time immersed in the culture. That indicates to us that you would fit in easily, that you wouldn't be caught out simply for not being a Frenchwoman if you were undercover there.'

'Am I being offered the position then?' she asked, folding her hands tightly in her lap to avoid them shaking so obviously.

'If we proceed, you will receive training, and then you will most likely be sent immediately to France on your first mission. We cannot discuss the work you will do until that time, but you must know that it will be dangerous work, and that your ability to converse in French, pass information along and work closely with other individuals will be imperative to the missions. My instinct is that you'll be most useful to us as a radio operator in the field.'

Hazel understood. It would be risky, but it was also important work, and if she said no, then she was hardly doing the best by her country or those she loved.

'I want to do whatever I can, no matter how dangerous the work is,' she said, sounding far more confident than she felt. 'I won't let you down.'

'If you are captured in France, the Germans will not treat you well for the mere fact you are a woman. I need you to understand that.'

She gulped. 'I understand.'

'You could be captured, tortured and killed,' he said bluntly. 'I'm not going to tell you otherwise, because we need men and women committed to the cause and prepared for anything. You are free to leave at any stage, which is why we don't want you proceeding if you don't understand from the outset what you're putting yourself forward for. You must fully appreciate the dangers at play here.'

'I understand,' she managed, finding the words hard to get out.

'Then take the night to sleep on it. Go home and rest, consider the position you would be putting yourself in,' Smith said. 'But this is a decision for you to make alone. No one is to know of this, of anything that we've discussed. Do you understand?'

She answered without hesitation. 'I do.'

'We will meet here again tomorrow at the same time. You must volunteer to work for us, and once you've done that, you'll be recruited immediately.'

Hazel took a deep breath. 'Thank you, sir. I appreciate your confidence in me and I won't let you down.'

He nodded and rose, then opened the door and stood back. Just like that, their meeting was over and she was left to think about what she was supposed to do. She wanted to help, of course she did, and she hadn't been lying about being prepared to do whatever she had to. So many men had given their lives already to this war, and if she could do something to make a difference, then didn't she owe it to her country to do so?

Now, there was not a doubt in her mind that she would be volunteering for this position, one she wouldn't even believe could have been offered to her if she hadn't heard it with her own ears. She pushed away thoughts of her parents, or John or her mother-in-law. She didn't need their permission to do this. Women were doing amazing things while their men were away, and she wasn't married yet, which meant her decisions were her own to make. And what decision could be more important and selfless than one to help their allies? If she could put her French to good use, then she would. And she wasn't going to let anyone stop her.

There was only one sentence that kept playing in her mind. *Fifty-fifty.* He'd said there was a fifty-fifty chance of not coming back. She gulped and steeled her jaw, head held high. She didn't know what she'd expected, but having as much of a chance of coming home as not making it wasn't something she'd ever truly thought about. Still, it didn't change her mind. It couldn't. Because they were at war. And war meant taking chances and facing the prospect of life never being the same again.

She turned back around and knocked firmly on the door. When Smith opened it, she smiled at him. 'Turns out I don't need the night to think about it. This is me volunteering,' she said firmly.

He nodded, not looking at all surprised. 'Welcome to the SOE.'

Hazel bit the inside of her mouth as she tried not to smile. Before the war, most of her family had expected nothing from her other than to become a good wife and be able to hold good conversations. It was why her mother had been so interested in sending her to France. Little did her parents know that one day they'd come to regret that decision, because she knew they wouldn't approve at all of what she was offering to do.

'So I'm in?' she asked. 'This is actually happening?'

He stood and offered her his hand. She stared at him for a moment before following his lead, placing her palm to his. 'Yes, Hazel, you're in. So long as you pass the training, which I'm confident you will, you'll be putting your skills to use in the field.'

She could hardly believe it.

'I wish you the best of luck,' Smith said, releasing her hand. 'You're doing your country a great service, and once this war is over, your assistance will always be remembered.'

Hazel beamed. 'You never told me what to tell my family.' It was the only thing she was worried about, because she had to tell them something, couldn't simply disappear in the dead of night, and she had to tell John's family something, too.

'To be honest, the less anyone close to you, including your immediate family, knows, the better. If they're ever questioned it would be better for everyone involved if they didn't know a thing.'

Hazel gulped. The weight of her decision was suddenly heavy on her shoulders. He still hadn't told her what to say; instead he'd told her what not to say.

'I understand,' she replied, her confidence slowly draining out of her.

'Good. I'll be in touch with more information, but you'll most likely spend a couple of weeks training and going through the recruitment phase. Then you'll head to Scotland for your paramilitary training should you pass the first level.'

She fought the urge to wrap her arms around herself as she listened to him speak. *Paramilitary training?* The idea of it made her head spin, but then she had no idea what she'd been expecting. Of course she needed training! It wasn't like she was going to be tucked safely in a room deciphering and translating messages. This was war.

'Godspeed,' Smith said, dismissing her.

Hazel swallowed and summoned her courage back, standing straight and taking a deep breath. 'And to you, sir. Thank you for your time.'

Hazel had never been so nervous in all her life. From the moment she'd told Smith she was officially volunteering two weeks earlier, to finding out what was required of her, it had been a whirlwind of activity. She was half expecting to wake from a dream, it was so surreal. Now, she was arriving at a house in the countryside that looked so peaceful from where she was standing, but was home to the SOE training and recruitment. The fact she was doing work that had previously been reserved strictly for men sent a hum of anticipation through her, adrenaline urging her on. And Smith's final words to her were still playing through her mind days later.

'*We need to set Europe ablaze. And women like you will be the ones doing this, because you can blend in and no one will suspect a thing unless you're caught.*'

'This is Wanborough Manor?'

She glanced beside her at the man who'd spoken. They'd travelled together on the train and he was pleasant enough, but Hazel had been so worried that it was a test that she hadn't known what to say to him. Was she supposed to let on what she was doing, discuss anything with him about their training? Or was he already undercover, travelling with her to see how easy it was to get her to talk? She'd already been given her undercover story, which they called their *legend*, and she wasn't stupid enough to let someone fool her before she'd even begun.

'I suppose it is,' she replied carefully. 'Shall we go in?'

They'd come to a quiet, peaceful area of Surrey, and an Elizabethan house loomed before them. She had no idea what to expect, but she did know that she'd be doing things here she'd never in her lifetime imagined.

There were two men outside the house and she approached them cautiously.

'We've been expecting you,' one of them said.

'I'm Hazel.' She gave her real name because she hadn't been told not to, although she chose not to reveal her surname to make her identity somewhat harder to verify.

'I know,' he said drily. 'This way.' Her travelling companion was speaking to the other man as Hazel was led away.

She guessed the beautiful manor had been requisitioned, as many had during the war, and she was sad to see how dusty and unkempt it was, even though it still looked so regal from the outside. She could imagine how it would have looked before the war, no doubt full of servants and with everything inside gleaming.

There was little time to look around, though, as she followed the man through the house, clutching her bag in one hand and her coat in the other. She played through her story in her head, something she'd been doing constantly for the past two days: she was a French student, loved art history and had friends in England.

'Sit.'

She looked up. The man she'd been following was pointing to a chair. She expected him to leave and for someone else to arrive, but instead he sat down.

'What is your name?' he asked in French.

Hazel gave a coy smile, ready to play her role. She was a Frenchwoman, so of course she wouldn't hesitate to answer in French.

'Hazel,' she said. 'And yours? Tell me, what is it you're doing here?'

'Ralph,' he said. 'Well done.' He was speaking in English now.

'If you want to check I have my story straight, I won't disappoint you,' she assured him. 'What I don't know is how to stay alive in the field. That's what I need help with.'

'You'll be fine,' he said. 'Just stay out of the cooler and you'll make it through.'

Hazel's eyebrows shot up and she cursed the fact that she'd reacted at all. 'The cooler?'

'It's where we send the failed recruits to cool off,' he explained. 'Build rapport with those around you, show us that you're capable of being in uncomfortable situations or meeting new people. Then we'll move on to training you.'

'Thank you for the advice,' she replied.

'Oh, and don't forget you can change your mind at any stage. This is dangerous work and we only want people in the field, man or woman, who have volunteered to be there.'

Hazel understood that. She was surprised at how often it had been said, though, especially when all of their men had been sent off without any concern for whether or not they wanted to be soldiers. But then she supposed the type of work she'd put herself forward for needed the person to be absolutely focused on the task. It was something she'd tried not to overthink for fear of changing her mind.

'Help yourself to a drink while you're waiting.' He stood, turned and pointed to a bottle of liquor and two glasses.

She stared at him, wondering if it was a trick. 'Excuse me?'

'It's more of an order. Enjoy.' And with that he left the room.

Hazel felt as if she was in some sort of dream world. She'd hardly ever had anything alcoholic to drink in her life, and she wasn't sure what to do. It wasn't that she wouldn't drink, but it seemed like a test to her.

'Hello again.'

She glanced back and saw the man she'd travelled up with. For some reason she'd expected to be with other women, even though it had been made clear to her that both men and women were part of the network.

'Seems we're supposed to have a stiff drink together,' he said.

'I see.' Hazel sat and watched him cross the room and pour amber liquid into the glasses. When he returned she stood and took one from his outstretched hand, then clinked her glass to his.

'To being here,' he said.

'To being here,' she replied, and took a small sip. The liquor burnt as it traced a fiery path down her throat and all the way to her stomach, and she tried not to cough.

She almost wanted to tell him that she was engaged, not to get any ideas, but as she bravely took another sip, eyes watering as she swallowed it down, she realised that she wasn't that girl any more. She wasn't John's fiancée, wasn't waiting for her man to come home and doing her best until then. She wasn't even truly *Hazel* any more. From this moment forward she needed to live and breathe her cover story. Today was the beginning of her new life, and there was no way she was going anywhere near the cooler.

She sat down again, reclined and smiled at her companion. They might be enemies for all she knew, which meant that she was about to charm this man and everyone else she came into contact with. She felt alive. For the very first time in her life, she'd chosen to do something, something that wasn't expected of her, something that no one would ever have expected her to do.

'What do you think we're supposed to do here?' he asked.

She smiled, feeling like an actor on a stage as her character gave her confidence and she breathed life into the person she was set to become.

'I suppose they want to see if we can hold our liquor,' she said, shrugging as she confidently took another sip. 'I'm more used to wine from one of our local vineyards, but this will do.'

He stared back at her, wide-eyed. For a moment she thought per-haps he hadn't understood her French, and then she realised that he sim-ply hadn't been expecting the first proper conversation he'd had with her to be in character. They didn't know who was watching them or what they were being judged on, though, so she wasn't taking any chances.

'Were you born in London?' she asked. 'I've only been here a short while. My parents sent me here to be closer to friends, but all I want is to go back home.'

By the time Ralph returned, she'd already filled her glass again, the burn no longer so bad when she swallowed, her body warm. She could feel her head starting to spin as she stood, the effects of the liquor so much greater when she was on her feet. She was surprised at how well she'd been able to tolerate it so far, although she was certain she'd have a decent headache in the morning. Hazel only hoped she'd done the right thing and the challenge hadn't been about temptation.

'We like to see how well you all do under the influence,' Ralph said. 'It can make it so much easier to become impulsive and forget one's legend.'

'I have no idea what you're talking about,' she said with a smile.

'I want you both to follow me,' Ralph said, beckoning with his hand. 'I have some things to show you.'

She followed, the other recruit falling in behind her. They were led into a room that was bare except for a table covered in tools, things that Hazel had never seen before. She took a few deep breaths, trying to block out the effects of the alcohol. She hated the way it had made her head feel woozy, whereas when she'd been seated earlier it had given her more confidence and made her feel like she could do anything.

'What are these?' she asked, about to reach out when a stern word stopped her.

'No.'

She pulled back her hand as if she'd been stung but continued star-ing at the contraptions.

'If you were out for the night and having a few drinks, and some-how your cover was blown, you could be captured and taken in for questioning.'

She slowly swallowed and stood up straighter.

'These are some of the things the Germans might use to get you to talk. For instance, this here,' he said, holding up a metal object that looked like a tiny guillotine and made her stomach churn, 'is excellent for taking fingers off. The enemy finds that the more pain they inflict, the more likely their subjects are to tell them everything they need to know.'

Hazel glanced sideways and saw that her drinking partner looked white as a sheet. She was trying her hardest not to let the shock register.

'And that?' she asked, her voice sounding shaky even to her own ears as she pointed at an unusual metal device that appeared to be a clamp of some kind.

'That could be to hold out a tongue or cut it off. But often they'll just use knives to get what they want.'

'How long would this go on for?' the man beside her asked.

He received a shrug in reply. 'Hours, days? Your guess is as good as mine. The best answer is probably until they get information out of you. Either way you'd probably be shot dead or left to rot at best.'

'So we mustn't get caught,' Hazel said. 'The point of your story is that no matter what, we mustn't get caught, and even if we've been drinking we need to be able to talk ourselves out of any situation and not let even the smallest mistake give away our legend.'

'I see we have a fast learner amongst us. Good work.'

'Is it true that we have just as much of a chance at coming home as dying over there?' Hazel asked.

Ralph leaned against the wall, his expression sombre. 'It's true. It's about even whether you'll make it home or not, and it's one of the reasons we give you every opportunity to pull out if you're not sure about what you're doing.'

'How many have you lost?' she asked, needing to know more about what she'd be facing. The more she knew, the better she could deal with it all.

'That's not information I can share with you. But I will tell you this,' he said, leaning forward. 'One of our operatives, a woman who was one of our best, was under suspicion for some reason. She was caught because she looked the wrong way when she crossed the road. It was as simple as that – their suspicions were confirmed instantly when they saw that she wasn't a true Frenchwoman.'

Hazel's mouth went dry. The weight of what she was putting herself forward for was starting to rest more heavily on her shoulders. 'She was killed for this?' She had to ask the question.

'Yes. Her life was over because of one thing she did that gave her away as not being French.'

'I don't believe you,' her travelling companion said, stepping forward. 'You're trying to scare us on our first day to see who turns tail and runs for the hills.'

'No, he's not,' Hazel said, finding her voice again. 'We already knew the chances, we came into this knowing the odds.'

'Take a look over these things.' Ralph gestured at the grotesque instruments. 'Familiarise yourself with them, train yourself to fear them enough that you won't ever let yourself be put in a position where they're used on you. You need to find a balance between fear and bravery, and remember that nothing is as crucial to you as living and breathing your legend, and staying smart every second of every day when you're in the field.'

Hazel absorbed his words. She wasn't in this to end up dead or tortured, but he hadn't scared her any more than she'd already been scared, either. This was her calling. She'd never felt so strongly about doing anything in her life, and she didn't even know what was required of her yet. All she knew was that whatever her field assignment was, she'd be responsible for helping to bring down the Nazis and their network, and that was all she needed to know.

'When do we start our training?'

'Tomorrow. If you make it until the end you'll be here for three or four weeks. You'll learn Morse code and be given instruction in explosives.'

A tremor ran through Hazel's body; she didn't know if it was fear or excitement, or perhaps a combination of the two. Never in her life had she thought she'd be learning about explosives or understanding how to translate and send codes. Yet here she was.

'Can we make a start tonight?' she asked.

'You don't get points for trying to be teacher's pet here.'

She laughed. 'You have me all wrong. I just want to learn everything I can to increase my odds of getting back home at the end of all this.'

She received a smile for her joke, although she noticed that her fellow prospect was not laughing. He had his arms folded across his chest, and his face was impossible to read, mouth in a tight line.

'What is it you want to learn first?'

'I want to know how to protect myself,' she said. 'If I'm caught and there's a chance of surviving, I want to know what to do.'

She'd always been the friendly girl, the happy girl, the girl who'd make a lovely wife and was a good best friend. But here, it was like she was playing a character, being someone she'd never dreamed she could be, and she liked this stronger version of herself.

'You'll need to pass beyond this level to get to weapons training, but I promise you that we'll teach you everything we can while you're here.'

She opened her mouth to say something in reply, then shut it when he started to speak again.

'To be honest, as useful as all that will be, your ability to speak perfect French and blend into your surroundings without being discovered is the best weapon you have. I can't stress enough that you must practise your language skills and become up to date on the current situation in France. The more you know, the more chance you have of not being discovered.'

'Thank you,' she said, relieved. If there was one thing she knew, one thing she'd excelled at in school and when she'd been sent abroad, it was how to speak perfect French and be mistaken for a local.

CHAPTER SIX

ROSE

BREST, FRANCE

1943

Rose walked out into the garden, noticing how everything was a little overgrown, so different to how their coastal home usually looked. Peter had liked everything to be perfect, and she'd made sure they had the people to keep it as he wanted. But that was before. She kept walking, not wanting to stare at something that reminded her so vividly of her husband.

She'd risen early to say goodbye to Charlotte and Sebastian, and now that they'd gone the house felt unusually empty again. Not for the first time she wished her maid, Maria, had come with her, simply so she had someone to talk to, someone to help pass the silent hours with.

Now, alone with her thoughts, she could only think one thing: missing Peter wasn't going to bring him back, and she'd cried so much for him she wondered if there was even a tear left in her body.

She clenched her jaw in a bite so hard she feared her teeth would crack.

There was one thing she could do, one thing that kept playing through her mind, and pregnant or not, she was damn well going to do it.

The Resistance needed help. They needed people prepared to do anything with nothing to lose, and they needed money; it just so happened she could fulfil both demands. Peter's death wasn't going to be for nothing – avenging him was what had forced her out of bed that morning. Once her baby was close to coming, she'd find a way to keep them both safe, but until then, having a child wasn't going to stop her. If Sebastian and Charlotte could be part of the movement, then why couldn't she?

She would take the day to mourn, maybe even the week. Then she was going to put a plan in motion. Next week, she wasn't just going to be the outspoken woman with a desire to do something to help the war effort and bring the Nazis to their knees.

Rose kept walking, imagining her husband falling into step beside her. At home, Peter had worked hard and their social life was often bursting at the seams, but here they'd liked a quieter pace, and they never entertained. She kept walking as she remembered Peter's warm smile. If he'd been here with her they'd have lain in bed until late morning, drinking inky coffee and indulging in croissants.

A noise pulled Rose from her thoughts and she noticed she'd walked further than she'd meant to. She stared with her mouth open at the sight of men running down the street towards her. There were three of them – all young, all looking terrified – and a cold, numbing terror passed silently through her.

She knew there was a reason why many of the homes around her were empty, how dangerous it was being here. Even her brother had warned her that she would need to be careful of the Germans, but she'd shrugged off his warning without paying it any heed, too lost in her own grief to care.

It finally dawned on her that she was indeed in the thick of it. Were these men part of the Resistance?

'Come with me,' she croaked, waving at one of them as he came closer, looking desperate. Her heart started to race when she saw the panic on their faces.

'Get out of here!' he yelled.

'Follow me,' Rose said, clearing her throat and sounding more assertive, hearing an edge to her voice that sounded more familiar to her than the weak rasp of earlier. 'I can keep you safe.'

The man looked alarmed, perhaps he was thinking it was too dangerous for her, but she would have told him not to be so silly if he'd even dared.

She rubbed her thumb over the big diamond on her finger, across the rough smaller diamonds on her wedding ring, too. They comforted her and gave her strength simply feeling their weight.

'Quickly,' she said. 'It's not far and you'll be safe.'

She wasn't scared for herself. But these men? They would surely be taken prisoner if they were found.

'This way. Quick!' he called to his friends.

Rose held her skirt up high and started to run, making for the road that would take them to her home. She had no idea where the Germans were or whether they'd be discovered on the way. It was telling that the streets were so deserted, everyone else locked up safely in their homes, but Rose had been walking aimlessly, lost in her thoughts, and she'd barely noticed her surroundings.

'Where are you taking us?' one of the men asked as he caught up to her.

'My home. I can hide you there,' Rose said firmly.

'We can't put her in danger like that,' another muttered. 'We're as good as dead as it is.'

'They can try to find you all they like,' she panted out as she kept running. 'But they'll have to get past me first.'

They kept moving, their pace fast. She had no idea if they were escaped prisoners of war or if they were part of some sort of secret military operation, and she didn't care. All she knew was that she wanted to save them.

'This way,' she said, pointing to a cluster of trees. She knew it would take longer, but if they weren't so exposed then maybe they wouldn't be seen.

Rose kept running, not checking to see if all three were still with her. She smiled, a combination of adrenaline and fear propelling her forward. It was the most alive she'd felt in weeks, and she was finally doing something useful, something to help.

'I have clothes,' she managed to pant out. 'We can get you changed and . . .'

She actually had no idea. How could she expect to miraculously keep them safe? Changing their clothes was hardly going to be enough to change their appearance. The only thing she could do was hide them, and hide them well.

'It's the big stone cottage,' she told them. 'We'll go through the back door.'

Suddenly a blast of noise ricocheted around her, an explosion that made her trip and fall to the ground. *What in God's name . . . ?*

Rose gasped. She looked down at her arm, blood trickling faster and faster down her skin, skin that was suddenly so terribly burning hot. She opened her mouth to say something but her vision blurred and she stumbled when she tried to get up, the damp leaves beneath her somehow pulling her back down towards them.

Big hands grabbed for her, strong arms pulling her to her feet as more bangs filled the air around them. They were being shot at!

Rose turned, unsteady as she saw one of the men she was with fire a gun. And then everything went silent.

'Run!' one of them ordered.

Rose ran fast, tripping every few steps, or at least it felt like that, but holding tight to the man's hand as they dashed frantically for her house.

Her breath caught in her throat, the wound in her arm sending shooting pains through her entire body, but she didn't have time to care or worry.

'Downstairs in the cellar,' she said. 'All of you.'

'It's the first place they'll look!' the man that had been helping her said, his eyes wide. She guessed he was probably twenty, maybe younger, and she hated the fear in his expression.

Rose paused, shut her eyes, thought for a moment about where they could be safe. There was a shed in the garden, but that would be too easily raided. The cellar had seemed logical, but perhaps her attic? She suddenly smiled despite her pain.

Peter's mother had given her a crib, his own baby one, and after so long trying and not getting pregnant, they'd brought it here. She hadn't wanted to have a nursery at home until they needed one.

She pointed upstairs. 'Go,' she said.

'What if we have to escape? We can't jump out the window up there!' complained one of the men.

'You won't need to.'

Rose hurried them into the room and showed them the closet. 'Get in.'

'There's no way we can all fit in there!'

'Just do it. *Quickly.*' She glared at them, then glanced down at her arm. She left the room and took her shirt off, hiding it under her pillow and getting one of Peter's long socks out of the drawer. She used her left hand and her teeth to tie it tight around her wound, not wanting to draw attention to the blood there.

Her hands were shaking so much, quivering from shock as much as terror. *I've been shot.* The three words kept echoing through her mind as she hurried, securing the tight knot and then stripping off the rest of her clothes. She stuffed them in her bottom drawer and quickly found a dress to pull on, then she raced back into the room where she'd left the men. She didn't know if they'd seen her through the open door or if they were already hidden, but given the circumstances she didn't care.

'Get in!' she ordered, seeing one of the men still standing in the room as she struggled to pin her hair up, trying to change her appearance.

'I can't fit. I'm going under the bed,' he muttered.

She forgot her shaking hands as she took charge.

'This is *my* home and I make the rules,' she ordered, taking a doll from the cot, also a gift from her mother-in-law, and wrapping it in a blanket. 'Get in the closet or walk out my front door and meet your fate.'

The man stared back at her but she held her ground, and seconds later she was pushing on the door to shut them all in, him included.

Rose took a deep breath and pushed the crib closer to their hiding spot. She could do this. All that determination and grit she'd had about doing something to help, well, this was her chance. She'd been in mourning long enough. She refused to look down at her stomach, her slightly rounded belly not big enough for anyone else to notice she was pregnant. She clutched the pretend baby, hoping whatever Nazi soldiers came looking fell for her ruse.

She forced herself to breathe normally as she started down the stairs. Each step felt heavy, her footfalls loud to her own ears. And then came the knock she'd been expecting. She heard loud noises and wondered what was happening, but she clutched the doll tight and refused to give in to any panic. Fear pulsed through her as she wondered if there would be retributions for the entire village for what she'd done. They wouldn't give up until they found the perpetrator.

Rose hurried the last two steps and ran to the door, pulling it open then quickly stepping back and patting her pretend baby. She held it close, making shushing noises at the same time.

Tears formed in her eyes and she didn't blink them away. She was pretending to be a scared mother comforting her child, which meant there was nothing wrong with crying.

'We're looking for French cowards,' the tall German officer said, in such good French she could hardly believe it. 'Men who think they are still soldiers. Step aside.'

She stared at him, wide-eyed, taking a few steps back. If he hadn't been the enemy she would have thought how handsome he was, but there was nothing about the cold blue eyes of the German that she wanted to admire. He was like a walking advertisement for Hitler's perfect Aryan race.

'There are no men here,' she said back, keeping her eyes downcast. 'I'm just trying to get my baby to sleep. Look around all you like.'

The officer waved his hand and she turned and went back up the stairs.

'Shh, my darling. Shhh,' she said, loud enough for the men to hear.

The German soldiers came into the house like bulls, knocking things over as if they took pleasure in ruining her home. She shut her eyes at a loud bang, wondered what they'd broken, but then realised that she actually didn't care. They could trash her house all they liked, but she wasn't letting them find those soldiers.

Heavy footfalls alerted her to the fact that someone, or more than one someone, was coming up her staircase. She moved into the small space between the crib and the closet, rocking her baby and holding it up to press her lips to its little doll head.

'Please, let me put my baby to bed,' she pleaded. 'There is nobody else in this house. Nobody but my child and I.'

'We'll see,' said the officer who'd been the one to knock on her door. 'Check under the bed!'

She knew German, and when he issued the command in his native tongue she understood immediately.

Rose held her breath, hoping one of the men hadn't decided while she was downstairs to change his position. She watched as the officer received a headshake from one of his soldiers. She kept jiggling the baby but stayed silent, not wanting to say the wrong thing or aggravate the situation. She also didn't want to make too much of a fuss of her 'baby' and have any of the men come too close.

Rose waited, the room full of strangers. She'd been worried about the hidden men sneezing or coughing or doing something to give themselves away, but now, staring at the Germans, she was worried about a whole lot more than that. She was a woman all alone, with the enemy.

She started to cry, and it didn't take any effort to summon the tears.

'Please don't hurt me,' she pleaded. 'Please, just let me put my baby to bed. You can take anything you like.'

The officer laughed at her and the other men all joined in. 'We are the conquerors. You can hate us all you like, and we *will* take whatever we want, with or without your permission.'

She started to tremble, looking down and nodding. She was scared. Scared of being raped, of them finding out her baby was nothing more than a doll, of being tortured. But mostly she was scared of the men she'd tried to save dying on her watch.

Help me, Peter. She silently pleaded. *Please, help me.*

'Take whatever you want, fill your pockets with food,' the German officer ordered.

There was still noise downstairs, and within minutes that noise doubled as the beat of the men's shoes thumped down the stairs and joined those below.

Rose waited, staying so still she could barely breathe. She waited until the noises stopped. Until the German voices were gone, until there was a final bang as the door shut. And then she dropped her baby to the ground, a silent scream straining in her throat.

The room started to spin, everything went black with bright white dots flashing into her vision. Rose saw the ground coming up to her, as if the floor was ready and waiting to swallow her, and there was nothing she could do to stop from falling.

'Help her!'

She heard the frantic, deep whisper as arms caught her and broke her fall, just as everything went cold, dark and silent.

Rose woke to the crackle of a fire, bathed in warmth as she stretched, eyes still shut tight. She could smell something good cooking, and she wondered what Maria was making for dinner.

She opened her eyes, faltered as she wondered where she was, whom the low voices belonged to that she could hear. And then it all came crashing back to her; what had happened, what she'd been . . .

'No!' she gasped. Where were the men? Had they been found? Killed? She remembered falling but once the room had gone black, she didn't know what had happened.

'Shhh.'

Rose tried to jump up but her legs buckled. Where was she?

'We don't even know your name.' A woman's voice made her turn. She regained her balance, stood more slowly and looked around the room.

The men were sitting there, in clothing that looked so familiar. It was . . . She smiled and reached her hand out to touch the wall, steadying herself. It was Peter's. They were all wearing clothing that belonged to her Peter.

'I hope you don't mind,' the woman said, smiling at her and making her way across the room. She'd been in the kitchen, where the delicious smell was coming from, and the men were all at the table.

'I, I'm sorry, who are you?' Rose asked, glancing down at her arm and seeing that it had been properly bandaged. It gave off not so much a burning, searing pain now as a deep thudding one.

'I saw what happened earlier,' the woman said. 'You were very brave. These men owe you their lives and none of us even know your name.'

Rose nodded, still feeling a bit wobbly. 'I'm Rose,' she said.

'Josephine,' the woman said, coming closer and touching her arm, her smile warm. 'I took the bullet out and cleaned the wound. You'll need to keep the bandage on for a while.'

Rose stared at her arm and then back at Josephine. 'Thank you.'

'We're all impressed by your bravery.' She laughed. 'Aren't we? This woman took a bullet for you and managed to pull one over on the Germans.'

A collective chuckle went up around the table and Rose felt her heartbeat slow, suddenly not so nervous about so many strangers being in her house.

'I did what anyone would do.'

'No,' Josephine said. 'You didn't. Because *most* people were hiding in their houses with the curtains pulled. You were the one running through the forest and then pretending you had a baby.'

Rose nodded. She didn't think she was anything special, but she appreciated this woman's kind words. 'When you have nothing to lose, it makes you brave. Or maybe just stupid.'

'Brave it is then,' Josephine said. 'And even when we don't think so, we always have something to lose.'

Rose didn't reply, but when one of the men pulled out a chair for her, she graciously took it. She could do with the seat.

'Thank you.'

'You'll need something to eat to get your strength up. It's only soup. There wasn't a lot left after those damn Germans raided the place.'

Rose nodded. 'Do you live near here?'

Josephine sat down when a chair was vacated for her, too. 'Yes. I'm staying in one of your neighbours' homes.'

'We wanted to say thank you,' one of the men said, and cleared his throat. 'What you did for us today, well, we owe you our lives.'

Rose shook her head. 'Please, it was nothing.'

'Your husband will be proud when he hears,' one of the others said, laughing. 'He'll no doubt hardly believe it.'

She tried to smile, but she felt it falter, couldn't make it stick. 'My husband, he's, well . . .' Her face flushed and a hot feeling rose in her throat, making her want to vomit. Rose took a deep breath. She needed to start saying it, start admitting to what had happened. 'My husband is dead,' she said simply.

Two of the men looked down, but one kept her gaze. The same one who'd not wanted to hide in the closet.

'I'm sorry,' he said in a low voice. 'We've lost so many men. I'm so sorry for your loss.'

Tears prickled Rose's eyes and a solitary drop escaped her lashes. 'Thank you.'

She bent her head and dipped her spoon into her soup, taking a mouthful and forcing it down. Then another and another.

'We've all lost someone we love to this war,' Josephine said.

'And how do you keep going?' Rose whispered.

'We find something to do to get back at those who've taken from us.'

Rose put her spoon down. 'Is that what you do? You help?'

Josephine gave her a look she couldn't decipher. 'Finish your dinner, then I'll take you upstairs to check your bandage.'

She went to open her mouth and say she felt fine, then stopped herself. There was something in the other woman's words, the way they were issued as more of an instruction. So she did as she was told as the men started to talk in low voices around her.

Rose watched as Josephine closed the door behind her and came to sit with her on the bed. There was something mysterious about her, even though she'd been nothing but kind and thoughtful all evening. Now, the others were staying quiet downstairs, the lights out and the curtains drawn. It was dangerous having them here at all, but strangely Rose felt comforted by their presence.

'You asked me a question earlier,' Josephine said, her voice hushed as if she was worried about them being overheard. 'Do you truly want to know the answer to it?'

Rose nodded immediately, knowing what she was referring to. 'Yes.'

'I know who you are, Rose. You see, I knew of your husband, Peter. I'm so sorry to hear that he's no longer with us.'

She felt her eyes widen. Is this why Josephine was here, because she knew Peter?

'How did you know him?'

'Are you aware of his generous donations?' Josephine asked. 'Or the fact that he risked so much to arrange funds and arms deliveries for us?'

'Yes.' Rose felt a surge of adrenaline rush through her body, the only time in weeks that she'd smiled without having to force herself to. When the boat he'd been travelling on had gone down, the good he'd done for France was the only thing she'd been able to hold on to. 'You're part of the Resistance, aren't you?' she whispered, hardly able to believe it.

Josephine's mouth turned up at the corners. 'So you're familiar with us?' She laughed. 'Are you also familiar with the fact that we weren't expecting Peter's lovely wife to turn up here? He'd promised us this place to use some time ago as a safe house, and when I saw you running in with three men in tow?' Josephine shook her head, still smiling. 'Let's just say that you took me by surprise.'

'He gave you our house to use?' Rose exclaimed. 'How could he do that without telling me?'

'Same reason we don't talk to our families or anyone else about what we do. The fewer people involved, the better.'

Rose nodded. 'So is this a recruitment?' she asked. 'You're telling me this because you want me to help you?'

Josephine folded her arms across her chest. 'Are you ready to help us?'

'Yes.' Rose exhaled the word as if she'd been holding it and waiting to let it go for ever. 'Yes, I'm ready.' She wasn't about to sit around and do nothing when so many good men were out there dying. Fighting for their lives against an evil that she wanted to help snuff out.

'The reason I didn't help you earlier when I saw you running is because I'm already hiding men, and I couldn't risk having my house raided,' Josephine confessed. 'We have a submarine arriving tomorrow night and we'll transport your men with them.'

'I'm sorry, you what?' Rose couldn't believe what she was hearing. 'A *submarine?*'

'We've been rescuing downed airmen,' Josephine said. 'It's danger-ous work, but if we didn't do it, they'd be captured by the Germans, tortured and then kept as prisoners – if they weren't shot after having their toenails pulled out and their fingers cut off, or whatever it is they do to them to extract information, that is.' She sighed. 'The submarines will be coming once a month. We need to transport the men to the shore, where they'll have rowboats waiting. This is our first mission, so we have to cross everything that it goes to plan.'

'I'll do it,' Rose said. 'Whatever you want from me, I'll do it.'

'You're certain? I'd say this isn't work for the faint-hearted, but from what I've seen of you, that would be an insult.'

'I've already told you, I have nothing to lose.'

She resisted the urge to touch her stomach. She was lying. She did have something to lose, but right now no one needed to know that she was pregnant, and she had no intention of telling anybody, not even Josephine.

'Welcome to the Resistance.' Josephine held out her hand and Rose shook it. 'I have a feeling that we'll all know your name by the end of this blasted war.'

Rose wasn't so sure about that. But she did know that she'd do anything she could to help. *Anything.*

CHAPTER SEVEN

SOPHIA

BERLIN, GERMANY

LATE 1942

'Alex!' Sophia frantically whispered. 'Alex!'

She was exhausted. She'd been shaking the entire way back on the train from her family estate, too scared to close her eyes and see the image of her mother's lifeless form hanging in front of her. The hatred sluicing through every inch of her, the desperation to seek justice, was the only thing keeping her going. Without it, she'd have collapsed to the ground and wished for death herself. Or perhaps fear of her father would have kept her open-eyed and shaking.

'Sophia?'

Alex was bleary-eyed, like he'd just woken up. She looked at her bed, saw how rumpled it was. She could hardly expect him to spend every moment hidden, but the fact he'd been lying there while she was gone, the fact that her apartment could have been raided and he could have been found before she'd even made it back . . . she fought a wave of emotion as it tried to choke her.

'You need to hide. Now,' she said, her voice wobbling. 'They . . .'

When she looked into Alex's eyes, her chin wobbled, and then a wailing sob erupted from deep within her as tears streamed down her cheeks and she fell to her knees. Alex dropped with her, cradling her and holding her tight to his chest.

'Shhh, it's okay. What happened?' he asked, rocking her as if he were comforting a small child.

Sophia cried and cried, let go of every emotion she'd been holding back since she'd left her family home. Alex kept holding her, mouth to her hair as he stroked her back.

'Tell me? Why are you back? What's happened?'

'My mother,' she eventually said, her breath coming out in a big shudder. 'He's killed her. My father, he . . .'

Alex held her back, looked straight into her eyes. 'Your father killed her?'

'She was hiding a family. A Jewish family,' Sophia explained, wiping at her cheeks and brushing her fingertips across her lashes. 'I got there and he killed them all. She was hanging with them, *with children*, strung up by their necks.' The picture of them all up there, of what she'd watched, what she'd seen, was crippling.

Alex pulled her close again and she hugged him back, but she knew they didn't have a lot of time. If her father or anyone else suspected that she could be doing the same as her mother, then they could arrive any moment.

'We need to get rid of any evidence, any trace that you've been here.' It was only now that she thought about Greta and their other servants. Would they be interrogated, too? Would her father actually be foolish enough to presume that they'd had knowledge of the Jewish family? That they'd helped to conceal them? She couldn't stand the thought of the women she'd known her entire life being questioned and tortured.

'I've been writing a diary,' he said, jolting her back into the present. 'I should have told you. I took one of your notebooks.'

'Keep it on your body,' she said, standing up. 'Any clothes, well, I'll be able to talk my way around those, say they're my boyfriend's if I have to. I'll deal with that. Are you sure there's nothing else?'

Alex shook his head. 'I have a photograph in my pocket. There's nothing else.'

It was awful to think they'd lived together for so long, yet Alex had nothing personal in the apartment.

She crossed the room and looked at her reflection. She was a mess. She had an excuse, and she wanted nothing more than to grieve for her mother, but she needed to pull herself together and get Alex and herself to safety. She needed to find out if there was any way of smuggling him out, if the train that would be taking the next load of Jews out of Berlin had left yet or not. And she needed to disappear herself, because no matter what happened, she couldn't stay.

She fixed her hair and wiped at her eyes, applying make-up to conceal her puffy red skin. She glanced at Alex, saw the concern etched on his face.

Thump, thump, thump.

Sophia's heart pounded as knocks echoed out.

'Open the door!'

She met Alex's terrified gaze as her hands started to shake again. There were only a few moments to answer before the door was broken down, she knew that, and the last thing she wanted was to look like she was hiding something.

'One moment!' she called out, watching frantically as Alex skidded on the timber floor in his hurry to hide and she ran to the door, pressed against it as if she could physically hold off the men on the other side.

'Open it now or we break it down!'

A single tear slid down her cheek as her mother's beautiful face flooded her memories. Everything she did from this step forward, she was going to do for her.

'I'm coming!'

Sophia reluctantly unlocked the door and slowly turned the handle, too afraid to look back and see where Alex was. Usually she made certain he was hidden first, made sure he was safe as could be, but not this time. The officers wouldn't wait that long, and if they were forced to smash her door down, they'd be relentless, certain she was hiding something or someone.

'Excuse me, but what are you doing here?' Sophia asked, summoning every ounce of strength she had and blocking the doorway, buying Alex more time.

'Move aside.'

She'd feared the Gestapo for a long time, but her fear was almost paralysing now.

She looked at their faces, the men standing there in uniform, smirking; or maybe she was imagining their amusement at her situation. She didn't know any more, her pain too deep, clouding her judgment.

'Do you have any idea who my father is? How dare you!' she said.

'Your father is the one who sent us here. Your mother was a traitor. Maybe you are, too.'

Sophia steeled herself against their words, surprised at how easily the lies flowed into her thoughts.

'My mother was a Jew lover,' Sophia snarled. 'How dare you compare me to her and her love of those filthy people?'

She stepped aside, hoping she'd given Alex enough time, praying that he knew how false her words were.

'Check everything!'

She stood, hands at her sides, teeth clenched so hard she feared they might break. Sophia watched as they looked under her bed, in her closet, behind her curtains. Everywhere a person could easily be hiding. It was when they circled back to her sofa that her heart almost stopped beating.

'Make sure there's no compartment in that sofa.'

'Excuse me?' she complained. 'If you damage my sofa—'

Two of the soldiers picked it up then set it down, shrugging.

'Nothing in there.'

'What about this?'

'You think a person could be in my *ottoman*?' She rolled her eyes. 'For goodness' sake, that's ridiculous!'

'Fire a shot.'

Sophia's mouth went dry. She didn't know where Alex was. She didn't know where he was hiding.

'The sofa *and* this,' he said, nudging it and meeting her gaze. 'If you're so certain no one is in there.'

This time she knew she wasn't imagining his smirk. Had her face given her away? Was she not as good an actress as she thought?

'By all means,' she said, her voice not wavering despite the turmoil inside her. She couldn't lose Alex and her mother on the same day. 'But my father paid for all of this. If you don't mind telling him that he has to have it replaced, then fire away.'

She thought that would stop them, thought the threat of her father would do something to halt their actions, but it didn't.

'Fire!'

The two shots straight into her sofa made her scream. They all laughed, every single one of them finding it so amusing to torture her like that.

Then they fired at the ottoman and her heart lodged in her throat, the noise of the shot reverberating through her. Then again. And again.

She shut her eyes, tried to pretend it was all a terrible dream.

'Any blood?'

She imagined Alex's bright red blood pooling through the fabric, seeping out on to her rug. Then another bullet fired at her head for harbouring a Jew. But there was nothing to see when she opened her eyes. No screaming, no blood, nothing.

'Good luck getting *Father* to buy you a new one.'

The soldiers walked out, laughing, kicking her door on the way past, and Sophia found the strength to shut it behind them before collapsing, her legs buckling beneath her as she slid to the hard floor and wept.

A noise made her look up. And then she leapt up and ran to her kitchen, to the cabinet that was still open from when they'd searched the room.

'That was close.'

Sophia bit back a scream as Alex's head appeared from behind the false wall he'd built, his dark brown eyes meeting hers.

'Oh, Alex! I, I . . .' She gasped for air. 'Thank God. I thought you were dead, I thought . . .' She couldn't even get her words straight as she whispered to him. She'd thought he might have dived into the ottoman to hide because it was closer, easier, but he was alive!

'We have to get out of here,' he said grimly.

'I know.'

The overwhelming love she felt for Alex right now was immediately overshadowed by everything else. Her mother was dead. Her father didn't believe she was innocent, otherwise he wouldn't have sent those men. Everything she did from this step forward could put her life and the lives of others in danger, could jeopardise their entire network.

She wanted to do more, needed to do more, but for now she needed to figure out how to get them both out of Berlin.

Sophia had never been so scared in her life. For the first time, she'd chosen to use her false identity papers during the day, terrified of using her real name now that she was under suspicion by the Gestapo. She'd fled with Alex in tow the night her apartment had been raided, knowing that if anyone recognised her, they'd both no doubt be killed. Twenty-four hours later, she was even more terrified than she'd been then.

She ran her fingers through her short hair, refusing to get sentimental over the fact she'd chopped her long blonde locks off to above her shoulders. Before, she'd looked just like her mother, but the rough cut made her look the complete opposite now. She rubbed her thumb over her ring finger, finding comfort in the weight and feel of her mama's ring resting there.

'What do we do now?' Alex asked, his collar turned up to brush his jaw but doing nothing to disguise his face.

Travelling at night and hiding in the shadows was slow, but somehow they'd so far managed to go undetected.

'We keep walking,' she said, knowing there was nothing else they could do but keep moving. They'd been walking for hours and Sophia's feet were rubbed raw, but she didn't know what else they could do.

'You don't need to do this,' Alex muttered, glancing at her. It was so dark but with the moon high in the sky she could just see him. 'I don't want you risking everything for me.'

She shook her head. 'Enough. Keep walking.'

Sophia kept replaying snippets of conversation over in her mind, remembering the person who'd collected the young Jewish man saying that it would be another few days before he was on his way to Sweden. She had to believe that they would be putting him on a train, like she'd done with others in the past. Getting Alex on that train was the only way she knew how to save him, and she'd guessed that tonight had to be the night. She just hoped the meeting point was still the same.

They kept walking, on and on, Sophia pausing only to take some food from her bag and pass half of it to Alex. She nibbled at the small piece of stale bread. Her stomach was growling with hunger, but she didn't have a lot on her and so didn't want to eat too much. It could be days before she was safe and had more food to consume.

When they reached the edge of the woods, Sophia recognised her surroundings. She'd escorted two small groups there before and walked them in, then walked back out to ensure they hadn't been followed. She knew it was the right place.

'This way,' she whispered, touching Alex's shoulder.

He followed her, then they fell into step beside each other again. Sophia knew they would surprise the others lying in wait, that they could be mistakenly killed by their own people, but as far as she could see, she and Alex were as good as dead anyway.

'Hurry,' she hissed, worrying that they might have already missed the train.

She roughly remembered where there was a small shack, and when she finally caught sight of it in the moonlight shining above them, she had to bite back tears. She reached for Alex's hand and held it tight for a moment, before holding both her hands up. He did the same, copying her, and they kept walking forward.

'Friends,' she whispered, leaning into the old, falling-down structure. 'We are friends,' she repeated.

They were greeted by a silence that seemed to stretch for ever, and just when she was about to give up hope, certain they were too late, a rustle sounded out in the bushes behind them. Sophia kept her hands held high.

'What are you doing here?'

She recognised Horse and dipped her head. Tears of relief started to fall then. 'This is my Alex,' she whispered. 'I need to get him on the train. *Please.*'

Horse waved to them both, and they disappeared into the woods with him, hiding low behind thick bushes. She quickly explained what had happened to them.

'Is there any evidence of what you've done for us in the past?' he asked.

She shook her head. 'No.'

'You'll lead them straight to us if you stay in Berlin,' Horse muttered. 'You need to get out.'

Sophia gulped. 'I know. That's why I came tonight.'

Alex's deep, gravelly whisper took her by surprise. 'Can she come with us?'

She looked frantically between the two men. 'I have my papers. I can get out of Germany on my own.'

Horse grunted. 'No, he's right. You go with them tonight. We'll have to move fast to make enough space, but we can do it.'

A rumble indicated the train was on its way; it was impossible to miss the deep noise as it started to come closer.

'You can do more to help us if you're gone. Make your way to France,' Horse said quickly. 'Move!'

He darted out of the bushes, and at the same time an entire group of men appeared from nowhere.

'What's happening?' Alex asked, clasping her hand tight.

Sophia moved quickly, pulling him with her. 'They've already bribed the conductor and train workers, but they can't stop the train for long,' she hissed. 'We have to hurry.'

When the train halted, it was an impressive sight. Even more impressive were the men rushing to open crates of furniture inside a boxcar. Sophia's heart skipped a beat when she saw the young man she'd helped only nights earlier, with no idea at the time that she'd be fleeing her country shoulder to shoulder with him.

She waited for the small group of Jews to board first, helping to seal the crate back up. And then it was her and Alex's turn. She hoped and prayed that no one had followed them, that dogs wouldn't be on the trail and come for the brave men who were helping them once they'd gone. When the train pulled away, those men would be hurrying to burn the furniture they'd emptied from the crates, then making their way back to their daytime lives, not letting anyone know what they did under the cover of darkness to help those most in need.

Sophia huddled close to Alex. It was just the two of them in the second crate, and she guessed at least six people were sitting silently side by side in the first.

'When we get to Sweden, if we make it there alive, I can't stay with you,' she whispered to him, dropping her head to his shoulder. 'I have to keep helping, I can't sit by and just—'

'I know,' he whispered, not letting her finish. 'Just promise me that when the war is over, we'll be married. Promise me you'll come looking for me.' He let out a deep, pained sigh. 'I would do anything to come with you, to help, but without speaking French or English . . .' His words faded.

Tears welled in her eyes but she refused to let them fall. It was heartbreaking that he felt so hopeless.

'Once the war is over, for two months, I'll wait every day at twelve noon outside that little church we could see from my apartment window. Promise you'll do the same?' she asked. 'If we're alive, that way we'll find each other.'

Alex squeezed her hand. 'I promise.'

As the train lurched and started to rumble forward, Sophia shut her eyes tight and prayed that they'd make it to Sweden alive. No matter how hard it would be to walk away from Alex, she would do it. She had to make her way to France, had to honour her mother and fight against Hitler.

Thank you, Mama, she silently whispered, thinking of all the lessons her mother had insisted upon, making sure her French was perfect. Her mother had liked Sophia to speak French with her, to remind her of her family, to make sure Sophia knew that she was as much French as she was German. Sophia couldn't possibly have known it at the time, but it was her mother's language that would make it possible for her to join the Resistance in France.

There she could honour her mother's homeland. Do what she knew in her heart was right. And the Resistance movement, full of women working underground to help fight the war, would be crazy not to take her on. She was a German woman with a French-born mother, had an intimate knowledge of the Nazis, could speak fluent French and had already proven she had the guts to stand up for what was right.

She was going to join the underground movement there, and she wasn't going to take no for an answer.

CHAPTER EIGHT

HAZEL

SCOTLAND

1943

They were stationed at Arisaig House now, in Scotland, and Hazel's exhaustion was like a persistent chill to her bones. The weather was cooler than she'd expected, and given the conditions the instructors kept putting them out in, she was surprised she hadn't frozen. Today they'd been stripped of their coats and anything warm to wear, and she'd been outside training all day with nothing to eat. She'd never been so tired or hungry, so close to collapsing. But she'd seen what happened to others who hadn't dug deep into themselves and kept going, and there was no way she was going to face the same fate after getting so far. She was determined to succeed and get to France.

She hauled herself into bed, reaching for a blanket and quickly wrapping it around herself. A bath would have been heavenly, even a few handfuls of warm water to splash against her face, but her legs wouldn't carry her any further. It was time for bed. It had been six weeks since she'd left home, and her initial four weeks at Wanborough Manor had been a walk in the park compared to what she'd faced in her time here. But it was almost over. It had to be.

Hazel shut her eyes, the burn beneath her lids starting to ease as she shut everything else out. She needed sleep. Deep down, she knew her superiors needed to be this hard on her, because if she couldn't withstand it here, then she'd never succeed in the field. But that knowledge didn't make coping with such long, tiresome days any easier.

She drifted into slumber, her body melting into the mattress. It was the best thing she'd ever felt, dropping into a deep, peaceful sleep.

'Get up!'

Hazel woke abruptly, stifling a scream as a man's rough hands shook her by the shoulders. She had no idea if she'd been asleep two minutes or two hours, and the hands didn't stop, fingers digging into her skin, pulling her so violently that she thought she was going to break.

A torch was pointed at her face, blinding her as she was thrown back down on to the bed.

'Get up!'

It was only then that she realised the man was speaking in German. She pulled herself up, blinking as the lights came on. She was shaking from exhaustion and fear, but she tried to assess the situation. A woman had started to scream, the men were still yelling, and . . . she blinked again, wondering if her eyes were playing tricks on her, if this could be a dream.

They're in German uniforms. They were German soldiers. Or if they weren't, well, they were doing a damn fine job of acting.

'What is your name?' the German demanded, his face so close to hers that she felt the spittle from his mouth land on her skin.

'Hazel. What is this about?' she asked in perfect French.

'Get up!' he yelled. 'Get up now!'

He was speaking in French now and she did as he said, reaching for her shoes and getting a kick in the side for her efforts. The room spun as she clutched her side, doubled over and trying her best to straighten even though the breath had been stolen from her body.

'Move!'

She stumbled, barefoot, leaving her shoes behind and fumbling her way forward. The soldier grabbed her shoulder violently and pushed her against the wall in the hallway.

'Why are you here?'

Hazel knew that this had to be a drill. Surely this was only a drill? Even if it wasn't, she knew she had to stick to her story anyway, for the safety of everyone involved. And if it was a drill and she didn't? Then she'd be sent to the cooler.

'My family sent me here to stay with friends. They wanted me to be safe.'

'You are a spy. We know that you aren't French.'

'A spy? I'm a Parisian as surely as you're a German.' She wiped at her eyes, moist from being woken so abruptly, full of sleep still. She was so tired, her legs ready to buckle beneath her.

'We've searched your apartment and found evidence. Tell us everything or you'll be shot through the head with the other traitors.'

'I don't know what you want from me, or who you're truly looking for, but I am not a spy. I don't even know what a spy would do.' She smiled. 'Please, sir, I think you have the wrong person.'

He laughed, a cruel sneer that made her fearful of what a real Nazi would be like. 'Maybe we could use you then, no? You have beautiful blonde hair and blue eyes, just what we're looking for.'

Hazel looked down, trying to appear embarrassed, thinking maybe she should be flirting with him to get him to be more gentle with her.

'I am a believer in this Aryan race you Germans talk about. It would be nice to live in a more pure world.' Just saying the words made her feel sick, but she forced herself to get them out.

'You expect me to believe that?' He laughed. 'Teach that to your fellow French and we might all get along.'

'May I go now? Or is there anything else I can do to help you with whomever you're supposed to be looking for?'

There went the cruel laugh again, and she watched as he reached into his pocket. He drew a lighter out and flicked it open and shut, his thumb brushing back and forth against the metal as he smiled at her.

She sucked back a breath, too terrified to take her eyes off him now.

'This might make you drop the story and tell me the truth.'

Hazel froze as he flicked the top back again, this time igniting it, the orange flame needing more coaxing as he rolled his thumb across the mechanism. His other hand shot up, grabbing her by the throat and shoving her backwards as he held the flame to her face. It was so close to her cheek, so close to burning her skin, to searing into her and leaving a mark that would for ever remind her of this night.

The lick of fire so close made her push her head back into the wall, a futile action as she couldn't get any further away and he knew it.

'Tell me. Why are you here? What is your name?'

'Hazel,' she whispered as tears clung to her lashes then slowly dropped down her cheeks, streaking across her skin. 'Please, let me go.'

He held the lighter steady, his breath too close, his body too close, everything about the awful man in front of her *too damn close*.

'Please stop,' she begged.

'What do you know about the Resistance?' he asked in a low, menacing tone.

'I don't know anything. Please, tell me what you want from me, but I can't answer your question because I don't know the answer.'

He lowered the lighter and flicked the cover back over. The smell was indescribable, the black smoke that had pungently been emitting from it seeming to curl around her face. She breathed a sigh of relief until she heard the metal flick again.

'Argh!' she yelped.

The flame had touched her hand, burnt into her skin, leaving behind a burst of heat that was getting hotter and hotter. He held it there, his grip tight on her wrist. She grabbed her hand back, stared at the tiny patch of scorched skin and then directly into the eyes of her torturer.

'You can hurt me all you like, but I can't answer your questions because I don't know the answers. I don't know anything because I'm nobody! Can't you see that?'

He grunted and put the lighter back in his pocket. She cradled her hand, able to ignore the burn but deciding that if she was indeed a French nobody then she would be horrified that her skin had been burnt and utterly surprised that any man could do this to her.

'Why would you burn a woman like this? Why would you pull me out of bed in the middle of the night when I've done nothing wrong?'

He shrugged. 'Maybe I'll come back again tomorrow night, too.'

He marched off and she was left standing alone in the hallway. She stared at her hand, surprised that she could no longer feel any pain there. Or maybe she was just in shock, too rattled by the entire experience to care about her singed flesh.

Hazel raised her other hand to her neck, her fingers carefully tracing her skin, soothing the place his fingers had been wrapped around as he'd held her back. Her legs were shaking but she forced herself to pull together and walked slowly back to bed. It had only been a test run, otherwise she wouldn't still be here, and it had been a fairly easy one at that. They might have targeted her when she'd been beyond exhausted, mentally and physically, but if she was out in the field? She'd probably be that exhausted on a daily basis. And no German who suspected her of being a British spy would have stopped at a little burn to her hand. A real Nazi would have held the flame to her face without hesitation, marking her for life, waiting until her skin melted beneath his hold.

A real Nazi would have kept pushing, would have tried harder to break her and not stopped until he did. And if he hadn't broken her and they truly believed her to be a spy, then she'd probably have a bullet through her head by now.

Hazel dragged herself out of bed the next morning. She sat on the edge, her back sore from the rough sleep she'd had, but when she glanced at the clock she was surprised to see how late it was. Then she looked up and noticed that the other two beds in the room were empty. She rubbed her eyes and stood, turning from one bed to the other. Had she missed wake-up? Was she out because she'd slept through?

She dressed quickly and went downstairs, surprised to hear chatter coming from the kitchen and dining room. Hazel prepared to be told she was done, that her time in training was over, but instead the men stopped talking when she walked in and two of them gave her a little clap.

'What is it?' she asked, looking over her shoulder, wondering who it was they were clapping for.

'You. You've made it through.'

She froze. She'd made it? 'Where are my roommates?'

One of the men, Paul, laughed. 'In the cooler. They've got a lot to forget.'

She knew then that they hadn't passed the test conducted during the night. She couldn't believe it. After all these weeks of training, to fold under their first proper interrogation? Perhaps they hadn't known it was a drill, had been too scared that it was real, and coupled with the exhaustion and . . . she stopped making excuses for them. The test had been worth it, because if her roommates had been in her circuit in

France, they would have given her up, and no matter how capable she'd proven herself to be, she'd be dead anyway.

'Well, I hope you've saved me some eggs,' she said, raising an eyebrow and taking her place at the table when Paul pointed to the seat beside him.

'Sure have, sleepyhead. Laid fresh this morning.'

After so long enduring powdered eggs, there had been nothing nicer than having farm-fresh eggs for breakfast in Scotland, even though she knew the little luxury wasn't going to last for long.

'So what's next?' she asked, as she helped herself to the food in the middle of the table.

'You need to brush up on your gunfighter technique like the rest of us,' one of the men who'd been training her replied, sitting back and nursing his cup of tea. 'And William and Eric are going to make sure you've mastered the silent killing technique.'

Hazel didn't allow her shock to register. She could deal with a lot of things, but the idea of killing a man with a knife made her stomach curdle. The thought of holding a blade and slicing through the skin of another human, of being responsible for taking a life, was almost too hideous to even think about. Her appetite had disappeared but she knew she needed to eat, both for her stamina and to make sure the others seated around the table didn't think she was too weak for the position.

'Morning.'

One of the other women training with her, Odette, stood cautiously in the doorway, the same uncertain look on her face that Hazel knew she'd been sporting. When the men clapped for Odette, as they had only moments earlier for her, Hazel beamed over at her. They'd done something incredible by surviving their training and getting this far, and she only hoped they both made it back from wherever they were sent – alive.

'We're just talking about silent killing,' Hazel said, wanting to warn her. 'Such delightful breakfast conversation, but then I suppose we can't expect much else here, can we?'

Laughter rang out and Hazel hoped her attempt at changing the subject had worked. When she'd said yes to volunteering, she'd thought of danger in the same breath as she'd thought about making a difference and hiding away to translate documents. Her language skills had been the thing to get her foot in the door, but it was her ability to learn and survive that determined whether she kept progressing or not.

Hazel ate silently, glancing around the table. There were only six men who'd made it through, and as far as she could tell two women, including her. By her estimates, at least a third of the recruits from those that had arrived at Wanborough Manor hadn't made it to Scotland, and with the dropouts last night, there were less than half of them now seated around the table. She cringed thinking about how many of them wouldn't make it back from where they were going, halving their numbers again.

'Once you've all proven yourselves with silent killing and mastered the full assortment of British and German weapons, you'll be sent to Hampshire and then given one final test.'

Their recruiter grinned at them all. 'I think it's time we dropped all and any pretences. You know why you're here and I know why you're here, and that means you need to be in as many mock situations as possible before you're put out in the field.'

They all sat silently, listening to him. It was the first time anything like that had been said, anything that wasn't skirting around why they were here and what they'd be doing, even though they'd all had a fair idea of the work they'd signed up for.

'Once you've been through your final paces,' he told them, putting his cup back on the table and leaning forward, 'you will be asked one more time if you're certain this is the work you want to be doing, and then we'll establish your best skills and place you accordingly.'

This was it. She'd done it. She only wished she could tell her parents what she was doing, how capable she'd proven to be, instead of sending them her nondescript letters that said how much she was enjoying her new translation job, as she'd been told to. She knew they'd never believe it anyway, the idea of her toting a gun or wielding a knife, let alone managing two cover stories and preparing to set out on her first true test in the field.

'Don't forget to keep up your letters home, maintaining your legends for your family at all times. You need to be your new identity from this moment on. Your life, and that of your fellow recruits, will depend upon it.'

'Will we all be sent to France?' Hazel asked.

'Those with the best French immersion skills will most likely be parachuted in, yes,' their recruiter said.

Hazel saw him look up and she turned to see why he was looking past her. There was Smith, her original recruiter, standing in the doorway, propped against the frame as he smiled at them all.

'So this is the best of the bunch, huh?' he asked with a smile.

His face was so different stretched into a smile, since she'd only seen him in recruitment and interrogation mode until now. She wondered where he'd been and what his ongoing role was.

'Certainly is. I'm just letting them in on a few trade secrets.'

Both men laughed.

'Going back to your question,' Smith said, coming into the room. 'You will receive specialised parachute training, those of you who will be deployed into the field in France, and some of you will stay in London, depending on what you're assigned to do.'

Hazel reached for the pot of tea, not caring if it had cooled. She needed something to sip while she listened.

'I'm here today to assist and observe, so ignore me unless you have questions to ask,' Smith said. 'I'm looking forward to seeing what you're all capable of.'

Hazel sipped her tea, trying to stay calm. It was like she'd been transported to a different place and time. How on earth was she in a room with special operatives in charge of putting together recruits to be parachuted – *parachuted* – into France? If she somehow managed to survive, she doubted her fiancé would believe even a word of it. Or her mother, for that matter. Or maybe she'd still be maintaining her story after the war, pretending she'd done nothing more than a typical woman's job while he was away.

Or maybe everyone would know her name, and those of the other Resistance members. Because the Germans had advanced too far already – she knew that and so did everybody else. Yet it was the Resistance making waves and tackling them head-on, and that was exactly why she was prepared to risk everything. She wanted to go to France. No matter what her posting or what her task, she was going to say yes.

Hazel stood, cleared her plate and cup and walked into the kitchen. She could decipher messages, drop passwords into conversations, recruit if she needed to and code. And she could kill. Never before had she even thought about whether or not she could take another person's life, and now she knew, that if it was a matter of life and death, she'd do it without hesitation. She'd have to.

She glanced down at her hand, the tiny red mark on her skin a reminder of what had taken place the night before. The Germans would have to do a lot worse to get so much as a reaction from her.

CHAPTER NINE

ROSE

BREST, FRANCE

1943

The days and weeks had passed quickly, and Rose could hardly believe that it was almost a month since she'd been recruited by Josephine. Now she was anxiously waiting for the cover of darkness, part of Josephine's covert monthly operation to ferry men to safety.

She sighed, feeling restless. The submarine was scheduled to come when the moon was but a sliver in the sky. Only then, once every four weeks, would they send the rowboats to shore to collect the allies needing transport, which meant that she had a dangerous ride on her bicycle ahead of her.

Rose touched her stomach, something she would never have done if she hadn't been alone staring out the window into the dusky early evening. She hadn't felt her baby move. She wasn't even sure she was supposed to yet, but she wasn't about to ask anyone, not even Josephine, for advice.

By her estimates she was about four months along now, which meant that soon her rounded stomach would be more noticeable, harder to hide from those she saw and worked with on a regular basis. She'd hide it for as long as she could, the baby growing inside her the only connection she had to Peter now.

She blinked and shook her head as if to banish all thoughts of him. These days she refused to go there, never let her mind wander to what could have been, but their baby was a constant reminder. Of why she hated the war, of what she was fighting for, of what she could have had.

Darkness would be upon them within the next half hour, and Rose took a sip of water and cleared her throat. It was time to go.

'Come on,' she said, knocking on the stairs to alert her visitors to come down. 'It's time.'

They would make part of the journey to the coast in the dark, but for the first part they needed some light to navigate their way by bicycle. From then on it was a slow walk, trying to avoid being seen by the German guards stationed all along the coast.

'We're ready.' The two downed British airmen, Thomas and Charles, whom she had been hiding for the past two weeks, made their way silently down the stairs.

The warm British accent made her smile; it had been nice listening to their perfect English, and she knew she'd miss their company terribly once they were gone.

'We have two bicycles and three of us, so I propose I sit on the handlebars and navigate,' she suggested. 'We need to make our way quickly, keeping hidden as much as possible.'

They nodded and she ushered them out the door. Her heart was pounding, every sense in her body on high alert. She'd saved these men, found them before the Germans could and rescued them from their parachutes. She was fast, and she had a home to stow them in, which meant she'd been in charge of their immediate rescue and getting them to safety. It had been Josephine's job to find somewhere to hide the damaged parachutes so no one found them and ended up chasing their trail. It had been an exhilarating four weeks, and Rose had lost men already who'd not made it past their injuries, but it was worth it for the two she'd saved. Her own injury had healed well, and she was surprised by how little she thought of the day she'd been shot.

Josephine had two men at her home, too, and there was another operative Rose hadn't met yet who would be ferrying her own men. And they were only the women in her immediate area. The thought of so many women up and down the coastline making a difference, saving their allies and making sure men made it home to their families, put a huge smile on her face.

'Come on.'

Rose waited for the men to steady themselves and then she hopped up on to the handlebars, wobbling to start with and then settling in. She'd have a sore bottom by the end of it, but she had no intention of complaining.

She held on tight, staying focused and scanning constantly. If they were seen, they were as good as dead. Up to a point, she could lie and pretend she was injured, announce her pregnancy or something, but covering for the men would be much harder. Their French was terrible and they'd be arrested or killed immediately.

The journey was bumpy and silent, and by the time she put a hand out to slow them down, reaching to touch the arm of her British driver – given that it was almost dark and she was worried he wouldn't see her signal – her bottom was completely numb. Every now and again she wondered if it was sensible to do things like this whilst pregnant, but she didn't dwell on the work she did. She couldn't. Otherwise she'd start to worry and overthink her actions, when what she needed to do was trust her instincts and do what came naturally.

'We need to hide the bikes now,' she said in a low voice. It was an eerie feeling, being in the dark, surrounded by trees that could be concealing Germans. A shudder ran down her spine but she pushed her fears away. 'I need them tucked away, but somewhere I can easily find them on my way back,' she said.

The men worked quickly and she stood with her back to them, straining her eyes in the darkness in case they were being watched. She was certain they'd have been shot by now if anyone had seen them, but she also knew that the enemy could follow them to learn more about what they were doing and where they were going.

'Come on,' she hissed once they were finished. She led the way, finding it weird that she was the one in charge of the soldiers. The respect all of the Englishmen had given her was incredible, their attitude making her feel like their superior. But then she figured they were simply grateful to be alive, and to have a way out of an enemy-occupied country.

Rose kept walking, careful with every footfall. She heard a noise and dropped low, waving her hand for the others to do the same. She lay still, her breath heavy and loud to her own ears, and listened for the crackle of footsteps, but no noise followed. She held her breath as she stood and lifted her head, certain the instant snap of gunfire would follow, but there was nothing.

'Hurry,' she said, moving faster now. The last thing she wanted was to be late to their rendezvous point and have to risk taking the men back home with her for another month. Not only would it be dangerous, but she wouldn't have the space to hide others, and they needed every hiding place they could find with so many downed airmen to rescue. Their network involved a lot of locals, but there were only a few of them tasked with getting the rescued men out of France.

After walking in silence for what felt like an hour, Rose slowed down once they reached the beach. They were close to where the men would be collected, and she prayed that there weren't any German guards patrolling this part of the coast.

'We need to lie down,' she instructed. 'No moving, no talking.'

Fingers around her wrist made her pause. The dark had completely swallowed the air around them, which meant it was almost impossible to make out the two men with her.

'Do you want me to dig out some sand?' he asked, his voice a whisper, and she realised it was Thomas. 'It might help to conceal us if we're partially submerged.'

She nodded and then realised he probably couldn't see the movement. 'Yes,' she whispered back. 'Good idea.'

They all dug into the sand and lay on their stomachs, facing the water. All they had to do now was wait, and pray that no one saw them. The wait seemed endless, but finally she heard it – the sound of an owl, a sound she'd mimicked and practised until she could make the noise as perfectly as the bird itself. She waited and listened again, just in case it was a German who'd figured out their calls.

The familiar owl sounded again, and Rose sighed with relief. It was Josephine. Rose made the noise straight back, twice, before standing and searching with her eyes frantically for her friend. In the end Josephine and her group almost ran straight over the top of them. Rose caught her arm, stopping her from falling, and pulled her down low. The two men Josephine had with her fell down beside them.

'Thank God you're here safe,' Rose whispered, hugging her friend tight.

'You too.'

They lay low, staying silent until another call was made. This time it was Josephine who made the owl noise back, and within seconds they were on their feet. Rose wondered if her friend's heart was pounding as hard as hers was.

Rose turned first to Thomas and wrapped her arms tight around him, fighting tears when he kissed her cheek. He'd lived with her for over two weeks now, in her house with her every hour of every day, and she'd miss his company terribly.

'You be careful with that arm of yours and make sure to tell your wife how much you love her when you get home,' she whispered quickly.

Then she gave Charles a hug, too, kissing his cheek. 'Get home safely,' she said. 'Now, head straight for the water. Wade out as far as you can – you'll be able to make out the rowboats further out into the water. They'll get you safely to the submarine.'

As soon as they moved away she breathed a sigh of relief and dropped low again, on her stomach and reaching for Josephine's hand. She listened, ears straining, making out the sound of water breaking as the men entered. Waiting was painful. She was certain she'd hear shots or German voices, but much to her surprise she didn't hear a thing.

She shut her eyes and saw Thomas and Charles smiling, imagined them clambering into the rowboats, felt their relief as they realised they were about to be saved and sent home. She imagined all this in her mind even as her body stayed on high alert, certain the illusion was going to be shattered. But miraculously it wasn't.

Rose stayed where she was, in the dark, burrowing further down into the sand beside her friend. It was too dangerous to leave just yet; they couldn't see anything and needed to wait until there was the tiniest slither of light to make their way safely. If the Germans found them now, well, they had nothing to hide. The English airmen were gone and the enemy could do what they liked with her. It would be Josephine she'd do anything to save, not herself.

Rose forced her eyes to stay open and made herself comfortable. Just her, the woman nestled beside her, and the tiny baby in her belly.

Rose's arms felt like they were going to break, they were aching so badly. The moment the sky had started to lighten she'd made her way quickly back to where the bicycles had been hidden, parting ways with Josephine. It was too dangerous for them to travel together; it was better for one of them to be caught than both.

Rose had uncovered one of the bicycles. She would have to come back for the other later and pray nobody found it in the meantime. Cycling home had been long and exhausting, and she was constantly fearful of being discovered, but she was almost there and in record time. As she neared her cottage she stopped, surveying the other houses, being careful to spot anyone who might be watching or lurking around. The homes closest to hers were full of supporters who'd risk anything to save their fellow countrymen and -women, but she was always cautious. All it took was one person, one traitor, to rip their network open and put an end to all the good work they were doing.

She breathed slowly, her heart beating fast, legs shaky from the exertion. Her stomach cramped but she did her best to ignore it. She'd had pains on and off for a few hours now, but she was certain it was hunger pangs given how long it had been since she'd eaten. Josephine was no doubt feeling the same from the sheer exhaustion of what they'd done.

Rose decided to walk now, going the rest of the way on foot and pushing the bicycle beside her. She felt uneasy, but that didn't surprise her.

She came closer to the house and went to place the bicycle around the back against the stone wall, but a low moan made her stop. *What on earth was . . . ?* She gasped and leaned the bicycle hurriedly against the side of the house, running to her back door. There was a woman lying there, curled into a ball. She was bleeding but Rose couldn't see where her wound was or what had happened.

'Help me. Please, help me.'

Rose dropped to her knees as her stomach twinged again. 'Tell me, what happened?' she said in a low voice, worried someone could be watching them or listening. 'Who did this to you?'

The woman turned on to her back slightly, eyes locking on Rose.

'Tell me your name,' the woman murmured.

'Rose,' she said, smiling down at her. 'I'll help you get inside. Come on.'

The woman shook her head. 'I . . . can't,' she rasped. 'Wrong . . . name.'

Rose stared at the woman, taking her hand and holding it tight. She needed to get her inside and fast.

'Are you looking for Josephine?' she whispered. 'It's too dangerous to go to her house. I'll hide you here.'

The woman grasped her hand back, her hold weak but the look on her face telling Rose that she was holding as tight as she could.

'Help me,' she murmured, trying to sit up. 'Please, help me.'

Rose somehow found the strength to pull both herself and the woman on to their feet. She looked down, wondered what the wetness on the inside of her legs was. She gasped, seeing blood and realising it was her own. A crippling pain tore through her belly and she fought not to cry out.

'You need to tell her,' the woman whispered, her lips cracked and dry as Rose stifled her own pain to stare at the woman in her arms. 'Tell her they need to know the fox has fallen down a hole. *Please.*'

Rose nodded, numb but determined to keep going no matter what was happening, not understanding the coded language but knowing how important it must be. But it was the baby. It had to be the baby. She was losing her baby, she knew it, and there was nothing she could do.

'Repeat the words to me, and don't tell a soul that you've found me. Only her.'

'The fox has fallen down a hole,' Rose repeated, her hands shaking as she managed to drag the woman with her. She reached out and turned the door handle, pushing the door open with her back as she did her best to haul them both inside.

She wasn't going to let this woman fall into the wrong hands, instinctively knowing how important she could be. Even if Rose was fighting for her own life and that of her child.

CHAPTER TEN

HAZEL

ENGLAND

EARLY 1944

Hazel's heart hammered so loudly she wondered if it was about to leap clean from her chest. This was the moment she'd been anxiously waiting for. She was beyond excited that she was finally going to be doing something, yet terrified that she'd be caught by the enemy the moment she landed.

She walked through the airfield beside her contact from the Air Liaison Section, Eddie, and gave him a tight smile when she noticed he was watching her.

'How are you feeling?' he asked.

'Scared,' Hazel replied honestly. 'But I'll be fine. I know what to do, I'm just not fond of heights.'

When he stopped at an aircraft hangar she took the chance to sit down, her knees knocking. It was time to run through everything again, and she was looking forward to doing so; it would give her the clarity and focus she needed. The more times she went through all the details, the more in control she felt.

She watched him as he carefully took out a map and leaned in closer to her.

'This is your dropping point,' he said. 'I want you to familiarise yourself again with where you'll be landing.'

Hazel stared at him, committing to memory what he was showing her. She blew out a breath. She knew she was joining a man and woman, that they'd be waiting for her in an old shed near her landing coordinates, and that she was being dropped in as their radio operator. But all the facts in the world weren't going to prepare her for the real thing and she knew it.

'There is one thing I want to talk to you about,' Eddie said, sitting down beside her.

'What is it?' she asked, curious.

'There are two tablets that every SOE agent must carry with them at all times. I have your two here for you.'

Hazel gulped. It felt like there were rocks in her throat. Why did she not already know this?

'What are they?'

'This,' he said, 'is Benzedrine. It will keep you awake if you need it to.'

'And the other?' she asked.

He nodded, holding up a small rubber something. She realised then it was a cover of some sort.

'This is an L tablet. It's lethal and you must keep it in this cover. Basically it's a death pill, and if you bite down on it, you'll be dead within two minutes.'

'It kills you that quickly?'

'I'm afraid so. Think of it as another weapon, something you have as a safety net if you're ever, well, if you're ever in the type of situation that desperately requires it.'

'Thank you,' Hazel said, taking the pills from him. She almost didn't want to touch the L tablet, hating the idea of being in a situation so dire she'd have to use it or even think about using it.

'I'll go through your equipment once more, but other than that you'll be in the air in no time,' Eddie told her. 'I'll give you a hot toddy before we drop you, so that's something to look forward to, I suppose.'

Hazel smiled her thanks. 'I hope it comes with a generous dollop of rum. I'll need it to steel my nerves.'

'Don't worry, love, it'll have enough rum in it to put hairs on your chest.'

She was nervous as a person could be, but his silly joke made her laugh. She took a deep breath as she looked out at the planes. There were some agents returning, the lucky ones who'd managed to stay alive in France and make it home, and a handful being sent out. She had less than an hour before she left the safety of England, and then her fate was entirely in her own hands.

All she had to do now was put her parachute overalls on and get ready to go.

The plane was vibrating so much that Hazel was certain her entire body was buzzing, her hands shaking, her stomach flipping so violently she was on the verge of being sick. Being so high in the air, knowing what was about to happen, what she was about to do to herself – it was beyond awful.

She knew they were close, that it wouldn't be long before she had to drop, but until then she was holding on tight.

'Here!'

She took the hot toddy that was being passed to her from the dispatcher when she heard his shout, willing her hands to stop shaking so she could hold it without spilling it all over herself. Hazel drank it down, hoping it gave her the courage she so desperately needed.

'See this?' he shouted, and if she hadn't been staring at him she probably wouldn't even have known he was speaking. The roaring of the plane's engines was so loud in her ears that she doubted she'd ever forget the noise.

She nodded and watched as he made a big fuss out of checking the line to show her how sturdy it was and then giving the hook they'd be using a few mighty pulls. The thought of free-falling and finding her parachute didn't work or wasn't properly attached had certainly crossed her mind. Then again, she knew her chances of surviving the parachute drop were significantly greater than surviving her time in France.

Something felt different then, the engine slowing or something, she didn't know, and when she passed the cup back to her dispatcher, she wished she hadn't drunk the entire toddy now that it was sloshing around in her belly.

She stared at the lights, watched as the dispatcher took a call from the pilot on the intercom. This was it. She knew this was the moment. She'd worried about her fiancé not coming home from war, but she suddenly realised that perhaps she had less chance of coming home now than he did.

Her dispatcher got up and took hold of the static line on her parachute, attaching it to the hook on the plane. Then he glanced at her before opening a hole in the floor of the fuselage. Hazel knew the drill, had gone over it many times so she knew what to expect and not to make a mistake, but everything seemed to be happening so fast now.

The red light came on, her signal to move, and she carefully sat, legs dangling over the edge of the hole. She didn't look down, kept her gaze up. Her stomach was churning now, diving and flipping, the anticipation almost too much to bear, but she never took her eyes off the light. It was still red. It was red. It was . . .

Green.

Everything changed then. The noise that had rumbled in her ears like never-ending thunder abruptly ended as the engines cut to slow the plane. She gasped, her lungs suddenly empty as she clenched her fingers and dropped out of the plane and into nothingness.

She'd had to move fast to avoid the slipstream, and as much as she wanted to scream as the cool air engulfed her, she stayed deathly quiet, eyes shut tight. And then she opened them, forcing herself to look around, to enjoy the once in a lifetime experience of falling from the sky. Hazel lost her breath, couldn't inhale as the impact of what she was doing caught up to her, and then suddenly, just like that, she felt free. She laughed, smiling so hard her cheeks hurt. This was it, this was what she'd been trained to do, and finally, *finally* she was here.

Hazel had never imagined anything like the rush of falling, then the static line pulled taut, jolting her back to reality as she thanked God that her chute had opened, keeping her from crashing into the ground.

She kept floating, like a bubble being passed gently through the air, and she thought about being a bird. About flying every day, seeing the world pass you by from above, and for the first time in her life she felt envious of the little winged creatures that she so often watched in the sky.

The descent was slow and magical, like nothing she'd ever felt, until she looked down and suddenly the ground seemed to be coming towards her at a rapid pace. The euphoria lifted then, disappearing like it had never existed.

She wasn't going to stop. She was going to crash. Oh God, she was going to break every bone in her body!

Hazel shut her eyes tight before quickly popping them open again. She was in charge, she was the one attached to this damn thing and she knew what she was supposed to do. As the ground seemed to open up, ready to engulf her, she realised she was doing fine. She was going the correct speed, was going to be all right so long as she didn't tangle in the nearby trees.

Oomph.

She hit the ground. Hazel scrambled to find her feet, everything she'd learned during her training coming back to her in a rush as though she'd done this all before. Of course she had, in training, only then she'd had backup and she hadn't been landing in a territory occupied by Germans. There was a chance they'd seen her already, which was why the quicker she found her contacts, the faster she'd get to safety.

Hazel struggled to release herself, the panic rising inside her, bile filling her throat as she thought about who could be watching her, what a bullet would feel like entering her body, a knife to her throat, a . . . She blocked her fears out, remembering her parachute protocol and moving quickly. Her contacts would be here soon, if they weren't already running towards her.

'Over here!'

She spun around, the urgent whisper surprising her. Hazel braced herself, then placed a hand on her weapon, ready to fight if she needed to, ready to use the knife that she'd had combat training to learn how to use. She knew not to trust anybody, couldn't believe this stranger just because she was another woman.

'Quickly!'

Hazel knew she had no choice but to confront the person calling her. She went to move, tried to look unflappable, and the woman darted out, surprising her with how fast she was. There was supposed to be two people, a man and a woman.

'Your contacts were captured barely an hour ago. We have to move now!' the woman said in rapid French.

Hazel quickly took off her parachute overalls, knowing now why they were often laughingly called 'striptease overalls' for how fast they had to be removed, and pulled out the little shovel she'd been given to hide her parachute with. The other woman stood guard but didn't offer to help as Hazel buried all evidence of her landing.

'Hurry.'

'Who are you?' she asked, still unsure if she was doing the right thing in trusting her. But they couldn't stand arguing all day when they could so easily be discovered, and she'd rather this woman than a German.

'Sophia,' she said quickly. She made a whistling noise, and within seconds another woman emerged.

Oh my God. It took only a second for Hazel to realise who was running towards her.

'What . . . ?' she whispered, dumbfounded.

Rose threw her arms around her in a quick hug before seizing her hand. Hazel grabbed the things she'd landed with, her suitcase containing the radio and her small bag.

'What are you doing here?' Hazel gasped.

'It's so good to see you!' Rose said, her voice low but her smile wide.

Hazel clutched her hand tight and ran fast alongside the two women. Now she knew who'd recommended her, and she couldn't believe she was in France, undercover, with the one person who'd taught her almost everything there was to know about the country in the first place. She was with Rose!

'We're posing as French students, same as you. Use the cover story you've been given and keep anything you don't know as close to the truth as possible,' Rose whispered. 'We've known each other for years, yet you two have only just met, that type of thing. Only lie when you absolutely have to.'

Hazel nodded, she knew all that already but she'd still listened carefully, and the enormity of what she was doing hit her like she'd walked smack bang into a solid wall. A lump formed in her throat and she thought of home; a warm fire, the sound of her mother humming as she sat down to knit, her father's laughter. Hazel pushed the thoughts away. There was no point wishing for home. She was here, and there would be no home to go back to if they didn't stop the Germans in their tracks.

She pushed herself to run faster, easily keeping up with the other two. This was what she'd trained for, this was what she'd wanted, and going home was no longer an option.

PART TWO

France, 1944

CHAPTER ELEVEN

ROSE

'You look like you've seen a ghost.'

She watched as Hazel looked up, eyes like saucers. The poor thing was shaking like a leaf.

'I feel like I have!'

They both laughed and Rose passed her old friend a cup of chicory coffee, hoping she wouldn't mind the taste of the substitute blend. It was nice to have a brief moment with Hazel. It had taken them hours to get back to her house, and Sophia had left them almost immediately to join Josephine and provide assistance after receiving word that there were allies scheduled to fly overhead.

'So you've been here all this time with Sophia?' Hazel asked, her brows furrowed. 'Was it you who recommended me for the job?'

Rose nodded. 'I managed to make my way here after Peter died. It seemed like the best place for me, even though it's crawling with as many Germans as Paris is.' She paused, taking a sip of coffee as she tried to warm up. 'I met Sophia under trying circumstances, but we've made a good team since then. We've been together almost six months now.'

Hazel had her fingers wrapped around the cup as she stared back at her.

'I was asked some time ago, once I'd proven myself, if there was anyone I thought was suitable for a similar role,' Rose explained. 'I mentioned you, of course. You were the only person I knew well enough to trust.'

'Dare I ask if you had another radio operator before me?'

Rose smiled. 'You've obviously heard about the mortality rate.' She shook her head. 'You were supposed to be joining my brother's cell, actually. He and his wife are working for the Resistance, too, and their cell has been short on a good operator.'

'Sebastian?' Hazel looked surprised.

'I know he'd love to see you again.'

'Is he all right? Why didn't I join them?'

Rose steeled herself, setting her cup down. She'd become better at keeping her emotions in check, so much calmer than before. Peter would have laughed – he'd been so used to her flying off the handle. 'We're not sure what happened, but we think someone my friend Josephine works with was captured, and another from their cell, so everything is in a state of chaos right now.'

Rose was quietly worried about her brother. He'd been supposed to arrive the day before with other members of his cell, but when she and Sophia heard word of the captures, she knew he'd have decided to lie low. Or else something had gone terribly wrong.

'I can't imagine, I mean . . .' Hazel took a deep, shuddering breath. 'Training is one thing, but actually being here is completely different.'

Rose sighed, seeing the light in her old friend's eyes, how excited and full of anticipation she seemed. It made her feel one hundred years old in comparison, or maybe she'd simply seen and been through too much. Perhaps she'd had that same light when she'd first told Peter what she wanted to do, how badly she wanted to help.

Rose finished sipping her coffee, liking the almost too hot burn as it slid down her throat and warmed her stomach. It was the quiet moments like this she relished now – the times of doing nothing that might have bored her in the past but now seemed like a luxury. It was what she was looking forward to most when the war was over.

'I know I've said it all in letters already, Rose, but I am so sorry about Peter,' Hazel suddenly said, taking her by surprise by changing the subject so abruptly. 'He was a good man, and from everything you said a lovely husband, too, and I want you to know how truly sorry I am, and also how grateful it made me that I attended your wedding all those years ago.'

Rose felt hardened to it now, after everything that had passed, as if she'd steeled herself so much against the pain that now it didn't hurt her. Until she was alone at night, in bed, trying to sleep.

'Thank you. I think perhaps it will hit me again once all this is over.'

Being helpful and joining the local Resistance had given her a purpose, something to wake up for every morning. As had looking after Sophia and nursing her back to health. They'd been through a lot together in the months since Sophia had almost bled to death outside her house. There had been so much else to do, so much to think about, that Rose had managed to push thoughts of Peter away.

It was her lost baby who haunted her the most, who played through her memories when she most wanted solitude.

'We might not be staying here long,' Rose said, pushing thoughts of her child away. 'We're operating right under German noses, and we've been working here for months. If we stay much longer they could find us or, worse, the locals will have to pay for what we've done.'

'What do you mean?' Hazel asked.

'You don't want to know,' Rose said, her voice so cold she hardly recognised it. 'But let's just say that when the Resistance disrupts them in ways they don't like, they find a way to make the locals suffer as penance.'

The floorboards above creaked and she saw Hazel startle.

'What was that?'

Rose pointed up. 'We have a guest,' she explained. 'We've been working with others in the area, rescuing pilots, but this one was injured and we couldn't get him out when the last of the submarines came through. He'll be gone with the new moon.'

Hazel looked uncertain and Rose understood how she felt. It was overwhelming, and all the training in the world couldn't possibly have prepared her for what she was going to be doing. If she hadn't been recruited on the ground as she had, Rose was certain she'd have looked just as worried.

'Gosh, I felt like I was top of my class during training and now I'm like a fish out of water!'

'Stop,' Rose said. She stood and moved around the table, holding out her hand and waiting for Hazel to stand. When she did, Rose opened her arms and hugged her friend long and hard. 'It's so good to see you again. We're sitting here talking, all stiff like we're strangers, and it's silly. It's been so long since I've seen someone from my past life, it's as if I need to be taught how to behave again.'

Hazel hugged her back and relaxed in her arms. 'It's good to see you again, too.' She sighed audibly. 'I definitely never expected to find a familiar face over here, that's for sure.'

Rose pulled away and wrapped her arms around herself. 'The work we do, it changes you. I didn't mean to be cold with you, but I feel different now. As if I'm not even connected to the old me, like I'm watching from above or something peculiar.' She knew how silly that sounded, trying to explain her feelings.

Hazel touched her arm before dropping back into her chair again. 'I can see that. I know you've been through so much and I haven't done anything other than be put through my training. I don't know how we're supposed to do the things they train us for, then simply return home at the end and pretend like nothing has changed.'

Rose nodded. She understood completely; her old life felt like a distant memory that she could barely reach out and touch. She couldn't imagine going home and being the same person again, especially not being able to divulge how active they'd been during the offensive in France.

'Hazel, I—'

A thump outside made Rose jump. She was used to the unexpected now, but a loud noise when they were so careful to be quiet and go unnoticed was unusual.

'Wait here,' she said, glancing at Hazel before hurrying to the door. She waited a second, then opened it a crack to take a look, ready to fight if she needed to. She was always on guard, always on edge, one eye half-open even when she was sleeping.

She gasped when she saw Sophia buckling beneath the weight of a man dressed in a British RAF uniform. Rose dashed out, calling for Hazel to join them.

'Help! Quick!' Sophia hissed.

Rose grabbed one side of him, taking part of his weight as her boots skidded on the damp grass. She slumped beneath him, trying desperately to stay upright.

'Who is he?' she asked Sophia as the man moaned. 'And how the hell have you ended up with him?'

'What in the world?' Hazel gasped.

Sophia collapsed just as Hazel reached them, darting to help catch the man as he grunted and slipped forward. He was filthy, his face covered in dirt and dried blood, his uniform torn and snagged.

'Found him,' Sophia panted as she let Hazel take over, 'crawling through the wooded area on my way back.' She stumbled to the door and held it open. 'I could hardly leave him, could I? Josephine had already gone.'

'What's your name?' Rose asked as they hefted him up the steps. One of his legs was working, but he was cradling an arm and the other leg was dragging and making him groan with every bump.

'Harry,' he muttered, barely audible.

And just as she was about to reply, he slipped straight from their arms and landed with a thud on the hard timber floor.

Rose stood dead still with the others for a moment, all of them frozen with the shock of what had just happened, before jolting into action.

'What do we do with him?' Hazel asked as Rose dropped to the floor beside him. She bent low and listened to his breathing. It was shallow but at least he wasn't dead.

'He's alive,' she said, glancing at Sophia. 'We can't carry him upstairs, so let's get him to the sofa and then we can check over his injuries.'

Sophia looked as though she was about to pass out, and Rose wanted her to rest. She'd been out for hours and the last thing Rose needed was for her to collapse from fatigue when they were on high alert.

'Samuel, get down here!' Rose called to the man who was sleeping upstairs. She'd told him not to come down unless he was told to, preferring to keep him well hidden until it was time to leave. There had been too many of their own caught by Germans in the past few weeks, their countrymen turning on them and giving information to the Nazis. They no longer knew who they could trust.

'Hazel, get hot water and towels. They're in the kitchen,' Rose ordered, kneeling beside their new patient as she waited for Samuel to come down to help her. 'I'll need bandages, too. Bottom cupboard.'

Samuel came down the stairs so quietly she didn't hear him until he was standing near her. He looked worried and she didn't blame him. He was so close to getting back home and away from an enemy who'd take pleasure in his capture; he was probably a nervous wreck.

'Help me lift him,' she said. 'I need to get him to the sofa.'

Samuel had his own injuries, but they were the least of Rose's worries right now. She needed to get this airman fixed up so they could hide him and figure out what to do. They'd only radioed in for one pickup from their circuit, and she'd need to figure out if she could take this one with them to the submarine drop-off or not. She wasn't meeting Josephine until the next day, and it was too risky to go over and see her before then.

'Let me help,' Sophia insisted, her voice hoarse as she stood. Rose looked up and saw how unsteady she was on her feet. Something was wrong; Sophia was never like this, always kept going no matter what as if nobody and nothing could exhaust her.

'No, sit there and rest. You need fluid and something to eat,' Rose said, taking command. They had a deep level of trust between them, and she knew Sophia would listen to her if she demanded it. She was more concerned about Sophia's welfare than her own most of the time, and given how many months Sophia had worked in France before turning up on her doorstep, Rose knew she was too strong to collapse merely from exhaustion. 'Hazel, how's that hot water coming?'

'Here,' Hazel replied, hurrying to her. 'What can I do?'

Samuel helped Rose to heft the airman higher up on the sofa, cushions propping his head and back. He moaned, his cracked, dry lips parting, every time they moved him. Once he was slumped there she stood back and swapped glances with Hazel. She was no nurse and yet there was Hazel waiting for her to issue instructions.

'I think we should clean his wounds as best we can, from what we can see. Then we can check him over properly once he comes around more.'

Hazel nodded. 'I'll bathe his face first,' she said. 'He'll need water and something to eat once he's awake again.'

Rose watched Sophia stand and slowly make her way into the kitchen. She knew how hard the other woman would find it to sit still and not do anything, but at least she wasn't doing too much. Rose's biggest worry was whether they were about to be raided, their door smashed in by soldiers who'd followed Sophia.

'What happened?' Rose called out as she carefully checked Harry's arm and took a clean towel, dipping it into the warm water and bathing the deep cuts and scratches etched into his skin.

'Everything's turned to hell out there,' Sophia called back. 'We didn't see any planes come down. Josephine left because she wanted to double-check we hadn't been followed. She's been frantic since Sebastian went missing, and she told me more from another network have disappeared from contact.'

Rose took a deep breath. She could cope with a lot, but being captured by the Germans? The things they could do to a person to try to extract knowledge weren't something she liked to think about. She had to remind herself that right now, they didn't know anything for sure.

'I got the package though,' Sophia said.

'What was the package?' Hazel asked, her voice low.

Rose shook her head, knowing Sophia would be furious that Hazel had asked so openly. She saw the hostile glare Sophia gave her old friend and cringed. The fact that the men with them were allies didn't mean they could disclose their secrets, not any of them, and Sophia was unforgiving when it came to protecting the work they did.

'How's his arm looking?' asked Sophia.

Rose kept going, checking his scratches, cleaning him up, pleased that everything looked fairly fresh. The blood hadn't long dried, and in some places he was still bleeding. But it was his leg she was most worried about, and she hadn't even examined that yet. The way he'd been resting it, she worried that there might be something too sinister there for them to treat with their crude supplies.

'Rose, we had the delivery confirmed for tomorrow night,' Sophia called out. 'We need to rest tonight, then get the package to the drop-off point and figure out whether it's safe to come back or not.'

It was the worst kind of news, to have to think about whether to leave the house or not, and there was obviously a lot Sophia was waiting to tell her. She wasn't looking forward to making the drop, that was for sure.

Samuel caught her eye and she smiled at him, not giving anything away. He'd trusted them this long, and the last thing she wanted was for him to think they weren't going to follow through on the promises they'd made him.

'You'll be on your way soon,' Rose reassured him. 'I promise.'

She kept going, methodically checking their new house guest over, wondering if he'd be the one to get them caught. Even if Sophia had been careful, she'd been trying to support the weight of a man twice her size. There was simply no way she'd have known if there were Germans hidden, watching her. 'Go back upstairs for now. It's safer there. Just bring down some new clothes for this one first, then we can burn his uniform.'

Rose sighed and stood. If the enemy had been watching Sophia, surely they'd have stormed the house by now, and a simple change of clothes for their guest wouldn't help at all.

'I'll be back in a moment,' she said to Hazel as Sophia reappeared. 'Keep going as best you can, and once he's patched up we need to strip him down and burn those clothes well enough so there's not even a thread of his uniform left.'

She motioned to Sophia with her head, looking towards the kitchen and walking to the corner with her. They stood close, heads bent, and she could tell from Sophia's eyes that something was troubling her. She'd seen that look on her face only once before, and that had been when they were both losing too much blood, side by side, and things were going horribly wrong.

'What happened?' she asked, keeping her voice deliberately low.

'No one has heard from Sebastian or Charlotte, but the other, the man Josephine has been working with, was confirmed as captured.' Sophia let out a breath. 'And the members of their cell we'd heard had been taken? It's confirmed.'

Rose felt her heart skip a beat, then thud rapidly. She was relieved Sebastian was still unaccounted for – no news was better than bad news, and she preferred to think of him as hidden somewhere safely – but she knew that Josephine would be devastated. Not to mention worried she could be given up.

'My guess is they're being interrogated right now, which means it's only so long before one of them breaks.' Sophia's tone was low, depressed. 'But I think we'd know if they had your brother.'

Or if he was dead. That was the missing part from what she'd said. They were either being interrogated or they were already dead. And if they weren't dead then they would be soon, or else they'd be sent to one of those horrendous camps, where it was a matter of *when*, not *if*, they perished. She knew her mind was racing, jumping to conclusions, but the chance Sebastian was safely hiding somewhere was seeming less likely by the minute.

'Any change in the pickup instructions for tomorrow night?' she asked.

'No,' Sophia said. 'But it's going to be difficult. There are German guards everywhere, more along the coast than ever from what I've heard. It'll be our hardest yet, and I doubt there'll be many more men we can rescue and get out. They're *everywhere*.'

'What we will do with any more we find?'

'There are rumours they'll have to be smuggled to Spain from now on, through an intricate network of helpers.'

Rose felt shivers go up and down her spine, the tiny hairs on her arms all standing on end. Up until now, they'd been so careful, and they'd done so many drop-offs that it no longer felt as dangerous as before. But Sophia wouldn't be scaring her if she didn't absolutely believe that what she'd been told was true.

'But we still go ahead with rescuing them, regardless?' Rose asked. 'At what point do we decide it's not worth the risk? That maybe we should' – she paused, hating the words she was about to say – 'leave them behind and focus on disrupting the Germans instead, with the other cells?'

'We radio Paris tonight,' Sophia said. 'It's the only way. And then they can communicate with London and follow their orders.' She looked sad, her mouth drawing down. 'We don't give up on any of them, Rose, not until we're told to. We can't.'

There was a chance they'd be found out, if the others talked, but they were all trained to keep their mouths shut. Giving away information about another meant certain death, and Rose knew she'd much prefer to die than give up her fellow Resistance members. But if they were spotted trying to get Samuel to the submarine, then they'd be found and tortured regardless.

'We have a radio here now, and that's something,' Sophia continued. 'If Hazel is as good as she's supposed to be, and she damn well better be, then we're going to be stronger than ever. It'll save me having to make that long ride out to the others in the circuit so often.' She sighed. 'Although from the looks of her, a feather could blow her over.'

Rose stifled her laugh. 'Have you ever heard the saying "don't judge a book by its cover"?'

Sophia made a face and shrugged, clearly unimpressed. 'She can prove herself to me and then perhaps I'll change my mind.'

Rose continued, ignoring the look Sophia was giving her. 'Look, we'll do the drop tomorrow night together, just you and I. But I doubt our newest visitor will be in any shape to be transported.' She turned to make Sophia a drink, certain she needed something hot to keep her going after the day and night she'd had. There was a watery soup that wasn't half bad still sitting on the cooker, and she wanted to make sure Sophia had some. 'Hazel will be great, trust me. I've known her a long time, and they wouldn't have sent her in if she wasn't one of the best.'

She took out two large mugs. They were low on bowls and it was often easier to sip their soup from a cup anyway. It was hardly worthy of a spoon, although she often used one simply to make it feel like she was having a proper meal.

'Have this and then get some rest. We don't need you tonight and you won't be any use to us tomorrow if you haven't had any sleep.'

'Sorry to disturb you.' Hazel's soft voice floated towards them and Rose turned, taken by surprise.

'Oh, it's fine. We're not keeping secrets from you, we just don't need anyone else hearing them.' She personally trusted their allies, especially given the help they were giving these two men, but if they were put under pressure? Tortured? She had no idea if they'd keep their mouths shut or give away their location and what they were doing.

'We have a problem. With Harry,' Hazel said, her brows drawn together.

'What is it?' Rose asked, putting down the spoon she was about to use to ladle the soup out of the pot.

'I was wondering if either of you have any experience in dislocated joints?' Hazel had been frowning, and now she was grimacing. 'That's the reason his leg is causing him so much pain, I think, or at least it's one of the reasons.'

Sophia groaned. 'I'll do it. After that I'm trudging up those stairs to bed though.'

Hazel looked relieved and Rose nodded. 'Let's get this over with.'

CHAPTER TWELVE

HAZEL

Hazel's hands had begun to shake when she'd leapt from the plane, and she wasn't sure if they would ever stop.

She sat next to Harry, reaching for his hand and clasping it when his fingers connected with hers.

'I thought I was supposed to be the scared one?' he said through gritted teeth, now fully conscious and holding on to her tight.

Hazel laughed, and with his hand in hers, she finally felt the shaking start to subside. 'Nice to see you awake again. You've woken up for the good part,' she teased, trying to keep the conversation light.

'Are you a nurse?' he asked, his breathing laboured, each inhale sounding too short and sharp to be comfortable. 'Is this some kind of makeshift hospital?'

'No,' she answered honestly, not about to lie to him. 'But just think of us as your angels, I suppose.'

'I'm feeling like the luckiest bloody guy on the planet,' he said, teeth gritted again as he tried to shift his weight. 'Rescued from the middle of nowhere by a beautiful woman, and now surrounded by two more. I think I must be hallucinating.'

Hazel smiled and looked up, watching as Sophia nodded at her. Rose was kneeling beside the sofa, hand on his hip area, near his thigh, and Sophia had his foot in one hand now, holding his ankle in the other, with a grimace on her face that told Hazel just how terrible the ordeal was going to be.

Her job was to focus on Harry, and she was taking her role very seriously, wanting to keep him talking and not tensing up as they prepared to manoeuvre his leg back into position.

'Harry, I want you to look at me,' she said, forcing a smile and looking into his eyes. 'Keep staring at me, just me.'

His lips moved, she guessed he'd been trying to smile, but then a thin bead of sweat broke out on his forehead and she felt his pain.

'It'll be over in a moment. Keep looking at me, keep—'

His scream tore through the room, and he didn't stop, moaning and crying out as Rose kept him still and Sophia did whatever she had to do.

'Harry, look at me. Tell me how you got here. What—'

'Done!' Sophia's voice and grin were triumphant when she made her announcement at the end of the sofa.

'Phew. Good work,' Rose said, standing and moving away.

Hazel stayed in position, still clutching Harry's hand. Or maybe Harry was the one clutching hers – she couldn't tell any more. All she knew was that he needed her to keep holding him and she wasn't about to let go.

'How are you feeling now?' she murmured, keeping hold of him as she reached back for a cloth and squeezed the water from it, then held it to his forehead and carefully wiped it. 'You were very brave.'

'I cried like a girl,' he muttered. 'No offence.'

She shook her head. 'None taken.' The truth was that most of the time it was the women she'd gone through training with who had been stronger than the men, so that expression was always going to make her laugh now.

'Can you sit with me awhile?' he asked. 'Unless you have something else to do?' He paused, his face showing his pain as he tried to adjust himself on the sofa. She'd bandaged his other arm, so he only had the one she was holding to move himself with. Hazel reluctantly let it go, her fingers slipping away from his.

'Of course. I'll get you something to eat, then sit here as long as you need me to.'

When he looked comfortable and stopped moving he met her gaze, a quizzical look on his face. There was some dirt clinging to his hair, and she had to resist the urge not to bend and smooth her fingers against his skin. 'What are three women doing out here alone anyway? And how do you speak English so well?'

Hazel took a big breath and stood. Had she already blown her cover? She was supposed to be a Frenchwoman, and one English lad had brought her guard down. 'Let me get you that food and then we'll talk.'

She rose and went to get soup from the kitchen, cursing herself for speaking such perfect English to their guest. She found Rose standing there, staring out the window into the almost-darkness.

'It's just me,' Hazel said, her voice low as she stood at the doorway, not wanting to startle Rose.

Rose nodded before drawing the curtains and turning to face her. 'It's fine. I was only thinking.'

'About whether or not we're about to be discovered?' she asked, knowing that any answer other than 'yes' would be a lie.

'I am,' Rose said simply, ladling soup into a mug as Hazel watched. She held it out to her and then retrieved a spoon. 'I'm afraid you've landed straight in the thick of it. You were supposed to be joining a larger circuit and working as their operator, but it looks like you'll be staying with us. And we need you to start radioing as soon as possible to notify Paris what's happened.'

'I'll do whatever I need to do here,' Hazel said. 'When they warn you that half of the recruits sent here won't make it out alive, you don't expect to be pampered and you certainly don't expect to be eased into the role.' It was the truth. She'd known what she was up for when she arrived, had volunteered for the role, and even though Rose was clearly fraught with worry, she needed to keep calm and deal with the situation she was in. 'Do you fear that we're sitting ducks and they're out there watching us right now?'

'Perhaps,' Rose said, touching the short curtain again before sighing and pulling her hand back, as if changing her mind about looking. 'But they'd be here already if they were. Sophia's right about that.'

'I'm going to see if I can get any food into Harry. Anything I need to do after that?'

Rose shook her head. 'We need you to get your radio operational, then we'll sleep. We all need rest while we have decent beds to lay our heads on. Tomorrow night, Sophia and I are going together to take Samuel to his rendezvous point – it's too dangerous for either of us to go alone. Only then will we know what our next move is, whether it's safe to stay or whether we need to make other plans.'

'Or maybe it's too dangerous to go together at all,' Hazel said, knowing she had to be honest with her old friend. 'We can't afford to lose both of you if the Germans are patrolling.'

'I know.' Rose gnawed on a fingernail, a nervous trait that Hazel had never noticed her do in the past. 'But they're always patrolling. We've both survived here this long, and we're careful. If there are two of us, well, we're both so aware of our surroundings, there would be a much higher chance of us going undetected.'

'But if they're lying there in wait, you'll never be able to hide,' Hazel pointed out. 'If operatives have already been captured near here, and heaven forbid you both were found, too, this area would be without—'

'Stop.' Rose put her hand up and Hazel shut her mouth. Maybe she hadn't needed to be quite so brutally honest.

'I'm sorry. I was trying to be practical, that's all.'

'You're right, of course you're right,' Rose said, rubbing her index fingers to her temple now as if she had a headache. 'I'll discuss it with Sophia in the morning. Get some soup into our guest, make him comfortable, then come into the back room with me. Sophia will give you your instructions.'

Hazel nodded, pleased she had her radio with her. She was better at operating the radio transmitters than building them, and she only hoped it hadn't been damaged when she'd landed.

'We need to get news back to Paris before anyone else is compromised. And they need to know we might have another delivery.'

Hazel hurried back to the other room, finding Harry slumped over and snoring. She took a moment to look at him, the light almost gone, and admired his face. She didn't suppose there was anything wrong with looking at him; she might be engaged to be married but she couldn't exactly help noticing a handsome man. Besides, it had been a long time since she'd last seen John.

Harry was tall, which was why it had been so hard to move him and poor Sophia had buckled beneath his weight so easily. His eyebrows were dark, almost black and darker than the thick shock of hair on his head. She could recall his deep brown eyes, too, had looked into them when he'd been braced for the pain about to be inflicted on him to put his leg back into position. They'd taken his trousers off him after that, cut them clean off his legs and washed him down before replacing them, awkwardly, with a spare pair from upstairs. So he looked like a civilian now, although how you could explain a man his age with an English accent . . . She shuddered. It wasn't worth thinking about what would happen if the house was raided.

She set the mug of soup down and moved closer, taking a folded blanket from a nearby chair to place carefully over him. He'd wake in pain and in shock, but for now he was warm and safe.

'He's asleep?' Sophia asked from the doorway, surprising her.

'Oh! Yes,' Hazel whispered, pleased the light was so dim so Sophia didn't see her cheeks flush at being caught staring at him. 'I thought you went up to bed?'

'I did,' Sophia said. 'But all I did was think about the messages you need to transmit. You haven't started setting up your radio yet? What have you been doing?'

Hazel wasn't sure if she was imagining the sharpness of Sophia's tone, or whether she was just being sensitive, but she wasn't going to push her.

'I was just trying to help with Harry,' Hazel said. 'I'll get on to it now.'

'Without a working radio, we're as good as dead. You're here as an operator, not a nurse,' Sophia said, still standing in the shadows. 'Here's hoping you're as good as Rose keeps saying you are, because the last thing I need is someone to babysit.'

Hazel obviously had a lot to prove.

Sophia led the way and Hazel followed her through to another room, where Rose had already put her case on the table. Hazel took a deep breath and sat in front of it.

'You can both go to bed,' she told them confidently. 'I'll radio any messages for you, and then tune into the BBC in case they're broadcasting.'

'No disrespect, but I'd rather stay up and watch,' Sophia said.

Hazel knew then that she hadn't imagined the sharpness in her tone earlier. She shrugged and ignored her, well used to having to prove herself.

'We can trust her,' Rose said softly. 'She's not the enemy here, Sophia.'

'We've been working together a long time,' Sophia replied. 'I can't help it if I don't trust her.'

There was silence around Hazel after that, the only noise her fingers placing all the parts. The metal was cool beneath her skin, and she worked instinctively, checking everything and setting up, trusting her ability. Minutes later she heard soft footsteps, and then a hand fell on her shoulder.

'She's gone to bed,' Rose said quietly. 'I know she can be prickly, but she doesn't trust easily. The truth is, we've been partners for so long, it seems odd to be working with anyone else now.'

Hazel nodded. She'd already figured that out.

'Sophia is one of the best agents in the field,' Rose explained. 'She's been lying low here with me the last few months, but before that she developed quite a reputation blowing up tanks and train lines. Sophia has been instrumental in setting up cells in the area and coordinating attacks and weapons drop-offs.'

Hazel paused, looking up at Rose. 'She's the one they whisper about? The woman they call "the fox"?' Hazel remembered hearing about her during her training, about the Resistance member who managed to pull off explosions and escape from the scene each time as if she'd never been there at all.

Rose laughed. 'She is. And I tell you, from what I've seen of her, the name suits her perfectly! She's as cunning as a fox, and just as clever and adaptable.'

Hazel smiled to herself as she worked. So Sophia might be difficult, but she was obviously very clever, and that meant Hazel wanted to prove herself to her even more.

The following night, after Rose and Sophia left for the rendezvous, taking Samuel with them, Hazel lay awake, listening to the soft patter of rain on the roof. She hated being left behind, knowing that her friends were in such danger, and yet here she was, safe and dry. She'd been in France less than two days, and she was still on edge, still shaking. She went to hold up her hand, then put it down again, not wanting to see the reality of her nerves.

She pushed herself up on her elbows when she heard Harry moan from the other side of the room. He'd not been in any state to be moved.

'Are you all right?' she asked, standing and walking over to him. 'I'm here.'

Hazel knelt beside the sofa, reaching to touch his forehead. He was clammy, and she worried that he had an infection. There was not much more they could do for him, and right now it was only the two of them in the house. Alone.

'Water,' he croaked.

She reached for the water she had nearby and used her other hand to help prop his head up so he could take a sip.

'Just a little. You don't want to flood your body with too much,' she said, letting him take another sip before putting the glass back down and helping to ease him back. She hesitated, then pushed some hair back from his forehead. 'How are you feeling now?'

He made a noise deep in his throat that she guessed was supposed to sound like a chuckle. 'Like I've been in a plane crash.'

It was Hazel laughing now, shaking her head at him. 'You're obviously doing fine if you can make jokes.' She waited, looking down at him, embarrassed that her body heated at the way he stared back at her. She hoped he couldn't see her hot red cheeks, because she knew they would be exactly that and she was embarrassed – she wasn't the kind of girl to go all weak-kneed over a handsome man!

'You never did tell me why you're here,' he said, the huskiness of his voice slowly clearing as he spoke. 'What are three women doing here alone? Weren't you going to tell me?'

She smiled. 'All you need to worry about is getting better, and the fact that you're lucky you were found by us and not the Germans.'

'I know how lucky I am,' he said, before groaning as he shifted position, trying to move from his back to his side. 'Trust me, I know.'

Hazel held out an arm for him to grasp and attempted to help him. He hissed out a breath and she winced, knowing what pain he was in.

'Do I have any hope of getting out of France?' he asked, looking into her eyes without breaking the gaze. 'And don't go sugarcoating it. I want the truth.'

She didn't want to lie, but it was part of her job now. She'd been taught to maintain her legend to get where she needed to get and do what she needed to do, and she could see no difference here. She needed to keep him calm and not give anything away about what they were doing.

'We'll do everything we can to help you,' she told him honestly. 'I don't know what else I can tell you, but there are some very friendly locals in the area, people who'd do anything to help someone like you.'

'I've heard about the Resistance movement, we all have,' he said, looking more comfortable, the vein that had been bulging in his forehead almost completely disappeared now. 'Do they operate around here? Is that why you said the locals are so friendly?'

Hazel refused to react, kept her smile fixed, made sure she didn't panic as she calmly breathed. It was good extra training for her, not letting her eyes give her away. 'I've heard about them, too, but the locals I've met are simply good families, women who worry about their own sons who haven't made it home. They only want to help, and I'm certain they'd shelter you and help you on your way if they had to.'

He nodded, seeming to believe her. She quickly changed the conversation, not wanting him to ask her any more about it.

'Tell me about home. Do you have brothers? Sisters?' She smiled, moving to sit across from him.

'I had a brother,' he said, looking away, making her wish she hadn't asked. 'The first thing I thought, when I was shot down and I

155

knew my plane was history, was that my mother wasn't going to have a child left.'

'I'm so sorry,' Hazel whispered, the room suddenly feeling terribly silent. 'There are so many families losing their sons, so many women losing their husbands. Every loss is heartbreaking.'

'I'm the younger one,' Harry continued, his dark eyes finding hers again, somehow making her feel warm, the silence of the room less painful when he wasn't gazing at the ceiling or at a spot past her head. 'He was always the sensible one, the smart one, the confident one. And now there's only me.'

Hazel didn't reply because there was nothing she could say to ease his pain and she didn't want to pretend there was. She only wished that she could tell him what she'd been through to get here, what she'd volunteered to do in an effort to make a difference in this war.

'You were lucky to get out of your plane alive,' she said, curious about how he'd managed to end up alive and on the ground. 'Will you tell me what happened?'

'I was hit but I was coherent – I hadn't been hurt then – so I jettisoned the canopy and unbuckled my belts, and detached my radio and oxygen supply,' he said quietly. 'I only had a split second, so I did a half barrel roll and just fell straight out of the cockpit. All I could think was that my parachute might not work, but I could feel it there. I had to believe in it, and I was a dead man if I didn't anyway.'

She nodded, chewing the inside of her mouth as she listened, feeling the fear within her, the churn of her stomach, recalling the similar experience she'd had. His eyes had come to life as he'd told his story, his lips curving into a smile as he shook his head and laughed.

'I still can't believe it worked,' he said with a chuckle.

'You were lucky to land where you did. To get out of there alive.'

'I was damn unlucky to hit some tree branches on my way down, though,' he continued. 'I got the worst of my injuries from hitting them. My parachute seemed to work but then I got caught and I fell from the trees. It felt like days, maybe it was hours, crawling further away from all the evidence, and some stroke of luck sent your friend past me just when I'd given up hope of a friendly face. I know there are terrible things happening to downed airmen, British and American, so to get to safety is amazing. Honestly, I hope you realise how bloody amazing it is.'

He'd been incredibly lucky. *Ridiculously* lucky, in fact. She only hoped his luck rubbed off on them and continued.

'Either you speak perfect English with a perfect accent for a Frenchwoman, or you're from the same place as me,' he suddenly said, catching her off guard.

So he hadn't believed her before. Hazel smiled but it was fake, and she forced her shoulders and body to relax to make her face do the same. If this was an interrogation, she'd have just given herself away. So much for passing her training with flying colours.

'I've let my guard down around you, and I shouldn't have,' she told him, not seeing any point in pretending otherwise. 'Don't ask any questions, especially when the others are back, otherwise you might find yourself without a group of women prepared to risk it all to get you out of here.'

He nodded. 'I just wanted you to know that it's nice to hear a familiar voice. I didn't expect to hear the lovely lilt of an English lass here, that's for certain.' Harry smiled. 'That came out all wrong. What I meant was that it's a nice familiarity.'

Hazel grinned back at him – she couldn't help herself. He was too charming and he knew it. 'Are you missing your wife or fiancée?' she asked. 'Or is it just a sweetheart you've left behind?'

This time it was Harry laughing, only he groaned as soon as he made the half-choked gurgle. Hazel jumped up and bent down, placing a hand to his chest. She'd suspected broken or cracked ribs from the beginning, and now she was more certain, but she had no idea what to do about it.

The door opened with a slam then, hitting the wall so hard Hazel was certain she'd felt the house jump from the shock of it.

'Quickly!' Rose shouted, running past them and legging it up the stairs.

Hazel's heart felt like it had leapt into her throat as she watched Sophia darting past, hot on Rose's heels.

'Get what you need and break the radio down. We're leaving!' Sophia panted out. 'There's no time to transmit.'

'Hurry!' Rose screamed from upstairs.

Hazel didn't need to be told twice. She saw Harry's panicked face, wished there was something she could do to reassure him, but there wasn't. She had no idea what was wrong, but something serious must have happened for them to storm into the house like that, ready to leave.

She hurried into the back room, checking her radio over and closing it inside the suitcase. She held tight to the handle, knowing it was the single most important thing in this house aside from them. In fact, it was probably more important than them.

Hazel ran up the stairs, breathless already, more from panic than exertion. 'What happened?' she asked as she grabbed her bag, the one she'd landed with and thankfully hadn't taken anything out of yet.

'No time, we're going now,' Sophia said, eyes wide as she held up her own bag and fled the room, calling over her shoulder. 'If we can move him we'll take him, otherwise he stays.'

Hazel's body went cold as she froze to the spot. Stay? How could they leave him behind?

'Downstairs, now,' Rose ordered, grabbing her arm. 'Grab whatever food you can carry in one hand or stuff into your bag, then pass it to me. We need to leave.'

She forced herself to follow Rose, taking each step as fast as she could. She followed her into the kitchen, grabbed what she could, wondering where they'd be spending the night, how everything had managed to change so quickly. What had happened to them out there?

'Get him up,' Sophia ordered, taking charge.

Hazel didn't question her, knowing it was in her interests to do what she was told. And the one thing she'd been able to find out about Sophia when they'd been told during training about 'the fox' was that she'd garnered the name from her ability to sneak about undetected, to elude everyone who wanted to capture her. That meant Hazel was going to do everything she ordered her to do right now, because she might just be able to save all their lives.

She wondered if Sophia knew that she was on the most wanted list, the one woman the Germans were determined to catch more than any other. It was a piece of information she'd overheard from Smith during her combat training and never forgotten.

'Harry, you need to move with us. Now,' Hazel hissed. 'Get up.'

She watched him struggle, put down the food to give him a hand. He grunted and let out a low moan as he managed to place his legs down. But getting on to his feet was almost impossible.

'We're going. Now!' Sophia called out, pushing open the back door with a bang. 'Give him this and then leave him.'

Hazel grabbed the broom that Sophia shoved in her direction, wondering how on earth she expected Harry to use it as a crutch in the condition he was in. But she saw the grim, determined set of his mouth as he stood on one leg and took it from her.

'Get me a towel,' he said. 'Anything I can prop on top so I can have it under my armpit.'

Hazel dashed back into the kitchen but Rose had beaten her to it, giving her two towels before hurrying back out.

'I don't want to leave him behind, either,' Rose muttered. 'But if it's us or him, we have to choose us. We're needed more than he is right now and there's no time to waste.'

Hazel agreed, she knew that in her heart it was the only way to think in this situation, but she wasn't going to give up without trying. She helped him with the towels and hated seeing the pain etched into every groove of his face as he took his first tentative step and then another.

'If you can keep up with us, I'll do everything I can to make sure you survive,' she said honestly. 'But you have to move now.'

Hazel saw the panicked look on Rose's face and followed her out, holding the door for Harry. She had her own things to carry, plus a radio to protect that was too valuable to their entire circuit in the area to lose, and hefting that around was heavy work. Their radio was the key to communicating with Paris and London, and connected them and others to their only lifelines.

'You're our pianist,' Sophia said, glancing back at her and using the undercover term for a radio operator. 'That means you're the most valuable of all of us, so I'll go first and Rose will be behind you. I want you in the middle whenever we're out in the open or approaching a new area.'

Hazel didn't say that every area would be new as they crept from Rose's former vacation house towards some woodland, about to pass other houses that could just as easily be home to foes as friends. But it seemed they had no other option.

'We'll stop when we can to radio Paris, but we have to move fast,' Sophia said briskly. 'I don't want our location discovered.'

Hazel glanced behind, saw how hard it was for Harry to walk, but she could also see how determined he was and she admired that. A lesser man would have collapsed within moments, unable to grit his teeth and push past the pain to keep moving.

'If he holds us up . . . ,' Sophia murmured, for her ears only.

Hazel nodded. 'I understand. We keep moving.'

Sophia was clearly in charge of their little group; Hazel could tell that already, and she wasn't about to challenge a woman who had such a formidable reputation. If she'd survived this long, chances were she'd be able to get them all to safety, too.

They walked and walked, keeping a steady pace, until eventually the darkness completely engulfed them. Any moonlight there was earlier had slowly disappeared behind wisps of clouds that had turned thick. It was too dangerous to continue.

'Stop here,' Sophia ordered.

Hazel tripped on a tree root or something sticking out of the ground, and was happy to stop walking. She could hear Harry's laboured breath behind them, although he'd been keeping up remarkably well, and she guessed he'd collapse the moment he was given permission to.

'What happened?' Hazel asked, staring at Sophia's silhouette. 'Why did we have to leave like that? Is Samuel safe?' She was full of questions after so many hours walking in silence.

Sophia turned her back and spoke without so much as looking over her shoulder, ignoring her questions. 'We need to secure the area, make something to shelter us all. Rose and Hazel, gather anything you can.' She looked around. 'As soon as it's light enough for you, you need to get that radio working.'

Hazel took that as her dismissal and knew she wasn't about to find out anything any time soon. 'What exactly do you expect us to find to make a shelter with?' she asked. They could barely see, let alone forage, and there were plenty of trees around to lean against.

'We need to save our energy,' Rose chimed in. 'Let's just hunker down here by these trees and move on before daybreak.'

'We're sitting ducks, especially with him,' Sophia replied. 'We'll have to move off the moment we have a slither of light.'

Hazel thought of the pill she'd been given, the one that could keep her awake for an extended stretch if she needed it to, but then she was certain it was supposed to be kept for far more dangerous situations than this. It was as much a comfort in her pocket as a worry.

'We all stay awake and rest then, to conserve our energy,' Sophia said, moving further away so they all had to follow her. 'Lean against a tree, have something to eat, and stay alert.'

Hazel did as she was told, trying to ignore Harry's grunts as he used his makeshift crutch. She'd help him once they were settled, but she didn't want to be accused of having a weakness. Sophia clearly had very high expectations, and she wasn't about to disappoint her.

She took her bag off and placed it beside her, more careful with the radio as she delicately set it down. Hazel leaned against the tree, pleased when Harry dropped beside her.

'How are you doing?' she asked.

'I feel amazing,' he grunted out, panting as if he'd run the entire way. She supposed he felt like he *had*, given the exertion he'd put himself through to keep up with them as they fled.

She held up a hand, touched it to his forehead and bit back her frustration. He was sweating profusely, too sick to be on the move, and she hated to think what damage he'd done to his leg already.

'How are the ribs faring?' she asked.

'I'll be fine after a rest. Don't go worrying about me.'

But she was. There was something about him that made her want to take care of him, to worry about him. Only she wasn't in France to nurse; she was here to make communications. Her job was to be the link between cells, to pass on vital information. That was her role, what she'd trained for, and she had to prioritise that above anything else, including her personal feelings.

She made herself as comfortable as she could, trying to make her body rest even though her heart was still pounding.

'We're going to have to talk freely,' Rose said, her soft voice even lower than usual. They all knew how easily sound could travel, especially conversation in the middle of the night. 'Harry, I'm going to give you the benefit of the doubt and trust you. But if you cross us?' She paused and Hazel listened, waiting for what she knew was going to come next. 'One of us will end your life without a second thought. We're all trained and capable, so take my word for it.'

Harry cleared his throat, probably so he could trust his voice to work. 'I wouldn't expect anything less.'

CHAPTER THIRTEEN

ROSE

Her back hurt, her feet were aching and Rose wanted nothing more than to curl into a ball and sleep. It had already been a long night, creeping towards the water, taking the long journey under the moonlight to get Samuel to safety, and every bone in her body was screaming at her to give up. But giving up wasn't in her vocabulary any more, not now that she'd become part of the Resistance. She was too proud to back down from her word, and too stubborn to stop doing something that she'd set her mind to. Besides, she was certain Peter was up there somewhere, looking down on her and smiling to himself about his courageous, capable wife. It was an idea that always made her smile, and gave her the strength to keep going every time she'd longed to walk away and find somewhere to hide until the war was over. She wasn't sure if he'd be furious or heartened that she'd stepped up to support the Resistance, but he would definitely be proud.

'Is Samuel dead?'

She turned at the sound of Hazel's voice. 'I don't know.' It was the only honest reply she could give. 'We got him there. Somehow we managed to weave our way to the beach undetected, and the rowboat was waiting. But then there were shots fired. We didn't know from where or how, but it was chaos,' Rose said. It felt like days ago, not mere hours. 'He could have been shot in the boat for all we know, or they could have rowed their hearts out and made it. I'm hoping and praying they did, but we'll never know.'

Rose was trying to stick to what had happened and speak matter-of-factly, but the truth was, she was heartbroken. She'd been so fond of Samuel, as she was of all the men she'd helped to save, but it wasn't his possible death that was causing her such pain. She was pleased for the cover of dark, preferring to be bathed in blackness so the others couldn't see the tears in her eyes. After she'd lost Peter and then her baby, she'd sworn she wouldn't ever shed another tear, but perhaps she wasn't as cold-hearted and closed now as she'd thought she was.

'Josephine was the woman who recruited me,' she managed to tell Hazel, the words hard to get out. 'She cared for me when I was shot and showed me what to do with the men I'd saved. She was there tonight, taking her own delivery, and I saw them grab her. They dragged her across the ground as she kicked and screamed, and for a moment our eyes met.' Rose wished they had something strong to drink with them, anything to help dull the pain inside her as she relived what had happened. 'I thought they were going to see, that they'd follow her gaze and see me hidden, but in that moment she looked away and started to scream and struggle. We took our chance to run, and within minutes we'd heard the single gunshot.' Rose shuddered, hot bile rising in her throat that she was forced to swallow back down. 'She was dead.'

'Is that why you wanted us to leave?' Hazel asked. 'Because you thought they'd followed you?'

Rose felt like all the energy had drained from her body after reliving Josephine's demise, and she was grateful when Sophia spoke up for her.

'No, but it's true they could have found us from that alone. There are more people now too scared to defy them, more who'd give us up than ever before. It's impossible with the Germans everywhere.'

Rose listened to Sophia, wishing things could have been different. There was so much she still hadn't told Hazel, secrets that were between her and Sophia alone. But with Josephine gone, that was going to have to change. They needed Hazel to be fully part of their little team, and there wasn't time for her to prove herself worthy – Sophia had no choice other than to fully accept her.

'If they'd captured and tortured her, she would never have given us up,' Rose told them, needing to be the voice for her friend who'd been taken. She shifted her weight, the ground rough beneath her. 'They could have done anything to her, *anything*, and she would have remained silent until the end.'

'Unlike your contacts,' Sophia said, words clearly meant for Hazel. 'They're why we had to leave like that. We had word they'd given us up, and the Germans showing up at our rendezvous like that was evidence it was good intel.'

'They what?' Hazel's voice sounded shaky. 'Who gave us up? Someone from Sebastian's cell?'

Rose nodded. 'Yes, the couple who were supposed to be meeting you. But we haven't heard from Sebastian directly yet. I'm hoping he's safe.'

'They gave us up, all of us,' Sophia said, glaring at Hazel.

'It's not her fault,' Rose said. 'Stop looking at her like that.'

'If they hadn't been on their way to meet her, they would never have been intercepted in the first place!' Sophia snapped.

'They might have been *her* contacts, but they were assigned to her by her superiors in London. What they did or didn't do has nothing to do with her,' Rose said angrily, not liking how hostile Sophia had sounded. She was one of the people in the world she was closest to now, but it didn't mean she approved of how blunt she could be sometimes. Sophia had been through a lot, and it often showed in her demeanour.

'Sorry if I'm a little annoyed at having to leave our bolt hole!' Sophia fumed.

'Enough,' Rose said quietly, her voice firm. 'There's enough going on without any of us being at odds.'

Sophia was silent. The only noise was the sound of Harry's still-heavy breathing.

'Of course, sorry,' Sophia said, surprising Rose by how quickly she apologised. 'It's not your fault, Hazel. They were members of our circuit, and they should have done anything to protect our identity and location.'

'So it's me they're after? Is that what you're worried about?' Hazel asked. 'Or is it just that you don't want me here for some reason? Is it because you want me to prove myself, or is it something else?'

'Hazel, they're after all of us,' Rose said. 'Honestly, they will take anyone they can from our underground network, because we've been causing such chaos for them. Last week others took out a major supply truck, and we've been couriering things right under their noses. The entire region has been destabilised because of the Resistance. What we're doing, it's working, and they hate each and every one of us.'

She had to smile as she thought about how successful they'd been recently. They might be out in the open with nowhere to shelter tonight, but it meant that what they'd been fighting for had worked, and that was something to be proud of.

'Tell her,' Sophia said, her voice softer now. 'It's me who's at fault. I don't trust easily, and you've already proven yourself if you've managed to come this far.'

Rose paused. 'We've been earmarked for assisting to cause disruption with trains and tankers. It's why we so badly needed a new operator in the area.'

'And these contacts, they might have given that information away?' Hazel asked.

'I doubt they knew enough to give much away, but they knew enough to compromise us personally.' Rose shrugged, even though the others could barely see her in the dark. 'Look, our cover was blown by people we should have been able to trust, but do any of us truly know our breaking point? We don't know how long we'd suffer to save another until we're in that situation.'

'I would never give anyone up,' Sophia said defiantly.

Rose shook her head. 'Maybe their families were threatened? If there was a gun to the head of your child or mother or brother, who are we to say we wouldn't say a word and expose the movement?'

There was no one they could threaten her with personally, but if her darling little child had lived? Would she have let that child be murdered to save the Resistance? She swallowed, repeatedly, always feeling the urge to vomit whenever she thought about that long, painful night with Sophia slumped beside her.

In a way, she felt she *had* given up her child for the cause, because she wouldn't have pushed herself the way she had if she hadn't been part of the movement. But blaming wasn't helpful, and it wasn't something she often let herself dwell on.

'I'd heard about women like you,' Harry suddenly said, his deep, low whisper of a voice helping to clear her head of the dark thoughts. 'We were all hearing whispers of the women, and men, who were sent here to slip undercover, report back to London and stop at nothing to succeed in their missions.'

The others stayed silent. It was Rose who eventually replied. 'So you speak French?' she asked, surprised.

He grunted. 'School French. Enough to have understood parts of what you were saying.'

Rose paused, wishing she could see Sophia's face. She knew she'd be angry that Harry was with them. Sophia had earned her reputation for being focused and overly determined, and she'd be even more furious now that he'd listened to their conversation.

'It's true. All the whispers, everything you've heard, almost all of it will be the truth.'

'Thank you for taking me with you,' he said. 'Once I'm strong again, I'll do anything for you, anything at all you need help with.' His French was slow, a little rusty, but she understood him. 'I will protect you all with my life if I need to.'

'Thank you, Harry. We'll be able to get you out if we get to the chateau we're heading for,' she told him, surprised by his words. 'Sophia's been there before, but we need to make sure it hasn't been compromised before we go charging in there.'

'Do any of you have husbands?' Harry asked, whispering in English now. 'They must be damn proud. I know' – he sucked in a breath, and Rose knew he must have been in pain – 'I would be,' he finished.

'My husband was killed,' Rose said quickly, not wanting to tell too much of her story. It was in the past and that's where she liked to keep it. 'I'd like to think that I'm making him proud.' There was so much more to it than that. Her heart ached for him every night, every part of her wishing he was still with her. She could hear his voice, the whisper of his words when all was silent, the warmth of his gaze. Her love for him hadn't wavered, and maybe it wouldn't be until all of this had stopped, until she was back in their home without him again, that the reality of her loss would sink in.

'Are you all widows then?' Harry whispered.

'I'm engaged,' Hazel said. 'But I may as well be a widow. I haven't seen him for such a long time, and I have this feeling that he won't make it home.'

There was a long stretch of silence before Sophia spoke. Rose knew she wouldn't be so open with her story; Hazel would have to wait to hear that, and she doubted Harry would ever hear it. Both of them had slowly shared fragments of their past, then more, until eventually they'd bared their souls, but Rose had known she was telling her story in confidence, and Sophia no doubt had felt the same. It was like an unwritten rule between them that they wouldn't betray the others' trust any more than they would give the other up under torture.

'No more English,' Sophia muttered to Harry. 'We're already close enough to being caught as it is.'

The wind had lifted, whistling through the trees, making the leaves crinkle and the night seem almost eerie as Sophia's low voice echoed between them. No one else said a word.

Rose thought of Josephine as they sat. She leaned her head back against the rough bark of the tree and shut her eyes, seeing her friend's smiling face, only to be replaced by a look of anguish, the fear and then determination in her final gaze. With Josephine gone, she supposed she had to take over as the circuit leader, only they were moving on and their wider circuit had been effectively torn apart. But they had the three of them, and they would either join a larger group or re-establish themselves elsewhere. She as circuit leader, to organise and recruit; Sophia doing what she did best and acting as their courier between circuits and gathering intelligence; and the newly arrived Hazel as their dedicated operator. They would make a fine team if they ever had the chance to find safety and actually work together.

'So where are we going?' Hazel asked.

Rose cleared her throat, emotion making it catch. 'The chateau. It's a safe house, or at least it was last time we heard. We can go there, regroup and link our circuit with theirs for the time being until we can establish ourselves elsewhere. We'll get you to make contact with London as soon as we get there.'

'Of course,' Hazel replied.

The others were silent and Rose thought of checking Harry, making sure he was actually doing as well as he was making out, but fatigue took hold and she found it almost impossible to lift her head. She needed to rest. They all did. If they were surrounded, then there was nothing they could do other than try to fight their way out, but if they were rested and careful when they set off again, they'd at least have a chance of making it to the chateau alive.

She settled back, shut her eyes and thought of Peter. She smiled as in her mind he turned, opening his arms wide as he always did when he saw her. Her lips parted in anticipation of his kiss, waiting for the moment that his warm mouth would cover hers. She sighed into him, her body melting into his embrace. When she looked up into his eyes, she felt at home, the way she had from the moment they'd met.

Rose felt silent tears slide down her cheeks, and she poked her tongue out to catch them. She swallowed their saltiness, refused to make a noise as she silently pulled herself together. Memories were dangerous, and tears were even more deadly, which was why she rarely let her guard down enough to shed them. Come morning, she wouldn't grieve for Josephine again until this blasted war was over once and for all.

A cracking sound stirred Rose from slumber and her hand shot instantly to her knife. She opened her eyes, kept her breathing steady as she blinked and looked around them. There was nothing, no one but the three people she'd travelled with, none of whom had moved from where they'd fallen asleep. Hazel was the first to meet her gaze, and she, too, seemed to have her ears pricked as she looked around them. It could have been an animal or even something shifting in the wind, but then again it could just as easily be a German moving quietly through the surrounding terrain.

Rose leaned forward, quietly nudging Sophia awake. She glanced across and saw Hazel on her knees, lightly shaking Harry, her hand slipping across his mouth when his eyes opened.

There was something reassuring about being with her old friend, even if everything had changed between them. She trusted her in a way she trusted few people now, and knowing how highly trained Hazel was made her even more confident in the other woman's abilities.

'We need to go,' she whispered to Sophia.

They both stood and Rose strained her eyes. They'd woken in time, but she knew Sophia would be furious that they'd all given in to slumber.

Staying on high alert, Rose moved to help Harry to his feet. Hazel was on one side and she on the other, and she could make out blood through his bandages from where it had seeped through during the night. They would have to tend to him later, though. There was no time now.

'Let's move, and I want everyone aware of their surroundings,' Rose told them. 'It's even more dangerous now than it was last night, and we can't have anyone see us approach the chateau.'

'Do you want me to try to radio first?' Hazel asked.

Sophia shook her head. 'No. I don't feel right about something. I'd rather wait until we're there.'

The other circuit should be well enough equipped to have lookouts. The chateau was legendary, gifted to the Resistance to use by a singer who was an ardent secret supporter. It had housed a great many Resistance members, local maquis who had banded together and put so much of their intelligence to good use. It was they who were responsible for blowing up railway lines and trucks, not to mention getting arms where they needed to be.

They started to walk, quietly at first, settling into a slow but steady pace. Harry was at the rear and she wondered if he'd be the one to get taken out, since he was slower and less agile with his terrible broom-crutch.

'How far is it?' Hazel asked, speaking quietly, only just loud enough to be heard.

'I think we'll be there in a few hours. Sophia?' Rose asked.

Sophia turned, rubbing at her eyes, no doubt as weary as Rose felt.

'I think we'll be three hours at least,' Sophia replied. 'Then we need to keep an eye on the place for at least an hour, see if there are any comings and goings. It might even take longer to ascertain whether it's safe there.'

Sophia had been there only a few weeks earlier, so if it had been compromised since then? Rose shuddered. It would be doubtful that any of them would survive.

'We'll rest again when we get close, and Sophia and I can take turns watching the house,' Rose instructed, still cautious as she walked, eyes still darting side to side with every step. It was an exhausting way to move, but it was the only way to stay alive if there were eyes on them. 'Until then, stay alert and keep moving.'

'What about our legends?' Hazel asked. 'Do we switch or stay with being university students?'

Rose glanced at Sophia and then wished she hadn't. She was in charge now, and she needed to get used to making decisions instead of waiting for orders to be given to her.

'We stick with our original cover,' she said firmly. 'We're students and this is our friend who's been in an accident. Although why three students would be traipsing around out here, I don't know.'

'We may need to switch covers when we take up residence at the chateau,' Sophia said. 'We'll need to change the way we work when we join up with them. They base the maquis there, the local section anyhow, and it's not somewhere we'll stay for too long.'

Rose nodded. 'We will all do whatever we need to, whatever they need us to do to keep things moving. We're already making a difference in this war, and we need to create more chaos, more discontent here in France to let the Allies take back control.'

CHAPTER FOURTEEN

SOPHIA

The chateau appeared as it always had to her, serene and quiet. Given how many men could be housed there at any given time, it was amazing that it could look so unthreatening, but right now it looked exactly that. Sophia was lying in the grass, straining her eyes as she squinted at the house. It was a beautiful property, and she imagined that before the war the gardens were always manicured, the home and grounds full of people who were employed to keep it looking perfect.

She pushed herself up and leaned against a tree for a moment, her soft palm pushed into the gnarled trunk. She'd learnt to deal with fear, how to process it and put it aside for the greater good, so when it started to pass through her in waves as she stared at the house, she pushed it down, swallowed it away as if the feeling was simply water.

Sophia liked being reminded of what fear felt like, because it stopped her from being reckless, gave her pause to think about what she was about to do. What she didn't like was when the feeling lingered. The night she'd left Germany, the day she'd fled with Alex, had been the start of her new life, her life without fear or worry or dread; this new life was about getting what she wanted and doing anything within her power to help the Resistance grow and become even better equipped. In the many months since then, she'd worked alongside so many members of the cause, and from the moment she'd set foot on French soil over a year ago, she'd hardly stopped to catch her breath. When she'd started out, she'd kept her head down and done whatever was asked of her, until she ended up losing the members of her cell and had no other choice but to start working on her own. A few months later she'd been shot, and that's when she'd ended up with Rose.

Sophia pushed away thoughts of the past and made her way back to the others, who were sheltering under a large tree, all seated in the shade. She was hungry, but now that she'd determined as best she could that the house hadn't been compromised, she wasn't going to stop. It was time to move, and fast.

'Everything looks fine down there. I want us to move in now,' she said.

Rose's eyes met hers for a moment. It was as if they could communicate without words now; they'd been working together as a team for so long that it was second nature understanding what the other was thinking, what they needed or wanted to do. She glanced at Hazel. Having a new, inexperienced operative joining them wasn't something she'd wanted or expected, especially when she and Rose had been so effective working together as a twosome.

'Sophia, you maintain the lead as we approach,' Rose instructed. 'I want us all to stay close, hands clear of our bodies or raised if they need to be to show that we're not hostile. Remember that these men don't even trust the locals now, nor anyone unknown to them, because things aren't as they were. With the Germans all over the countryside and coast, it's harder to know who to trust, who's faithful to the new rule or the old.'

Sophia nodded and collected her bag from the grass where she'd discarded it earlier, then placed it over her shoulder as she waited for the others to collect their things. When she saw Harry struggling she went to help him, but Hazel beat her to it. She saw the way Hazel smiled at him, a shy, flirtatious smile that made Sophia want to scold them. Harry might be in pain, but she was certain he'd have caught the look Hazel had flashed him.

'Get a move on,' she ordered, glaring at Hazel. She felt a pang, wished she hadn't been so harsh, but seeing them like that, seeing that look and remembering what that felt like . . . Sophia shut her eyes for a second, let herself remember, let herself go back in time.

Alex had made her feel like that all the time, even when they'd been teenagers sneaking kisses and holding hands whenever they could.

She inhaled, slowly, imagining him beside her, talking her through what she was doing. He would have loved this, would have been the first to volunteer to do something, *anything*, to help, and she almost wished she'd brought him with her. There were plenty of Jewish Resistance members, more than she'd ever expected, but then they had good reason to hate the Nazis and want to go undercover to help to bring them down.

'Why the frown?' Alex would say, stroking her shoulder and tickling his fingers all the way to her chin. *'It doesn't suit you, looking so cross.'*

She'd laugh. He always made her laugh. *'I've got too much to worry about.'*

'Don't waste time worrying about me. You've done enough of that already to last a lifetime.'

Sophia clenched her fists thinking of the way they'd been separated, the way they'd been forced apart, the way he'd been driven to seek refuge and hide in her apartment like a prisoner. She would never understand how he'd managed to stay sane, but he had, and she could only hope that the man she'd left behind would one day find his way back to her. It would be a miracle, but if she didn't believe, then she wouldn't be able to keep moving forward and doing the things she needed to do every day. Without Alex in her mind, his words in her head, his face in her memory, she would never have transformed into the woman she'd become.

'Come on,' Rose said, touching her back as she passed her, jolting her from her thoughts. 'Lead the way.'

Sophia walked quickly to get ahead and then set the pace. She could die today, or tomorrow, but at least she knew in her heart that she was fighting for the right side and always had been.

They kept walking, the irregular thump-thump of Harry at the back of the pack the only noise out of place around them. When they were closer, Sophia held up her hands slightly, keeping her head down. She'd walked in like this the last time she was here; she hadn't even told Rose that the first time she'd arrived with a package she'd been asked for a password by Pierre, the fearsome leader of the French Resistance fighters in the region. At the time she'd known to be scared, but she hadn't known who he was.

She recoiled, thinking about the way he'd shoved the butt of his gun to her chin, not caring that she was a woman. An enemy was an enemy, and it was clear how ruthless Pierre was from that very first encounter. When she'd insisted there was no password, he'd thrown her down and yelled for someone else to come for her, until she'd been quick enough to think of something to change his mind. There was a whistle, one she'd had to learn before to get the attention of rural fighters deep in a wooded area where she'd been tasked with couriering arms and supplies almost a year earlier, one of her first assignments after she'd landed in France. She'd pursed her lips and softly whistled the tune, then paused and done it again. When he'd burst out laughing and held out a hand, she'd taken it reluctantly, until he'd pulled her hard into his body and kissed her on both cheeks before letting her go again.

'So it's true. Our little fox still lives, she's not a legend,' he'd said triumphantly, referring to the name she'd been given for her many successful covert missions to blow up enemy lines.

Sophia had insisted she wasn't worthy of the title, but he'd made a fuss of her and invited her in, interested in the information she'd brought him, written into the silk lining of her skirt, and the package she'd kept carefully hidden in her purse during her travels.

She doubted Pierre would still be here now – he was too important to be in one place for long – but her memory of his blatant brutality was a warning for what could come as they entered.

Sophia was starting to grow concerned at how easily they were approaching the house, wondering if in fact everyone she knew was gone, until she heard a noise in the distance. She sniffed the air, her senses alert, aware that the men who lived here all smelt like they hadn't bathed in at least a year.

'Stop,' she murmured, holding her right hand up high to alert her group.

A man suddenly appeared, rifle cocked, and she smiled, thankful to recognise him. She didn't know his name, but she did know his face.

'Fox,' he said, nodding.

'We need somewhere to stay,' she said quickly, gesturing to the others. 'This is the rest of my circuit. Our house was compromised. We moved before they had a chance to find us and we haven't been followed.'

'Who's he?' the man asked.

She glanced back at Harry and noticed how terrible he looked. His face looked pained and his skin was slick with sweat.

'He's British RAF. We rescued him after a plane crash, and we couldn't get him on the last shipment with our other packages,' she said.

'Get inside. We're still pretty full in there, but we've lost a lot,' he said. 'They're on to us, in more ways than one, and we're short on supplies.'

Sophia had thought as much. 'What do you need?' she asked as they walked to the front door.

'A damn good radio operator,' he said without hesitation. 'Ours have all been taken out.'

'We happen to have one, and she's the best you'll find,' Sophia told him, pointing to Hazel and watching as she held up her hand. She'd been hard on her since she'd arrived, she knew that, but right now Hazel was valuable to the cause and she was going to stand by her, at least in front of the others. She knew part of her problem was the jealousy slowly simmering inside her at no longer being Rose's closest ally, not that she'd ever admit it to anyone. 'Tell her what you need and she'll do it. We even have our own radio with us.'

'You still our best courier?' he asked her.

Sophia smiled. 'I'm the best at everything I do,' she said confidently.

'Then we have a job for you. For all three of you.'

She had a sinking feeling in her stomach for some reason, but she didn't let her concern show on her face. She nodded. 'Of course. And him?' Sophia asked. 'You're fine with him staying here until we can find a way to get him out safely?'

'If he keeps his mouth shut and doesn't die on us, he's fine. But he'll have to figure out a way to make himself useful.'

Sophia knew that was the best she could expect. 'Fine. Now let's go in and get this radio set up, and then you can get someone to tell our operator exactly what it is she needs to communicate.'

A new man leaned against the doorjamb once they'd all gone in, his face and hair dirty, his skin tanned dark. Once he had a shower and cleaned up, she imagined he'd be handsome, but right now he simply looked exhausted.

'Where's Pierre?' Sophia asked.

His face turned to steel. 'Gone. I'm the new Pierre.'

Sophia let the words sink in, the fact that someone as strong and committed as Pierre had been taken out.

'And you are?' she asked.

'Mathieu,' he said. 'Once we get comms with London, we should have a new delivery of arms within days. Without it, we'll all be gone,' he said, before turning and walking away. 'We're waiting for a broadcast, a warning, so get your girl on the radio and don't let her off it.'

Sophia nodded before slowly turning on the spot and looking at the house she was standing inside. The rooms were full of men. They were definitely in the minority.

'I'll find somewhere for Harry,' Rose said to her, 'check him over and make him comfortable, and you and Hazel can get to work.'

Sophia touched Harry's shoulder as she passed him, returning the smile he was giving her, and walked side by side with Hazel to find someone who could explain what they were here to do.

'How long will it take you to set up?' Sophia asked, anxious to get their transmissions out as quickly as possible.

'I'll work as fast as I can, but it'd be easier without you breathing down my neck!' Hazel replied as she opened her case.

Sophia looked down at Hazel, saw how flushed her face was and knew that she'd been too hard on her. Something had changed within her, she'd lost the way she used to trust others, the softness that had made her want to help everyone and anyone when war had first broken out. She took a deep breath and sat down beside Hazel, placing a hand on her wrist. Sophia didn't have to like her, but she didn't have to make her job any harder than it already was.

'I'm sorry,' she said, finding the words almost impossible to say. 'Let's just get this information sent as quickly as we can.'

Hazel glanced at her, surprise written all over her face in that one quick look. 'It's fine.'

'It's not fine,' Sophia muttered. 'None of this is fine, but we have to do the best we can and not get caught in the process.'

She slowly took her hand away, liking the warmth that had travelled from Hazel's skin to her own. It felt like a long time since she'd touched somebody like that, just had the press of her skin to another person's. Maybe she was starting to lose her mind after so long working undercover.

'I need to transmit what happened to Josephine, is that correct?' Hazel asked.

Sophia was impressed at how quickly she was working, the radio appearing operational already as Hazel held one side of her headpiece to her ear.

'We need Paris to know that the cell in Brest has been compromised,' Sophia said, her heart starting to race. 'Then I need you to attempt communication with London, or at least start listening to the BBC.'

Hazel nodded, but it was obvious she was no longer focused on Sophia and more interested in the job at hand. Sophia had known she would be good, of course she had, but still, it was hard to trust someone new when you knew nothing about them, yet your life depended on them. Hazel might be highly trained, but she'd never actually worked in the field before, and that made Sophia nervous.

They sat in silence, Hazel tapping and staring intently at her instruments, and Sophia wondering how much longer they'd be alive. Surely her luck had almost run out? She'd been here much longer than any of the other members she'd met, and maybe she'd just been more determined, had more to prove because she was German, but she'd somehow earned a reputation to equal the top operatives.

After an hour she stood and stretched, silently leaving Hazel and going in search of food. When she returned, she set a cup of tea beside her new operator friend and sat down to sip her own. Rose was going to fix them something to eat, and Sophia wanted to stay close to Hazel in case she needed any assistance.

'Sophia,' Hazel suddenly said, her tea untouched and cold at her side by now. 'You're not going to believe what I'm hearing. I made communication with London earlier, to relay our message. But I've been listening to the BBC since then and . . .' Her voice trailed off and Sophia watched as she scribbled on her notepad.

'What have you found out?'

'I need a moment,' Hazel said, her focus absolute.

A deep male voice interrupted them, and Sophia turned to see Mathieu behind them. She didn't trust him – the sharp, cold stare of his eyes unsettled her – but then perhaps that's how she'd appeared to Hazel when they'd first met.

'German radar units along the coast are being taken out,' he said, his voice low as if he didn't want to be overhead. 'The Allies should be bombing trains soon, and we'll be further disrupting supply lines and tankers.'

'You'll need us to be part of this?' Sophia asked.

He nodded. 'But we need your pretty little girl here to do her job first, otherwise we'll be going in blind.'

Sophia watched as Hazel turned then, her stare so cold it rivalled Mathieu's. She felt a little shiver of pleasure surge down her spine. Maybe she and Hazel could become good friends after all.

'The *girl* has done her job,' Hazel said matter-of-factly. 'Your arms delivery will take place two days from now, and the Allies will be landing in Normandy within the next fifteen.'

Sophia looked between them, trying not to smirk.

'You're certain?' he asked, gaze narrowed.

'You do your job and I'll do mine,' Hazel replied tartly. 'The message was a poem but it was clear. Within fifteen days.'

He stared at her for a moment and then suddenly mobilised, his boots heavy on the stairs as he disappeared.

'You're good,' Sophia whispered, feeling a warm sense of camaraderie between her and Hazel for the first time as she watched her giggle to herself. She wasn't going to trust her just yet, but she suddenly wasn't so opposed to her, either.

'I'm used to being treated as if women are somehow second-rate to men,' Hazel said. 'But just because I'm used to it doesn't mean I like it.'

'So you've got a reason not to like being second-guessed by a man, then?' Sophia asked, completely understanding her sentiments.

'Something like that.'

'What's going on up here?' Rose appeared at the top of the stairs, holding two bowls of what Sophia guessed was going to be soup. 'Our little operator seems to have got the men downstairs all in a flap!'

They all laughed and Rose sat on the floor beside them after passing them their bowls.

'Let's just say she's already proven herself,' Sophia whispered, not wanting to disturb Hazel now she was listening in again to her radio.

'Didn't I tell you?' Rose asked.

Rose had her eyebrows raised but she was smiling, and Sophia gave her a quick shrug in reply. But as they sat in silence, the only noise the quiet sipping of soup from spoons, Sophia wondered how long they'd be together. If it was true that the Allies were preparing to land in Normandy, they had a lot of work to do to assist them. The war might finally be close to being over, but that meant even more dangers for everyone working underground.

CHAPTER FIFTEEN

HAZEL

Hazel sat quietly with Harry. She might have known Rose longer than anyone else here, but for some reason it was Harry she had the strongest bond with. Perhaps it was because they were both English, or newcomers, or maybe both. Sophia had started to thaw, which was a relief, but Hazel still felt like the new recruit amongst a team of highly experienced spies and soldiers. Even if they weren't traditionally trained, and despite a fair amount of chaos, the maquisards that were based here certainly seemed capable, determined and ready for action.

'Can you tell me anything you have planned?'

Harry's voice was a pleasant surprise and pulled her from her thoughts. His dark eyes were warm, his smile easy as he spoke to her.

'Or is it that fiancé of yours you're deep in thought about?'

Hazel shook her head when she saw his mouth curve into an even bigger grin, knew that he was teasing her. 'I suppose you're feeling better after that big sleep, are you? If you're well enough to make jokes about me, that is.' She glanced away, embarrassed and not quite sure whether he was being friendly or something more.

She was pleased to see him smiling, and for the first time, his brow wasn't covered in sweat. He actually looked better. She probably looked worse; she'd sat up late after she'd finished working, playing the poem she'd listened to over and over in her mind, and it was torturous not to be able to share it with Harry.

'So which was it?' he asked.

'I wish I was daydreaming about him,' she confessed, then laughed because she realised it had come out all wrong. Now she was the one giving confusing signals! She wished it was John she was thinking about and not Harry; it must have been lack of sleep jumbling her mind. The fatigue was scrambling her thoughts. Or perhaps Harry was reminding her how she'd once felt with John.

'Should I be worried about our safety here?' he asked, his tone more serious now.

'Probably,' she admitted, not about to lie to him. There was no point pretending with Harry. He had eyes and ears, and that meant it wouldn't take him long to figure everything out, if he hadn't already. They were as safe here as they could be, given that they were in German-occupied France. 'How are you getting along having to speak French?'

They spoke English to him a lot, but of course everyone at the chateau spoke French and she wondered just how much he'd been able to understand and whether he'd been frustrated that he couldn't respond easily.

'It's been a long time since I've tried to speak the language in conversation.' He laughed. 'I can get by, but I don't sound like a local and I give myself away fairly quickly.' He paused, catching her eye. 'Unlike you.'

She could understand why he was so curious. It was only natural, but he knew enough and she wasn't about to engage, no matter how charming he was. She ignored the question in his gaze.

'You need to be careful here,' she cautioned him. 'If they have any suspicions about you or what you might know . . .'

'Why would anyone be suspicious of me?' he asked, eyebrows pulled together, clearly perplexed. He grunted when he shifted his weight and she cringed for him, feeling his pain.

'Look, even British agents get turned here. For all they know you've been saved, captured and turned.' Hazel hated even having this conversation. 'All I'm saying is that they're hot-headed and they hate the Germans with the fiercest of passions. I know who you are, and you know who you are, but I just want you to keep your head down and stay out of trouble.'

She couldn't help worrying about him, and she hated that she was letting her emotions control what she was thinking right now. But she felt an obligation towards her fellow countryman. Wasn't that why she was here? To help their soldiers and their country? She stifled a groan. She was much better when she was working; the moment she was following orders or sitting at her radio, she blocked everything else out.

'You're worried,' he said simply.

She looked at his leg, the way he was holding it, how uncomfortable he looked every time he tried to shift his weight, which was often.

'It's nothing. I mean, it's something but it's nothing I need to talk about,' she mumbled. 'I'm going to let you rest, see if some sleep might help your pain.'

'I shouldn't have walked on it at all and yet I managed miles on it,' Harry said. 'I'll be fine, it's just going to take a while, that's all.'

'Get some rest, Harry. I'll come past and check on you again later.

'Stay safe,' he replied, his smile sweet as he met her gaze again.

She smiled and held up her hand, for a fleeting moment thinking of bending down and pressing a kiss to his cheek. But she didn't. Instead Hazel forced herself to turn around and walk out the door, shutting it behind her.

She stood against it on the other side, listening to her own rapid breathing, feeling the up and down motion of her chest as it rose then fell. What was it about being in a room with Harry that made her feel less like the trained agent she was, made her go from the woman who was so capable she could barely believe it, to a young girl stupidly attracted to a man who wasn't her fiancé? She balled her fists and pushed off from the door, heading off to find the others.

'Hazel!' She looked up when she heard her name called.

It was Sophia.

'Everything good here?' Hazel asked, walking quickly over to her.

'Yes and no,' Sophia said, breathless. 'We need to act quickly. Can you message London?'

She nodded. 'Of course.'

They walked together briskly, back towards the room she'd set up in. 'What's happened?'

'We need to confirm the delivery of arms,' she said. 'Mathieu is very anxious because if we don't receive it, then we're as good as useless.'

Hazel hurried down the hall to the staircase.

'Will we be involved in directing the delivery in?' Hazel asked. 'Or do you want me staying close to the radio?'

'Fairly certain we will be, I think it'll be all hands on deck,' Sophia replied. 'We need to keep you safe, though, especially since you're SOE-trained. That makes you one of the most valuable operators in the region, and most of the trained people here are dispersing.'

'They'll be starting their disruptions soon?' Hazel asked, pausing outside the room they were about to enter.

Sophia was frowning, her mind obviously on something else. 'Yes. Mathieu said they have plans to disrupt a train line because there's been intelligence about a shipment of enemy arms coming in. But they can't see any way to take it over without losing too many men. Option number two is simply to blow it up.' She sighed. 'The only other skilled operator they had is working to send incorrect messages that the Germans can intercept, to try to keep them expecting attacks in the wrong areas.'

Hazel shuddered. She didn't want to ask what had happened to all the other operators they must surely have had at other times.

'What is the exact message I'm to send?' she asked Sophia, taking a deep breath before picking up her earpiece and preparing to work at her radio.

'We simply need to clarify the drop and the coordinates,' Sophia said matter-of-factly. 'And once that's done, I'd say you and I are going to be standing in a field with torches, directing that plane.'

Rose touched Hazel's hand and made her jump.

'Sorry, I didn't mean to startle you,' Rose said, giving her an apologetic look. 'Everything fine with you?'

Hazel nodded, glancing over at Sophia as they walked.

'Is Sophia still giving you a hard time?' Rose asked, her voice low as she leaned in closer. 'I can say something to her if you'd like me to?'

Hazel shook her head. 'No, Sophia's fine. She's been less hostile since we arrived here.'

'Well, that's a relief. She can be slow to thaw sometimes.'

Hazel laughed and she saw Sophia head towards them from the corner of her eye.

'What's so funny?' she asked as she came closer.

Hazel shrugged and Rose laughed, but the moment was over before it started when Mathieu motioned that it was time to leave. The arms shipment was soon to arrive, and they needed to be in position.

As Sophia left them to discuss something with Mathieu, Rose and Hazel kept walking, easily keeping the same pace.

'Was Sophia like that with you, too?' Hazel asked. 'The way she was with me, I mean.'

'It was different with us, and we've been working together for months now,' Rose said. 'She has her own story to tell and I have mine, but . . .' Rose's voice trailed off. 'I was pregnant, Hazel, and I lost my child. Sophia and I were together at the time, we'd just met and we were both—'

Hazel had stopped walking. 'You were *pregnant*?'

Rose had an almost expressionless look on her face, and Hazel didn't know how to react.

'The night I lost my unborn baby feels like a lifetime ago,' Rose murmured. 'I'm telling you because I want you to know that Sophia and I went through a lot, *she's* been through a lot. But when she lets you in and starts to trust you, she'd take a bullet for you and you wouldn't find a more capable, genuine woman. You just need to keep proving yourself to her.'

Hazel started to walk with Rose again, their pace faster now as they headed for the woods. There was chaos around them, men dashing out and making their way in the same direction – they'd be hidden further away with vehicles to transport their loads.

When Sophia caught up with Hazel and Rose, they'd been walking in silence for a few minutes. It was nice to have her arrival as a distraction – Hazel hadn't been able to think of anything other than what Rose had disclosed to her, and it was more than clear that Rose didn't want to talk about it further.

Hazel wrapped her arms tight around her body as the air started to cool.

'There's nothing quite like directing a weapons drop-off in enemy-occupied territory in the middle of the night,' Sophia said grimly.

Hazel made a sound that was supposed to be a laugh but ended up sounding more like choking. 'Exactly what I'd hoped to be doing on a Saturday night!' she said.

Rose laughed. 'Sophia loves this sort of thing. She lives for it.'

'The success of this mission isn't directing the plane perfectly, it's unloading those arms and getting back without being killed or followed on the way,' Sophia told them matter-of-factly. 'And then we get our little star operator to communicate our success and await our next orders.'

Hazel gritted her teeth, refusing the urge to grind them. It all sounded so simple, but it was anything but. She hated the idea of waiting out in the open for so long. What if someone had betrayed them and the Germans were lying in wait? Hazel shuddered, but she kept her concerns to herself.

'Did you go through the same training as I did?' Hazel asked Sophia in a low voice as they walked through some tall grass. For some reason she'd been thinking a lot about her training recently, wondering who'd made it through and whether they'd been prepared well enough or not. 'I don't know what I was expecting, but the worst of it for me was the mock interrogation. I keep wondering how awful a real one would be.'

'I know. I went through it all, too,' Sophia said. 'I also remember my parachute into France well, that feeling of freedom as you flew through the air, only to be replaced by terror as the ground raced up to meet you. I remember thinking I was about to pee my pants!'

They both giggled. It would have sounded peculiar to anyone listening, and nothing about the reality of parachuting had been funny, but in hindsight she could still remember the feeling well and had worried about the exact same thing.

'It's so different being here to what I imagined,' Hazel confessed. 'I suppose I had this glamourous idea in my head, even though I knew what I was coming to and what to expect.'

Sophia was silent for a moment, but it was a comfortable silence between them now.

'When I first arrived, I was so determined to prove myself, to show the others they could trust me even though my father was German and I'd grown up there,' Sophia said. 'I don't know what I expected, but I knew I wanted to help.'

Hazel watched Sophia, still able to make her face out perfectly in the fading light. Her jaw looked hard, her fists clenched at her sides as she walked.

'Why did you join?' Hazel asked, curious now. 'Aside from turned former German agents, are there any other Germans here?'

'I'm French now,' Sophia said abruptly. 'My mother was French and proud of her country, and I am, too. That's who I identify with.'

Hazel looked at Rose and received a shake of her head, nothing more. Maybe she shouldn't have asked. No one said a word until Sophia cleared her throat and spoke quickly, as if it was something she wanted to get over with and not linger on.

'I hid my boyfriend in my apartment in Berlin, away from the entire world, to keep him safe. When Jews were being killed and beaten and taken, I kept him safe for as long as I could,' Sophia said. 'I know he's safe now, but even if he wasn't, I'd be here fighting just like I am now. My mother's nationality was my ticket into this game, and I want to make her proud. She was, *is*, my hero, and I know that she would have been immensely proud of how long I hid Alex from everyone, including my Nazi father, right beneath their noses without being caught.'

Hazel was speechless. Did Rose already know all this? She scolded herself. Of course she did, she and Sophia were close, but Hazel was struggling to comprehend that the woman she was working with had a Nazi for a father!

'So your father—' Hazel started, but didn't finish her sentence before Sophia interrupted her.

'I shouldn't have called him that. He is nothing to me. *Nothing*,' Sophia spat out. 'When I joined the Free French in London, I vowed then and there to leave my German identity behind me. And every package I courier, every time I disrupt anything to do with the Nazis, I take pride in the fact that I didn't stoop to their level. When so many did, when so many of my people were too scared to say no or too impressionable to see the truth, I listened to my heart and my brain. Just like my mother always encouraged me to do until the day she died.'

Hazel didn't say anything further and the silence engulfed them again.

Before the war, a friend confessing a story like that, opening her heart in such a way, would have made Hazel hug and comfort her. But this was different. This was war, and they all had their own reasons for doing what they'd chosen to do. Sophia didn't want pity or comfort; she clearly wanted revenge, and to see civility restored in the country she'd grown up in. No amount of comforting was going to give her those things, and Hazel certainly wasn't going to try to soothe her with words.

'We need to sit and wait now,' Sophia said, pulling out a piece of paper and using a tiny torch to see properly. 'I'm certain the coordinates are correct. Let me look again.'

It wouldn't take long for darkness to completely engulf them, and Hazel let Sophia check while she took out a piece of bread for them to share. Her stomach was starting to get used to much smaller amounts of food, but since they'd arrived at the chateau the hunger pains had become worse. There wasn't a lot to go around.

'Did you see those chickens out the back?' Hazel asked Sophia once she'd finished and was folding the paper into her skirt.

'I certainly did.' Her smile told Hazel she'd probably had the exact same thoughts. 'Once the others leave, those chickens will be in the pot.'

Hazel grinned back at Sophia, and Rose looked at them as if she was wondering what on earth they'd been whispering about. But as they found the exact position, they stopped talking, the reality of where they were and what they were doing setting in. All of the men had slowly arrived, too. The women had heard the rumble of engines as they'd made their way closer, but they were hidden out of view and no one from the convoy had dared to come near them. It wasn't worth it. Some of the men would lug any loose arms out on their backs, as many as they could carry, but there would be boxes as well and those needed proper transportation.

'It'll be here soon,' Sophia whispered.

They were sitting close, shoulder to shoulder, and when eventually they heard the rumble of a plane approaching after hours of lying in wait, and Sophia checked the time and the coordinates yet again, they knew it was time to act.

Hazel dusted herself off, gripping her torches with one hand. They positioned themselves, Rose standing near to her and Sophia slightly further away, as a shudder went through Hazel's body, her ears straining, eyes wide and heart pounding. What if it was a trap? What if they were about to be gunned down by an enemy plane?

She waited until the right moment, then held up her lights, waving one in each hand. Then as the rumble intensified, the plane coming closer to the large area of grass where they were waiting, she flashed the lights like she'd been taught, indicating where the drop-off was.

Wind gushed towards her, made her lose her breath as she held her torches so tightly she was certain her knuckles would be white. These were the arms they needed to keep fighting, and she'd managed to do her part to make the night a success.

The boxes, attached to parachutes, drifted to the ground. It was surreal – these packages containing goods to kill men and blow up trains, fluttering down to earth like flowers. Hazel felt the ridiculous urge to laugh even though she was shaking in her boots. And then the thump of boots behind her made her laugh suffocate in her throat. When she spun around, she saw they were their men, but for a moment she'd half expected to feel the butt of a rifle to her head and the hard-packed ground coming up to meet her face.

'Good work.'

She turned to see Mathieu standing behind her. Hazel nodded but kept watching, overseeing what was happening, still anxious about being caught.

'You three will be in charge of blowing up the Paris-to-Brest railway bridge,' he said, so calmly it was as if he'd just informed them they were on kitchen duty and would be in charge of cooking the evening roast.

'I have men set to cause mayhem all through the area, but you'll have the best chance of making it there, and a better chance of talking your way out of trouble if you encounter it.'

Hazel gulped. 'Of course.'

Sophia's hand touched her back then, and she was pleased her friend was standing so close.

'We won't let you down,' Sophia said.

'Do we leave in the morning?' Rose asked, sounding slightly out of breath.

'Tomorrow midday, you'll need to be on the move. I'll be leaving at daybreak, and some of the others by mid-morning.'

Hazel's heart was galloping as if it were in a race. It seemed her work for the Resistance had finally truly begun.

CHAPTER SIXTEEN

ROSE

Ever since Rose had started to work with the Resistance, she'd felt a strange sense of calm. Perhaps it was the fact she was filled with purpose, or that she had nothing to lose, but she felt oddly in control and capable in her role. Even now, as they walked endlessly towards their target, she wasn't so much nervous as filled with anticipation. Finding out they were charged with blowing up a railway line bridge had been a surprise for her; it wasn't the type of work she'd done before, but her friends were highly trained and she was more than confident in their abilities.

'I'm sure if we were stopped by Germans, we'd easily talk them around,' Hazel said. 'Three pretty young students taking a walk in the woods? They'd be putty in our hands.'

Rose laughed and noticed Sophia roll her eyes, but she also saw her smile, which told her that Sophia was definitely defrosting where Hazel was concerned. She was glad, because they were both important to her, and it made it much easier if they all got along.

'How much further?' Rose asked.

'We'll walk for another half hour, maybe an hour,' Sophia said. 'Then we need to lie low until we have the cover of darkness.'

The sky was clear and Rose was grateful; it would make the moonlight easier to see by later in the evening, which would make working simpler, but the downside was they could be seen if they weren't careful.

'It's going to be a busy few days,' Hazel said, and Rose glanced back at her. She was hefting her radio around in a satchel, since they'd all decided the suitcase she'd been issued with originally looked out of place and too obvious. Although Rose had offered to take it for a while since it must have been so heavy, Hazel had declined. It seemed that she liked to keep it close. 'The lorries of ammunition will be blown up shortly, and the petrol supply should be next.'

Hazel knew everything that was happening, and she'd been instrumental as the point of contact throughout the morning. Rose liked having her on her team. She was capable and calm, and they could radio instantly after their attack to confirm what had taken place and to receive any new orders.

'Plan Violet is in full force,' Rose replied. 'After all this time, I can't believe we're finally going to start gaining ground back here. Their cables will be down soon and there should be explosives detonating everywhere!'

Eventually, when they were all exhausted and breathing heavily, Rose held up her hand.

'We need a rest,' she said. 'Surely this is as good a spot as any?'

She waited for Sophia to disagree, but to her surprise she nodded. 'We need a little water and something to eat,' she told them. 'We can share some cold meat.' One of the men had come back with rabbits for dinner, and Harry had taken them to the kitchen to cook the meat, no doubt in an effort to start pulling his weight around the place. They'd all been grateful for the stew the night before and some cold cuts to take with them on the road.

Rose looked around and noticed something in the distance. A small building that looked like an old, falling-down barn or stable. 'Do you see that?' she asked, pointing down into a field. 'Maybe we should stop there instead?'

Sophia took a few steps forward, hand up to shield her face from the sun. 'I'll go take a look,' she said. 'It's safer that way.'

'I can transmit from the roof if I can scramble up there,' Hazel said, moving closer, her shoulder brushing Rose's. 'You'll have to help me up, but the signal will be better.'

Rose put a hand on her arm. 'Sophia's right, she's best to take a look first.'

'If it's safe, we can wait there until dusk. Good spotting, Rose.'

They waited, leaning against a tree and catching their breath as Sophia moved quickly towards the old structure. Rose always expected the worst; she waited for a gunshot, for a shout, for an army of the enemy to lurch towards Sophia, but thankfully nothing untoward happened. Inside the stable could be another matter entirely, though. It could be occupied, it could be under surveillance, it could be—

'Rose,' Hazel said, her hand falling to her shoulder. 'Just breathe.'

Rose smiled. Trust Hazel to notice that she was falling apart with worry. It was unlike her, so maybe that's why it had been so obvious. 'I always prefer to be the one risking my neck,' she said quietly, 'than the one watching.'

'So I've noticed.'

They stood silently, side by side, until Sophia finally emerged and waved to them. They set off towards her, not rushing in case for some reason they were being watched. They were simply three students wanting to immerse themselves in nature and have a picnic out in the open, and they had to make every part of their cover story believable, from their words to their actions.

Sophia collapsed and leaned against the old stable or barn or whatever it was. It was so ramshackle in appearance that Rose wasn't sure herself about leaning so heavily on it, but it was a relief to have somewhere to operate from, albeit temporarily.

'I can't believe we're actually doing this,' Rose said as she passed the others some bread before taking a small bite of her own piece. Her stomach growled loudly in response. 'I mean, rescuing airmen and couriering packages was one thing, but blowing things up?' She laughed. 'It's unbelievable. Never in a million years would I have imagined myself doing anything like this.' Peter had thought her desire to drive an ambulance was extreme, so she could hardly imagine what the poor man would think if he could see her now!

Sophia chuckled but Hazel stayed quiet. It was usually the opposite.

'I can believe it,' Sophia said. 'I'm ready to blow up anything that's used by the Nazis.'

They sat in silence for a while, chewing their bread and taking turns to sip water from the bottle Rose had been carrying. She nudged her hand past the explosives materials to put the leftover food back, careful with her movements even though she knew the bag was safe until they actually detonated the device.

'What are you most looking forward to, once this is over?' Hazel asked.

Rose wasn't sure. She honestly wasn't sure. 'I don't know. I mean, this is what pulled me through after Peter's death and then after I lost . . .' She sighed, not wanting to mention the baby. 'I haven't thought past the work we're doing here, I suppose.'

'I want to find Alex,' Sophia said, her voice low and surprising Rose with her honesty. 'I have to believe he's still alive, otherwise I don't think I'd be able to keep going. After everything, after what I've seen and fought for and witnessed, I just need to believe that once this is over I'll have him to return to.'

Rose reached for Sophia's hand but her friend pulled away and stood, pacing a few steps away and then back again. It wouldn't have been easy for her admitting that, and Rose only wished that she'd let them comfort her instead of feeling as if she had to be the strong one

198

all the time. Of all of them, the war had affected Sophia terribly, made her live through horrible things, and her heart went out to her whenever she thought about how she'd been forced to flee Germany.

'I just want to go home,' Hazel admitted. 'Or at least I think I do, but then I don't know how I'll go back to just being the old me.' She shrugged. 'Does that sound crazy? I mean, I'm still me but I feel so different now. I liked earning money and being part of something bigger, instead of being told what my future is supposed to hold.'

'We're all different now,' Sophia replied. 'We're not the women we were, because we've been forced into situations we should never have had to confront. We'll never be the same, no matter how hard we try.'

Hazel nodded and Rose watched her, understanding how conflicted she felt. The war had taken her fiancé away from her, and her comfortable life had been pulled out from beneath her. Of course she wasn't the same person any more. Rose certainly didn't feel like the same woman who'd been happily married and living in a beautiful big home in Paris before the war, either.

'I'm going to clamber up there now,' Hazel said, pointing to the roof. 'Anyone fancy giving me a hand?'

Rose nodded and set the water bottle down before walking around the dilapidated structure to look for the safest point. 'We could boost you up here?' she suggested, seeing one side of the stable looked sturdier with the roof completely intact. 'But you'll have to work quickly, I don't want you up there for long.'

Hazel already had her aerial out and the length of cord connected to it, and she quickly climbed up on to Rose's shoulders. Sophia gave her a push, trying to help her as she scrambled to get up. Finally she made it, and with a triumphant smile down at them, set to work.

'She's determined, I'll give her that,' Sophia muttered.

'She's better than just determined. She's damn good.'

Sophia laughed. 'Fine. I've been hard on her, but you two have history. I was never going to trust her with my life without her proving herself to me first.'

'I know. It's been just the two of us for a long time.' She knew it must be hard for Sophia. If it was her, she'd definitely feel threatened by the past she shared with Hazel.

Rose kept an eye on Hazel as Sophia kept scanning the trees around them, careful to keep watch and make sure they were safe. Rose knew Hazel was fast, but seeing the speed with which she tapped her codes was incredible.

'The RAF failed to destroy their targets, so all circuits are mobilised!' Hazel announced, her voice full of excitement. 'The train lines must be blown up tonight!'

'You're certain?' Sophia asked impatiently.

'Stop second-guessing me, I know what I'm doing! We're—'

'Hazel!' Rose yelled, as a cracking noise echoed out and without any other warning, the roof suddenly collapsed with a series of thuds as it fell to the ground. She ran to the door, waiting for the billows of dust to settle, waiting to see if she could see Hazel on the ground. Where was she? Was she dead?

'Hazel!' Sophia gasped, pushing past Rose as she stood gaping, and leaping over some of the fallen-in roof.

It was Sophia who reached Hazel first, dragging her out and patting her back as she coughed and spluttered. Rose quickly retrieved the wireless, hoping it wasn't too badly damaged.

'You didn't have to do anything quite so dramatic to prove the message was correct,' Sophia scolded, still holding Hazel as Rose offered her water.

Hazel coughed. 'It's up to us,' she spluttered. 'The others will be cutting cables and derailing trains, but we need to blow that bridge or any part of that line up, and then get as far away as we can.'

Rose shivered despite the mild weather. 'We can do it. Of course we can do it. It's why we're here.'

'Is my radio broken?' Hazel asked, rubbing her head.

Rose nodded. 'It's fixable, except for the aerial. I think that's as good as gone.'

She packed it all up into Hazel's satchel, adrenaline starting to course through her veins. This was it. This was what they'd all been waiting for, and now they had to do their part to make the Allied landings a success. London and Paris were counting on them!

'Come on, let's rest a little and plan our attack,' Sophia said. For the first time, Rose thought she looked rattled, although maybe she was just nervous herself and imagining it. 'We're going to have a very limited window of time, and the place could be heaving with bloody Germans.'

Rose glanced at Hazel one more time, hoping she wasn't hurt. It had been a fast, brutal fall.

'You're certain you're going to be—' Rose started.

'Don't worry about me,' Hazel said, coughing and clearing her throat. 'I'm tougher than I look.'

Rose already knew that. 'I think we all are,' she muttered.

'What?' Sophia asked.

'Tougher than we look.'

Hazel laughed and then suddenly they all burst into laughter. Rose leaned back against the old stable wall and hoped it wouldn't collapse; Hazel sat there with cobwebs in her hair and all covered in dust; and Sophia stood there in the middle, bent over, giggling like Rose had never heard her laugh before.

'There's nothing funny about any of this,' Hazel said, still grinning. 'It's awful and scary and bloody terrifying. Why are we even laughing?'

Sophia shook her head. 'Because if we weren't laughing we'd be crying.'

'Sophia, you have experience detonating explosives. What about you, Hazel?' Rose asked, wiping her cheeks to brush away stray tears from her silly laughing episode. 'I mean, this isn't just a little bomb, this is . . .

'I'll take charge,' Sophia said. 'But Hazel will know what to do if anything happens to me.'

Rose wasn't surprised – she knew a lot more about Sophia than anyone else – but Hazel?

'Don't look so surprised,' Sophia said, walking off and looking anxious again. 'I'm not the only one trained by SOE, remember?'

CHAPTER SEVENTEEN

SOPHIA

Sophia scanned the open fields around them, anxious to start moving again. She hated the feeling of being a sitting duck, as if they were inviting the enemy to find them by staying in the same place for too long. She'd stayed alive before meeting Rose by moving often and always staying in small groups or working on her own, and she didn't want to become complacent. If anything, it was more dangerous than it had ever been now that an Allied attack was imminent.

'When did you train with the SOE?' Hazel asked, appearing beside her. 'I don't even know how long you've been here.'

They stood side by side and Sophia waited before answering, not wanting to be short with her. She'd told Hazel bits about her past, but her new friend was obviously still curious.

'After I left Berlin, I headed for London,' she said. It felt like an eternity ago; so much had happened since then. 'I found my way to the right people, offered my services, and although they were suspicious of a German woman suddenly wanting to assist, I was able to prove myself to them.' Sophia paused, thinking back. 'I've been in France for well over a year now. I was the same as you, the moment my training was over I was earmarked to be sent in.'

Hazel was standing close and Sophia almost wished she'd bump into her, brush her shoulder against hers. She craved just the simple act of having someone casually touch her. Before she'd left Germany, she'd been used to a closeness with her mother that she knew would never be replaced, and she'd had Alex with her all the time. Now, she missed it. The wall she'd built around herself had kept her safe, but it had made her feel a deep-set loneliness that she was starting to resent.

'Did you tell your recruiter about your mother and your Alex?' Hazel asked softly.

'I did. And I was able to tell them about my work in Berlin, rescuing Jews and working with our network to smuggle them out of the city.' She laughed. 'That and the fact that I excelled at explosives training made me a valuable asset.'

They were silent for some time, the only noise the soft echo of birdsong in the trees nearby.

'Can I ask you something, about your training?' Hazel said.

Sophia turned and gave Hazel a quick smile. 'Anything. Of course.'

Hazel looked uncomfortable and Sophia hoped it wasn't her who'd made her so. She glanced over her shoulder and noticed that Rose was sitting slightly away from the old barn now, her back against a tree. She was probably trying not to listen, but no doubt their voices were carrying the short distance.

'Do you believe you could kill a man?' Hazel finally asked, her voice so soft it was almost a whisper. 'I mean, with a knife to his throat or with his own weapon or . . .'

'With my bare hands?' Sophia finished for her, knowing they'd both been taught the same methods of killing.

'Yes.'

Sophia nodded and took a deep breath. 'I know I could because I already have,' she confessed. 'The night I ended up on Rose's doorstep, I'd been shot. But I was quick enough to grab my knife and kill one of the two men. The other was so shocked that it gave me time to grab the dead Gestapo's gun and shoot him, too.'

Hazel's face showed her surprise. 'Oh, well, I see.' She stumbled over her words and Sophia wondered what she was thinking, whether she was horrified or proud. 'Was it easy? I mean, did you second-guess yourself?'

'You don't have time to second-guess yourself,' Sophia told her, remembering the feel of the blade in her hand, of squeezing the trigger, of looking down at two dead men and knowing that her hand had taken both their lives. 'There's a split second between them killing you, or you killing them. The only time you have to think about it is after.'

'Thank you,' Hazel said, placing a hand on Sophia's shoulder, her eyes so filled with honesty that Sophia wished she'd never been so hard on her in the first place. 'I needed to hear that.'

'Come on,' Sophia said brusquely, not knowing what to say with Hazel looking at her with such compassion. 'We need to go through what we're doing.'

She walked over to where Rose was sitting and dropped down to the ground. Hazel did the same.

'Are either of you familiar with the bridge?' she asked.

Hazel shook her head, but Rose nodded.

'I am, but I can't say I've ever taken a lot of notice of it,' Rose said.

'Me neither,' Sophia confessed. 'But we don't need to know it well to understand what we need to do. The only unknown is how well patrolled that area is, and we're not going to know that until we get there and survey it with our own eyes.'

'I think it's too dangerous to watch it for too long,' Hazel said. 'We're more likely to be found, and the Germans could have intercepted any of the recent messages.'

'I agree,' Sophia said. 'But we need to be careful that we're not caught before we lay our explosives. We need to spend a short time watching, and then when we run down, we need to put everything in place fast and get out of there quickly.'

'What do you need us to do to help?' Rose asked.

'I'll set the explosives,' Sophia said. 'We have two hand grenades and I need you each to have one, in case you have to throw it. We have a short delay, approximately ten minutes, so it will give us just enough time to get out of there. We don't want any longer, though, in case it's discovered.'

'Or we're discovered,' Hazel muttered.

'Exactly,' Sophia said.

'Let's have something to eat and get on our way, then,' Rose said. 'It'll be dark in a few hours or less.'

They sat quietly and took the food Rose passed them, and Sophia thought how amusing it was to have a bag containing grenades and food sitting so casually beside them.

A couple of hours later they walked confidently across the field. They'd surveyed the railway bridge, and there was no doubt it was dangerous. But night was starting to fall and if they were going to do it, they needed to act fast.

'The biggest problem, aside from those bastards, is that we could end up being caught in an explosion by one of our own,' Sophia muttered. 'Who knows how many local fighters have mobilised?'

They'd decided to walk as far as they could without trying to hide. That way, they could try to talk themselves out of trouble and pretend they were lost and not doing anything wrong. Sophia had suggested the plan, and even though she was the first to admit it wasn't her best idea, it was the only one that got them close to the railway line without doing anything suspicious.

'If we can't get to the bridge, can we blow up the line on this side of it?' Hazel asked. 'We're surely better to blow up something than nothing at all?'

Sophia agreed. 'Yes. We'll decide once we're there.'

They all stayed quiet as they continued their approach, and Sophia almost jumped out of her skin when an explosion echoed out, a dark cloud rising in the far distance.

'Run!' Sophia ordered, holding tight to her bag and moving as fast as she could. Rose and Hazel kept up her pace, one on each side of her, and as they neared the train line they heard dogs barking, the noise carrying to them on the wind. Another cell must have blown up something nearby! It was the only explanation. There had been no planes droning overhead, and now they had even less time to set their plan in motion.

'I don't think we have long,' Rose panted beside her. 'They're going to be everywhere soon. The patrols will be—'

'Let's just do it here,' Sophia said, knowing that being cautious was better than being dead, even though she hated not making it all the way to the bridge. She slowed down, tried to catch her breath and glanced back at the others. Hazel was walking with one hand on her hip, clearly winded, and Sophia knew how heavy her radio equipment must be to haul around like that.

'You're certain?' Rose asked.

Sophia nodded and looked down the line, not seeing anyone. The bridge was too far away – they would never have made it without being seen – and here at least she had a moment to think and place her lines carefully.

She didn't need to ask Rose or Hazel to cover her, because they were already in place. The moment she dropped to her knees beside the line they were on either side of her, and she looked up to see Rose pass Hazel a grenade. She set to work, still hearing dogs on the wind, their just-audible yips sending shivers through her. It was her greatest fear, a dog being set on her, and she knew from what the Germans had done to Jews in Berlin that their dogs didn't hesitate to rip a person to pieces as they screamed and begged for mercy.

She worked quickly, instinctively knowing what to do, her mind quiet as she focused on laying the wires and preparing her explosion site. Once she was done she reached into her bag for one of the pencil detonators they had luckily received in the last drop. She crushed the end of the copper tube with the heel of her boot and checked she'd broken the glass vial, then moved on to the inspection hole to check it was unobstructed. Then she carefully inserted the end of the pencil into the explosives.

'We need to go!' Rose hissed. 'I can hear a rumble, there's something coming.'

Sophia ignored her and checked her work, ran through everything in her head, closed her eyes and felt the temperature around her. It wasn't cold, which meant the timer should be accurate for ten minutes; it usually only went off later if it was freezing.

'There's someone coming. I can hear . . .'

'Move!' Hazel ordered, her voice deeper than usual, her hand on the back of Sophia's jacket and yanking her up. 'We need to get out of here and fast.'

She stood and squinted, looking down the line. There was company on its way, that was for sure. Sophia packed away her remaining equipment and grinned down at her handiwork, before following behind Hazel as she set the pace. They walked quickly, heads ducked, chins tucked down as if they were cold and trying to use their jackets' collars for warmth.

But the rumble was fast approaching now, the unmistakable sound of trucks or tankers or something – not a train because the noise was all wrong – and Sophia made the mistake of looking behind them.

'Incoming!' she hissed. 'Head for the trees!'

They started to run then, and as darkness started to fall around them Sophia prayed that time was passing more quickly than it seemed to be. How many minutes had gone by? When the bomb went off they'd at least have a head start because of the disruption it would cause.

The yells of men told her they'd been seen, and she was smart enough to know that they were within plain sight, that with everything going on they would be seen as traitors the moment they were spotted running. But what else were they supposed to do?

'We're not going to make it,' Hazel cried. 'I need to break my radio up, I can't have them taking it!'

'Stop it!' Sophia yelled at her. 'Just keep moving!'

'She's right, we need to—'

Boom.

The explosion was bigger than Sophia had imagined. As she stumbled, hand shooting out to save her in case she fell, she looked over her shoulder and saw the grey clouds of smoke billow up, visible even in the fading light. Shouts erupted, bellows from Germans who had started to gain on them but were now caught in the chaos of the explosion. She grabbed Hazel's grenade from her, fingers fumbling with it before she threw it with all her might and then started to run again.

Terror surged through her. All these months, she'd evaded capture. She'd almost started to believe she was untouchable.

But she'd only been fooling herself.

'Run!' Rose shouted, holding her bag close, her other arm pumping as she ran as fast as she could alongside her.

Sophia gasped as Hazel roughly snatched her hand, pulling her along. She stifled a scream as her ankle collapsed, twisting on something that snared from the ground, but she didn't slow down. They had to move fast.

They were surrounded by the enemy now. If they didn't find their way to safety, they were as good as dead.

'It'll take time for them to regroup,' Sophia managed, panting as she whispered, a familiar wave of calm grounding her and clearing her thoughts. 'We'll be gone before they even start searching for us.'

The silence from the other two women told her they weren't so optimistic, but Sophia refused to be anything other than certain of their survival. She'd faced worse odds before, they all had, and there was a reason they were all still alive and so many others weren't.

'Hazel—'

'No!' screamed Rose, leaping in front of her and pushing her back.

The Nazi had appeared from nowhere, pistol raised, the barrel pointed skyward now as Rose fought against him, pushing him away. Where had he even come from, and why was he alone? As Sophia staggered to her feet, the gun went off, the blast making her ears ring, making everything silent around her as she watched Hazel move behind the soldier.

They'd talked about death, about whether they were capable of killing a man with their bare hands the way they'd been trained to do. Sophia swallowed away the bile rising in her throat as she watched Hazel's hand tremble.

The silver of her tiny blade shone as Hazel sliced it against his throat, blood spurting out as Rose fell backwards, released from his grip.

Sophia caught her and pushed her back up, lunging forward to retrieve the pistol.

Hazel was frozen. The fallen Nazi was at her feet, blood staining his otherwise immaculate uniform.

'Now we really need to go,' Sophia managed to say, taking Hazel's knife from her and wiping it clean on the soldier's shoulder as she took charge. She passed it back to her friend as she surveyed the trees around them, hoping they weren't about to be ambushed, knowing their location had just been given away. They'd have dogs sent to find them, men scouring every blade of grass for them now. 'Move!' She grabbed Hazel's hand and yanked her along with her.

It was kill or be killed. And she knew without a doubt now that she could trust Rose and Hazel with her life.

CHAPTER EIGHTEEN

HAZEL

Hazel's body had started to shake so badly, she felt as if she was about to start convulsing. It was worse than the night she'd parachuted in, so much worse.

She'd killed a man.

Only hours earlier, she'd confessed to Sophia that she didn't know if she could do it, if she could actually take the life of another human being. But Sophia had been right; when the decision was right in front of you, it was an easy one to make. If Hazel hadn't killed him, if she hadn't whipped her blade out and sliced it clean against his skin, Rose would be dead.

'Just a bit longer,' Rose panted, her run as sluggish as Hazel's.

They'd been on the move for hours. It was well and truly dark; night had fallen long ago and yet they still hadn't stopped moving. But if she didn't stop soon, she was certain she'd collapse and never get back up.

Hazel's stomach heaved and she tried to swallow it down, only the feeling wasn't going away. She finally slowed, hand against a tree as she doubled forward and retched, vomiting over and over again until there was nothing left in her stomach.

'We still need to keep moving,' Sophia whispered to her, taking her hand. 'But let's walk for now.'

She was relieved to hold Sophia's hand, taking some of her strength. It also stopped the shaking.

They were all panting heavily, all exhausted, physically and mentally fatigued as well as desperately thirsty. After some time walking, the three of them side by side as they stumbled across the grass and tripped on tree roots, thankful at least for the moon guiding them, Sophia spoke.

'I know roughly where we are, and there are some farmhouses coming up. I don't think we should avoid them.'

Hazel gasped. 'You want to turn up on the doorstep of some farmhouse and hope they take us in?'

Sophia squeezed her hand, a warmth in her touch that Hazel hadn't felt before. 'No. I want to find a farmhouse that has a barn, and sneak in for somewhere warm to spend the rest of the night.'

Hazel breathed a sigh of relief.

'It's a good plan,' Rose said. 'It's too dangerous to stay out in the open, but I think we've put enough distance between us for now.'

They kept walking, silently trudging along, and when they finally came across a farmhouse in the distance, they moved more slowly, cautious of where they were and what they were doing. It was impossible to know where was safe and who they could trust.

'Look, there's a barn or something there. It's close to the house, but if we move quietly I think we'll be fine,' Sophia said, using her torch to look ahead before quickly turning it off again.

Hazel was thankful to follow Sophia's orders. It was easier than trying to think for herself while she processed how close they'd been to dying only hours earlier.

'We can hide by the cluster of trees there, then move in one by one.'

Nothing further was said as they made their way closer. Hazel's breath hiccuped in her throat as she tried not to make a noise. Sophia held up her hand for them to wait, and she darted across the short expanse of field from where they were hiding. The creak of the barn door sounded deafeningly loud in the dead still of night, and Hazel half expected the farmer to come running from the house or enemy fire to ring out, but nothing happened.

Rose went next, touching her shoulder before darting off after Sophia. And a few minutes later, Hazel pushed off from the tree and ran as fast as she could. Within seconds she was in, too, pulling the door behind her and finding them in complete darkness. She rummaged for her torch and quickly turned it on, hands still quivering, at the same time as Sophia.

'My torch won't . . . ,' Rose started, banging it against her hand, but her words fell away.

At the same time as Hazel locked eyes with two goats, the smell of animal filled her nostrils. It wasn't awful, but it was unfamiliar to her, and she supposed it was a mixture of their hair, the hay and the dung on the ground. She looked over her shoulder, wondering what other animals she was about to find lurking, but one of the goats butted at her arm and distracted her from her worries.

She smiled and scratched his head, and the goat stretched his neck out as she moved her fingers under his chin.

'I think he likes it,' she whispered.

'He?' Sophia scoffed. 'Try she! Now you hold her still and I'm going to see if we can milk her.'

Hazel grimaced, putting her arm around the goat and cuddling her as Sophia passed her torch to Rose and got down on all fours. Within moments she had milk squirting out and the goat couldn't seem to care less.

'Do we have a bottle still, or did it get broken?' Sophia asked.

Rose pulled out the bottle that had contained their water and held it while Sophia milked the poor goat. If they hadn't been so parched and desperate, it would have seemed funny.

When she'd finished, Sophia held it up and took a sip before passing it to Rose. Then it was Hazel's turn and she sipped the warm milk, grateful to have something liquid in her dry throat even if it wasn't a taste she was used to.

'We need to rest,' Rose said. 'I'll take first watch and you two take a nap. We need to be gone before dawn.'

Hazel nodded and bedded down in the hay. The goats seemed unsure what was going on, but finally the one they'd milked came over and lay down beside her. It started to chew on her hair and Hazel pushed it away, keeping her hand on it for a moment as she fell instantly into a deep slumber.

'Wake up.'

Hazel jumped, heart pounding as she pushed up, disorientated and sore. The night before came flooding back to her and she realised she'd been snuggled up close to the goat. It was probably the only reason she was so warm instead of frozen-to-the-bone cold.

'My radio,' Hazel croaked at Sophia. 'I need to see if I can get it working.'

'No.' Sophia shook her head. 'We already know it's damaged from the fall yesterday. We don't have time to fix it and the last thing we need is to be tracked to here when we're so close to the chateau. Let's go.'

Hazel pushed her hair from her face and stood, reaching for her satchel and pulling its strap over her shoulder. The weight of the radio was familiar, almost comforting, even though it pulled her shoulder down uncomfortably with it.

Sophia shook Rose awake, and Hazel ignored the growl of her stomach as they dusted themselves off and followed Sophia's lead out the door. There was no farmer holding a gun waiting for them, nothing but the steamy, misty morning air as they shut the door quietly behind them and hurried off. Soon they would be at the chateau. Soon they'd be far from the explosion, far enough to be as safe as anyone could expect to be in the middle of occupied France.

They walked in silence for a long time, and Hazel wondered if her friends' legs burnt as hard as hers did from their gruelling run the night before.

'I'm sorry I slept through my shift,' she said, feeling guilty about sleeping the entire time.

'You deserved it,' Sophia said firmly.

'And when we get back, you'll be the one working to fix that radio and start transmitting while we rest,' Rose added.

Hazel wondered if they were going easy on her because of what she'd done, but she didn't say anything. Besides, they were right. Once they were back, she'd be frantically trying to work her radio and there wouldn't be a moment's rest for hours.

When they finally made it back to the chateau, her legs almost collapsed beneath her. She walked up the steps, clutching at the door as she passed it.

'Hazel?'

A noise escaped her throat that sounded like a yelp to her ears as Harry appeared in front of her. His arms opened and she fled into them, clutching on to him and sobbing against his chest. She couldn't believe they'd made it back. She couldn't believe what she'd done. She couldn't . . .

'Hazel, it's all right. Everything's going to be fine,' he whispered into her hair, his arms so warm and strong around her, holding her together. 'Whatever happened, it's over now.'

She breathed in the scent of him, held him close, giving herself a moment to get her emotions back in check. When she finally pulled back, Harry held her in his arms and looked down at her, concern etched into his face.

'It's good to have you back,' he said in a low voice.

Hazel nodded, lost for words.

'Where are they all?' Sophia's voice broke through her thoughts, and Hazel watched as Harry's face changed. His hands fell from her arms.

'They're out working in small groups. Something about following orders and causing mayhem,' he said.

Hazel took a deep breath and patted the satchel that was still over her arm. She looked up at Harry and something inside of her warmed all over again.

'I have to get back to work,' she said.

Harry nodded. 'I'll fix you something to eat.' And then he stepped forward, oblivious to the fact Rose and Sophia were in the same room. Harry dropped a warm, slow kiss to her forehead and squeezed her arm, not saying another word as they stared at each other for a long moment, before she reluctantly pulled away to dash upstairs.

Sophia and Rose both followed her, but neither said a word about the way Harry had welcomed her. She was pleased, because she had no idea how she felt about what had just happened between them, let alone what to say in response.

'It's no use,' Hazel muttered, cursing herself for ever climbing on that old roof to start with as she fiddled with her set. 'It was damaged in the fall, and maybe it banged into a tree or something when I was running as well, because I can't get it working.'

Her frustration was making her top lip damp with sweat, and her heart was thumping loud. She took a deep breath and then started all over again, tinkering with her machine. This was why they'd been given suitcases to transport them in. If she hadn't put the thing in a satchel, then it might not have become so damaged.

'Someone's back,' Sophia said, frowning and disappearing.

Hazel kept working, letting Rose watch her back as she sat in the attic. But within minutes there was the heavy footfall of a man, and then Mathieu appeared with Sophia behind him. Hazel stopped what she was doing when she saw the unusual expression on Sophia's face, her eyes wide and her bottom lip tucked beneath her teeth.

'Rose, I need to speak to you,' Sophia said. Mathieu stood, still and silent as stone beside her.

'What is it?' Rose asked.

Hazel went cold, waiting, dreading what she was about to say.

'Mathieu would like you to do a solo courier operation.'

'What?' Hazel all but hissed. 'I thought we were supposed to be working together? Why does he need her?'

Sophia looked as worried as she felt, but it was Mathieu who spoke.

'There was another woman, an agent,' he said in a low voice. 'She was preparing to go undercover as a cosmetics representative, but she was taken out recently. Rose is a good match for her. She can use her identity.'

'*Taken out?*' Hazel asked, her voice barely a whisper, and she glanced worriedly at Rose. Her friend had stayed silent, her expression impossible to read.

'The others believe she took her pill, the one issued to you before your parachute jump,' Sophia said.

Hazel's hand instantly went to her pocket, feeling the bump of the pill she had sewn in there in case of an emergency. She couldn't imagine deciding to swallow that, but then the idea of being tortured and losing the opportunity to live, giving up others when you couldn't survive another moment of it . . . She breathed deeply, worried for Rose. 'So you want Rose to take her place? Using her cover?' she asked Mathieu.

'She's going to get you the part you need from another cell, and take money and codes with her,' Mathieu said. 'She'll fit the role perfectly.'

'The identity has already been created,' Sophia explained. 'I would have been the logical choice for courier work in the past, but the

Germans are more suspicious than they've ever been. She's the right age, she fits the description, and most importantly she's actually French. There is nothing she can do or say that would make them suspicious.'

Hazel knew it made absolute sense, but it was hard not to think of Rose as her old friend from their old lives. When she was training, it was about looking after herself and doing her job, taking calculated risks and understanding the consequences. The problem here was that she knew Rose and cared deeply for her. Hazel was going to have to use that to fuel her work, to make sure she didn't make a mistake that could cost her friend her life.

The room suddenly felt too small and stuffy for Hazel, and even though she wanted to scream at Rose that it was too dangerous, she didn't say a word.

'I'll rest for a few hours, then make myself up and get going. I suppose I need to move fast?' Rose asked.

'Yes,' Mathieu said. 'I'll leave you a moment, then report to me downstairs.'

Hazel let the words sink in and exchanged glances with Sophia. She knew Sophia would be just as worried, but she'd probably never think to stop either of them from partaking in an important mission.

'Take this,' Hazel said, holding out a part for a radio that she'd found in the attic but that was of no use to her repairs. 'It might help someone else in the other cell.'

Rose opened her arms and hugged her tight, and then held on for some time, standing silently in the room while Sophia watched on.

'There's been news of Sebastian,' Sophia suddenly said, wiping at her eyes, at tears that Hazel knew were mirrored in her own eyes. 'Mathieu said that Sebastian was asking questions, trying to find you.' She was staring at Rose as she spoke. 'It's so good to know that he's still alive, but there was no mention of his wife. The others passed him when they were blowing up petrol tankers, but he had to return to his own cell.'

'You'll all make it home. We have to believe that,' Hazel replied, not knowing what else to say. 'You and Sebastian and his wife, you'll survive, Rose. You will.'

Sophia gestured that it was time to go downstairs, and Hazel took one last look at Rose before sitting back at her desk. Tears burnt her eyes. If only she hadn't broken the radio, then perhaps Rose wouldn't have been sent at all. She thought of Harry downstairs; suddenly all she wanted was to run to him and hold him and sob against his shoulder again. But she was stronger than that.

She was an undercover agent, and she wasn't going to let this or anything else crack her.

'You look beautiful,' Hazel said, admiring Rose as she stood before her three hours later. 'Ravishing in fact.'

Rose laughed and rolled her eyes. 'If only I had someone to be ravishing for, hmm?'

She joked, but Hazel knew the truth of the pain beneath her easy words. 'I'd tell you to be careful, but I know you will.'

'Come here,' Rose said, her case discarded as she opened her arms and stepped forward. They were all so tired, but Rose suddenly looked a million dollars, certainly not the same woman who'd woken in a barn with goats earlier in the day.

They embraced and Hazel held her tight, not wanting to let go. 'We still have so much to share. You make sure you come back as quickly as you can.'

The trip was important, they all knew that, and Rose's mission was vital to their success. Without Hazel radioing, all the small cells around them would become invisible, cut off from the others, because she was the only highly trained operator at the chateau – or within miles, from what she'd been told.

'Your red lipstick is amazing,' Hazel told her, admiring how it accentuated her full mouth when she pulled back.

'It's Elizabeth Arden,' Rose told her with a wink. 'I had one too many in the bag I was given, so I left it here for you and Sophia. But I don't take Sophia for the red-lip kind of woman.'

They both smiled. Sophia was amazing, but she was probably too focused on her job to be overly worried about lipstick. Hazel, on the other hand, was more than happy to receive the gift.

'I'll wear it every day and think of you.'

Rose gathered her things and Hazel watched her go. She had a long walk ahead of her to the train station, and from there it would be a dangerous journey that made Hazel shudder to think about. But Rose was a Frenchwoman; she had nothing to hide about her lineage, and the fewer lies being told, the less likely anyone would be caught.

'We'll miss you,' Hazel said as Rose walked out the front door.

Hazel held her hand up and watched her go. When she turned she saw Sophia standing not very far behind her. She'd been watching their exchange, perhaps the whole time.

'She'll be fine,' Sophia said. 'Rose is as good as they get. And besides, she's fearless. Nothing and nobody will rattle her.'

Hazel wondered if Sophia felt like an outsider sometimes to the history Rose and she had, but if she did, she didn't say anything.

Sophia smiled and took her hand. 'I'm putting you to bed. You need some sleep before you start staring at that blasted radio again.'

She was too tired to disagree, and having Sophia so obviously looking out for her was a nice change.

CHAPTER NINETEEN

ROSE

Rose held her head high and kept her shoulders straight. She knew she looked glamourous, more like she might have before the war, or at least before Peter had been taken from her, and it gave her the confidence to play her character. The red lipstick had transformed her in front of the mirror, and she'd taken one look at the face staring back at her and known she could do it. It was like looking at the old her, the *Parisian* her. Only she'd not expected to see that face again any time soon.

'I'm a confident sales representative for cosmetics,' she murmured to herself, her lips barely moving. 'I love make-up. It's my passion.'

She needed to live and breathe her new legend. She'd always loved fashion and make-up, like any of her friends with money to spend. But that life seemed, well, a lifetime ago, and since then the closest she'd come to being the glamourous woman she'd once been was brushing her hair out at night and twisting it up off her face before bed.

Rose clutched her bag tighter, not thinking about what was inside. She had codes written into her silk underskirt and two small parts in her case that could be used to build a new radio or repair an old one, as well as money. If she was caught, she'd be killed. It was as simple as that. Which was why she wasn't going to get caught, because she wasn't going to let herself get put in that position.

She had a special pass, since her work meant she had to travel, so the Gestapo shouldn't bother searching her like they would most others. Besides, she had the advantage of creamy white skin and bright blue eyes, features the Germans seemed to like well enough even though her hair was brown and not blonde, and something shared by the original agent whose place she had taken. It was the reason why she'd been unfortunate enough to be earmarked for the role in the first place. She only had to hope none of them took *too* much of a liking and tried anything on. The thought alone made her stomach turn.

It was never going to get easier however often she did this, she knew that, but she had to remember why she was doing it. She and she alone could keep the various cells working. If the Normandy landings went ahead and they were able to keep disrupting the Germans, then they might actually win this godforsaken war.

Rose reached the station and looked around. There were Gestapo waiting, watching, laughing amongst themselves. But this time she didn't have to fear them. She straightened her shoulders and pinned a bright smile firmly on her face. She was Roseanne DuBois and she was the best make-up representative in the country!

Rose tried to sit up straight but her body kept slumping forward every time she fell asleep. She'd been on the train for some time, and now that it was dark she was trying to let herself sleep, only it was almost impossible to do sitting upright. There were no private sleeping cars, so Rose had to sleep in her seat, freezing cold and uncomfortable, rather than sleep in a car with men. There were few women on board and she didn't want to put herself in that position.

She rubbed at her eyes and then realised she'd probably ruined her make-up. Rose wiped more carefully across her skin, clearing her throat as she shifted and trying to make herself more comfortable. Surely the journey was almost over? She wanted to get rid of the package, dispose of the message she had to relay and then breathe a huge sigh of relief. She was wishing she hadn't brought their spare parts with her.

Rose sat and listened to her own breath going in and out, trying to enjoy the motion of the train and the solitude of her journey. She'd hardly spoken to anyone since she'd left the chateau. A nod to the Gestapo man who'd asked to check her papers, followed by a brisk thank you as she'd boarded the train. Then another nod to yet another German, before finding her seat and refusing to make eye contact with any of the other passengers. Given how long she'd lived with Sophia, and how often she'd had a house guest waiting to be rescued, she'd become used to having someone to talk to, or simply with her, at all times, so solitude was an unusual notion now.

It was also the first time she'd truly let herself think about what she'd left behind when they'd fled her house by the coast.

My baby. She let the words move slowly through her mind, mentally grasping them and replaying them over and over. *My baby. My baby.*

Sophia had helped her bury the baby she'd delivered, so early that he hadn't had a hope of surviving. He'd been months too soon, but still, he'd been perfectly formed. His head and body tiny, small enough to fit easily in the palm of her hand. Her heart had broken in a way that couldn't even compare to losing Peter when she'd looked at that little human who had come too early to join the land of the living. Her body had been wracked with pain, the blood had covered the bed she'd managed to crawl up on, and then she'd managed to pull herself together and wrap her tiny, unviable child in a towel. All night she'd held him, sobbing, stopping only to crawl over to Sophia on the bed beside her and make sure she hadn't died. And then she'd realised that her new guest wouldn't survive without her help, and she'd placed the baby down and pushed her own pain aside to save another.

Sophia had repaid her that favour a hundred times over. She'd helped her to bury her child, holding her when she'd cried, despite the physical pain it must have caused her to even rise from the bed. And then she'd been her one and only confidante – they had both been to each other – and from then on Rose had vowed to do anything to keep Sophia safe. She would happily take a bullet for her strong-willed, capable friend if it meant ensuring she survived the war and made it home to her Alex. At least Sophia still had someone to return to, could hold on to the hope that she would be in her loved one's arms again.

'Do you speak German?'

Rose jumped at the intrusion, the man's voice shaking her from her thoughts. A tremor of fear circled through her as she collected herself, quickly smoothing down her skirt to make sure it hadn't risen up.

She forced herself to smile at the man despite the fact he'd almost made her jump out of her skin as she'd stared out the window into nothing.

'A little,' she replied, not wanting him to know that in fact she spoke quite excellent German. 'You . . .' She smiled, pushing her shoulders up into a little shrug, and switched from German to French, hoping he might understand. 'Frightened,' she said. 'I do not know the word for *frightened*.'

He laughed, understanding when she jumped and flapped her hand to her heart. She hated how handsome he was, how easy the smile of this Gestapo man was when he no doubt was as cruel-hearted as the rest of them.

'I understand,' he said back to her, conversing again in German. 'I'm sorry.'

She could see the irony in him apologising to her. If he only knew what she was carrying, he'd be smacking the back of his hand in a practised arc into her cheekbone instead of extending his hand politely. To him she was merely a pretty French girl, nothing more.

'Kurt,' he said, his smile wide, eyes sparkling at her as if they were two people meeting at a dinner party rather than in her country, which his country had conquered. 'And you are?'

She took his hand, slid her palm to his warm, soft one. She was freezing, but he was dressed in a big, warm coat and had no doubt been enjoying a private car.

'Roseanne,' she replied, holding his hand just long enough before retrieving it and folding both hands back into her lap.

'You're freezing,' he said, frowning. *'Cold,'* he said again, as if he was unsure of how much she could understand. He rubbed his hands together and then blew on them. 'Here,' he said, shrugging out of his overcoat and gesturing for her to lean forward.

Rose's skin was crawling at the mere thought of taking his coat, every part of her wanting to rebel against any offer of kindness from a man like him, but she gratefully accepted it and moved over so he could sit beside her. She snuggled into it, knowing that her ice-cold bones would soon start to thaw. It was so big that she was able to ball her hands inside, too.

She wondered if he would get into trouble for lending it to her, but she supposed he didn't care what anyone else thought. There were other people around them, but no one dared to look at them, and the other Gestapo on board probably had better things to do than worry about one of their own flirting with a Frenchwoman.

'You are travelling alone?' he asked.

Rose nodded and pointed to her case. 'I sell make-up,' she said slowly, pointing to her lips for effect and pretending to put on lipstick. 'I have to travel.'

He smiled and she wondered if they were actually so different. Sometimes she thought that not every member of the Nazi Party could be so terrible. Surely many of them had joined merely to blend in and save their families, while knowing in their hearts that what was happening was wrong. But then she thought of Sophia, the secrets she'd confided in her about finding her mother that day, the way her father refused to spare even his once-beloved wife when she was found to be keeping Jews safe in their home.

'Ah,' he said, nodding and gesturing to her face. 'You are so beautiful, you must be very successful.'

Rose laughed and raised her hand to hide her mouth, glancing away coyly. She needed to play the game, and Roseanne was single and would surely be attracted to a handsome young German paying her so much attention.

'You must miss home,' she said, careful to say the words slowly so she didn't give away her knack for languages. 'Are you, ah, married?'

It was Kurt grinning this time. 'No,' he replied. 'No wife. And you?' He glanced at her hands, no doubt looking for a ring. She'd entrusted her wedding ring to Hazel while she was gone, and as she rubbed her thumb across her fingers, she felt bare without the weight of it there.

'No, no wife,' she said, knowing she'd made a mistake but expecting him to laugh at her mistake.

He did, grinning at her and shaking his head. *'Husband,'* he said slowly, 'you would have a *husband* if you were married.'

She giggled and hated how easy she found it to be silly and immature. She was fortunate that she looked so youthful and could pretend to be unmarried and in her early twenties.

The train slowed then, suddenly jerking, and Kurt threw his arm out to stop her from shooting forward. His hand brushed her and he smiled and pulled back.

'It was lovely meeting you, Roseanne,' he said as the train groaned.

It wouldn't be long before they were at the station, and she knew he'd have work to do now. He might be about to check identity cards and passes again, perhaps search bags, and she gritted her teeth as she made herself smile back at him. It was a dangerous liaison to be having, flirting with Kurt, but it would have been even more dangerous if she'd ignored him and been rude when he'd clearly been so interested.

'I hope to see you again,' she said, shaking her head at how stilted her words sounded. It pained her to speak a language she knew well so poorly, but she was enjoying playing her character, like an actress performing on a stage.

'Let me,' he said, taking the coat from her shoulders when she leaned forward, before putting it back on himself. He bent down and reached for her hands, nodding. 'At least you warmed a little.'

She nodded. 'Thank you.'

As the train continued to slow, Kurt stepped sideways and reached up, his hands closing over the handle of her case before she could protest. Instead she sat frozen, waiting, certain that he was about to open it – or worse, that the handle would give way and her case would fall open, the pieces she was carrying spilling all over the floor.

'Here,' he said, passing it to her.

'Thank you,' she said again, ready to pass out as her fingers clenched the handle and she pulled it closer to her body.

He gave her one last look, his mouth still tilted up to make his entire face light up, and then finally walked away.

Rose had thought she was tough. She thought she had nothing left to live for and nothing to be scared about. But Kurt had shown her how close she'd come to being found out, how easy it would have been for him to ask to look inside her case. And then she would have found out just how easily the charming young German could turn into a cruel captor, of that she was absolutely certain.

Rose prepared to stand, holding on as she rose, legs frozen cold, her toes locked and aching as if she had frostbite. But she kept the most pleasant look on her face that she could muster and pushed through the pain. All she had to do was deliver the codes to the other cells and pick up the radio parts, make appearances at a couple of stores that were in the business of selling make-up to at least make her cover story look legitimate if anyone was observing her, and then get back on the train and return to the chateau.

Her role was clear and her job simple so long as she wasn't stopped and searched. All she had to do now was convince everyone between here and there that she was indeed a glamourous young woman passionate about her job.

She might not feel glamourous anymore, but she certainly knew what it meant to be passionate about a job.

CHAPTER TWENTY

HAZEL

Hazel smiled at Harry and wished he didn't make her pulse quicken with one brief glance and one very cute, dimpled smile.

'I'm worried about you.'

She shook her head as he stared at her, his dimples disappearing into a frown.

'Please don't,' she said quickly. 'I made the decision to come here and I want to do what's needed of me.'

He sighed, his smile slowly returning. 'Where do they even find women like you?'

She shrugged. 'There are plenty of women doing amazing things at home, too. When you get back, you'll see.'

He reached out, his fingers gently brushing hers. Hazel stayed still, her breath catching in her throat as his fingertips fell to rest over the back of her hand.

'I don't need to be told how amazing our women are,' he said, voice low and husky. 'Because I'm not that kind of man. But I do worry about you. About all three of you.'

'You do?' she asked, wishing she had the willpower to pull her hand away. Instead she kept dead still, liking the warmth of his skin touching hers.

'It's you I worry the most about, though.'

She needed to tell him again that she was engaged, needed to make it clear that his advances weren't welcome. She'd made a new career based on lies and deceit ever since that first meeting when she was recruited by the SOE, but for some reason she couldn't make the words come out of her mouth when it came to Harry.

'I . . . I . . . ,' she started, looking up into his dark eyes. They were seated on the ground, backs up against the wall. There was a decent space between them, the only connection made by his outstretched arm.

'I don't think I'll be here much longer,' Harry said, giving her a moment to collect her thoughts. 'The last thing they want is an injured ex-pilot holed up for too long.'

Hazel disagreed that the others would be getting sick of him being there, but he was right about not thinking he'd be there much longer. Almost a day after Rose had left, she'd finally patched her radio together again, although it was only a temporary fix. Now that she'd been in direct contact with Paris, her next job was to confirm the rescue of a handful of Allied airmen and have them smuggled out to Spain. As well as listening and waiting on more news of the Allied invasion.

'I'm engaged to be married,' she said, the words just blurting out.

He didn't pull his hand away, instead started to move his fingers again over hers. 'I know. You've told me that already.'

She gulped. 'I don't want to, well . . .'

'You don't need to say it,' Harry said. 'I know.'

Hazel felt better now she'd said it, pleased she'd at least tried to explain, but it didn't change the way she felt. And she had a feeling it wasn't going to change anything about Harry, either. There was something between them, something that was impossible to ignore, and she knew he felt it just as keenly as she did.

Hazel heard someone calling her, a muffled shout from another room, and she knew she needed to get back to work. She'd stopped only for a quick break and something to eat, her head pounding from hour after hour concentrating at her desk. After confirming Harry's collection, she needed to get to work pinpointing exact positions for drops for other cells ahead of the landings. But she knew her work would be hindered by having to fiddle with her set to try to keep it working, and it would be like that until Rose returned with the part she needed to fix it properly.

She reluctantly pulled her hand away from Harry's, but he surprised her by tightening his grip, fingers firm against hers as he tried to keep her still. His skin was smooth and warm, reassuring even though it was also so obviously forbidden.

'Come here,' he murmured.

Hazel hesitated, stared down at him. She shouldn't. She needed to leave, needed to put distance between them before something she regretted happened, before . . .

To hell with it.

Hazel dropped back down again, her breath ragged. Harry's eyes fell to her mouth and her lips parted involuntarily as she lowered to her knees. They were both still until Harry's hand rose, his palm soft to her cheek as he gently caressed her skin.

She made the final move despite her mind screaming out to her to stop. She'd been thinking about it for so long, but she'd never had any intention of following through and turning it into reality. Hazel slowly, carefully touched her mouth to Harry's, the lightest of kisses as their lips brushed. She paused, his breath hot against her, his body so warm and inviting.

'We shouldn't,' she whispered.

Harry didn't answer her with words. Instead he leaned in and kissed her again, for longer this time, his mouth firmer, his lips moving against hers and making her skin tingle.

'I have to go,' she finally said, heart racing as she dipped down to kiss him one more time.

'Then go,' he whispered back.

Hazel reluctantly stood, looking at Harry one last time, knowing from the heat in her face that her cheeks would be stained a dark shade of pink. She'd never, ever thought she'd be unfaithful to the promise she'd made John, and it terrified her how easily she'd done it. But everything felt so different now, as if she were a different person leading a completely different life.

But she had to get him home safe. She needed to be able to do her job without worrying about him, needed to stay completely focused without any distractions, and that meant helping him and any other Allied airmen in the area out of France and on their way back to England.

Harry. His name circled her mind as she hurried upstairs to the attic, her little bolt hole away from the hustle and bustle of the rest of the big house.

She should be thinking about codes, and instead there was a handsome man with lips like silk against hers who had infiltrated her thoughts.

'Do I even need to ask where Harry is?'

Hazel bit her lip, turning on the staircase and finding Sophia standing at the bottom, arms folded and a knowing smile on her face. She tried to remain expressionless.

'Well . . . ,' Hazel started, clearing her throat and thinking quickly what to say in her defence.

'No need to explain, I didn't say a thing,' Sophia said with a laugh, making Hazel grin. 'Do you want me to take over for a bit so you can have a longer rest?'

Things had changed between them now, and for the better. Mind you, after what they'd been through, there was little they didn't know about each other, and very little they wouldn't trust the other with.

Besides, not having Rose with them had brought them closer; they were both worried about her, and not knowing where she was or whether her mission had been a success was no doubt playing on Sophia's mind as much as it was Hazel's.

'I'll be fine,' Hazel said, forgetting all about Harry and refocusing on her work. 'I'm only worried that being on the radio so long could give up our position.'

Sophia nodded, following her all the way up and into the small room. 'Look, if we were in the city, I think we'd need to be extremely careful. We'd have to be on the move after every transmission.'

Hazel agreed. 'I know. But for all we know, we're not as isolated as we think here. What if I'm compromising our security? What if we're not being careful enough?'

She listened to Sophia sigh as they sat down. Hazel was at her desk and Sophia was on the bed, facing her.

'How's the radio holding up?'

Hazel groaned. 'It's terrible! I have to keep trying to patch it up, and I lose the connection all the time.'

'Rose will be back soon. As soon as she's here, we move on.'

'I think we need to. We're safer on the move than being sitting ducks for the Germans.'

Sophia lay back on the bed, no doubt deep in thought. She was the most introverted of them all, even though she was their natural leader. But the reason she was so good was because of the way she could read a situation, the thought she put into everything they did before they did it.

Hazel tried to tune into the BBC again once her communications for the day were over, but the signal kept fading out and her frustration was rising. Not to mention the fuzzy feeling in her stomach, the gnawing sensation she'd had ever since Rose had left. Something didn't feel right to her, only she didn't know if it was merely worry over her friend or something more.

CHAPTER TWENTY-ONE

ROSE

Rose's palm was clammy against the handle of her case as she walked. It was heavier this time. She'd thought the trip back would be easier because it was her second time and she knew what she was doing, knew what it was like getting past the security checks and into the train, how she felt playing her role. How wrong she'd been.

The case was certainly weighing her arm down, and she had to grit her teeth and force herself to keep walking, a smile fixed on her face as she pretended it wasn't just about taking her arm off. In truth she could walk for hours if she had to – she was determined enough – but her stamina wasn't her concern. It was being stopped. It was someone touching her case. Because this time, she had a crucial radio part and additional aerial with her, as well as explosives that she'd been given in case they needed to do more to assist before the landings.

The wind was cool on her cheeks but Rose welcomed it, enjoying how it felt against her flushed skin. She wanted the war to be over as much as the next person, but she also loved the work she was doing. Her racing pulse might unsettle her, but she was good at what she did, and something about that understanding always sent a sense of pride through her.

She noticed Gestapo and flashed a smile, not slowing her pace. She would be in the train station soon. Once she was inside she'd be able to show her pass, flirt if she had to, then find a seat and keep to herself until it was time to board. Only once she was seated and the train was moving would she start to relax.

Rose took comfort from the click of her low heels, the rhythmic noise soothing her as she kept up her fast walk. She was almost there, she was in the station, she was . . .

'Roseanne?'

Her heart felt like it jumped with a thud to the concrete beneath her feet. Rose sucked back a breath and turned, knowing from the thick German accent who it had to be.

'Kurt!' she exclaimed, waving at him and grinning as if he was the best thing she'd seen all day.

He pushed off the wall he'd been leaning against and strode over, his smile wide, just like it had been that night on the train. She thought again what a shame it was that he was a Nazi. Not that she was even interested in other men, her heart was still full to brimming for Peter, but the thought still crossed her mind.

'Are you heading back again so soon?' he asked in German.

She nodded. 'My, ah, business,' she said, 'it is all' – she paused for effect – '*finished.*'

He gestured in the direction she'd been heading and matched her pace as they slowly walked side by side.

'If I wasn't working,' he said, eyes as bright as his smile, 'I would have asked you to have dinner with me.'

She blushed, her cheeks hot, only it wasn't because she was flattered. The burn inside of her was anger at the fact that a man who was an intruder in her beautiful country thought she would be swooning over the idea of dinner with him.

'That would have been . . . ,' she said, laughing. '*Wonderful.*'

'Let me take your bag,' he said, taking her by surprise as he reached for it, his hand grazing hers as he clasped the handle. 'Please.'

Rose felt her heart sink for the second time in less than a few minutes. She let go – she had no choice unless she was about to refuse him – and his eyes narrowed the moment he took it from her.

'It's heavy,' he said, no longer walking as he looked from her to the bag.

'So much make-up,' she explained quickly. 'And I took some magazines, ah, *catalogues* of new cosmetics that I can show to my customers.'

She realised she was speaking too rapidly, her German suddenly too fast for someone who was supposed to have only a limited grasp of the language. Rose smiled and laughed, flashing her eyes at him, doing her best to flirt when inside a voice screamed at her to run. She'd blown it. She knew as surely as she knew her own name that she'd blown it.

'Magazines?' he said, his smile returning. 'Oh, of course. Of course.'

She started to walk again, trying not to panic, letting him hold it for her, the tension within her slowly starting to subside. There was some shouting then and she glanced back, saw a couple being pulled aside, followed by more raised voices. She had no idea what was going on but Kurt stopped and walked back a few steps, calling out and then looking back at her.

'May I see your pass,' he said quietly, looking more like a guard and less like a friendly face now. 'I should have checked it before.'

Rose tried to stop her hand from shaking as she reached inside her jacket pocket for it. She smiled at him when she passed it over. 'Of course,' she said. 'You know me, sorry, I didn't think to show it to you.'

He silently took it from her.

'Will you be able to sit with me?' she asked, smiling. 'On the train ride back?'

He looked up at her, still holding her pass. When another Gestapo officer joined them, her mouth went dry as if every bit of moisture in her body had been drained away.

The other man gestured to her case. She smiled. Kurt looked at her again, frowning now, then assuring the other man that he'd met her before and that nothing was amiss. She watched on with a smile, acting like she had no idea what they were talking about.

Until she heard the words she'd been dreading from the other man. *'Open her case and look.'*

Had someone betrayed her? Were they looking for someone? Why was she being searched? This man was obviously Kurt's superior given the way the younger man nodded, ready to obey orders.

Kurt met her gaze again before dropping the case to the ground and bending to one knee. Her lungs screamed, her body shook, her face froze into a smile. She had a knife on her body. She could stab him or the other man, slit their throats if she had to, just like Hazel had done to the German near the train line. But then instead of a chance at life, she'd be shot in the head by their comrades before she had time to see the bullet coming.

Rose's breath shuddered out as Kurt looked up. His face was blank, the smile long gone as he instead searched through her things, clearly confused. He lifted the catalogue that was on the top, pushed aside the pots of make-up and lipsticks, and then his hand hovered. Rose waited, barely breathing. When he asked quickly for something sharp, her heart sank – a sharp blade cutting through the lining that she'd so carefully sewn in herself to hide what she was carrying.

He pulled out a thin sheet of paper first, paper that had codes on it for Hazel. The Gestapo couldn't take possession of it!

She lunged for it, her movement fast, jerking down and forward and snatching it from him. Arms grabbed at her, roughly hauling her back by her stomach as Kurt jumped up to take it from her. But Rose was fast, far too fast for them. She didn't bother to use her elbows to slam into the guard who had her from behind. Instead she frantically bit at the paper, tearing it with her teeth twice and quickly chewing.

Kurt snatched what was left from her but she'd already eaten out the middle of it, which meant there would be no way it could possibly make any sense to any of them. His hand clamped around her jaw, trying to prise her mouth open, but Rose swallowed, gagging as she tried to push the paper down her throat. There wasn't enough saliva, she hadn't chewed it for long enough, but she was not going to give in until she'd forced it down.

'You bitch!' he swore in German, holding his hand back and slamming it into her face.

She wanted to scream as pain echoed through her body, the crack loud, knowing he'd broken something, maybe her cheekbone. But instead she swallowed through the pain, opening her mouth wide once she was done to show him it was gone.

He'd dropped down again, and she struggled against the hold the other man had on her. By now there were other guards, even civilians looking on, no doubt wondering what was going on and who she was.

She saw him find the explosives at the same moment a rifle butt slammed into her head from behind. For a moment she saw the concrete coming up to meet her, but then everything went black.

CHAPTER TWENTY-TWO

HAZEL

Hazel smiled to herself as she puckered up and carefully applied her bright red lipstick. She'd used it the day Rose had left and the two days since, and she liked that it made her feel closer to her friend. She'd thought about her a lot since she'd left, wondering what she was doing and when to expect her back, but the truth was she might not see her for days and it didn't necessarily mean anything had gone wrong. Or at least that's what she was telling herself.

She walked upstairs, back to the attic she was regularly transmitting from, reaching for her pencil the moment she sat down. She twirled it between her forefinger and thumb and settled down. This was the moment she'd been dreading. She needed to confirm the drop-off coordinates for Harry and a small group of other rescued airmen and an injured SOE agent, and the moment she did that, the reality of him leaving would start to set in because he'd be gone within hours.

She didn't want to see him go, but he needed to get out of here. His leg wasn't healing well despite the amount of attention she was giving him, but she knew only basic first aid; it wasn't as if she were a nurse.

'Hazel?'

She looked up, turning when there was a light knock at the door.

'Hello,' Hazel said, smiling at Sophia.

'I'm heading out,' she replied. 'I wanted to see if you'd managed to confirm Harry's passage?'

She grinned. 'Fingers crossed. He should be on his way tonight if I manage to get the final confirmation.'

Sophia came forward, surprising her by putting her arms on her shoulders and then drawing her closer for a hug, dropping a kiss to the top of her head.

'They say you're the fastest they've ever seen at transmitting messages to London.' Hazel laughed and hugged her back. It was awkward because she was still sitting, but she appreciated the affection. It still surprised her whenever Sophia was so kind, even after everything. But that day she'd killed the Nazi had changed something between them, even though neither of them had ever spoken about it again.

'I'm lucky. Being a country mouse is definitely better than being a city one!' She used their code terminology – radio operators were often called country or city mice depending on where they were transmitting from.

'Don't be so hard on yourself. You're good at your job. Better than good, you're great.' Sophia stepped back and Hazel felt a strange shiver pass through her.

'You're not leaving, are you?' she asked, keeping her voice low in case anyone was listening to them. The way Sophia had come to her seemed strangely final in a way. She hoped there was nothing going on that she didn't know about.

'No, of course not. I just, well, I don't know. I'm worried about Rose, I suppose, and I feel, oh, I don't even know what I'm trying to say.' Sophia's brows were knitted close together, like she was trying to figure something out.

Hazel stood and hugged her again, holding her for longer, knowing how overwhelmed she'd felt at times and wanting to do anything she could to comfort Sophia. What they were doing, it was tough mentally, had made Hazel question so many things, but the one thing she'd never questioned was how dedicated Rose and Sophia were to the cause.

'It's like a little safe haven here, isn't it?' she said, finally letting go of Sophia.

'It feels too safe. I don't feel right about something, but I don't know why.' She let out a deep, audible breath. 'I definitely want to leave when she gets back. The more I thought about what you said, about how we could be compromising our safety . . .' Her words trailed off. 'I just thought she'd be back by now. It's making me jittery.'

Hazel knew what she meant. 'Look, if they knew we were here, if there were teams out there tracking my signals? They'd have stormed the place by now. There's no way they would let me send another message.' She didn't mention Rose because she shared all the same worries.

'I know, you're right. But I felt safe at our last place, too. I never would have thought anyone there would have betrayed us.'

Hazel patted Sophia's shoulder before turning back to her radio. She hadn't had any messages come through yet.

She listened to the door open and shut, and then Sophia's footsteps slowly receding. Her stomach swirled, something unsettling her, but she pushed the feeling away and settled back down to work.

She put the headset to her ears and carefully sent her message by code. They had a delivery of arms scheduled to come in, and it was the best way to get Harry safely home, not to mention the other men. Certainly a whole lot better than having to smuggle him through a network of people to get him to Spain.

CHAPTER TWENTY-THREE

ROSE

Rose sat alone. They had her in a room, a cell, and she had no idea how she'd got there. All she knew was that she was sitting on concrete, her back to a wall, and she was dripping wet. She'd only woken when they'd thrown a bucket of cold water over her as she'd been lying on the hard floor, the puddle of water spread around her. She was shivering, her entire body convulsing, but she'd done her best. She'd twirled her long hair up and managed to knot it in place, with a few pins that had still been hanging from her hair helping to keep it in place, so it wasn't dripping down her back. But she'd decided to keep her clothes on instead of stripping off to dry. There was no point risking her clothes being taken if they weren't on her body, because at least with them on she could dry out slowly and then stay warm. If she even lived that long.

Footsteps echoed out and she sat up straight, ready to look fear in the eye. They could scare her all they liked, but she wasn't about to let them think they could get her to give anything away. Her only priority now was keeping her friends safe, and she would say nothing, *nothing*, to give their location or existence away. It would start to get dark again soon, she was certain of it, unless she'd been out for so long that she had lost an entire night.

'Here she is,' a man said in rough French, 'our lovely new prisoner.'

She stared at the man as he walked into the cell, his smile verging on cruel. He was eating a slice of bread and she looked away from it. He was trying to tease her, trying to make her salivate so she'd beg him for food. Only he had no idea just how stubborn she could be.

'You might be a fool, but you're beautiful,' he said, his accent thick. 'We could still all have a lot of fun with you.'

Rose gulped but she defiantly stared back at him. Rape would be a fate far worse than death for her, but every Gestapo in the region could rape her and she still wouldn't talk. Scream, *yes*. Cry, *certainly*. Vow to slaughter every last one of them? *Until my dying breath.* But she would *not* let them torture her into giving her secrets away.

'Tell us who you work for,' he said. 'I want to know everything. We've already found the others, so you have nothing left worth hiding.'

She sat silently, her lips slightly parted, her breathing shallow. She didn't believe him for a second. Who was he even pretending to have found?

'We know where you came from and where you were going back to. It's only a matter of time before we know everything.'

Still she didn't say a word, but the hairs on her back slowly prickled as she thought of Hazel and Sophia being captured.

'Stand up!' he barked.

She glared at him but grudgingly did what he said. She would do whatever they asked, so long as they weren't asking her to talk.

He strode closer, the bread long gone as he wound his arm back and pummelled his fist into her stomach.

'Arrghh,' she cried out, hating the pained noise that escaped from her throat.

'Tell me what I need to know,' he said in a low voice, stroking her hair as she tried to stand from her doubled-over position. 'Then I can be gentle with you.'

She shook her head and he punched her again. Rose doubled back over, and he hit her a third time, slamming her back against the concrete wall. Tears escaped her eyes, as she cried out, yelping in pain.

He walked away then, striding from the cell and calling over his shoulder.

'You will talk,' he said. 'I am good at making women talk. Eventually.'

'Bastard!' She spat out the word but it came out low, barely audible, her lungs screaming as they tried to work. She gasped for air as she listened to his footsteps echo away from her, struggling to breathe, struggling to move. Struggling to stay coherent.

They couldn't know anything; it wasn't possible. They might get close, but there was no way they could trace her back to the chateau.

Rose shut her eyes, willing sleep to find her to take away the pain. She'd expected Kurt, knew he'd be furious that she'd deceived him, but in a way she'd expected to be able to sweet-talk him. To play on the attraction he'd had to her, beg for forgiveness, give him a few titbits of information to get him to trust her, to make it look like she was wanting to be turned.

But her captor wasn't Kurt. And that man? She was certain he'd taken great pleasure every time his fist had connected with her body.

The shaking had stopped. When, she didn't know, but her body had finally warmed enough to stop convulsing from the cold, her clothes no longer wet to her skin. But her feet were still like icicles, and no amount of jumping up and down or flexing and wriggling her toes had helped.

Rose sat still, ears pricked. She'd had very little contact with anyone since her arrival, but she knew there must be others in cells nearby. It was so dark where she was, the only light an old lamp in the corner.

And that was only ever turned on in the short time it took them to interrogate her.

Today would be worse. They'd thrown icy water on her, pretended that they knew everything about her friends when she was certain they didn't, flexed a few tools that were supposed to terrify her into talking for fear of them being used on her. None of that had worked, of course, which meant that today she was certain they'd start doing dreadful things to her instead of merely threatening to.

She heard footsteps, soft at first but then becoming louder. It would no doubt be the same man, the one who made her feel sick just by looking at him. Her eye was swollen from having his fist slammed into her face so many times, and her jaw ached. But it wasn't like she was being fed anything, so at least she'd been able to rest it.

'*Bonjour*, my love.' The thick German accent made her cringe, his words making her skin crawl. She knew that was exactly the reaction he wanted, but she could barely look at him when he flicked the light on and pushed open the cell door.

'What, not even a "good morning"?' he asked, speaking in German now.

She sighed and stood, not wanting to be curled into a ball in a submissive position with him standing over her. She kept her back straight and her expression neutral.

'Good morning,' she said in perfect German.

'Ah! She has a voice!' he said, his sarcasm not lost on her.

She waited to see what he would say to her next.

'Are you hungry?'

Rose nodded. There was no point lying; anyone in her position would be starving hungry. She actually had no idea how long she'd been captive, but she was certain it was long enough for Hazel and Sophia to know that something had gone terribly wrong. She thought of their safety constantly, hoped they weren't locked in a cell somewhere, or worse. And Sebastian. Would her brother and his lovely wife still be safe? She'd been fretting about them since her capture, too. Was he still alive? Were they both safe?

'Tell me what the codes mean,' he said plainly. 'All you need to do is give me something, some piece of information, and I'll have breakfast sent down to you.'

Rose thought for a moment, wondered whether she could tell him something trivial in exchange for something to eat. If she didn't have something soon then her energy would diminish completely, and she needed to stay physically and mentally strong.

'I know nothing of importance,' she replied, deciding to stay standing so she didn't feel so inferior beside him.

'We know you are a *courier*,' he said, spitting out the word. 'You are transporting information and devices. That means you have information to give me. You are working for someone.'

She knew there was no point flatly denying her involvement in the Resistance movement. They'd caught her with evidence. She was guilty, and there was no getting around that fact.

'I know nothing because I was paid to take those things,' she said quietly. 'I needed more money, so I said yes, and they told me I had to make it back or I wouldn't be paid. I am guilty.'

He smiled as if he believed he'd been the one to push her into finally talking, as if his tactics had succeeded.

'You see? So much easier when you talk.' His laugh was sinister, or maybe she hated him so much that she was imagining the cruel undertones. 'Perhaps we can be friends after all.'

Rose nodded, forcing a tight smile. 'I would receive a package, but I never saw who was delivering it. My job was to leave it near a train station,' she lied.

'That is all?' he asked.

Rose smiled. 'Yes. I don't want to get into trouble. I never meant to do anything wrong.'

'I will get you something to eat. I am a man of my word,' he announced as he turned around. 'When you're ready, you will tell me the rest.'

She watched him go, knew the second she saw him hesitate he was going to turn and say something else.

'If you don't tell me everything?' he said in a low, quiet voice. 'Then you will *never* eat again. I promise you that.'

Rose didn't doubt him. He liked her being passive, and if she didn't stay that way, she was certain her life would be short and miserable. She could die here, and no one would care. But she didn't want this filthy Nazi to get the satisfaction of seeing her take her last breath.

He returned with a piece of bread, covered in dripping, and a chipped cup half-full of water. She took it gratefully.

'Thank you,' she said, eyeing the piece of bread, her mouth full of saliva as she anticipated her first bite. She didn't care what it tasted like or how old it was; eating something, *anything*, would help her to stay alive.

Rose waited for him to leave before eating. Her stomach growled and groaned loudly in response, but she ate slowly. She chewed every tiny mouthful well and swallowed it down before pausing and taking another, wanting to feel full, knowing it might be the last thing she ate for some time. She sipped the water, too, a few little mouthfuls before finishing the piece of bread. She was still hungry, but it had taken the worst of the pains away and she knew it would give her more energy for whatever her captor had in store for her next.

She sat against the wall, the concrete so hard on her bottom that she felt as if her bones were protruding through her skin. Rose shut her eyes and willed sleep to find her, the cold seeping back through her body, chilling her right through as she imagined Peter's smiling face, imagined how warm she'd feel in his arms, the strength of his embrace.

'Get up!'

Rose was jolted awake by the rough voice, followed by something loud banging. She jumped up, bleary-eyed, realising she'd been asleep but not having any idea how long she'd been out.

'Get up!'

There had to be others. If it was only her he wanted to rouse, then why wouldn't he be standing in her cell?

Her door opened and she waited for instructions. A man pointed, one she hadn't seen before, and she obeyed, walking out and standing still. She wanted desperately to glance back, but he was holding a gun and the last thing she needed was to be smacked with the butt of it again and suffer more injuries.

There were more footsteps and she wondered who was there, but still she didn't look. Was she being taken out to be executed? She trembled at the thought even though she knew they wouldn't kill her yet. They hadn't tried hard enough to extract information from her; there was still so much they would do to her before they gave up on what she did or didn't know. The Resistance had been too disruptive for them not to question her hard. Surely?

'Walk!' The command was shouted and she started to move. It didn't take long before a guard pushed a door open and she stumbled out into the bright morning sunlight, the glare causing her to squint her eyes until it was like looking out from behind pinpricks.

But as her eyes adjusted and she was roughly shunted in the back, she realised what was happening. For whatever reason, they weren't going to interrogate her any more here. The cattle car was waiting for them on the tracks, already full of others. Rose stepped forward and clambered up when she was told to, looking at another woman who looked hungrier and far sadder than she about their situation.

Her heart bled for them all, seeing the looks on their faces, the haunted gazes staring back at her. These women would have children. Husbands. Grandchildren even. Their pain was so much worse than hers would ever be. The men would have wives they were desperate to protect.

The door was shut with a bang, and Rose stood up, clinging on to the sides. As they were juddered and shuddered every which way, she bravely held her hand to her heart and looked at the others crowded in with her.

'Have you heard the news?' a young man murmured, just as Rose opened her mouth.

She shut it and shook her head. 'What news?'

'It's happening. The Allies are coming, and soon.'

The smile on Rose's face grew so big she couldn't stop it. So it was true, it was happening. She didn't care how he knew and she certainly didn't ask questions, but it gave her a quiet hum in her chest, told her that perhaps all was not lost. 'Join me,' she said proudly, hand still on her heart. 'We'll sing "La Marseillaise" until our throats are hoarse and we cannot sing a breath longer.'

She started to sing their anthem, softly at first and then louder as her voice stopped quavering after so long being quiet. It didn't take long before others joined her, and soon every prisoner was defiantly singing their song – their French song that would be like torture to the Germans' ears.

'France for ever!' she yelled, before launching straight back into the anthem with all the gusto she could muster.

When her throat was hoarse from singing and the train began to slow, Rose felt some of her confidence start to fade. She looked around, wondered where they'd been taken and why. If the Germans were worried about an impending attack, why would they have brought them even closer to Normandy? Or perhaps they truly didn't know where to expect it. Maybe all their codes and incorrect messages had worked after all!

'Get out!' The words were shouted as the side of the car slid open. It was another prison. She'd hoped for that and not a longer trip to a camp near Germany, even though she knew they were both merely different forms of evil.

A guard grabbed her hair, dragging her down and shoving her forward. Tears burnt in her eyes but she refused to shed them. She just had to stay alive long enough for the invasion to happen. If she survived that long, she might just make it back home alive.

CHAPTER TWENTY-FOUR

HAZEL

'I should be happy about leaving.'

Hazel didn't care who could see them. She stood on tiptoe and threw her arms around Harry's neck, kissing him boldly on the lips. It would be the last time she'd ever see him, and engaged to be married or not, she was going to kiss him.

'You should definitely be happy about leaving,' she whispered in his ear, holding him tight. His body was warm against hers and she wished she'd been brave enough to kiss him days earlier. Perhaps then she'd have been able to spend more time with his arms encircling her.

'If anything changes, if you ever want to find me . . .'

Hazel pressed a finger to Harry's mouth. She couldn't think about him once he'd gone. She didn't need to be wondering *what if* and being miserable thinking of him if she ever made it home. All she wanted was the sweet memory of his kiss and the warmth of his body against hers when he held her.

Harry shuffled back a step and she hoped she hadn't leaned on him too hard. He was still limping badly, and she was certain he was gritting his teeth and braving the pain so she wouldn't worry about him.

'Here's my address,' he said, passing her a scrap of paper from his pocket. 'Memorise it then throw it away. Please.'

Hazel took it from him and stared at it, committed the address to memory immediately.

She stood still when he leaned back in, his lips soft as he stole one last kiss. He held his mouth to hers and they stayed like that, her tears trickling down to meet their lips. When he stepped back this time, he fanned his fingers down her cheeks and gave her a glimpse of his dimpled smile.

'Goodbye,' he whispered, fingertips brushing her arm before falling away.

She nodded, biting down on her bottom lip. *'Goodbye.'*

He limped away from her then and she stuffed her fist against her mouth, biting down on her own knuckles and staring at his back as he left. Harry never turned back, never looked at her one last time, and she held that memory of his smiling face in her mind as she fled back up to the attic. The men that had taken him were trustworthy, they were good at what they did, and so long as he managed to keep up, he'd be gone by nightfall.

There was nothing left for her to do, but the attic felt like her safe place. She lay down on the small bed up there and tucked her body into a ball. She'd been strong for months, and now she felt so hurt, it was like a knife had been embedded in her stomach.

Harry was gone, and instead of being overjoyed at him being safe, she was miserable. It was selfish and stupid, but it was the truth.

It was dangerous for them to have another shipment so soon after the last in the same location, and they were all starting to get nervous over the lack of contact from Rose, but they needed the weapons. It was too soon to know whether something had gone awfully wrong or whether the delay had simply been inevitable, but it wasn't stopping any of them from worrying. And Hazel hadn't received any information back that suggested something had happened. Which meant she needed to stop worrying and stay positive. Rose was alive, she had to be, and all her fretting wasn't doing anyone any good.

She listened in to her radio, smiling when she picked up the soothing voice of the BBC presenter. She stretched out, eyes shut, hearing every word even though to someone else she might look as if she was asleep.

And then she heard something that changed everything.

'Sophia!' she screamed, forgetting her usual muted tones, the fact that she always spoke quietly and quickly, and only to her intended audience, not the entire house. 'Sophia!' Hazel scribbled down the words, the poetry that she was certain meant . . . She sucked back a breath and went through it one more time. It had only taken her minutes and she was certain of the meaning.

'What is it?' Sophia asked, breathless as she suddenly appeared at the top of the stairs, leaning in the doorway.

'It's happening,' Hazel whispered, hardly able to believe it. 'They're going to be landing in Normandy soon. We have targets to attack, and we're to disrupt as much as we can before and during the invasion.'

Sophia's eyes widened. 'You're certain?'

'Yes, I'm certain!' Hazel said excitedly. 'Tell the others. They must do as they've been instructed.'

Sophia turned and took a step down before spinning around. 'I wish we knew where Rose was. I don't feel right.'

Hazel knew exactly what she meant. 'We need to stay safe, Sophia, in case there are urgent messages to be sent out.'

She nodded. 'I'll brief the others, you stay tuned in. And then rest a little. We need you well rested before all this starts to happen.'

Hazel doubted she'd ever be able to fall asleep now, but Sophia was right. Her heart skipped a beat as she carefully put her headset on, groaning when the transmission faded and she had to try to fiddle with her radio again. She needed Rose to ensure she could keep getting messages out, and most of all, she needed to know her friend was still alive.

Hazel stirred. She stretched out an arm, surprised to see darkness surrounding her. How long had she been sleeping? She'd doubted she'd be able to get even a wink of sleep, but she'd obviously been more tired than she'd realised. She went to sit up, swinging her legs down, and froze.

There was thumping. Then a bang. She stayed still, listening to her own breath pushing in and out. What was going on down there? Was that what had woken her up?

Hazel carefully put her feet down, not making a sound. She padded softly across the floor and listened at the door, wishing she hadn't shut it properly. She didn't dare turn the knob. Something was wrong. Something was happening down there that shouldn't be.

She kept her ear tight to the timber. And then her blood ran cold, her skin instantly turning to ice, every tiny hair on her body standing to attention.

The muffled bang was unmistakable. She stifled a scream, the silent call for help caught in her throat.

They'd been found. There was no other explanation. When she heard another bang, this one louder, followed by screams and shouts, she knew they were under attack. Suddenly gunfire exploded downstairs, and Hazel leapt into action. She grabbed for the radio, pulling it apart. They couldn't take the radio; it was the only piece of equipment that was truly crucial. It might need fixing, it might not be reliable, but it was still a valuable radio and she wasn't going to let anyone get their hands on it.

She hastily took it apart, knowing she couldn't take everything with her. It wasn't pitch-black yet, so she was able to see enough, but the truth was she knew the machine so well that she could have figured it out with her eyes closed.

Hazel turned, scanned the room and decided to hide some of the pieces. She ran to the window first, cringing as more gunfire echoed out from downstairs. She pushed the flimsy curtain aside, looked down and gasped when she saw the commotion. There were Germans everywhere. She definitely wouldn't be able to get the radio out, because her chances of getting away from the chateau herself were . . . She dashed back to the radio pieces. She knew it was unlikely she'd get away. The only positive was that the Germans were wasting their time here instead of preparing for the landings, which meant the intelligence must have been correct. They couldn't know where and when it was happening!

Hazel stashed one part under the pillow on the bed, then another piece high in the wardrobe, standing on tiptoe to reach it. After scurrying over to the bed and pulling it out, yanking hard with all her might, she packed the rest of the radio in her satchel. She pulled up two loose floorboards and stuffed the satchel inside, then replaced the boards and hefted the metal legs of the bed back across the floor. The noise would have alerted anyone to the fact someone was up there, but they'd have eventually come looking anyway.

Hazel glanced around the room, knew there was nothing else she could do. She could have taken the pieces of the radio and strewn them outside, getting rid of them individually, but she had to believe that someone would survive, that one of her own would come frantically looking for the parts she'd hidden. If Rose returned and they were all gone, she would be able to transmit at least.

She pushed the curtain aside again, praying that no one would see the movement. The only light now was from the moon, sitting high in the sky and illuminating the roof for her. She pushed the window open and climbed up, the narrow opening almost too small to squeeze through. The roof was steep and she had no idea how she was going to safely clamber down, but her only other option was to open the door and walk down the stairs into certain death.

She looked down and wished she hadn't. It was like the night she'd jumped from the plane into France, only then she'd had a parachute to stop her from falling and smashing all her bones.

She heard shouting and loud footsteps, knew they were coming upstairs. Hazel fought the urge to freeze and await her fate, half sliding, half scrambling down the first part of the roof. Her feet crashed into something hard, the jarring feeling shooting up her legs and through her body, but she didn't pause. A gunshot echoed out, a bullet whirring too close to her for comfort, and she glanced up, knowing they were on to her whereabouts.

Hazel scurried as fast as she could, staying low, sliding down the next part of the roof and then wriggling. She dropped, hands scrambling for the downpipe as she slid the rest of the way. It gave way, breaking and sending her spiralling to the ground, and she landed with a loud thump on the grass below. The wind came out of her with a big gasp and she struggled to inhale again, but she didn't have time to stop and feel sorry for herself. She rolled over, used her hands to push herself up and staggered away, running towards the wooded area, arms pumping as she sprinted for the trees. She saw others, knew she wasn't alone, but they were shooting back, retreating but probably trying to find somewhere safer to position themselves. She had nothing. No gun, no knife, *nothing*. Her training had taught her to kill a man with her bare hands if she had to, and she'd already proven to herself that she had the guts to do it, but nothing was going to help her against men with guns, men who were hunting her and every other Resistance member.

There was no way she was getting out of this. She was as good as dead. If they caught her, she'd never say a word, which meant days of pain before they'd finally kill her.

CHAPTER TWENTY-FIVE

SOPHIA

Sophia clung tightly to the tree. Her arms were scratched, her skin bruised and torn from climbing the trunk and pushing her way up the branches. She'd been near the back door when they'd been raided. She'd been about to go up and look for Hazel, wanting to see how she felt about Harry's departure and make sure she wasn't too worried. It was obvious there was something between Hazel and Harry, it would have been obvious to anyone, and she'd hoped for her friend's sake that Harry made it home safely.

She shuddered as she listened to screams below, squeezing her eyes shut and wishing she could block it out. Her natural instinct was to drop down and fight, to do anything she could, but her bare hands were nothing against the men below toting guns.

Hazel.

Sophia dug her fingernails into the trunk, the pain inside her impossible to comprehend. The only other time she'd even come close to this kind of pain was seeing her mother . . . She pushed away the memory, refusing to let it in. There was nothing she could do. Nothing.

She could try to drop slowly, quietly, or she could try to sneak up on one of them and take a gun, but the probability of either of those things working was almost nil. Her training was clear; she had to do whatever she could do to protect herself. She had to hide and wait and get up to the attic. She had to secure anything she could that was left in the house, and then get to the next closest cell and re-establish.

'Let me go! I have nothing to say!'

Sophia's blood ran cold as she heard the scream. Icy, painfully cold. In the moonlight Sophia could see Hazel, held on each side by Gestapo, her legs kicking frantically as the men each clutched an arm. She was like a wildcat, scratching and clawing and squealing.

Whack.

Sophia gasped. One of the men had clearly had enough. His fist connected with Hazel's face and she went limp, falling to the ground. The other man gave her a kick before hauling her back up. She stumbled, blood dripping from her nose and down her top – the lights from one of their vehicles had suddenly perfectly illuminated her face. There was silence for a moment, or perhaps it was the ringing in Sophia's ears that made everything else silent for her. And then Hazel started to fight again.

Sophia listened to her friend yelling and wished she'd just go quietly, knew they'd probably go easier on her if she was meek and mild. But Hazel was a fighter, and she knew in her heart that she would never give anything away.

She waited for a gun to fire, for the blast that would take Hazel's life, but instead she heard her friend swear as they dragged her away, feet trailing in the dirt as they hauled her to one of their trucks.

Before, the lawn and trees had been full of gunfire. The maquis had battled hard, but she knew most of them were dead, strewn across the grass. There would be Germans dead, too, but she guessed they'd lost fewer. They were the ones who'd taken them by surprise, which meant they were always going to come out victorious. Hazel had been so worried about staying, about their location being discovered, and Sophia had been the one insisting they wait until Rose was back. She blinked away tears. Rose was gone. It had been days since they'd waved her goodbye, and she would have returned by now if she could have. They should have left; they could have left a coded message and disappeared, moved on so they had less chance of being found.

A pain in Sophia's side intensified and she slipped one hand from the tree and pressed it to the soreness. She was surprised to feel moisture, a stickiness that she hadn't been expecting.

What happened? What was . . . ?

Sophia lifted her hand and rubbed her fingers together. It was blood. Had she been shot?

When she'd been running, she'd felt pain, a stinging, burning sensation against her side, but she hadn't had time to react. All she'd cared about was getting away, running past anyone in her way and finding somewhere to hide. She'd been terrified they'd have tracking dogs, that they'd find her and she'd be sitting up the tree with nowhere to go. And then she'd seen them with Hazel and . . .

Sophia held on, feeling woozy now that she'd touched the blood. She'd been through worse. That night she'd first met Rose, landing on her doorstep in the middle of the night, slumped and bloodied against her door. This wasn't as bad as that.

Sophia shut her eyes tight again, waiting, knowing it was too soon to go down yet. If she was going to cling to a tree and watch her friend be taken, then she was going to make damn sure that she made it count. Her only problem was that she had no idea how she was going to travel the sixty-odd miles to the next cell on her own if she did manage to escape. With no help, no transport and a gunshot wound that would make her journey almost unbearable.

Sophia made her way as carefully as she could down the tree. She had no concept of how long she'd been waiting, clinging there in the dark, but there hadn't been any noise for what she was certain were hours. If she waited longer, then she risked them coming back to check the house over in the daylight, especially if someone they'd captured talked and gave any information away. She stretched once she landed, her legs heavy and achy from being in the same position for so long.

The risk now was that they'd left someone in wait. There could be someone hiding, watching to see who emerged and came back to the house. If only she had a weapon. But she didn't and she was going to have to risk it.

She walked quickly but was as careful as she could be. She headed straight for the house. The moonlight was almost completely covered by a mist of clouds, which made it nearly impossible to see. But she kept going, determined, knowing she had a small window of time, one opportunity before the sun rose. She had to gather what she needed, secure what she could and then head north before it started to get light.

Sophia entered the house. She strained to listen, her breath loud in her own ears as she waited, expecting to hear something, but there was nothing. Only long stretches of silence greeted her, so different from the house that had been heaving with people up until a short time ago. They were fortunate in that so many of the maquis had gone. Even though they might have had a chance at surviving against the Germans if they'd been here, they would have lost so many more men and all of their plans would have been interrupted. As it was, she had no idea how she was going to warn the other cells, get word to London and Paris before things got worse. How much did they know? How many cells were they infiltrating?

She refused to think about Rose. Rose would never have talked, nothing would have made her give up her friends or anyone in the Resistance, but she hadn't made it back and that meant something had definitely gone awry.

Sophia stopped when she saw the first body. Face down, a huge wound through his back. She didn't need to turn him over to know he was dead. As she moved through the house there were more. Bodies were strewn everywhere, not all of them theirs, but most. There was blood splattered across the walls, pools of it seeping into the floor, and she was thankful there was no smell yet or she'd have been gagging with every step she took.

She stopped to touch one man, slumped against the wall. Sophia placed her fingers to his neck, waiting, silent as she hoped to find a sign of life. But as with all the others she'd come across, there was nothing. She moved fast, eyes straining as much as her ears to see. There was only one place she needed to go, and that was upstairs. Hazel had been taken, but that didn't mean her equipment had. She hurried, focused on where she had to go and not letting herself think about anything else. Creaks echoed out from under her feet, but she'd quickly realised that the likelihood of anyone surprising her now was almost non-existent. If they were lying in wait, she'd have been long dead by now.

She placed one foot on the stairs, about to race up, when a noise made all the blood drain from her face. Sophia paused, spun around, her heart in her throat.

'Halt.'

Sophia came face to face with a German. He was crawling, his face screwed up in pain, but his intent clear. He was holding a gun but his hand was shaking and she quickly moved out of his line of fire. He groaned and tried to follow her, but she was too fast for an injured soldier fallen to his knees.

'Halt!' he screamed, but it came out as more of a plea, his voice faltering as she stared at him.

Sophia dodged his aim again, cringing when he fired the gun. It shot through the wall to her left, and she knew that she had no choice but to disarm him. He might be injured, but his desire to kill her was strong, and she wasn't going to walk away from him only to have him shoot her in the back.

She'd passed another dead German on her way in, and she was furious with herself that she hadn't taken his gun then and there. She made her way back and found him, bending to push him over. He was heavy and she had to shove him hard, her heart in her throat as she listened to the shuffles of the other man near the staircase, rattled now after being so certain she was the only living person left in the house.

She collected the pistol, checked it and made her way straight back to her enemy. There were many things she could have done; disarming him by overpowering him and killing him with her bare hands had been her first thought, but this was safer. And if she died or hurt herself right now? Then thousands of maquisards, the rural French Resistance fighters who relied on them, who were so vital to their movement, would be effectively left in the dark.

She walked closer, stood over him from behind. He went to move, went to turn around and take aim, but she was already waiting, pistol head high. A cool rush of calm passed through her body, her mind clear as she stared at the enemy in front of her. Sophia squeezed the trigger, pulled it back and held the gun steady, refusing to look away when the bullet entered his head and killed him before he'd had a chance to do the same to her. This time when she stepped over him and started up the staircase, she kept the gun with her, ready to take anyone down who dared to stand in her way.

Her heart was racing, pounding in her chest as she took the steps two at a time. She paused at the top, dizzy and pressing her hand against her side as she nudged the door open and scanned the room. It was silent up there, but everything had been upturned. Sophia glanced where the radio had been, where she'd last seen Hazel sitting, her back to her. Hazel had turned and smiled, laughing at something when she'd teased her about Harry. She hadn't known at the time that they'd never share another moment like it.

Sophia gasped, the weight of everything that had happened, what she'd survived, what she'd *done*, hitting her. She fought the urge to fall to her knees, to give up, to berate herself for sitting in a tree and watching her friend get taken so brutally. But she couldn't. *This* was how she helped her friends. *This* was what they'd want her to do.

She took a moment instead, inhaled deeply and positioned herself in the middle of the room. She grabbed a pillow off the bed and took the pillowcase off, smiling when she saw a wooden piece from Hazel's radio fall to the bed. She left that and quickly tore the pillowcase, fastening it tight to her side now that the bleeding had started up again. Then she looked around, knowing the other parts must be hidden in the room. Hazel must have heard what was happening and had a chance to hide the parts, and she'd obviously broken it down. The trick now was to find them all, and hope that she hadn't tried to run with the rest of the radio.

Sophia remembered the secret boards in the room. She knelt beside the bed and leaned down lower, squinting and seeing nothing. The bed had been moved, but not very far, so she hauled it out from the wall and shoved it away as far as she could. On hands and knees, she felt around, glancing behind to make sure no one had followed her, that no one was about to surprise her with a gun pointed to her head.

No one was there, but she was still unnerved about being in a house filled with so many dead bodies, and possibly another not-dead one.

She kept feeling around and connected with a groove, a slight imperfection that didn't fit against the other board, that made her certain she'd found it. Sophia scrambled forward some more, tugging at the board and then the one beside it. She grinned when she uncovered the hole and stuck her hand inside, connecting with a bag of some sort. Quickly she pulled it out, recognising Hazel's satchel, and making sure there was nothing else there. She opened it, looked inside and saw the metal parts she'd been hoping for. She had no idea where else to look, but Hazel had obviously broken the machine down into parts so the entire thing couldn't be discovered too easily. She might even have had a simple piece on her.

And then she saw something that made emotion clog her throat, tears filling her eyes almost instantly. It was Hazel's red lipstick, the one Rose had given her before she'd left. She reached for the Elizabeth Arden case, holding it tight, fingers clenching around it as she thought about her friends, the only other two women in the world she'd ever trusted that way. They both meant the world to her, and now they were gone. She opened the case and carefully swept the lipstick across her lips, leaning into the little mirror above a large piece of bedroom furniture. It was filthy and the light was still impossible, but she could see enough to make sure she wasn't drawing on her face. Once she was finished, she slipped the case into her pocket, a little something of Hazel's to remember her by. Then she rummaged around, found one of Hazel's shirts and quickly changed into it, grateful that they were a similar size.

Sophia froze when she heard a noise. Her ears pricked, body on high alert. It could have just been the old house moving, it could have been anything, but she knew it was time to get out. She frantically searched for the other piece, knowing there had to be another part, pulling down books from the bookcase. Then, frustrated, she opened the wardrobe, yanking things down and then standing on tiptoe, arm extended to feel around.

Got it! She connected with a piece of cold metal, exactly what she'd been looking for. She quickly put the other pieces in the satchel and walked on silent feet across the room and back down the stairs, placing the strap of the satchel across her neck to drape diagonally between her shoulders. She hoped she'd found it all, did a quick check and ran through everything in her mind. She'd been trained in radioing, too, only it had been some time since she'd worked the equipment herself.

It was silent now, and she hoped it stayed that way until she left. Sophia made her way to the kitchen, knowing her efforts would be fruitless if she didn't have something to eat or drink or both with her. There was a meat safe that had been turned into a real safe some time ago, and she was thankful she'd been trusted with the code. She turned the dial, put in the correct numbers and reached in for all the money the safe held. She quickly stuffed it into her satchel, along with two papers she saw in there containing codes that could be useful.

Sophia then turned and scanned the kitchen, the space a mess from so many people using the same house. She opened a cupboard, looked for something, *anything*, to eat. She found some bread and put the chunk into the satchel. It would have to do. She fetched a mug and filled it with water, gulped it down and then turned to go. There were some old bicycles out in the shed, and she knew they were her only hope to get away fast enough. On foot she'd be too slow.

She kept glancing around outside, scanning the trees and thinking every shadow was the enemy, but she saw no one. When she reached the shed she hauled the rickety old door back and found an equally rickety-looking bicycle staring back at her, beside a crate half-full of apples. The bicycle was propped against a stack of old crates and covered in cobwebs, but she didn't care. She quickly wiped it down, using her hand to get the dust from the seat and the webs from the handlebars. Then she took some apples to fill her satchel with, put the satchel in the basket at the front and pushed the bicycle out, wobbling as she got up on the seat and started to pedal. She struggled over the grass, pushing as hard as she could past the gnarled apple trees in the orchard. At least with her bag full of fruit she had a cover story, since she could be taking them to a friend or a relative, and with any luck they might help her to avoid detection.

She had a long ride ahead of her, but all she was going to think about with every push of the pedal were the thousands of maquisards who were relying on her. She was the only one left from the chateau, and if the message hadn't been received by everyone that the landings were imminent, then they could lose the war. They needed to disrupt the lines and cause mayhem to ensure the German focus was anywhere *but* Normandy.

She gritted her teeth and settled into a steady rhythm.

There was no way *that* was happening on her watch.

CHAPTER TWENTY-SIX

HAZEL

Blood poured from Hazel's nose and down to her mouth, slipping past and dripping from her chin. She kept her face tucked close to her knees, refusing to let so much as one tear fall. She was stronger than that. No one was going to see that they'd defeated her.

No one.

She wondered what had happened to Sophia, whether Rose had been dead for days and they hadn't even known. She squeezed her eyes shut, tried so hard to push the dark thoughts away, imagining her friends lying on the ground, bodies contorted, life squeezed from them.

She'd lost everything. *Everything.* The only thing she had left now was her bravery, her strength at refusing to say anything that would give her friends and her colleagues away. They could beat her all they liked, but she'd never talk.

Hazel lifted her hand, cringing when she parted her lips, the pain of moving after the beatings she'd received almost too much to bear. She touched her breast, felt the pill sewn into the pouch there. All this time it had been with her, a constant companion of sorts, an option if she was pushed to her limits.

She imagined swallowing. She'd been told she would be dead within seconds, maybe a little longer. If she used her fingernails to get it out, if she raised the pill to her lips and put it under her tongue, if she bit down on it . . .

Hazel dropped her hand, fisting it instead. *No.*

She wasn't a coward, and she wasn't about to give up now. There was a chance she could escape. There was a chance she could live, that she could help others, that she could be useful in the war again if she survived.

Swallowing that pill would be the easy way out, the coward's way out, and she was strong enough to keep going. At least for now. The vehicle lurched and she slammed back, hitting her head and wincing. She tried to see where they were but it was still so dark. She'd been somewhere first, a house, where they'd asked her questions and taken pleasure in using their fists and boots on her, but now . . .

'Get out!'

She stumbled as a rough hand reached for her, yanking her arm so hard she wondered if it would disconnect from its socket. One of her eyes was almost closed over, the swelling rapid, but she used her good eye to look around, to try to get a bearing on where she was. If she had the chance to escape, she needed to be armed with as much information as possible.

Hazel did her best to walk without stumbling as she was shoved forward, wondering how long they'd travelled for. She'd woken at one point, which meant she must have passed out, so she didn't know how many hours they could have been driving.

A push from behind almost sent her sprawling, but she lifted her feet just in time to step into the building. There were guards nearby, and a shiver ran through her as she realised she was in a prison. It must have been commandeered by the Germans, and she wondered how many others were being held there. Would she be thrown in with men? Would they . . . She gulped, staggering as she tripped on something, her eye completely swollen over now. She thought of Harry, tried to summon happy thoughts and push away the terror of being raped and beaten and tortured. She just needed to focus on his smiling face. Had to believe he'd made it safely away.

The butt of a rifle slammed against her elbow. She stopped, almost numb to the additional pain. A metal door was pulled back and she was pushed forward. She stood, suddenly overwhelmed with tears when the door was shut with a slam.

It might only be a short reprieve, but it was enough.

She slowly, silently sank to the floor as she looked around, her strength disappearing now she was being left alone. There were narrow beds, lumps that she presumed were people sleeping on them, but other than that she couldn't make anything out.

Hazel curled into a ball, the concrete as cold as ice and eating into her skin as she huddled tight. She was so tired, all she wanted was to sleep.

CHAPTER TWENTY-SEVEN

ROSE

Rose gritted her teeth and tried to stop them from chattering. She was so, so cold, and no matter what the time of night or day, her bones never seemed to thaw.

Someone new had arrived into their already packed cell during the night, and the poor girl was still curled up on the floor, her body curved around itself as if she was fruitlessly trying to protect her stomach and face.

'Hey,' Rose said, placing a hand on her shoulder and gently shaking it. 'Wake up.'

They were in a cell of all women, and she gathered that most of them were suspected of being part of the Resistance. She had no idea how she herself was still alive. Perhaps she'd done a half-decent job of convincing them that she was a good Frenchwoman who'd done something wrong, feeding them little bits of information that seemed helpful.

'Argghhhh,' the woman moaned.

She slowly rolled over and Rose kept her hand on her, wanting her to know she wasn't alone. The woman pulled her hands from her face and Rose gasped at her swollen, bruised eye, but then she stifled a scream, falling to the ground beside her.

'Hazel?' she whispered. 'Oh, Hazel, what have they done to you?'

Even with the blood-matted hair and contused eye it was unmistakably Hazel. Rose cradled her, pulling her up and holding on to her as they both cried.

'You're alive,' Hazel whispered through badly swollen lips. 'We were so worried about you.'

'What happened?' Rose asked, carefully taking strands of Hazel's hair off her face. 'Where is Sophia?' Her stomach twisted and she wished she hadn't asked.

'I don't know,' Hazel said. 'I don't know what happened to her. But they came for us, they knew where we were and . . .' Her voice trailed off and Rose held her and rocked her as if she were a child. 'We were supposed to be working in small groups – there were too many of us coming and going. We put ourselves at risk.'

'I'm sorry I never made it back to you,' Rose said, trying hard not to break down and cry. She'd been so strong, so stoic through her whole ordeal, but seeing Hazel like this, both of them being in the cell together, it was almost enough to break her.

There were moans and murmurs from around them, and Rose helped Hazel up, wanting to get her off the cold concrete. Her hands were frozen, her face ashen probably from the shock as much as the conditions, and they only had one tiny bed to share. But they'd fit if they tucked up close together, and their body heat would help.

With the two of them lying side by side, Hazel's back to her chest, she ran her hand up and down Hazel's thigh, trying to help thaw her out.

'How bad is it?' Hazel asked, her teeth chattering. 'What do they do to you?'

Rose took in a deep, shuddering breath. She couldn't deny Hazel the truth; it would make her better prepared. 'It's bad,' she said. 'It's . . .'

She chose her words carefully. 'They beat you, and then they offer a little something, to get you to talk. They try to pretend they aren't so cruel. You need to give them something.'

'Have you told them anything?' Hazel whispered.

Rose was still cautious, didn't trust any of the women in her cell. They hadn't done anything wrong by her, and they all seemed nice enough, but they were starving and desperate to be released; who knew whether they would use information to get out? She shook her head, just a tiny movement, and she knew Hazel would have felt it.

'Are we near Normandy?' Hazel whispered.

'Yes,' Rose replied.

'We'll be safe soon then,' Hazel said, chattering still. 'It's happening.'

Rose took a deep breath and held Hazel tight. She needed her old friend to survive. She could die, was prepared to die if she had to, but not Hazel. Please, God, not Hazel.

CHAPTER TWENTY-EIGHT

SOPHIA

Sophia's legs were burning. There was a deep, painful heat building in her calf muscles and sweeping up into her thighs, pushing down into the balls of her feet and then tingling up every inch of her. Her hips were achy and her hands gripped the handlebars so tight that her knuckles were white. But she never stopped pedalling.

She'd been going for perhaps two hours, she wasn't sure. But the sun was now high in the sky and a constant beading of sweat had formed above her top lip and greased her forehead. She was hot and wet, but nothing was going to stop her. Thankfully she'd been to the other cell, almost a year ago, before she'd even met Rose, so she had a rough idea of where she was heading and how to get there.

It was a long journey, though, and she knew the reality of that kind of bicycle ride. Her hands would be blistered, along with her feet. She'd be so hungry and thirsty that she'd collapse with exhaustion, her legs buckling beneath her the moment she got off. But nothing was going to slow her down or squash her determination. *Nothing other than a German.*

Up ahead she would pass through a small village, and she knew there was a chance she could be stopped. There would be a patrol there, perhaps guards watching and waiting where she couldn't see them. Sophia kept on, taking one hand off the handlebars to swipe across her upper lip, not wanting to ruin her lipstick and look a fright if she had to flirt with danger.

She kept pedalling – another ten minutes, then another, perhaps half an hour – and then she saw them. The Germans *were* waiting, standing there, looking around. They were talking, looking unworried about life, and as she approached she forced a huge grin and waved out, wobbling a little and then laughing at herself as she did it again once she was closer.

'Hello there!' she called out in German as she passed by.

One of them laughed and smiled back, another grunted. She smiled at the one who looked least impressed of the three of them, and grabbed an apple from her basket and tossed it to him.

'Enjoy!' she called out.

She puckered her lips and blew a kiss, knowing the men would probably love her full lips covered in red lipstick. This was why female agents were so good; it was easy to flirt with a man and give the impression that she was nothing more than a silly girl, and most of the time they bought it.

'Stop!' one of the men commanded.

She inhaled deeply, slowing and putting one foot down to stop and steady herself.

'I'll be back past again soon!' she said in a sing-song voice. 'Off to give these apples to my grandmother and check she's all right. Would you all like one?'

She picked one out, then another, offering them and grinning when the two men took them. She kept eye contact, glancing away every now and again as if she were shy in their company.

'Let her go,' the closest man said. 'Come see us on your way back.' The knowing look he gave her made her want to retch.

She waved and pedalled off, terrified she would wobble and tip over. Her legs were already shaky, her balance terrible, and they'd been so close to seeing what was in her basket. The radio parts, the money, the codes . . .

Sophia gulped and kept going, not rushing, not wanting to alert them. She wasn't even halfway yet, and she had to keep going.

Sophia had started to slow. She'd been going for hours. How many, she had no idea, but she'd been cycling all day and her movements were getting sluggish. She had recognised the house, a small, nondescript cottage that was set well back from the road, and she was heading towards it, so close to collapsing but refusing to give in.

She neared, wobbling as she put one foot down and then dropped the bicycle and staggered off, her remaining apples careening from the basket and leaving her satchel to fall on to the grass beside them. Sophia stumbled as she tried to reach for it, her legs seizing and crying out to her to lie down.

'Stop!'

She looked up and into the eyes of a man she'd never seen before. His gaze was menacing, reminding her instantly of the Gestapo, but he was wearing plain clothes and she knew she was at the right place.

'We were ambushed,' she croaked out, desperately in need of water. 'I have what I could save. I need . . .'

'What's the password?' he demanded, pulling out a knife and grabbing her by the hair, yanking her up.

She flapped her hands, clawed at his grasp, but when the cool blade of the knife pressed to her throat, she stopped moving.

'I don't know the password!' she insisted. 'But I have been here before. They used to call me the fox.' Please not the *password* game again!

He laughed. 'Try again.'

She heard someone, knew at least one other person had joined them outside, but she couldn't look over her shoulder to see.

She inhaled, let her body go slack, remembered her training. These men were tough and strong, good fighters and prepared to do anything, but they hadn't received the dedicated training that she had in London. They were often too quick to act, and not fast enough to listen first.

Sophia breathed deep again, feeling the blade, feeling his hands on her, knowing instinctively that his grip with one hand wasn't solid. She spun then, using one hand to smack the knife away and the other to push him. She took him by surprise and jumped back once she'd got away, touching her neck, knowing he'd nicked her with the blade.

'Don't ever do that to me again,' she spat out. 'I've travelled all day on that wretched bike to get here, and I have an urgent message, not to mention a radio and money for you.'

Her would-be captor glared back at her, eyes narrowed. He would have been handsome if he hadn't been looking like he wanted to kill her. She let herself glance around then, saw there were in fact two more men outside and more in the small house looking out.

'How can we trust you?' one of the other men asked, arms folded across his chest.

'You can trust me when I show you this,' she said, opening the satchel so he could see inside and then throwing it to him. He caught it easily. 'That's all the money from the chateau and something to start building a radio with if you don't already have one. I'm the only one left. The others were either already gone, killed when we were ambushed or . . .' She swallowed, her mouth dry. 'Taken. My friend Hazel was taken.'

'Wait, *Hazel?*' The man straightened, his face changing from harsh to warm. He gave her an odd kind of half-smile. 'My sister, Rose, was working with an old friend of ours named Hazel.'

Sophia could have cried. 'Sebastian?' she asked quietly. 'You're Rose's brother.'

He nodded. 'Where is she? Is she safe?'

Sophia shook her head. 'I'm so sorry. She didn't return from her last job, and Hazel was taken last night. I'm the only one left.'

Sebastian nodded, holding his hand out. She clasped it, his palm warm against hers as he shook her hand. There was suddenly so much left unsaid between them, and there was nothing she could say to reassure him as she broke their connection. His face was gaunt, his eyes pained as he stared back at her, but a noise from behind made her turn. It was Pierre. She'd thought he was dead from what they'd been told upon arrival at the chateau, but clearly he'd simply moved on.

'Pierre?' She smiled when he walked towards her with open arms.

'Little fox, come here,' he said affectionately.

'The Allies are landing in Normandy,' she told him, starting to feel dizzy. 'We have to act now, we have to . . .'

She went to move but her legs buckled, and when she looked down she saw the dark red stain on her top. She'd forgotten about the bullet. All that time, riding past those soldiers, and . . .

The grass rushed up to meet her, the sky spinning when she looked up.

'Catch her!' she heard Pierre yell as Sebastian lurched towards her.

Blackness engulfed Sophia as someone caught her under the arms, the world whirling as she shut her eyes and gave in to the darkness cradling her.

Sophia stood and stretched, moving to the window to look out. She'd had a restless sleep, as always, hearing noises and certain that they were about to be raided. It had been five days since she'd arrived, and her blisters and bullet wound had finally started to heal. Her legs were still aching and she'd been so exhausted when she'd arrived, but it was the worry for her friends, the sadness for all the lives that had been taken when hers had been spared, that had taken the biggest, most lasting toll on her.

She had a big night ahead of her tonight, and she was thankful that she'd been able to wake early. More than a few hours' sleep and she'd do nothing but toss and turn, more exhausted than before she'd gone to bed.

The shipment of arms was arriving soon, and it was she who was going to guide it in, just as she'd done in the past with Hazel. Since that terrible night at the chateau, she'd taken over radioing, and even though she wasn't nearly as fast or talented as her friend, she'd managed to do the job well enough and build a new radio from the parts she'd brought and what was already at the house. Some of the men, including Sebastian, had gone the night she'd arrived, their target a transport line that ran to Normandy, and she'd taken over the role of communications to ensure they were aware of what was going on at all times.

She kept replaying the conversation she'd had with Sebastian over and over in her mind, wishing she'd had the chance to get to know him better. She could understand why Rose was so fond of him; there was a kindness about him when he spoke, a warmness in his gaze that reminded her of Alex. And just like her Alex, there was a strength about him that made others look up to him. Sophia had been able to tell how much Sebastian's men respected him by the way they stopped talking to listen to him, following his orders without question.

The poor man had been consumed with worry about his sister, though, not to mention his wife.

'I was under no illusions about our work here, but I never expected my sister to become so involved.'

'She's very good at what she does,' Sophia said. 'She saved my life once and I would trust her to do it again in a heartbeat.'

'You know,' he'd said with a laugh, 'she used to drive our parents mad sometimes. They were desperate for her to settle down, but until she met Peter, she was so outspoken and determined to have her voice heard, they wondered if she'd ever marry. I suppose her work here shouldn't have surprised me so.'

'And Peter settled her down?' Sophia asked. The Rose she knew was quietly determined, and would stop at nothing to help their cause.

'No, Peter loved my sister for who she was. He liked her opinions and her intelligence, and all he ever wanted was to make her happy.'

Sophia nodded. 'And your wife? What news have you had of her?'

Sebastian met her gaze and she wished she hadn't asked. 'I've had no word for days now. It's the first time we've been separated since . . .'

She waited as he cleared his throat, as if he was wondering whether to tell her something or not.

'She left the Resistance for a short time and had to travel back to Paris. For family matters,' he said hurriedly. 'But since her return we've worked side by side.'

'I can't offer you empty promises about their safety, because we all know the reality of being here,' Sophia said, placing a hand to his shoulder. 'But I can promise you that if I have the chance to help Rose, I will do anything in my power to save her.'

Sebastian gave her a long stare before opening his arms and holding her tight. She'd held him back, feeling oddly comfortable in the embrace of a man she hardly knew. But there was a familiarity about Sebastian being Rose's brother, a connection to the people she'd lost.

'Hazel was very close to my family,' he said as he pulled away. 'If there's anything we can do to help her, if you have any word at all . . .'

'Rose and Hazel are both my family now, too,' she said. 'You focus on your work and finding your wife, and let me worry about them.'

Sophia brushed away tears as she thought of Sebastian's drawn, tired face as he'd walked away from her. She pushed away her thoughts and readied herself, then went out to the kitchen to find something to eat, pleased that the house was empty. She was the only woman amongst an ever-growing group of men coming and going from the house, and although it didn't bother her, she liked the few quiet moments she had. The night before, they'd been planning their next mission, ready to target the trucks that would be travelling in convoy and filled with German arms. The idea of the chaos they would cause was enough to put a smile on Sophia's face, but she also felt the pressure of the part she had to play weighing heavy on her shoulders. She had set the coordinates and she would guide the plane in. She was effectively in charge of arming hundreds of men.

Sophia looked through the grubby window and saw a few men outside. She headed out, calling to them and beckoning for them to follow her.

'We're going now?' one of them asked.

She nodded. 'We are.'

Sophia climbed aboard her bicycle, and two of the men did the same, coming with her to keep her safe and assist her as needed. By the time they had a blanket cover of darkness, all three of them were in position, tucked behind trees. Soon they would hear the faint sound of trucks in the distance, and men would be arriving on foot and hiding.

The rumble soon alerted her to the fact that the plane was coming in on time. She listened to her thumping heart and then stepped out. She raised her light and turned it on, using it to guide the plane, signalling and standing bravely as it came in. From then on it was a blur. Men appeared from nowhere in the dark; boxes were unloaded and carried away; and the plane disappeared into the sky again, leaving them in the field alone, in the dark, their breaths clouding around them.

'Let's go,' Sophia ordered, going back to find her bicycle.

The moon was high and when the clouds finally drifted out of the way, its light guided her. She took a moment to look up, to smile and remember the nights she'd spent with Rose, transporting soldiers under the crescent moon to the waiting submarines. It seemed like a lifetime ago.

A pop sounded out, in the distance, but loud enough to make her pause.

'What . . . ,' she began, her voice a whisper as she spun around, mouth open.

The noise that echoed around her was louder this time, jolting one of her companions back, his body staggering and then falling to the ground.

Sophia started to run, her arms pumping, not knowing where the enemy was or how many there might be or . . .

Boom.

The noise was a bang, an explosion of sorts, but when the force entered her body all she heard was a *thwack*. Heat billowed through her, starting as a sharp sting and quickly reaching a crescendo when it exploded inside her.

She grabbed at her abdomen and sobbed as she spiralled down.

'I've got you!'

Someone grabbed her, someone had hold of her, strong arms pulling her and then throwing her up in the air. She thought she was on someone's shoulders, that she was being carried like a sack of potatoes, but she had no idea.

The only thing she knew was that she'd been shot, that her body was so hot, as if she was on fire. It was the third time she'd had a bullet enter her body, and there was no mistaking what had happened to her.

Or that it was someone friendly who was carrying her.

'Alex?' she mumbled, laughing as she bumped along in the dark and gunfire sounded around them, her mind all foggy. She tried to push past the haze, tried to make sense of where she was as everything blurred.

'Alex?' she asked again.

She could see his dark eyes, feel the warmth of his embrace, the smile that had always greeted her whenever she'd arrived home.

'Alex,' she whispered again.

Alex had her. Or maybe she was dead and that's how she'd found him.

'*Alex,*' she whispered one last time, before shutting her weary eyes and feeling every ounce of life drain from her body as she did so.

'You're going to be fine. We're going to get you home.'

Sophia opened her eyes, then shut them quickly. Home? Was she still alive?

Pain exploded in her abdomen again, and when she opened her eyes just enough, slits to peer through, everything was still fuzzy, pain blurring everything around her. There were people working on her, doing something. Was she back at the house?

'Argghh!'

She heard a noise, realised her mouth was open, that she was the one making it.

'You're doing great. The bullet's out, we're just stitching you up.'

She went to resist, to move, but her hands were being held down, keeping her still. Sophia fought the waves of pain, knew she'd been shot, that they were trying to help her, but it hurt so badly.

'Sebastian?' she asked, wondering if it was Rose's brother.

'Sebastian's not coming back. He's gone,' came a rough, hoarse reply. 'We were fired at when we were trying to explode the German tanks. We lost men.'

Sophia started to cry. She couldn't help it. Tears streamed down her cheeks. How would she ever tell Rose that her brother was dead?

'We're not going to let you die. We'll get you out of here,' the same voice said.

Alex was her home. She wanted to tell someone that, but when she opened her mouth all that came out was another moan. She wanted Alex. All she wanted was Alex.

She sobbed then, unable to stay strong any longer.

She wanted Alex. She wanted her mother. She wanted the life she'd had before the war had taken everything from her.

'Last stitch.'

Sophia heard the words but she couldn't form a reply.

She wanted it over. The war. Her recovery. The death. The fear.

All she wanted was to find Alex again, to feel his arms around her, his whispers against her skin. Everyone she loved had died, and Alex might have, too, but she had to believe he'd made it. Without Alex, she had no one and nothing to return to.

'You're our little hero,' a man said. She didn't know if it was the same man as before or someone else; there were a few of them peering down at her.

'I'm no hero,' she managed to mutter.

'You are,' he said again. 'The delivery was a success and we're going to blast the hell out of every last German on that train line tonight, mark my words.'

Sophia managed a smile. It didn't feel like a success, but at least it hadn't been for nothing.

'Tonight you're going to rest, and tomorrow we're taking you somewhere safe until we can get you back to London.'

CHAPTER TWENTY-NINE

ROSE

Rose listened. The noise of battle was so close, she could feel the buzz of the planes in her bones. They were Allies. They had to be the Allies. Which meant the Germans were slowly being defeated. The landings must have been a success.

She'd become accustomed to the deep, gnawing ache in her stomach that had been there for weeks now. Or had it been days? The beatings and questions felt like they'd been going on for a lifetime. The pain of being so hungry was something she could never fully ignore, but she'd started to become more used to it. She wondered if it was her body's defence mechanism, something that happened when a person was forced to exist on so little.

The door lurched and she cringed, instinctively moving closer to Hazel. Her friend was asleep, as were all the others, or at least they were lying down and pretending to be. They were all so hungry, so cold and miserable, and she expected every day to be her last. Maybe the last for all of them.

A new prisoner was roughly shoved in, and Rose kept her eyes downcast until the guard disappeared, the door locked behind him.

She leapt forward then and touched the woman's face, seeing how badly they'd beaten her.

'I'm a friend,' she said quickly. 'We all are in here.'

The woman smiled up at her, surprising Rose. The light was dim but not dark enough that she couldn't see properly.

'They'll come back for you soon. They never leave you for long,' Rose explained quickly.

'It doesn't matter,' the woman whispered, moving and taking something from her waistband.

Rose was on her haunches and she moved back a little, worried until she saw that it was a crumpled piece of paper. There was a stirring behind her and Rose turned to see Hazel, rubbing her eyes and putting her feet on the concrete.

'What is it?' Rose asked.

The woman passed it to her and Rose read the words quickly before scanning them again, excitement building within her.

Take courage! We're on our way!

She read the words again, and again, over and over, before passing the note back and turning to Hazel. Rose grabbed her and held her tight, hugging her as tears streamed down her cheeks.

'We just need to stay alive a little longer,' she whispered. 'They're coming. It's truly happening.'

The next day, Rose and Hazel sat huddled together. Another woman was coughing, she'd been doing so for hours, and they were a sorry-looking bunch, all half-starved and looking close to death. But something was happening. The planes had continued to fly over, the air assault in full swing, and the bombs and gunfire had been going on all day. No guards had been to see them, there had been no heavy footfalls, but there had been yelling outside and it was obvious the mood had changed. The fighting was so close to them, the noise of war sending thrills through Rose as well as pangs of terror.

'The Americans are at the gates!' a guard yelled.

Rose screamed along with everyone else, terror blending with excitement blending with hope as they heard the frantic scream from outside.

'They're here! The Americans are here!'

She held Hazel's hand, sitting still, hoping they wouldn't be killed before they were saved.

'We're going to make it!' Hazel said softly to her, her tear-stained cheeks a contrast to the brightness of her eyes.

'We are,' she whispered back, grasping her hand and rocking back and forth. Could they truly make it out of this alive?

They weren't going to die. They weren't going to die!

'They've really come for us.' Hazel's words were barely loud enough to hear. Rose watched her as she stared straight ahead, before leaping to catch her as she sobbed and fell forward.

'They're going to save us, Hazel,' she said. 'The Americans are here!'

Rose breathed deep and gripped Hazel's hand.

'I want to go home,' Hazel said quietly back. 'I want to go home to London. I want to see my family and lie in my own bed.'

Rose understood. She craved home, too, even if everything would be different than before. She wanted to eat, to forget the deep gnaw of hunger in her belly that pained her every minute of every hour of every day.

A series of bangs echoed out as shots were fired outside. The door to their crammed cell opened and a soldier rushed forward.

'Harry?' Hazel muttered.

'Hazel, get up!' Rose ordered, wondering if her friend was becoming delirious. Why would she think Harry was here?

Hazel blinked up at her, eyes wide.

'Get up!' Rose said again. 'Quickly!'

She scurried to her feet and Rose got a tight hold of her arm. It was over. Their nightmare in the prison was over.

Tears streamed down her cheeks and made her choke as she held tight to Hazel and watched the commotion around them, the world spinning as she tried to focus, tried to digest the reality that they'd been so close to death. The soldier scooped Hazel up, and Rose somehow managed to walk beside him as they moved through the prison. Outside, her eyes teared up from the bright light. She was squinting hard as if she'd never seen the sun before.

She looked across at Hazel, saw her matted hair and her bruised face, her cheeks so gaunt. How had they managed to survive?

'It's over,' she told Hazel, collapsing into her friend as the soldier left them, calling out orders. There were soldiers everywhere and her head started to spin as she tried to watch them, tried to figure out what was going on.

'It's over,' Hazel muttered back. 'We're going to make it home. We're going to be fine.'

Rose started to laugh, her ribs screaming in protest at the movement. They were going home!

'*Vive la France!*' she whispered.

Hazel laughed back, tears streaming down her cheeks. '*Vive la France* indeed.'

EPILOGUE

PARIS, FRANCE

1945

Rose

When Rose had first learned that Peter had died, she'd felt as if her world had ended. Darkness had engulfed her, snatched away her happiness and with it any excitement or anticipation about the future. But walking now to the little memorial she'd made, her tears were replaced by a smile, the sadness she'd carried all those years barely a whisper against her skin. Just as her time in prison, the pain and suffering she'd endured before being rescued and finally sent home, was like a silent murmur in her mind that she was mostly able to ignore.

She smiled when she looked down at the little girl whose hand she was holding. *Her* little girl. Coming home to find that her brother and sister-in-law had both been killed hadn't surprised her, not given their work with the Resistance. But finding out they'd had a daughter and that Charlotte had given birth and smuggled her back to Paris, that she'd found Maria and begged Rose's old maid to keep her safe? That she and Charlotte must have been pregnant at the same time without her knowing? That had been the biggest surprise of her life. And Francesca was like the daughter she'd never had, a reminder of Sebastian with her thick dark hair and even darker eyes, and Rose felt like she now had something, *someone*, to live for.

She'd been holding Francesca's hand, the little girl happy to toddle along beside her, stopping a hundred times or more to touch a blade of grass or admire a bird in a tree, or sometimes even to pick a flower. Nothing had ever felt more special than having her palm clasped to Francesca's, her wonder at everything giving Rose a new perspective on the world through the eyes of a toddler.

When she shut her eyes, now she saw a future: Francesca as a beautiful young woman, love and laughter, grandchildren even. She would have done anything to have Peter by her side, and her brother, but nothing could bring them back from the dead.

'Will you blow Uncle Peter a kiss for me?' she asked, bending low and pressing a kiss to Francesca's soft little cheek.

She received a big kiss in return instead, and Francesca clamped her hands to Rose's face, forcing her to look at her when she stared into her eyes. It was the kind of spontaneity that took Rose by surprise every day, made her smile when she least expected it.

'Thank you, sweetheart,' she whispered.

Francesca was frowning, but when Rose dropped a wet kiss to her nose and laughed, the frown disappeared.

'I'm not sad, just missing Uncle Peter.'

Today would have been his birthday. If he'd been alive they would have started the day in bed, eating breakfast and planning their day. Peter had always taken the day off work on his birthday and hers, the only days that he cleared his schedule and refused to go to his office or talk business even for a moment. They would indulge, eat, make love and laugh. It was always one of Rose's favourite days of the year, and it was the one date that was always hard for her to pull through now. Without Francesca she'd have buried her head under her pillow and refused to rise until the day had passed.

'Come on, darling,' she said, standing and taking Francesca's hand once more. 'Let's say our prayers and then go back home. We have our visitors coming soon.'

Rose had buried a tiny box of Peter's things beneath a beautiful oak tree before she'd left Paris for the coast, in one of her favourite places to walk, since she had no remains of his to lay to rest. She'd planned to put down a plaque, something special so anyone passing could read it, to keep him living on and to give her something to reflect upon. But she realised now that the old pocket watch he'd inherited from his grandfather and his favourite silk handkerchief resting beneath the earth was enough. She was carrying a flower, and when they reached the tree she bent low to place it at the juncture where the trunk met the ground.

'I'll never forget you, my darling. Not for as long as I live.'

Francesca tugged at her hand, loosening their grip, and Rose let her go. She could toddle off for a little bit; this was a moment in time that Rose needed, just a minute or two until next year.

'Thank you for loving me. Thank you for believing in me and always letting me be myself, challenging you when most wives would have agreed with anything their husband said. No man will ever live up to the memory I have of you.' She brushed tears from her cheeks as she smiled and touched her palm to the tree. She held it there, feeling the energy from the oak that stretched so high up into the air.

'I hope you are free and watching over me, seeing me with little Francesca. She is a breath of fresh air, and everything I imagined our own child would be like. If Sebastian has found his way to you, and Charlotte, make sure they know how loved she is. She will never want for anything in her life, and I love her as fiercely as I loved you.'

Rose felt a tug at her leg and saw Francesca was back, holding on tight to her, wanting to be picked up.

'Happy birthday, Peter,' Rose whispered, pushing off from the tree with her hand and stepping back.

She scooped up her little girl and pressed a kiss to the top of her head, dark curls all messy from an afternoon of play.

'Come on, sweetheart. Let's go.'

She loved the weight of Francesca in her arms, the smiles and the affectionate looks and touches. It had warmed her heart, and every day with her made her realise how important every sacrifice had been, why every life they'd lost in the field had been for something greater. They'd fought for freedom, for all the children out there who deserved a safe and free world to grow up in. It had been a huge price to pay, but one day she hoped Francesca and all the other children in France would listen to their mothers, aunts and grandmothers tell stories about the war and understand just how much they'd given up for them.

'Are you looking forward to meeting Auntie Sophia and Auntie Hazel?' she asked Francesca. 'I bet they'll love meeting you!'

By the afternoon they'd be together again, the first time seeing one another since they'd been separated, and she couldn't wait. They would always have a special bond, a shared understanding of what they'd endured. Without them she might be reflecting on the past and wondering if she'd dreamed up the whole thing – that's how unlikely it was that three women from three very different backgrounds had ended up wielding guns and knives and getting some of the most important messages out of and into France during what she was certain would be remembered as the bloodiest and most sacrificial war ever known to man.

And what she'd shared with each of her friends – with Sophia that night she'd lost the baby she'd been so desperate for, and the nights huddled with Hazel in the German prison, so close to death – would never leave her. They were a part of her soul, the memories engraved into her very being, and she would love those two women like sisters for the rest of her life.

HAZEL

'I still can't believe we're here,' Hazel said, arm linked through Sophia's as they made their way up the steps to Rose's beautiful Paris home.

Sophia let go of her, and Hazel watched her knock on the door, her smile wide when she turned. 'I know. It's . . .'

'Surreal,' Hazel said for her when Sophia struggled to find the right word.

They had been as close as sisters during their time together, all amazed that they'd somehow managed to stay alive when so many hadn't. But she was still nervous, restless about how they'd get along now and what they'd say to one another. Hazel had missed them both terribly, thought about them often, but until Rose had made contact asking if they'd like to see one another again, they hadn't been in touch.

Within seconds the door was thrown open and a very excited woman held the door.

'Are you Sophia or Hazel?' the woman asked, holding the door still.

Hazel laughed. 'I'm Hazel. And here I was thinking it was the wrong house when you answered the door.'

'I'm Maria. Rose is this way. Please, follow me.'

The moment she saw them Rose screamed and ran across the room. Hazel opened her arms and hugged her, not letting go as tears streamed down her cheeks and Rose cried against her shoulder. Then Sophia took over, holding them both at the same time, her arms tight around them.

'It's so good to see you!' Rose whispered.

'And you,' Hazel said. 'I can't believe it.'

They finally parted and she watched as Rose dabbed at her eyes, looking at them in disbelief, as if she simply couldn't believe they were standing in her home.

'Rose?'

They all turned when Rose's housekeeper called her, and Hazel stared in disbelief at the little girl she held in her arms.

'Mama,' the child babbled, wriggling to get away. 'Mama.'

She watched as Rose dropped to one knee, arms outstretched, and the girl leapt towards her, pudgy little arms around her neck as she sat on Rose's hip.

'Mama?' Hazel asked in a low voice.

Rose's smile was bigger than Hazel had ever seen before. 'This is Sebastian's daughter,' she said. 'My brother had a little girl.'

Hazel froze. *'Had?'* She glanced at Sophia and saw her nodding, as if she knew something Hazel didn't.

'He was killed, he and Charlotte both. Maria here,' Rose said, gesturing towards her housekeeper, 'cared for her until I came home. It seems Charlotte came back here to give birth sometime after I last saw her and before she was caught.'

Tears welled in Hazel's eyes as she watched them together. It was clear Francesca adored Rose; the love shining from her little face was unmistakable.

'I'm so happy for you,' Hazel said as she moved closer to Rose. 'I'm sorry for your brother, I know how much you loved him, but what a wonderful thing to be able to raise his daughter as your own for him.'

Rose leaned in and kissed her cheek, and they looked into each other's eyes for a moment. When she stepped back Sophia opened her arms, holding Rose close and whispering something that Hazel couldn't hear. They embraced for a long time, and when they stood back, Sophia and Rose both had tears in their eyes.

'She's beautiful, Rose,' Hazel said, stepping forward and stroking the little girl's hair. 'How lucky to have a second mummy as delightful as you.'

They all stood and chatted, clucking over Francesca and admiring her chubby little cheeks and cherubic smile, until the child struggled to get down and toddled off after something. Rose turned to them all then, her smile making it impossible for Hazel not to return it.

'My husband would have loved having you all here today. He would have liked nothing more than to hear about some of our adventures and escapades, and to share stories about what we had all loved and lost over the years,' Rose said bravely. 'I lost the love of my life to the war that we all so bravely fought, but it makes my heart happy to know that we made it, and that you both made the journey here to see me today.'

Hazel had tears in her eyes listening to Rose's words. They had an unbreakable bond after what they'd been through together, one that nothing could shatter.

'Peter loved his champagne, and I found a few hidden bottles the other day when we were sorting through some of his affairs,' Rose said. 'So I propose we sit down to a long lunch with free-flowing champagne and raise a glass to my husband, in case he's looking down and watching our little get-together.'

Hazel wrapped an arm around Rose's shoulders and squeezed, smiling over at Sophia on her other side. To her, it sounded like the perfect day.

Sophia

Sophia's face was hurting from smiling so much. It had been a difficult choice deciding to come, but she was pleased she had, and that it was just the three of them. And she was also pleased to have been able to whisper to Rose that she'd seen Sebastian, that she'd been in his presence before he'd been killed. She'd wanted to tell her but never known how, not wanting to write it in a letter and . . . She sighed. She was just pleased she'd finally said the words she'd been needing to say to her. She also understood now what he'd meant when he'd spoken of his wife having to return to Paris for family matters.

'It's hard to believe we're all here, isn't it? I mean, who would have thought we'd all make it?'

Rose and Hazel laughed, holding up their glasses, and Sophia did the same before taking a long, sweet sip of champagne. Only between the three of them could they ever laugh or even smile about what they'd been through.

'I've been hesitant to mention it, but you're wearing a ring,' Rose said. 'Dare I ask if you found your Alex?'

Sophia's neck warmed and the heat rose all the way to her cheeks. It was ridiculous blushing when she had nothing to be embarrassed about with her friends, but something about falling in love with Alex all over again made her feel like a lovesick teenager.

'I did,' she said quietly. 'I returned to Berlin to find him, and three weeks later he met me just like we'd always planned.'

Rose's smile told her how pleased her friend was for her, but it was Hazel leaning in and waiting for more. They might not have been best friends immediately, but she couldn't feel any closer to Hazel now if she tried.

'Tell us,' Hazel said. 'I want every last detail!'

Sophia took a little sip of champagne, smiling to herself when she thought about that day. After recovering enough to travel to London, she'd stayed there until the war had ended. As soon as she was able she'd returned to Berlin, anxious to find news of Alex.

'I never believed I'd find him,' she said quietly. 'We'd planned to meet outside a church near my old apartment. I was so scared of being back there after everything that had happened and what we'd done, but I also had this feeling that I wanted to see the Germany I'd loved as a child. And I desperately wanted to find Alex if he was still alive.' She cleared her throat, emotional as she relived the events. 'Only, the Berlin I remembered was gone. It was in ruins. I don't know why, but I wasn't expecting to see the city like that.'

Rose and Hazel were watching her closely, hanging off her every word, and she smiled as she remembered the moment she'd finally crossed paths with him again. She would tell them some of it, but some parts were for her and Alex alone.

She looked around, the wind slapping at her cheeks. She'd sat too long. When she'd told Alex that she'd never forget him and never give up on seeing him again, she'd meant it. He was the love of her life and he always had been, and if she had to sit here all day for the next three months waiting, then she would. But the not knowing was heartbreaking, as was the devastating thought that he was gone and she had no idea, that he'd been reduced to ashes and yet she sat every day waiting to see his smiling face.

She'd told him that one day, when she returned to Berlin, she would wait every day from noon to late afternoon, for two months. What she hadn't anticipated was how very long that was, how long each minute felt, the hours passing by as an almost impossible stretch of time.

Sophia stood, her mind miles away. It had been a long time since she'd allowed herself to think about her mother, the memories long buried to make way for happier ones from her childhood. But being back in Germany had brought everything flooding back, waves of memories and sadness hitting her like a gale-force wind to the chest. And her father . . . She shook her head and started to walk, as if the action itself would rid her mind of him. If she saw him now, or any of the Nazis she'd known and hated, she would simply cross the street and ignore him. If she didn't do that she'd probably murder him. The thought had crossed her mind, making him pay for what he'd done to her beautiful mother, to the wife who'd been so loving and loyal to him, the woman he should have done anything to protect.

'Sophia!'

Sophia stopped, every thought she'd been turning over in her mind falling away. Had she imagined someone calling her name?

'Sophia!'

She slowly turned, eyes shut, not wanting to get her hopes up, to believe that . . .

'Sophia!'

'Alex?' she whispered, his name barely leaving her lips. She opened her eyes, heart full of hope. And then she saw him. 'Alex!'

Sophia ran faster than she'd ever moved in her life. She sprinted towards him, eyes locked on the man's frame as he moved towards her. His hair was too long, his cheeks brushed with stubble, but she knew it was Alex. She would never forget the way he moved, his height, the way his smile stretched his cheeks wide.

'Sophia!'

His arms opened as she ran into him, screaming as she thumped hard against his chest, holding on to him tight.

'Oh, Sophia, I can't believe it's you.'

'I've waited every day,' she sobbed into his chest, 'for three weeks I've been here. Waiting for you.'

She couldn't let go, couldn't take her hands off the man she'd fought so hard to protect and spent so long away from. She'd thought it would be awkward, that he might be nothing like she remembered, that she'd perhaps imagined how she truly felt about him. But how wrong she'd been.

Alex put his hands on her shoulders and pushed her back a little, staring down into her eyes. His vibrant green-brown irises were dancing. His face was gaunt, cheekbones hollow, but his happiness at seeing her was written all over his face.

'It's taken me a long time to get back to you,' he said, stroking her cheek with his thumb and slowly lowering his face to hers. 'But I kept imagining this.'

He brushed his lips against hers, his touch so soft as their mouths moved slowly, softly together. Sophia sighed into him, kissing him back, her arms still looped around his neck. She could have kissed him all day, was lost in his touch, amazed by the years that had separated them and how it now felt as if they'd never spent a day apart.

'I've missed you,' she murmured when he finally pulled away, his mouth still so close that she could feel his breath against her skin. 'I thought you were dead, I thought I was never going to see you again.'

'You look beautiful, just as I remembered you,' he said, his mouth covering hers again, hands at her waist.

'How did you get back? What happened to you?' She sighed and placed her cheek to his chest, listening to the steady beat of his heart, feeling him breathe.

'Can we go somewhere safe?' he asked quietly. 'I don't like being here in the open.'

She nodded and reluctantly lifted her head. It must be surreal for him to be here, out on the streets of a city that had taken everything from him, a city that had held him hostage in her apartment because of its hatred for *who and what he was. She'd fought for him, but she'd never come close to understanding how he felt.*

'I have a room, the place where I've been staying. We'll be fine there.'

She held his hand tight and smiled up at him. It had been such a long time, and yet now it felt as if they'd never been apart. They walked in silence, through the ruined streets like they had never been able to do as adults together, hands clasped together. Sophia was no longer fearful, prepared to spit on the cobbled stones at any Nazi she knew and passed, but she didn't want to live with so much hatred bubbling inside of her, and she knew that Alex wouldn't, either. He'd lived with it long enough.

'Sophia, I need you to know that I can't stay here. I can't be back here,' Alex said in a low, quiet voice.

She gripped his hand even tighter. 'I know.' The possibility of staying in Germany, of seeing her country become great again, had seemed real only moments earlier. But now she was with him, she knew how childish the thought had been. Besides, she'd made peace with being French, and she didn't mind staying that way.

'Come,' she said as she led him down a street. She was staying in a lovely little hotel, and she'd advised the owner that her husband might be joining her when he returned. She doubted Alex would mind the little lie if it meant being together.

Soon the house came into view, and she kept hold of Alex's hand as she led him inside. There was no one about, and she took him upstairs with her. Perhaps she should have tried to go back to her own apartment, but her father had owned it and she didn't want to run the risk of finding him there, or of the awful memories flooding back when she set foot in there again.

'Here,' she said, shutting the door behind them. 'We'll be comfortable here for the night.'

Alex smiled and she laughed at him, suddenly self-conscious. His eyes travelled up and then down her body, before he met her gaze once more. She raised an eyebrow, heart pounding as he took a step towards her, not saying a word. Sophia's fingers fumbled on her jacket buttons, but as she took that off, Alex shrugged off his own coat. She watched, mouth dry as he then undid the buttons on his shirt and peeled that off, before kicking off his boots. He was so thin she could barely believe it, his bones jutting out but his muscles lean, as if he'd been doing something to keep himself strong. She almost didn't want to know, hated the thought of him being hurt, abused and starved.

She pushed the thoughts away and kept her eyes on him as they stripped down.

'Come here,' he commanded, voice as rough as gravel.

She gulped and walked one step forward with only her slip and under-garments on. Alex reached for her, ran his fingers over her shoulders and then down her arms, the pads of his fingers soft to her skin. She gasped when he ran his fingers back up her middle, skimming her stomach before taking her slip off her as she raised her arms.

His fingers twirled over her scar, the big incision curling down her abdomen from when she'd been shot that last night before she'd been sent back to London. She looked at it and felt it often, a reminder of what she'd survived, what she'd managed to endure during her time in France. Alex glanced at her, met her gaze, but he didn't ask questions. Instead he kept touching her, stroking her breasts. He went still, his eyes hungry, and then in one swift movement he had his arms around her and was walking her backwards, to the bed, pushing her back so she landed with a thump on the mattress. Alex's mouth closed over hers and she kissed him like it was the last kiss they'd ever share, desperate to feel every part of him against her.

'I've missed you,' she whispered. 'I've missed this.'

She had him back. Her Alex was back. Tears filled her eyes as she wrapped her arms and legs around him, wanting him closer, wishing they could stay like this for ever.

'I love you.'

Sophia snuggled closer to him. This was the safest and happiest she'd felt since leaving him, or perhaps since she was a child. Safe in his arms, with no war raging outside, no waiting for knocks at the door, or being found *out. It was going to be a different life for them now, a life she'd never truly imagined they would ever live.*

'What are we going to do?' she asked, turning on to her side, lifting her head and resting her chin on him as she stared into his eyes.

'I'll go anywhere but here,' he said, breaking their gaze to look out the window. 'I can't . . .'

'Shhh,' she said, reaching to touch his face, to make him turn back to her. 'You don't have to explain. We can go anywhere.'

'All I feel out there, all I see, is hatred,' he said. 'I can't ever forget what they did to us, what they did to my family.'

Sophia gulped, knowing they'd need to have difficult conversations, to open the pain that would be so raw again as soon as they started to delve beneath the surface.

'What happened to them, Alex? Are they all gone?' she asked, her heart close to breaking for him.

'They're gone. Every single one of them,' he whispered. 'Gone like they were never here in the first place.'

Sophia breathed deep, thought of his mother, full of so much love for her family, for her son.

'We both lost our families, Alex. You know I lost my mother, but . . .' Sophia bit down hard on her bottom lip as it quivered. 'My father is dead to me, too. It was his order that killed her, and if I saw him, if I had the chance to put my hands around his throat and—'

'Sophia,' Alex said, his thumb gentle against her shoulder as he stroked her. 'Enough. We've had enough violence to last us for a lifetime, and as much as I want to kill every Nazi bastard, we're better than that. We both are.'

He was right, of course he was right.

'Can you tell me what you've been through? Where you've been?'

He chuckled and kept stroking her skin, lulling her, healing her with his touch.

'Can you tell me?'

'Do you really want to know?' she whispered, wanting to tell him almost as desperately as she needed to keep it secret, to keep it buried inside and never let it out.

'I know that the woman I fell in love with did things that no woman should ever be expected to do,' he whispered, pulling her up higher so she was closer to him, so he could kiss her. 'You might have felt like a little fish in a very, very big pond, but every life you saved, every person you shielded from harm in your apartment, will for ever remember you as their hero.'

A tear slipped down her cheek and she watched as it fell to his chest, then another and another after that.

'I did what everyone should have done,' she said. 'There is nothing special about helping someone who needs it.'

Alex's fingers thrummed across her skin. It had been so long since they'd been intimate, so long since she'd felt his fingertips on her, smelt his skin and tasted his mouth. Yet here they were, as if nothing had changed. She whispered to him some of the things she'd done, things she'd never share with anyone else, and his smile warmed her when she finished.

'You're quite the girl, huh?' Alex said. 'When I lay awake at night, wondering when I'd be found, I imagined you undercover, doing that type of work. I knew they'd never manage to stop you.' Alex's words were soft. 'The Gestapo was so close to me sometimes I was sure I could feel them breathing down my neck, I'd wake with chills in the night. And yet there you were, working right beneath their noses without a second thought.'

He was wrong of course; she'd had many second thoughts, but then she'd always thought of what her mother had died for, what Alex's family had been persecuted for, and she'd kept on going. She'd had to. And now she was fortunate to be able to talk to him about what she'd done, because he'd known the risks she was taking and the network she was part of long before she'd formally joined the Resistance.

'Would you consider moving to Sweden with me?' Alex asked.

Sophia kissed his chest and then wriggled further up to kiss his lips. 'What's it like there?'

'Beautiful,' he said simply. 'It will be a beautiful place to live and raise our children. We'll grow old there and make a new life for ourselves, a life we can be proud of in a country that has done her best to be kind to us.'

'Children?' she asked, trying to sound surprised. 'Here I was thinking we were simply lovers.'

'Very funny,' he said, grabbing her hands and pressing a long, lingering kiss to her fingers, stirring feelings long forgotten within her. 'There had better not be any other boyfriends you're stringing along.'

'Not one,' she said truthfully. 'I shamelessly flirted my way out of many a bad situation, but I never gave part of myself to another. I promise you that.'

His smile was crooked, and it broke her heart to see how thin his face was, as if someone had sucked all the stuffing out of it, his cheekbones pointed and face gaunt. He was still handsome, but she was looking forward to fattening him up a little.

She didn't want to know what he'd done, who he might have been with. It was better to be oblivious, because they'd been parted a long time and the only thing that mattered now was the future.

'I still can't believe you survived,' she murmured. 'It's a miracle.'

'All my people,' Alex said, shaking his head and staring away from her. 'I don't even know how many are left from Germany. The things they did to them, the deaths, the gas chambers, working them in those camps with no food until they starved or collapsed from exhaustion.'

'It's over,' she told him. 'We'll never forget what they did, what they took from you and the part of my soul I had to give to survive, but it's over. It's time for us to rebuild our lives, wherever you need that to be. So long as we're together, we'll make it.'

'So will you marry me?'

'Yes,' Sophia said without hesitation. 'I think we should find someone to marry us at once, tomorrow even. What do you say?'

'I say that I can't wait for you to be my wife.' Alex's voice was husky and she felt emotion clawing at her throat. 'I've waited all this time to say that. All these years.'

'I'd do it all again,' she whispered through her tears. 'To save you, to do what I did, I'd do it all again if I had to, just to get to this moment.'

He looked deep into her eyes. 'I don't have anything to give you, Sophia. Nothing.'

'I only need you,' she whispered back. 'You're enough for me, and I have enough for both of us.'

His eyebrows drew together, making her laugh. 'What do you mean? Your father isn't . . .'

She held up her hand. 'Don't ever speak of him. He doesn't exist to me,' she said quickly. 'It's my mother we can thank.'

'I'm not sure I understand,' Alex said, looking confused still.

'The day I ran out of the house, the day he killed her, I took her jewellery,' she told him. 'I buried some of it near here without telling you, before we left that night, and I've already dug it up. I only sold two diamonds to help get me to London all that time ago.'

Alex grinned, then started to laugh. 'You little fox! Here I was thinking we didn't have a penny to rub together!'

'I'm going to wear her diamond wedding band when we marry, and everything else we can sell to start over somewhere.' Sophia sighed. 'At least that way she didn't die for nothing.'

'I'll never let you forget her,' he said. 'I'll never let us forget any of the loved ones we lost. We mustn't ever stop talking about them, letting their memories live on.'

'One day, will you come back to France with me?' she whispered, thinking how much she loved the country she'd worked in, the locals embracing them and doing all they could to help. From the moment she'd landed on their friendly soil, she'd felt right at home.

'Of course.'

Alex leaned forward and kissed her, slowly at first and then more urgently. She ran her fingers through his hair and pushed him back, climbing on top of him and straddling his thighs. Her hair fell around his face as she kept her lips on his, kissing him and pressing herself even harder to him. There were memories pushing at the surface, always wanting to take her back to where she'd been and what she'd done, but this made all of those thoughts go away. This was what she'd been wishing for, waiting for, fighting for.

'I love you,' Alex whispered into her ear.

Sophia kissed him fiercely. 'I love you, too.'

When Sophia finally finished her tale, Rose was dabbing her eyes and Hazel had tears flowing down her cheeks. But their smiles told her they were happy tears.

'I wish you'd brought him with you,' Rose said. 'Perhaps next year? And if you want a proper marriage celebration, a ceremony your friends or any family can attend, you're welcome to have it here.'

Sophia couldn't help the smile spreading across her lips. 'You would do that for us?' she asked.

Rose nodded. 'You're like the sister I never had. You both are. And that means you're welcome here or at my home in Brest anytime, if you can bear to go back there after what we went through.'

'You haven't told us about you,' Sophia said, turning to Hazel. 'All these hours and you haven't mentioned John?' Sophia found it hard to say his name, so close to slipping and saying 'Harry'. It had been plainly obvious to her that Hazel had fallen for the dashing soldier they'd rescued, but Hazel had been engaged to another man, and she doubted her friend would have turned her back on her duty, even after all they'd been through.

HAZEL

'I, well . . .' Hazel sighed. 'I might need another drink to get my story off my chest!'

Sophia laughed as Rose leapt up and reached for the bottle of champagne, quickly topping up Hazel's glass.

'Don't leave us in suspense!' Rose said with a grin, before filling her own glass and Sophia's as Hazel watched on.

'John isn't my husband,' Hazel said, glancing first at Rose then Sophia.

'Husband?' Sophia exclaimed. '*Husband?* You never said you were married!'

Hazel giggled and leaned back, wondering what on earth her friends would think. But then, they'd been there with her through far worse, and she doubted either one of them would judge her for falling in love with another man.

'When I arrived home, it was months before John returned. And when he did, I found out through a friend that he'd been home almost a week without sending word to me,' she said, remembering the moment so vividly as she recounted the day to her friends. 'I walked to his house with a heavy heart, wondering if I'd ever feel for him the way I did before the war, but it turned out he'd already made that decision for me.'

'What? How?'

She laughed. 'It's kind of funny now, but at the time I thought my poor mother was going to die from the shock of it all.'

Hazel shut the front door to her parents' home and started walking, ready to see the man she was engaged to. She toyed with the ring on her finger, the small diamond now so foreign to her as she rubbed her thumb over it. She'd only recently started to wear it again, and the weight of it, the touch of it against her skin, was unusual, somehow making her feel claustrophobic just having it there. John's family had been distant when she'd seen them recently, his mother no longer excited about seeing her and chattering about how wonderful it would be to have her son home. Now, it was almost as if she'd managed to upset her somehow, which was ridiculous given what they'd all been through and how long she'd been away for.

She was no longer wistful thinking about John, or maybe she was. But there wasn't the same sense of warmth within her any more when she thought about him, no longer an ache within her to see the man she'd promised to marry. Now there was a swaying of uncertainty confusing her, like being in a storm at sea. Either the feeling would pass once she saw him and threw her arms around him and it would all come rushing back, or the swaying would intensify and she'd want to throw herself overboard. Or maybe her mind was still on someone else, someone forbidden who she'd been trying to forget about all these months.

She quickened her pace, doubting that it would be a case of the former. Maybe her problem wasn't with John; maybe it was because she no longer felt like the same young girl who'd fallen for him and lovingly waved him off to war. The woman she'd become during the war . . . she was nothing like the woman he'd proposed to. Would he ever believe she could shoot a gun and disarm a man as fast as he could, or even faster? That she'd survived working undercover in France and lived to tell the tale, only she'd kept everything to herself, bottled it up inside so that she was almost ready to explode with it? That she was one of the women that had been whispered about since the war had ended, muttered about by the Gestapo, who'd have loved nothing more than to have seen her with a bullet through her brain? Who'd tried to kill her and so nearly succeeded?

Harry had seen a version of the real her, the Hazel she'd become, which was why it had been so bittersweet saying goodbye to him. Pretending she hadn't loved him more in the stolen moments they'd shared than she'd ever loved a man before, including her fiancé.

She'd never be the naive young woman she'd once been, and she was certain that the men who had been away serving would never feel the same, either, but at least their families and friends knew something about what they'd been doing. No one would ever know what they'd seen, how they'd coped or the decisions they'd made, and they all had their own demons to face, but she had to pretend like nothing had changed when it had. She'd seen how a man could treat a woman, how he could show her the same respect in the field as he would another man, and she'd become used to it. When her recruiter had told her that both genders were treated equally and had to be for the success of their work, she hadn't realised the full extent of his words. But she'd certainly become used to the idea.

And now she was about to go back to the role of doting fiancée, with no idea why her beloved hadn't bothered to contact her and had instead returned home to his family without calling on her. It wasn't going to be easy, but she'd given her word to him that they would be married, so she needed to grit her teeth and get on with it, and perhaps hope that time would heal her wounds and help her transition back into her old life.

She kept walking, slowing when she finally saw his home. She had a few more houses to pass, and she took her time, taking deep breaths and readying herself for what she knew was going to be an awkward encounter.

Hazel knocked firmly on the front door, stepping back to wait. She hadn't so much as received a letter from John since she'd been home, and she was so anxious she was breathing fast.

The door swung open and she was suddenly face-to-face with her future mother-in-law.

'Oh, hello, Hazel,' she said, glancing behind her and giving her a worried look. 'I suppose word has travelled quickly.'

Hazel nodded. 'I've heard he's home. How wonderful for you to have him back safely.'

John's mother gave Hazel a long, considering look. 'You haven't heard?'

Hazel shook her head slowly. 'Heard what? He is all right, isn't he? Has something terrible happened? Is that why he hasn't called on me?'

She watched as his mother pushed the door open properly and beckoned for her to come in. Something strange was going on, only Hazel had no idea what it was.

'I'm sorry, love, this isn't something I agree with but there's nothing I can do about it. Come with me.'

Hazel followed, her anxiety giving way to panic now. What had happened to John? What was going on?

'I don't mean to intrude,' Hazel said quickly, wishing she hadn't come. 'If there's a better time or . . .'

'John, you have a visitor.'

Hazel opened her mouth to say something, but no words came out. She stared at the man who'd half risen from his chair, his hand on the shoulder of a beautiful brunette, the other woman's eyes wide as she stared back at her.

John looked as handsome as he always had. His dark brown hair was thick and she watched as he pushed it off his face when some fell over his forehead, his gaze flitting from her to the woman beside him and back to her again. And just like that, the ball of anxiety deep within her, the feeling of being unsteady at sea, lifted. She should have been heartbroken, she should have dropped to her knees and sobbed or screamed the house down, anything, anything but have to bite her lip to stop from laughing. Because it was so obvious that this beautiful young woman, her stomach bulging from pregnancy as she shifted in her chair, was with John. Her John.

'Hazel, I wasn't expecting you,' John stuttered, so unlike his usual composed self. 'I . . .'

She looked at his mother, who was shaking her head, then she turned her attention to the man before her.

'Tell me everything, John,' Hazel said, pleased with how confident her voice sounded. 'I deserve to know what's happened here.'

'I'm sorry,' he said simply. 'I should have come to see you.'

'Yes, you should have.' There was no excuse for her to find out this way, not after she'd waited for him, and she didn't want him to see how secretly happy she was, even if his actions had embarrassed her.

'This is Pénelopé,' John said, gesturing towards the other woman. 'She's my . . .' He shut his eyes for a moment before stepping closer to her and speaking in a lower voice. 'Pénelopé is my wife. I met her in Italy.'

'And you didn't think to write to me, to contact your fiancée, and mention that you'd married another woman? That you had a baby on the way?' She wanted to be hysterical and make him see how appalling his manners were, but she was mostly irritated that he'd put her through this when she could have found out months, weeks ago and not fretted so much about him coming home.

'I don't know what to say.'

'We're so sorry, my dear. We were looking forward to welcoming you into our family.'

Hazel felt sorry for his mother when she spoke.

'Thank you,' Hazel said warmly, not about to be rude. 'I'm understandably hurt after waiting so loyally for John to come home, but there's nothing to be done about it now, I suppose.'

John went to say something but she shook her head. 'Here,' she said, taking the ring from her finger and holding it out to him.

'No, you don't need to give it back,' he said quickly.

She laughed. 'I don't want your ring as a reminder of our failed engagement.' She pressed it into his palm and stepped forward to place a kiss to his cheek. Maybe he'd fallen in love with the Italian woman, or maybe he'd simply got her pregnant and had to marry her, but either way she was strangely relieved.

'I wish you happiness,' Hazel said honestly. *'You shouldn't have ended our engagement like this, but I do hope you'll be happy.'*

Hazel looked at his mother, wringing her hands near the door, then his new wife with one hand protectively to her stomach. This Pénelopé had left her family behind to follow John, given up everything to be with the man whose baby she was carrying, and Hazel actually felt sorry for her. Perhaps John didn't even want to be with her but had decided to honour his unborn baby instead of the promise he'd made to Hazel.

'Can we speak in private?' he asked.

Hazel shook her head. 'There's no need. Please just let me be.'

John touched her elbow and she fought the urge to tear her arm away, knowing it was silly. 'It was different over there, Hazel. If I could explain what I've been through, what it was like being away from home and the things we had to do, I would. I promise you, I would.' His hands were shaking and she could see the trauma of what he'd experienced reflected in his eyes, knew instinctively how much he must have struggled. Perhaps he still was.

'I understand what you've been through,' she said.

'No, you don't. I mean, you can't. No woman can understand.'

Hazel could have laughed. If only he knew. He might have been away much longer than she'd been, but she was fairly sure that she'd seen and done things that would easily rival his experiences. It also told her that he'd never been the right man for her.

'The war has changed us all.' Hazel was ready to leave, she didn't need this to drag on for any longer than it already had. 'Goodbye, John.'

She didn't turn when he touched her arm, didn't listen to his words or those of his mother as she heard her raise her voice and scold her son as if he were a child still. Instead she walked out with her head held high. Her vision should have been blurred with tears, her face bright red from the humiliation of what she'd just found out, heart racing, but it wasn't.

Instead she was wondering how to tell her mother, but then that would be easy. She'd done nothing wrong, so her mother could gossip and moan about John and his family with her friends, her father could be angry that someone had broken a promise to her, and her friends could rally around and cluck like hens about what an awful thing John had done to her. And then she'd be free.

Free.

There would be no more covert operations, no more risking her life or worrying about being caught and killed. And she was free to marry whomever she pleased and to do what she wanted with her life. She'd had a taste of being independent and being treated as the equal to any man, and she wanted that for the rest of her life. Damn it, she was going to demand it!

So instead of crying and running down the road, she burst out laughing and tilted her head back as she walked, letting the sun warm her face and sink into her skin. Her fingers were almost itching to find a pen, to write a letter to the one person she'd tried so hard to forget about and should never have pushed from her thoughts or her heart.

The chains were gone. Nothing was holding her down, not now.

It was time to start her life over again, and she couldn't wait.

'You married Harry, didn't you?' Sophia asked, shaking her head like she could hardly believe it the moment Hazel stopped talking. 'You found him!'

'I did,' she confessed. 'I'd never forgotten his address – he'd given it to me before we parted ways – and I wrote him a letter telling him how I felt about him, and that I was no longer engaged to be married.' She laughed. 'Writing that bloody letter was almost harder than working in France with you lot!'

They all sipped their drinks, and Hazel spoke again before either of her friends could. 'John arriving home with an Italian wife should have broken my heart, but it didn't. I had to pretend to be sad when I told my parents, when I was in fact jumping for joy inside. And the rest, as they say, is history.'

'You do realise that we could all see it even when you two couldn't, right?' Sophia teased. 'It was almost painful to watch you two falling in love.'

Hazel shook her head. She'd known, of course she'd known, that Harry was the one for her, but she'd been engaged. It wasn't like she could have acted on her feelings.

'I suspected as much,' she confessed. 'But never in a million years did I expect to end up married to the man. Things turned out pretty well for us,' she admitted, talking about more than just her finding Harry. 'I mean, after what we went through, I couldn't ever imagine coming back home and pretending like our war experience was no different from anyone else's. *Because it was different.*' She cleared her throat and looked each of her friends in the eye. 'One day the world will talk about us. It will start as whispers about the women who infiltrated France. They'll talk about disguises and gasp at the type of training we might have done, the fact that we knew how to kill and code and courier. One day, maybe by the time we have grandchildren, we'll be able to smile, knowing the women who made history, those women they speak about with such admiration . . .' She had tears in her eyes now but she didn't bother trying to brush them away. They fell and she continued on, not scared of crying. 'We are those women, and it makes me so proud thinking about what we did. Sophia, we're so fortunate to have men in our lives who know the kind of women we became, because they saw us for who we truly are.'

Sophia held out her hand across the table and Hazel squeezed it, but it was Rose who looked like she needed the comfort, her shoulders shaking as she bravely, openly cried in front of them without turning away.

'I'm so sorry for your loss, Rose. Truly I am. We both are,' Hazel said. 'I didn't mean to exclude you. It must be so hard for you to hear about us and—'

'Don't say it,' Rose said, dabbing at her cheeks. 'It's enough to see you both happy, to see that you're loved. I had years with Peter, and it's enough for me knowing that he would have wholeheartedly approved of everything I did. He would have been in awe, but he also always knew how brave I was, that I wasn't afraid to stand up for what was right or share my opinions.'

'Must have made for interesting dinner party conversations, then,' Sophia said with a giggle. 'What in the world did his friends think of him, having such an outspoken wife?'

Rose sipped her champagne as they waited for her response, and Hazel did the same, taking a small sip of hers.

'It did and they couldn't stand me! But, Sophia, I'm so pleased that you found your Alex. You deserve to be loved and to get your chance at happiness with him.'

'I wish the end of the war had been different for you,' Sophia replied, her voice low.

Rose squeezed Sophia's hand as Hazel watched on. 'So do I. But I married a man I loved and he treated me with so much love and respect that no man will ever live up to his memory. But don't ever think I'm not bursting with happiness over you both!'

'Truly?'

'Look who I have,' Rose said, pointing to Francesca. The little girl had fallen asleep, her head tucked into a deep cushion on the sofa, her pretty little mouth open as she slept. 'She's my reason for living now. She makes every day worth getting out of bed for, every demon worth facing.'

'Our men fought that war, on the ground, day after day,' Sophia said. 'My own countrymen, my own father, fought against everything I believed in.'

Hazel held her hand tight across the table, listening to her friends talk.

'But it was what we did that won the war, I'm certain of it. Our networks and our people undercover in France, we changed the outcome, and we need to be so proud of that.'

They were thoughts Hazel had already had, things she often pondered in the early hours of the morning when her husband was fast asleep beside her. If she hadn't helped, hadn't been part of their amazing network of men and women, maybe she wouldn't have had a safe bed to sleep in at all.

'Shall we toast those in our networks who didn't make it?' Rose asked.

Sophia held up her glass of champagne, and they clinked them gently together. 'To the fallen,' she murmured.

Hazel held up her own glass and smiled before taking a sip. 'Can we all promise one thing?' she asked. 'Can we all meet, every year, here or somewhere equally wonderful?'

'We'll meet here every year, no matter what,' Rose said firmly. 'But next time you must bring your husbands, and in years to come, your children, too.'

'Then it's a deal,' Hazel said.

'We'll be here. Absolutely, we'll make it every year, no matter where we are,' Sophia agreed.

They all sat in silence for a moment, before Hazel cleared her throat. 'To us,' she said, holding her glass high.

'To us,' the others said in unison.

This was right; being together, celebrating their highs and mourning their losses. Hazel was certain they'd be friends for ever, until they were old ladies sitting in their rocking chairs, laughing and whispering about the things they'd done when they'd been young enough to risk it all. She laughed and smiled through her tears at her friends. After everything they'd been through, nothing could be more perfect than tonight. *Nothing.*

ACKNOWLEDGMENTS

One of the most amazing things about this book is that so much of it is based upon fact. Of course, Rose, Sophia and Hazel are all completely fictional characters, but the truth is that any one of them could have been real. During World War II, so many women stepped up into roles that women had never dreamed of doing before. The women who were recruited by the SOE in London, or those in France recruited by the Resistance, were incredibly capable, brave women, and the work they did most certainly had a huge impact on the eventual outcome of the war. They were highly trained and determined to make a difference, and they will for ever be remembered for their bravery. Many didn't make it back home, but their contributions to the war will live on for ever. There is still a lot of secrecy around much of the work they did, but there is enough to piece together just how incredible each and every one of those undercover women was. In the words of wartime leader Winston Churchill, their task was to 'set Europe ablaze'.

When I talk to young women and girls about writing, I always tell them something I was constantly told during my high school years: girls can do anything. We can't do everything at once, but we can do anything we set our minds to, and this feminist fact was as true during World War II as it is today. I hope that you feel as empowered reading this book about my brave Rose, Sophia and Hazel as I felt writing it!

I had tears in my eyes reading the true accounts of the undercover female agents in France, for so many of them did the most amazing things and were killed so young. Others managed to survive through luck as much as skill, and I've tried to successfully balance this story with heartbreak as well as hope. It was one of the hardest stories I've ever created, but in many ways it has also been the most rewarding. Some days I had to walk away from my laptop to pick up my children from school, haunted by the scene I was working on, or by the research I'd just completed. But as much as the stories haunted me, they also made me hungry to tell the tales of my fictional characters, no matter how tough the creative journey.

As with all my books, I have a very small but important group of people to thank. First of all, thank you to my readers for buying my books. I read every email, every review, every mention I'm alerted to on social media, and I thank you for taking the time to read my stories and correspond with me.

Thank you to my incredible team at Amazon Publishing – I'm so proud to be published under the Lake Union imprint. Sammia Hamer, Emile Marneur, Bekah Graham, Victoria Pepe, Katie Green and Jessica Gardner, thank you for being such a fantastic team. I always know I'm in great hands with you all in my corner, and there are many more people involved behind the scenes there too.

I'd also like to thank Laura Bradford, who has been my agent for seven years now, and will hopefully be my partner in the publishing world for many more years to come.

My days at home as a writer are very solitary – except when I'm surrounded by my children and trying to work of course! But the quiet times are made less solitary thanks to my daily writing partner, Yvonne Lindsay, and daily emails from fellow authors Nicola Marsh and Natalie Anderson.

And finally to my most important support crew . . . my family. I am so lucky to have a job that allows me to work full-time as well as parent full-time, and even though it feels like an impossible juggle sometimes, I wouldn't change it for the world. Although without an amazing mother and husband to help me at every step of the way, the juggle might just be impossible!

I love hearing from readers, and I personally respond to every email and social media message. I also enjoy chatting to book clubs, so if you want me to Skype into your book club meeting or answer questions, please do contact me through my website, www.sorayalane.com.

While you're reading this book I'll already be busy at work on my next women's fiction title, so don't forget to follow my author page on Amazon to be alerted of my next release!

ABOUT THE AUTHOR

Photo © 2014 Carys Monteath

Soraya M. Lane graduated with a law degree before realising that law wasn't the career for her and that her future was in writing. She is the author of historical and contemporary women's fiction, and her historical novel *Voyage of the Heart* was an Amazon bestseller.

Soraya lives on a small farm in her native New Zealand with her husband, their two young sons and a collection of four-legged friends. When she's not writing, she loves to be outside playing make-believe with her children or snuggled up inside reading.

For more information about Soraya and her books, visit www.sorayalane.com or www.facebook.com/SorayaLaneAuthor, or follow her on Twitter: @Soraya_Lane.

42085763R00197

Printed in Poland
by Amazon Fulfillment
Poland Sp. z o.o., Wrocław